MOTHERLESS CHILDREN

DENNIS FISHER

Printed in the United States of America

First Printing, 2012

ISBN-13 978-1475194166

For my family

"The difference between you and me is that I know what I am. I may not like it, but I have it figured out now. You? You still think you're some other person, some better form of yourself."
--Danny Tobin

Prologue

It was no kind of day for flying.

As he sat on the helipad, Trey Evans could feel the wind gusts buffeting his chopper, rocking the huge machine on its skids. Looking out through the co-pilot's door while he waited for the EMTs to load the kid into the rear of the big BK 117 C1, he could see the wind sock at the edge of the helipad at full stretch while the branches of the trees lining the access road shook and shivered, their leaves raining down.

This is not what I need today, Evans thought.

It's not like he hadn't flown in some terrible weather before. God knows he had. Evans had spent a total of 22 months in Iraq and he'd seen weather over there that made the nor'easters here in New England look like sun showers. Sandstorms that popped up out of nowhere, cutting visibility to less than zero, wind shear so bad that it had blown a Blackhawk piloted by a buddy of his 40 meters flat sideways into an apartment building in Baghdad.

And the heat? Forget it.

He'd once forgotten his flight log in his chopper after a training flight and had gone back out to grab it a few hours later. Evans had just come from the makeshift on-site gym and was wearing mesh shorts and a tank top. He'd only sat in the pilot's seat for four or five seconds while he snatched the logbook from the floor, but the Blackhawk had been sitting on the tarmac in the sun uncovered and he'd ended up with second-degree burns on the backs of his thighs.

Evans's crew had surely racked up its share of bodies. No doubt. He knew they had. But he hadn't seen any of it up close. Whatever killing they'd done, they'd done because they'd had to. No choice. And the nature of their missions had always kept them far enough removed from their targets that the only time they saw the results of their work was on CNN or Al-Jazeera.

Mostly it was like a video game: see a target on the screen, push a button, no more target. That's how they thought about it in the moment, and Evans never spent much time dwelling on it later. He'd done his job. That was all.

And none of it had really fazed him. At least he hadn't thought so at the time.

It wasn't until much later, when he'd been back home that the shaking had started. It was hardly noticeable at first, just a slight tremor in his hands when he picked up a glass of water. He'd ignored it then, convincing himself that it was his imagination. Guys like him didn't get the shakes. That was for the guys on the ground, the ones who went house to house and room to room, never knowing whether they'd turn a corner and find a hajji with an RPG or twist a doorknob and wake up in a VA hospital in Germany, their legs somehow having gone missing.

But within a few months, it had worsened to the point that he was having trouble holding a pen or brushing his teeth without making a mess. His doctor had told him there wasn't anything wrong that he could find, and referred him to a neurologist up in Boston, but

Evans had never gone. Not because he was too tough or too ashamed, like some of the guys he'd known. No, he hadn't gone because he knew his problem wasn't physical and he knew it wasn't going to get better.

Only worse.

Evans had never had any of the post-combat fever dreams that many of his buddies had. No night sweats, no phantom insurgents popping up in the hallway. Instead, he got the shaking, and he knew as he sat there, watching the trees bend and shake, that his days in the cockpit were numbered. He would have traded his lot in a second for every nightmare and flashback that anyone wanted to give him, because no matter how bad those were, he knew he could still fly with them.

But not with this. No, not with this.

He looked down at his hands, trembling like those of old pensioner and thought: Won't be long now.

The rear door on the chopper slammed shut and Evans turned to see the EMT settling into his seat in the back next to the gurney, double-checking the fasteners that held the bed in place. He nodded at Evans.

"All set," he said.

Evans nodded and grimaced as he looked through the windshield. The sky was mostly blue now, with just a few scattered clouds pushing eastward toward the ocean. An ugly late-season tropical storm had torn through eastern Massachusetts the day before, knocking out power in a number of communities and causing coastal flooding up and down the South Shore. He'd seen video on the news that morning of a large chunk of the seawall at Nantasket Beach in Hull breaking loose and dropping beneath the foam of the Atlantic as a perky reporter in a $250 rain coat stood in the foreground and made the excellent observation that at least the carousel had survived. Fucking TV.

The rain had ended overnight and the sun was now trying to peek out, but the wind was still howling, straining the branches of the old oaks and willows that dotted the grounds of Plymouth's Jordan Hospital. The hospital was a small one, but it was the only MedFlight station between Boston and the Cape and so it served as a transfer point for critical patients from several area hospitals who needed to get to Mass General or Boston Medical Center quickly.

The kid in the back of the chopper had come up by ambulance from Hyannis early this morning and was on his way to Mass General to see a team of trauma specialists. He'd been in the front passenger seat of a car that had been T-boned by a box truck during the height of the storm last night. The truck driver had swerved to avoid a tree branch and looked up to see that the light had turned red. He locked up his brakes trying to stop, but skidded into the intersection, slamming into the right side of the Honda Civic the kid was in. The Civic flipped onto its left side and slid across the intersection, coming to rest against a parked car. Neither the driver nor the passenger, a 17-year-old named Alex Cone who was a serious baseball prospect, was wearing a seatbelt. The driver had been thrown halfway out of the car and was pinned underneath when it stopped, dead before the paramedics got there. Alex had taken the brunt of the impact, and by the time the firefighters had gotten there with the jaws of life and ripped the roof off the Civic, he was barely hanging on. He had a broken femur, six broken ribs, a shattered clavicle and a mass of internal injuries and lost two pints of blood. From what Evans could tell, the kid was pretty well fucked.

As he guided the chopper off the helipad, Evans felt a familiar tightness in his stomach. He'd often felt like this before missions, but never once in the four years he'd been flying MedFlight. He couldn't say what, but something just felt off.

Evans shook it off, and pushed the helicopter northward. A few minutes before he'd lifted off, Evans had gotten a weather briefing from the MedFlight comm center in Boston and heard that the winds aloft were still gusting in the fifty to sixty-miles-and-hour range, so they'd told him to stay low for the trip up. Evans climbed as he passed over the high school and a small collection of houses before banking right and following Route 3 north toward Kingston and Duxbury. He normally liked this trip, an easy thirty minute ride over some of the prettiest countryside in New England, dotted with cranberry bogs and white-steepled churches. But the weather, coupled with his worries about the tremors, were conspiring to make this one nothing but a chore.

Evans climbed past 500 feet as he turned slightly inland and moved to the western side of Route 3 as they passed over Duxbury's southern edge. He was about to radio the comm center and give them an ETA when the EMT's voice came through the headset.

"Hey. What the hell is that?"

The EMT, a young guy named O'Connell who was just out of the Coast Guard, had his face pressed against the right-side window as the chopper banked right. From that angle, O'Connell was essentially looking straight down at the trees below. Evans shot a glance through the passenger side window, but couldn't see much of anything, just a kettle pond sitting a few yards from the highway.

"What's what? It's a pond," Evans said.

"Yeah, no shit. I'm saying, what's that thing over there, toward the middle? And there's another one on the left over there. Are those downed trees? Oh shit."

"What? Probably just trees knocked over last night, like you said. So what?" Evans said. By now they were past the pond and Evans was coming out of the turn and climbing.

"No no no. Fuck man, I think those were people. I think, damn, I'm not sure. But those weren't trees dude. Make another pass, go back." O'Connell's voice had a little edge to it that Evans recognized: adrenaline, fear and a little excitement mixed in.

"What for? To see a bunch of logs? I'm all set with that."

"No man, you gotta loop back around. I'm telling you. Those were not trees. They weren't round or tree-shaped. How many times you flown over that thing? You ever seen that before?"

"A lot. But I'm not looking down either. That's not even the issue, though. That kid next to you is about half a step from a wooden box. He needs to get to Mass General. Now."

O'Connell had taken off his harness and slid forward between the front seats in a low crouch. "I get that. I'm the EMT here, remember? But he's stable and sedated and thirty seconds isn't gonna make a difference either way. I'm telling you man, I've seen my share of floaters. Those were bodies. Bet it."

Evans knew O'Connell was right about the kid. He wasn't getting any better or worse in the next minute. He was more worried about the prospect of what they'd find if he did turn around. A small part of him already knew, but he wasn't interested in removing the doubt that remained. Still...

"Fuck. *Fuck*, man. Ok, get your ass back in your seat and strap in."

Evans pushed the stick over, squeezing it tight to calm the shaking and banking hard left, making a wide loop around the pond, coming in from the southwest. He dropped his altitude a bit, making a low pass over the barren area surrounding the water, skimming over what looked like the charred trunks of evergreens still somehow standing upright, and while he was still fifty yards away he could see them. Two, then three, now seven or eight dark shapes bobbing on the surface of the pond, the wind whipping the slate gray water into tiny whitecaps around them. On some low, instinctive level he knew what they were before his eyes confirmed it. His stomach dropped as he pulled the chopper up over the line of pines and maples at the northern edge of the clearing.

O'Connell was right on. That kettle pond, one of hundreds like it in the lowlands around here, was a graveyard. A fetid, ugly little graveyard.

One

I woke with a chill.

My eyes were still closed, but I knew from the brightness on my eyelids that the room was filled with sunlight, as it often is in the early mornings. I lay on top of the sheets and the late-summer sun coming through the windows and skylight of my room should have been warm upon my skin. But as I slowly drew myself up and out of sleep's grasp, there was no heat, none of the pleasant warmth that should have been there. Instead, I felt a long finger of cold on my spine and it stayed there as I rose and walked to the window and looked out at the beach and the sea beyond.

The day was bright and clear, a high, crystalline blue sky spreading out above the water. The sky bore no traces of the low, black curtain of clouds that had hung over the coast for most of the last thirty-six hours as a tropical storm twisted and turned and blew, dumping more than six inches of rain in the process. From my window I could see driftwood and large branches strewn around the sand, and the ocean still was whipping furiously, the normally placid waters of the Atlantic now churning with four and five-foot breakers topped with lacy white foam. The dunes, diminished already by decades of car and foot traffic and millenia of tidal pushing and pulling, had taken a beating in the storm and there were now deep channels as well as small rivulets cutting through them that hadn't been there a day earlier.

As I stood at the windows, the summer wind flowing in

through the screens all around the room did nothing to remove the chill from my skin. I'd felt it before, a handful of times, and I did not relish its return. I did have a good idea how to get rid of it, though.

Ten minutes later I was out the door and running along the sandy lane in front of my house at an easy warm-up clip. I quickened my pace as I made the turn onto Warren Avenue, heading north, and started pushing it harder as I worked through the hills on the way into town, feeling my legs warm nicely with the effort. The sun was still below the trees, but the air was warm and thick and by the time I cruised into downtown Plymouth, three miles into my run, I had worked up a nice sweat and shaken off the uneasiness I'd woken with. I'd left my watch at home, but figured I was doing a comfortably hard 7:15 per mile pace or so. Tree limbs littered the sidewalk and streets of downtown and several times I was forced to run out into the middle of the road to avoid deep standing water left by the storm. There was a crew from the power company with a cherry-picker working on the power lines near the old courthouse and a pair of Plymouth cops stood nearby drinking coffee and watching. One of them raised a hand as I went by.

"Danny, what's up, kid?" he said as I passed.

I waved and kept going, not wanting to stop and feel the chill again.

I was nearly at the turnaround point of what would be ten miles when my phone went off. I had it tucked into a small zippered pocket of my Camelbak and I was cruising along at a nice steady pace, coming out of downtown on Water Street when the phone jarred me out of my running cocoon. I stopped quickly and yanked the iPhone out of the pocket and checked the caller ID.

BLOCKED.

Ugh. That meant one of two things, neither of which was good. Either it was a telemarketer looking to give me a great deal on a family pack of pajama jeans, or it was work. I wasn't sure which was worse, but given that it wasn't even 8 a.m. yet on the Saturday of Labor Day weekend, my money was on work.

Awesome.

I hit the Answer button and gritted my teeth, prepared for my weekend plans to take a left turn straight down the crapper.

"Tobin."

"Hey man, it's Tex. Where you at?"

"No."

"Whatcha mean, no? That wasn't a yes or no question. So, where you at?"

"It's irrelevant. And you know why? Because I'm off today, so whatever steaming pile of crap you have lined up for me, you can shovel it on to someone else's plate. I'm going to finish my run, then I'm going to plant myself on the beach with a cooler and look at pretty girls and drink beers until I either pass out or get lucky, whichever comes first. So, no, Tex, where I am does not matter. Not today."

Laughter. "Child, please. There isn't any 'whichever comes first' in that. You'd be asleep in that beach chair by noon, and with your Irish tan? You'd be

19

six shades of red by dinner time. Plus it's too windy for the beach today. It'll be a sandstorm. But the good news is, I'm here to save you from all that. We caught one. Actually, you wanna be picky about it, we caught nine."

"Nine what?" I asked.

"Winning scratch tickets. I'm calling you from my new villa in Zihuatanejo right now. The hell you think I mean? Nine bodies, man. They're pulling them out of a pond over in Duxbury right now."

I sighed and dropped onto a nearby bench. I pressed the heels of my hands into my eyes, hoping when I pulled them away I'd find myself on the beach instead of sitting here, knowing I was headed for a weekend full of misery. It didn't work. I blew my breath out and stood.

"You okay? You sound like you sprung a leak," Tex said.

"I'm fine. But we're not even up. Simmons and Morgan are. They haven't had a case in, what, a month or six weeks. We haven't even tied up the Ramirez thing yet."

"I know it, believe me. I was loading up the boat when the captain called me. Supposed to be going over to Cutty Hunk today with the boys," Tex said. He had three sons, 14, 12 and 9. "But this thing already looks like it's going to turn into a major shitshow. The locals are there, we're about to come and get in their business and there's already talk that the feds might be on the way down from Boston. So, the captain said he's giving the Ramirez case to S and M so we can get on this thing. He's paying us a compliment, he said."

My turn to laugh. Dropping nine bodies on us, on a weekend. That had to be the worst compliment ever.

"Who found them?"

"MedFlight guys on a run up to the city. You know Trey Evans?"

"Sure."

"Him. Said he was keeping it low on account of the wind higher up, so when he flies over the pond, the medic in the back is looking out the window and sees them. Said there wasn't much doubt what it was, but he looped around again anyway to be sure and then he made the call."

"Yeah. All right, look. I'm downtown right now. Give me an hour and swing by and pick me up at my place."

"Bet," he said. "Oh, and Tobin?"

"Yeah?"

"Bring your waders."

I stood looking out at the water of Plymouth Harbor for a minute. The surface was white with foam and the few boats that hadn't been hauled out before the storm were bouncing wildly on their tethers. In the distance, I could see the Myles Standish monument sticking up incongruously out of the pines and firs of the state park over in Duxbury, a concrete and bronze anomaly standing high above the deep green forest.

As I turned to head back, I felt the cold return, working its way down my spine as I ran.

Two

I made it home in just over thirty-five minutes, hammering it hard south on 3A till I hit the entrance to my road. Calling it "my" road was sort of ridiculous, considering it was also the entrance to Long Beach, the town of Plymouth's public seashore. But that's how I thought of it. I'd spent every summer of my life on this beach, chasing plovers along the flat, wide beach, playing hide-and-seek in the dunes with my cousins and learning to swim in the waters of the frigid Atlantic. In the 1950s, my grandfather had been granted one of a handful of permits to build a summer house at the northern end of the beach as part of a weird, ill-conceived effort by the town to raise some extra tax revenue. A carpenter by training, he'd spent three summers designing and building the house with my dad and his two brothers. It was a two-story beauty with an open first floor that was always flooded by sunlight and a second-floor loft that had been my grandparents' room, then my parents and was now mine. On mild nights, my cousins, my brother and sister and I would sleep outside on the wide oak-planked porch that wrapped around all four sides of the house, trading exaggerated tales of our day's adventures until the rhythmic sounds of the waves lulled us to sleep. The next day, we'd do it all over again.

When my grandfather died, the house passed to my dad, the oldest boy, and we continued to spend most of July and parts of August there every summer, making the nine-hour drive up from our home in Virginia. The beach house was my parents' oasis. My father was a mathematician and worked for the federal government, but I never knew exactly which agency or what his actual job was until much later. All we knew as kids was that he was gone a lot and when other grown-ups asked him what he did for a living, he smiled and started talking enthusiastically about his work as a statistician for Commerce. I don't think anyone ever made it through more than thirty seconds of that without changing the subject. The nature of my dad's job meant that my mother was left alone to raise my brother Brendan, my sister Erin and me. She had graduated from William & Mary with a degree in English and in another life would have been a teacher or writer, but I never heard a word of complaint from her. Never. She knew exactly who my dad was and what he did when they married and, as his only confidant, she knew it was important.

Still, it was a stressful life for her and my dad and our trips to Plymouth were their release. The tension that had built up all year would begin to seep out as soon as my father pointed his yellow Ford Bronco north on I-95. He'd walked into the dealer and paid cash for the truck, opting for the larger straight six. The Bronco was completely out of character for my dad, a lifelong Chevy man who'd owned nothing but sedans. But he loved that truck. My mom, on the other hand, tolerated it. But, on those trips north, the farther away from D.C. we got, the more relaxed she and my dad became. I could always tell when we'd crossed the border into Massachusetts, because my mom would crank down her window as soon as she saw the sign, not wanting to miss a second of the salt air. By the time my dad turned off 3A and dropped the Bronco into four-wheel drive for the mile-long drive along the sand to the house, he'd have the sleeves of his shirt--always long-sleeved, always white--rolled up to the elbow and my mother's long red hair would be in a ponytail, tied with a satin ribbon the same shade of yellow as the Bronco.

When my mom died three years ago, my dad had decided the time was right to let the beach house go. The Plymouth town fathers for years had been looking for a way to get rid of the ten houses that still sat on Long Beach, which was not only technically public land but was now bordered on two sides by protected wetlands. Several of the original owners had sold their houses back to the town at a nice profit, but the other families knew what they had and weren't going anywhere. So they'd cut a collective deal with the town that allowed us to stay indefinitely, but with one major catch: the houses could never be sold. When a current owner died or wanted to divest himself of his property, he either had to transfer it to a member of his family or sell it back to the town of Plymouth at "fair market value." Brendan, who is three years older than me, had moved to California after college and didn't get back east much, and Erin...Erin was gone. So I'd bought the house from my dad for a dollar and one of my Patriots' season tickets.

I thought about all of this as I jogged up the steps to the front porch and went inside. I dropped my keys, phone and Camelbak on the counter and grabbed an apple and Gatorade from the fridge on my way upstairs. Reggie, my black Lab/Rottweiler mix, was dozing on the floor, splayed out in a rectangle of sunlight beneath the windows on the west side of the room. I reached down and patted his stomach on my way in. He groaned quietly and rolled onto his other side, lazily licking his chops. Tough life.

After a quick shower, I dressed in jeans, a navy blue Massachusetts State Police polo shirt and waterproof Keen hiking boots. I went over to the armchair by the window and slid it and the throw rug it sat on to one side, exposing a 16-by-16 inch square cut into the hardwood floor. After moving into the house full time, I'd had my dad help me install the small gun safe up here. My grandfather had never anticipated this being a year-round residence, so he hadn't put in any closets in the loft. It was just open space with a small bathroom on the east side. I put in my key, opened the lid of the safe and took out my gun, a Sig Sauer P226 .40. I clipped it to my belt in a nylon tactical holster, relocked the safe, put the rug and chair back in place and headed downstairs.

By the time I walked into the kitchen, Tex was pulling into the sand-and-crushed-shell driveway. He was driving his personal car, a dark green Subaru Outback wagon. He came up the front steps two at a time and opened the screen door. He was wearing dark jeans, a blue denim work shirt and black tactical boots. The shirt had an embroidered patch on the left chest that read, "2008 National SWAT Pistol Championships."

"You ready?" he said. "Captain just called, wondering where we were at."

"I'm set."

Reggie came racing down the stairs, bounding straight for Tex, his nails clattering on the hardwood floor. Tex bent down and bear hugged him, rubbing his head while Reggie sloppily licked his face. "OK, OK boy," Tex said, laughing and wiping his face with his sleeve. He grabbed an old tennis ball that was lying nearby and tossed it up the stairs. Reggie sprinted after it.

"Man, that dog is ugly. He'd scare the shit out of Halloween," Tex said.

"That's my life partner you're talking about there. Be gentle."

I'd gotten Reggie from an SPCA shelter two years earlier and despite his questionable parentage, he was about the most gentle, good-humored dog you could ever ask for. Tex was right, though. Reggie was as ugly as homemade sin. He wasn't so much black as sort of a sickly brownish-purple that my dad had once said reminded him of a rotting eggplant. One of his eyes was yellow, the other was grey and he had a bald spot on his left hindquarter in the shape of an upside-down question mark, minus the dot, where he'd been burned with a coat hanger by his previous owner. I figured it was some sort of cosmic reminder of his crappy past as well as his convoluted family tree.

"Let's get before he comes back down and gives me a heart attack," Tex said.

I grabbed my phone and keys off the counter and locked the door behind me. We climbed into the Subaru and Tex backed out and headed for the beach exit.

"Doesn't your mom get tired of you driving her car all the time?" I said as we bumped down the sandy track.

"You know the ladies love this thing."

"If by ladies you mean the Golden Girls and dudes hauling kayaks on the roof, then yes."

"Kayaking is good exercise," Tex said.

"So is zumba, but I'm not trying to do that either."

Tex eased the Subaru onto 3A and headed south for Route 3. Frank Teixeira and I had been partners for more than two years, but we'd known each other for nearly ten. He had been one class ahead of me at the academy and we both ended up at the barracks in South Boston. After doing his time in the cruiser, Tex had gone into narcotics, spending four years building a reputation as a smart, clear-headed investigator and carefully cultivating a network of street-level informants. As he'd risen through the ranks, so had his sources, and even though he'd been in homicide for three years now, he'd kept those relationships up. Tex was a full-blood Portagee, born and raised in New Bedford, but he had gone to college down in South Carolina and had somehow come back with a southern accent. The drawl was straight Old South, but to New Englanders they all sounded the same, so the accent,

28

combined with his last name, had earned him the nickname Tex.

"I only got the rough outline from the captain about this thing, but even that is a fucking mess," Tex said as he accelerated onto Route 3 north. "Like I said, Evans was headed up to Boston early this morning, around 5:30 or so, and the EMT riding in the back notices some weird shit floating in a pond. So, Evans swings back around for another look and they get down low and see what they think are eight or ten bodies floating in there. He calls the comm center up in Boston, tells them what he saw, they call the Duxbury cops and they send a car over. I'm sure these guys figured they'd find a bunch of dead trees or other debris, but they were on the phone to us ten minutes after they got there. That was around seven o'clock I guess, and so the Duxbury guys and our crime-scene guys are there. I guess they've already fished a couple of them out. They were in rough shape, but there was enough there to tell they were both females. It ain't much, but none of it's good."

I sighed and looked out at the traffic heading south to Cape Cod, backing up as everyone scrambled to make the most of the last few days of summer. Many of the cars and SUVs were towing boats or had kayaks strapped to the roof, the drivers and passengers headed for a long weekend on the water, building love seats out of sand and having late afternoon drinks at The Beachcomber. And we were headed for what? A day of bodies rotting in the sun.

29

"Nine bodies. And we're sure these are homicides?" I asked. It was an inane question. No one knew anything at this point in the investigation, but I was grasping for something, anything that would get this mess out of our hands and into someone else's.

"Naw, man, I'm sure this'll turn out to be just like that other time we had all those people who accidentally drowned together in like six feet of water."

"Eat it."

Tex laughed, an incongruously high-pitched thing that still caught me off guard after all this time. It was a laugh that belonged to a nine-year-old girl or Justin Bieber, not a 6'2" homicide cop with a shaved head and full-sleeve tattoos on both arms. "The first question I have is, why were the locals so quick to call in the staties? I mean, I get that it's a big mess and a lot to process, but why not take a swing yourselves before calling us?"

"This is Deluxe-bury we're talking about here. I bet they haven't had nine homicides in the last thirty years, let alone all at once. These guys are busy breaking up high school parties on Friday nights and fights over parking spots at the yacht club. I'm not even sure they have a homicide squad, to be honest."

"I guess, but look at it from their point of view. That's the kind of case that a guy can make a career on. Even if he doesn't put it down, he does good work and busts his ass on it, it's a shot at getting out of double-A and into the big leagues, no?"

"We're the big leagues now? I know I am, but I always thought of you as more like Crash Davis or

Ozzie Canseco--allllmost there, but not quite. I guess we're about to find out."

Tex grunted as he turned left off East Street onto a weedy unpaved access road. We only got about twenty yards down the rutted track before he had to pull to the side and park. The road, turned to two-inch deep mud by last night's monsoon, was choked with emergency and support vehicles. Tex opened the center console in the Subaru and took out his gun, clipped it to his belt.

"Never know when you might have to shoot someone," he said. "Especially if the FBI is here."

The FBI wasn't there, but everyone else was. We climbed out of the car and slogged through the mud toward the end of the line of vehicles, where the yellow crime scene tape was stretched taut between two maples, snapping wildly in the wind as the remains of the storm pushed through. Our captain, Dave Winthrop, was standing a few yards away in a group of four or five other cops, talking. I caught his eye and he broke away from the group and waved us over. He was somewhere in his late 40s and was dressed, as always, in a dark suit and red tie. Even traipsing around out here in the slop, I knew he'd walk away without a speck of mud on his clothes. I'd once asked him if he slept in a suit. It went over like a fart in church.

"Gentlemen. Let me bring you both up to speed," Winthrop said. "We don't know much more than what I told Teixeira on the phone. I spoke with the Duxbury chief and the officers who were first on scene and there's not a lot to go on. This area is well-known to the locals as a place that teenagers come to drink and do

31

whatever it is teenagers do, so the Duxbury cops are in here pretty often. But mostly at night."

"So it's gonna be a tough ask to figure out a time frame for when these bodies were dumped," I said.

"If, in fact, they were dumped and not killed here, yes, that's accurate," Winthrop said. "One of the Duxbury cops who responded to the call this morning said that he was in here on patrol Thursday night and didn't see anything. Granted, he didn't dredge the pond, but that at least gives us some sort of starting point."

I looked around at all of the cars parked on the access road, the two dozen cops, crime scene techs and other guys walking around. "I guess we can forget about any actual forensic evidence on this one. Any hope we had of finding useful tire tracks or footprints disappeared when the first cruiser pulled in here."

"Well, detective, the scene itself is a hundred and fifty yards that way," Winthrop said, indicating a narrow path leading through a stand of dead trees behind him. "That area's been locked down tight. Only people over there are our crime scene techs, a couple Duxbury cops and the guy from the medical examiner's office. So don't despair yet."

"Yeah, let's wait till we get over there and see the nine dead people before we do that," Tex said. "Can we take a walk, captain, or is there anything else?"

"No, that's all for now. Go ahead. But, just so you know, our good superintendent called me about twenty minutes ago, asking to be kept up to date on this. As you may know, she lives in Duxbury, just a mile or so down the road. She's fairly eager to have this one taken care of quickly and quietly. Emphasis on the quietly part."

Tex cut his eyes sideways at me and gave a barely perceptible shake of his head. The superintendent, Susan Cooper, was a political hack with no police experience who'd gotten the job eighteen months ago in return for her family's generous support of the governor's reelection campaign. I had no use for her and had clashed with her last year on a case involving a state senator whose son was a witness--and maybe more--to a double homicide. The senator wanted his kid out of it, I resisted, Cooper sided with the senator and that was that. Except for the part where I'd let a reporter for the Globe know that he might want to ask some pointed questions of the prosecutor about the senator's son. That had earned me an official reprimand and an unpaid one-week vacation.

I rolled my shoulders, let out a deep breath and nodded, more to myself than anyone else. "OK, captain. We're on it. But, you know, murder investigations tend to be sort of messy and un-quiet."

"I'm aware. What I'm telling you, though, is that there is very high-level interest in this case. It's why you two are on it and not those two rodeo clowns, Simmons and Morgan. So my advice is to put this one down. Yesterday. Superintendent Cooper feels some attachment to this case and those victims. She's taken some ownership of them, I guess you'd say."

"I hear you, captain. But you can tell Cooper that the dead belong to me."

We walked over to the trees and headed up the short path to the clearing where the pond sat. There was a small white tent set up about 50 yards away and several people milled about outside of it. That would be for the bodies. The sun was well above the trees now, and the temperature was already in the low 80s, headed for the 90s. Direct sun wouldn't be doing the bodies any good. The clearing itself looked like it was about a quarter of a mile square, with the pond sitting roughly in the center. This part of Massachusetts is lousy with ponds, some tiny little puddles, others that could be considered small lakes. I'd once heard that Plymouth County alone had 365 ponds, and it wasn't unheard of for someone to find a body or two in one of them on occasion. But most of them don't end up as mass graves.

We headed for the tent and introduced ourselves to a pair Duxbury cops standing near the front entrance.

"Those two are the only ones you've pulled out so far?" Tex asked, nodding his head toward the tent.

"Yeah. They brought them out maybe a half hour, forty minutes ago," said one of the cops. He was built like Chris Farley, but with less muscle definition. Sweat poured off his forehead and his uniform shirt, which I guessed was once tan-ish, was soaked through and was now roughly the color of old pus. His name tag said Flanagan. "The ME is in there now, giving them a first look, trying to get a rough time of death. Won't be easy though, them being in the water and all."

"I don't suppose there were any driver's licenses floating next to them," I said.

Flanagan snorted. Or maybe it was a laugh. Really hard to tell. "Sorry. No IDs, no clothes and no hands."

"Wait. What?" Tex said. "No hands?"

Christ. I dropped my head and rubbed the back of my neck. Tex stuck his head inside the tent and quickly came back out. I looked up at him, raising my eyebrows. If nothing else, that told us that we could take everything but homicide off the table. Most drowning victims don't cut their hands off before going for a swim. I looked at Tex again and saw that he had already recovered and was back to gathering data. He had his small, spiral-bound notebook out and I knew he'd be putting down a detailed description of the scene and what we knew at this point.

I turned and walked into the tent, knowing I had to see what was in there. The two bodies were laid out side-by-side on blue tarps. They were naked and one looked to be in her late teens or early twenties, while the other appeared to be somewhat older, although it was difficult to tell for sure. I squatted on my heels next to the older one. She had a long, arcing scar that went from her right cheek over her nose. It looked fairly old and it marred what was probably once a very pretty face. I looked closely at the stump of her left arm. The skin around what would have been her wrist was pinched tightly and the bones were severed cleanly, no serrations that I could see. I stood up and walked around to the other body and found the same kind of wounds on both of her wrists. I stood and pulled my iPhone from my pocket.

"All right if I take a picture of one of the wrists?" I asked the ME, a guy named Mitchell who I'd worked with on a few other cases over the years. He was approximately a hundred and thirty-seven years old but was sharp as hell and had an absurd recall of the smallest details of cases he'd worked decades earlier.

He shrugged. "Sure. I don't think she minds."

I snapped three pictures of each wrist on the girl on the left. There was something about the wounds that was bugging me, but I wasn't sure what. And the scar on her face could be helpful in making an ID, if we ever got that far.

"First impressions, think they drowned or died before they went in?" I asked.

"Too soon to know for sure, obviously, but I'd put my money on them being dead when they went in. You saw the wrists. Even if someone was holding their hands down, I'd expect to see some sort of evidence that they struggled when their hands were being, ah, removed. Tearing, stray cuts on the arms, like that. But there's nothing, just clean cuts. So I'm thinking they were dead when their hands were taken. Then they were brought here and dumped."

I nodded. "Any guesses on how long they've been in the water? They're in pretty rough shape, especially this one," I said, pointing to the girl on the left. The body was severely bloated and large swaths of skin had fallen away from her arms and legs, leaving a patchwork of alternating mud, exposed muscle and skin. She had long hair that had probably been jet black but was now the sickly greenish color of a parking-lot oil slick.

"I was thinking about that before you came in," Mitchell said, walking over to the body on the right. She was the smaller of the two and had bleached blond hair, cut to chin length, and had obviously been quite pretty at one point, as well. "There's a pretty clear difference in the decomp level between the two, so I'm thinking they went in at different times. No way to know whether they were killed at different times, but I'd say that they definitely were dumped separately, maybe as much as three or four weeks apart."

I let that sit for a minute, studying the two bodies as I considered what Mitchell had said. "So that means..."

"Right. Someone's been using this place as their personal dumping ground. For a long time."

Three

I left Mitchell and the bodies in the tent and found Tex outside chatting with Flanagan and his partner. We excused ourselves and headed for the pond. On the way, I told him about my discussion with Mitchell and showed him the photos I'd taken of the wrist wounds.

"You see anything odd about them?" I asked.

"Aside from the lack of hands, you mean? They look very neat and clean, no mangled bones or anything. So probably not done with a saw, at least not a hand saw. I don't even think a power saw would be that clean."

"And there aren't any serrations on the wounds at all. You ever seen anything like that before?"

Tex shook his head, handed my phone back to me. "Nope. Drug gangs generally don't take the time for this kind of stuff. It's two in the back of the head in an alley and that's it. And they want us to find those bodies. These guys obviously didn't, and on the off chance that we did, they weren't going to let us ID them."

"So we're really at square one here," I said. "Their faces aren't going to be easy to ID either after sitting in the water for however long."

"Know who might be able to help though? I worked with this guy from ICE down in Miami a couple, three years back on a takedown of a nutjob crew from a Mexican cartel. They were bringing big loads of coke and heroin into South Florida in a fucking mini-sub that they'd bought from the Chinese somehow. They were running the dope up the I-95 corridor, working with MS-13 and a couple of other gangs on contract. We helped ICE set up on this bunch in Medford and ended up taking down 18 or 20 assholes. Anyway, this dude knows everyone and everything in the gang world, so I'm thinking it might be worth giving him a shout to see if this sounds familiar. Never know."

I nodded. "Definitely. You have his cell or email? Send him the pictures."

"Yup."

We stopped by the edge of the pond and I texted two of the photos to Tex and he emailed them to his ICE contact, asking him to call when he got them. There was remarkably little activity at the pond itself, just one Duxbury cop, a uniformed trooper and four crime scene guys. Two of the CS techs were loading another body into a black zippered bag, while the other two were in a small Zodiac about 30 or 40 yards out in the water, guiding it back to the shore.

As I watched the boat slow and the techs hop out, I noticed a man standing just on the other side of the crime scene tape, inside a stand of trees on the western edge of the pond. He was wearing jeans and a hooded sweatshirt despite the heat, and black sunglasses and was standing perfectly still, just watching the recovery operation. It's normal to see rubberneckers at crime scenes, especially when the word gets out that there might be dead bodies involved. But there wasn't a house within a mile of this place, so this guy must have walked in from the road or...I don't know what.

I started walking across the clearing toward him and as I did, he turned slightly and looked directly at me. He gave a short nod, turned and walked into the trees. I shouted "hey" and broke into a jog, but he kept walking and by the time I reached the tree line, he was gone. I looked at the ground where he'd been and the mud was undisturbed, not a footprint anywhere.

Tex was on the phone when I got back to the pond. I caught his eye and he pointed to the phone and nodded, indicating that his ICE contact had called back. I watched the crime scene techs work while I waited for him to finish the call. They had brought three more bodies out of the water and were in the process of getting a fourth into the Zodiac. I wandered over and looked at the three new bodies. All females, and again, all naked. But with two big differences: All of these corpses still had hands and they all had massive trauma to their chests, what looked like shotgun blasts at first glance.

What the hell was going on? We already knew that there had been at least two separate dumps here, and now it looked like maybe there was more than one person dropping bodies here. I suddenly felt very, very tired.

I turned as Tex came up behind me. "Tell me you have some good news," I said.

He smiled and looked down at the three bodies laid out by the edge of the pond. "Hey look, hands. Huh," he said. "I do have some good news. That was my guy from ICE, Chris, on the phone. He said he'd seen that same kind of wound a couple of times down there."

"He say what it was from, by any chance?"

"Sure," Tex said. "It's from a machete."

"And I thought you said you had good news," I said.

He smiled again. "That is good news, kid. It gives us a little piece of thread we can start pulling on, see where it takes us. Start to unravel some shit."

I looked down at the three dead women lying a few feet away. The sun was starting to work on them and I could see a dozen or so green bottle flies buzzing around them, as well. "Let's do that," I said. "I'm done with this fucking place."

Four

We were sitting at a high-top table on the upstairs deck at the Cabby Shack, having lunch and trying to process what we knew about the case so far. The restaurant occupied a prime spot on the Plymouth waterfront, overlooking the harbor and the long jetty that sheltered it from the open Atlantic. It was a favorite locals haunt, but today, like most of the summer, it was swarmed with tourists and bikers. I'd lived here for years and still couldn't figure out why Plymouth turned into Daytona Beach north between Memorial Day and Labor Day, with bikers flocking to town every weekend. They were mostly friendly and of the I-bought-a-$40,000-chopper-as-a-midlife-crisis-reward type, so no one really minded. I liked the burgers at the Shack and they had Mayflower IPA on tap, so I came here a lot. Plus, I could look across the harbor to Long Beach and see my house. I was having the jalapeno burger and Tex had a pizza with chorizo and linguica. I pitied his wife and kids having to use the same bathroom as him tonight.

"OK, so let's lay it out," I said. "Nine unidentified victims found in a pond that hasn't been used for years. No real time frame for when they were killed or when they went into the water. No sense of where the primary crime scene or scenes might be. Two of the victims had their hands amputated by what we think is a machete at some point, probably post-mortem. Is that about right?"

43

"Don't forget the part where we're supposed to have this solved already because the suits are uncomfortable," Tex said. He finished the last slice of pizza, wiped his hands on a paper napkin and pushed his plate aside. The waiter came by with two more diet Cokes and cleared our dishes.

"Right. So how do we get from where we are now--which is exactly nowhere--to there?"

Tex cracked his knuckles and then rubbed his hands together. "All right. I think, given the facts we have right now, that we can safely say that we're not looking for one offender. I've never seen one killer do that kind of work alone. I don't see this as some lone head case picking these girls off one at a time. It just smells like something else to me."

"I'm with you on that, but what are the other options? You said, and I agree with you, that it doesn't fit for a drug crew."

Tex shook his head. "Definitely not. They typically don't fuck around with killing women like that. Maybe one here or there if someone's gonna testify, they need to send a message or something like that. But this? Nah. There wasn't any message in this. This looks to me like straight business."

"But what kind? Whose?"

"Always with the damn questions."

My phone buzzed on the tabletop.

"Tobin."

"Dan. It's Mitchell. Got something for you."

"I hope so, cause we got zero right now."

"Yeah, well, listen, it's probably not much. But we got all of the bodies out of the water and those two that you saw were the only ones without hands. But all of the later ones had those same wounds to the torso, probably from a shotgun."

"Huh. OK. What's that mean?"

"Beats me. You're the detective."

"Right. Thanks."

"Any time. One other thing, though."

"Yeah?"

"We pulled a male out of there too. Eight females and one male. Dark skinned, but not black. I'd guess maybe Native American or even some kind of Latin descent."

"No shit. That's something. Thanks. What's your guess on when you'll have prelim cause of death on any of them?"

"What do you mean? Oh hell, I thought you guys were still here when that happened."

"When what happened? What do you mean?"

"When we went to transfer the two bodies you saw in the tent to body bags, we rolled the blond over on her stomach and the hair on the back of her head sort of separated and fell to the sides."

I was getting impatient. I didn't need the play-by-play on this. "Cut to the chase, man. How'd she die?"

"OK, sorry. There was an entrance wound in the back of her head, just below the occipital ridge. Small one. I'd guess a .22, like that. Small caliber, anyway. Bullet went in, rattled around, and never came out."

I glanced at Tex, who spread his hands out, palms up. I made a gun with my thumb and forefinger and he let out a low whistle.

"OK, thanks. Listen, lemme know if anything else pops up."

"Will do."

I looked at Tex, who was staring at me expectantly.

"So," he said.

"So we might want to revisit that whole drug gang thing."

"Yeah?"

"Think so. Mitchell said the two we saw in the tent took one small-caliber slug in the back of the head. No exit wounds, obviously. And the rest of the bodies they pulled after we left had what are probably shotgun wounds to the torso instead. Oh, and the other interesting thing is that one of the bodies is a man. So eight women and one man," I said.

"Mmmm. And what do we think about that?"

"I know what I think: no idea. I was hoping you might have some insights."

"Well, given what we know now, the drug thing fits a little better for the two in the tent. Quick, efficient. But what about the others? They don't fit," Tex said, absently rubbing his hand back and forth on his shaved head. With his bald dome, wraparound Oakleys and inked-up arms, he fit right in with the biker crowd here. "Unless...didn't you say Mitchell thought that they might not have all gone in at the same time?"

"Yup. He was pretty sure that the blond in the tent hadn't been in the water nearly as long as the dark-haired one. Probably a month or more difference. But they were the ones with the same wounds."

"So maybe this is a long-term project for these guys. Someone gets out of line, gets clipped and they dump the body there. Could have been doing it for months or years, who knows? At some point they change up weapons because it's a different shooter or the gun gets lost or whatever."

"Makes sense. But why all the women? That part still doesn't fit. You said yourself those guys normally aren't much for killing women. And why Duxbury? Someone trying to drive down property values?"

Tex nodded. "All good questions. I think we should find some people to start asking."

I pushed away from the table and grabbed my phone. "Let's start by finding the owner of that pond and see what his story is."

"Done. I talked to one of the Duxbury guys while you were in the tent with Mitchell and he gave me the guy's name. DeSilva, DeSalvo, something like that. I have it in my notes. Anyway, Flanagan said the guy bought the property about five or six years ago, right after the fire and hasn't done shit with it since then."

"Fire?"

"Yeah, that's why the place looks like a target range for Predator drones. It was a functioning cranberry farm for a long time, but it burned to the ground one night, took out half the surrounding forest, too, as we saw. So after that, the owner at the time took his insurance money and moved to Florida. The current owner came in a few months later with a cash offer and bought the land and then...nothing."

"That sounds like something we should poke at with a sharp stick," I said. "We got an address or phone number for this guy?"

Tex smiled. "Indeed. Let's take a walk."

We left the car at the restaurant and walked down Water Street through the herds of tourists wearing brand new, stiff-brimmed Red Sox caps and Black Dog t-shirts. The temperature was well beyond 90 now and the smell of the roving packs of Midwesterners had reached dumpster-behind-a-diner levels. We cut up the hill away from the harbor on Brewster Street and reached the relative calm of Court Street. Even though it was only one block removed from the furor of the harborside tourist traps, Court Street often was much less crowded and, therefore more tolerable in summer. Dotted with antique shops, upscale clothing stores, cafes and bars, it had the small-town New England feel that attracted so many people to Plymouth every year. Tex stopped and watched as a column of motorcycles roared past, fifteen or twenty bikes long. He rode a red Ducati Monster for almost ten years, but as the boys had gotten older Kim had begun casting progressively more venomous glances at the bike and Tex had finally caved and sold it last year. Given the choice, there's no question in my mind he would've rather surrendered one of his kidneys. But he wasn't given that choice.

He sighed as the last of the bikes rumbled by.

"Hey, look," I said. "There goes your lost youth."

"Gives me a rash," he said, shaking his head. We'd stopped in front of a white clapboard-and-brick building diagonally across Court Street from the old courthouse. The ground floor had blacked-out windows with stenciling in both English and Portuguese on either side of a huge Brazilian flag decal. The English read "Brazil Store." A set of four brick stairs led up to the glass-fronted door, which also was blacked out. The top two floors of the building, like many of the others on this stretch of the street, comprised apartments. Most of them housed families of recent immigrants from a hodge-podge of countries: Brazil, Cape Verde, Portugal, the Dominican Republic, Ireland and who knows where else. Plymouth might have still been the very definition of white bread New England in most people's minds, but in reality it was becoming more and more diverse by the day and the town's schools were now filled with kids who were learning English as a second language and had come here in the last couple of years.

"What's in here?" I asked.

"Our man DeSilva," Tex said, glancing down at his notebook. "Paolo DeSilva. Flanagan said he came over here sometime last year to talk to him and let him know about some kids who had been fucking around, driving their daddies' Range Rovers around in the mud on his property. Said DeSilva couldn't have cared less. Just nodded and didn't say a word."

"Maybe he'll care more about a bunch of a corpses," I said.

49

Tex shrugged and led the way up the stairs and opened the door. Inside, the shop was small, bordering on claustrophobic. It was maybe twenty feet square, with a small glass-front counter along the wall to our left. An ancient gray manual IBM cash register squatted on top of the counter. It was coated with dust and looked like it hadn't been used since the Carter administration. A couple of metal shelves mounted on the wall behind the counter held nothing except for a wireless Internet router, a cable modem and stack of Playboys about a foot tall. The counter was empty and, as I looked around, so were most of the shelves. There were two aisles with double-sided shelving units holding a few cans and boxes of Brazilian food products, as well as some novelty items. A rack displaying Brazilian newspapers and magazines stood to one side of the door and a pair of yellow soccer jerseys with the number 10 and the name Kaka on the back hung in the window. There was no one in the shop and a door to what was probably the office on the far side of the store was closed. I saw a small surveillance camera in the upper corner of the store, facing the front door where we'd come in. Unlike the cash register, the camera looked to be brand new and active. I waved at the camera and held up my badge case.

A few seconds later the rear door opened and a small, ancient-looking man stepped through, with two much larger men following. The small man was wearing loose-fitting black pants and a white guayabera that hung on his frame and looked to be nine sizes too big. Black huarache sandals covered his feet but couldn't hide the dark yellow toenails hanging over the ends. He had dark, almost olive-colored skin and with his gray, wispy goatee, the overall effect was something like Mr. Miyagi's derelict older brother. He was no more than about five feet two inches tall and if I passed him on the street I doubted I'd even notice him, but there was something in his eyes and his manner that commanded attention. His two goons, both of whom were well over six feet tall and had the look of roided-up wannabe MMA fighters, leaned against the wall near the door to the back room. Both of them wore dark sunglasses and untucked t-shirts over their jeans. The older man stood about four feet away from us and simply stared, waiting for us to speak. He didn't seem at all surprised to find two state troopers standing in his store on a Saturday afternoon.

"I'm Detective Tobin, this is Detective Teixeira. We're with the Massachusetts State Police. We're homicide investigators and we'd like to ask you a few questions about some property you own up in Duxbury if you have a minute," I said, holding out my credentials. The man didn't even glance at them, just continued looking at Tex with a completely unreadable expression on his face. I looked at Tex and shrugged.

"You speak English?" Tex asked.

The man simply stood there. No reaction at all. Tex nodded and switched to Portuguese, speaking rapidly and gesturing often with his hands. After about thirty seconds he stopped and waited for the man to answer. He seemed to consider what Tex had said for a moment, then let a thin-lipped smile creep across his face, revealing teeth that, if anything, were an even sicklier shade of yellow than his toenails. The man answered Tex, spitting his words out in a tone of voice that was clearly full of disdain. I noticed Tex clenching and unclenching his fists as the man spoke, though his facial expression never changed. When the man finished speaking, he handed Tex a business card. Tex glanced down at it and gave a short, unamused laugh and turned to me.

"I told him who we were and why we're here and asked him whether he was in fact the owner of the Duxbury property. He was kind enough to confirm that he was the owner and then said some rather unkind things about my ancestry. The Brazilians speak a dogshit version of our beautiful language, but I believe he said something about my mother and a mule. Or maybe a goat, I'm not sure. He's also lawyering up."

He handed over the business card, which bore the name and address of a lawyer in New Bedford, Mario Santos. I didn't know him, but either way, it meant we were officially wasting our time with Miyagi here.

"Well, I'm proud of you for not shooting him."

"So far," Tex said. "The day is young."

"Fair point. So that's a pretty quick trigger on the lawyer. Looks like our guy here is a pro."

"No doubt. If he's handing out his lawyer's card like Halloween candy, he's been through this a time or two," Tex said. He cracked his knuckles and looked Miyagi up and down again. "OK. This isn't going to get us anywhere. He didn't even blink when I told him about the bodies. He knew. And I'm sure he speaks

English just fine, but let's go see Santos and see what's up."

Tex looked at the man for a few seconds, then leaned in and said a few words in Portuguese to him in a low voice. Miyagi's eyes flashed anger for a second and when Tex finished speaking, the man turned and shuffled into the back room without a word, shaking his head, his pack mules following silently.

"What was that?" I asked, as we walked down Court Street in the midday heat toward the car.

Tex smiled under his sunglasses. "I told him Kaka was a pussy and he played like a coward in the World Cup."

Five

On the way back to the car, I called the office and had them get busy looking into Miyagi. I was almost certain that nothing would come up under the Paolo DeSilva name in terms of a criminal record, but we might get some other property records that could give us names of other people to bother. If not, I figured we might be spending some quality time sitting in front of the Brazil Store seeing who came and went and tailing Miyagi when and if he ever left that store. While I got that started, Tex was on the phone with Santos, Miyagi's lawyer, trying to arrange a meeting. He hung up as we got to the car and climbed in. Tex backed out of the spot and wheeled the car toward Water Street.

"So Santos said he got a call from DeSilva early this morning, telling him to expect a call or visit from the cops at some point today. He wouldn't tell me anything else about the conversation, but I think it's safe to assume that someone hipped DeSilva to the fact that there were cops crawling all over his property," Tex said. "Then he calls Santos and sits back and waits for us to show up. Like you said, this isn't his first rodeo."

"No doubt. I've got the boys back at the barracks looking at DeSilva's history, see if we can find something useful. But I'm expecting a whole lot of nothing. Guy like that isn't going to have a jacket full of liquor store hold-ups and carjackings."

"Unlikely."

"So is Santos gonna make time for us today?"

"Even better. He's coming here. He said he was on his way over here this afternoon anyway, so we're going to meet him for a beer around four."

I glanced at my watch. Two fifteen. "Good. Gives us time to get our thoughts together and figure out some strategery. I have a little idea rattling around that might turn into something."

"Can't be worse than what we got now."

"Nope. It might even be better."

"Wouldn't that be something?"

We drove back to my house, slowly snaking our way through the weekend traffic choking the parking lot at Long Beach. It was nearing low tide and the beach was full of people. I tried not to think about the fun I was missing and just pictured a slew of fat girls in bikinis that were three sizes too small laid out on their stomachs. It wasn't working.

Tex parked in my driveway and we went inside. I grabbed two bottles of water from the fridge and we settled in on the front deck, looking out at the water. I propped my feet on the railing, chewing over what had happened so far. There were a lot of things that didn't make much sense, starting with there being nine bodies in a pond in the first place. There are a lot of places to hide bodies where they'll never be found, or at least not in any time frame that the killer would care about. A lot of times, even the killers who have planned out their crimes in minute detail and thought of every contingency tend to lose their minds when it comes time to dispose of the body. I'd once worked a case where a woman who'd been taking beatings from her boyfriend for three years had shot him four times while he took an afternoon nap, then drove way the hell up to New Hampshire with his body in the trunk. She stopped to buy lottery tickets and a handle of gin at a big state liquor store in Nashua and got caught when she opened the trunk to load the booze in full of view of about a dozen people in the parking lot. I almost felt bad for her. Thing is, most of the time, if you just go a hundred yards or so into the woods and dig a grave, it's going to be a very long time before anyone ever finds it.

So that was bugging me, as was the fact that two of the bodies didn't have hands, while the rest did. But the thing that was really pulling at me was guy I'd seen standing in the trees at the crime scene. I hadn't mentioned it to Tex, mostly because I wasn't even sure what I'd seen. If the guy was just a citizen, trying to catch a glimpse of the action, then why did he take off? And if he was something else, why show himself? I didn't see any advantage or percentage in the guy hanging around the scene if he was somehow involved. You'd think he'd want to be as far away as possible. Or maybe he'd just been a heat-induced hallucination, who knows. And where the hell had he gone? I had no answers for any of this.

"So what are we hoping to get from Santos?" I asked Tex. "You know him?"

"Yeah, he's a decent guy, for a lawyer. Him and my old man go back. I'd see him around when I tagged along with my dad to the Portuguese-American club once in a while. He defended that kid from Mattapoisett

57

a few years back who ran over the football players who'd been whipping his ass every week for like two years straight."

"That was him? He got the kid off, if I remember right."

"Yup. Sold the jury a story about the kid having post-traumatic stress disorder from all the beatings he'd taken. Probably helped that the kid looked like Linus and sounded like Beaker. Made a nice victim. I think he ended up with some reality TV deal out of it, too."

"Of course he did."

"As far as Santos goes though, I'm not sure we're going to get much useful info out of him on this. He was already making noise to me on the phone about how his client is a respected businessman in Plymouth and a faithful member of St. Peter's and all that shit, saying he bought the Duxbury property as an investment and planned to build some condos there, but then the housing market tanked and his financing dried up or whatever."

"Forget about the question of how a guy who owns a convenience store that doesn't seem to actually sell anything is getting a loan in the first place."

"That's none of your business."

"Right." My phone buzzed in my pocket. I dug it out and saw that it was the office. "Tobin."

"Hey Danny, it's Harris. Got some data for you on DeSilva. You ready?" Harris was a detective in the Computer Crimes Division and probably the best guy I'd ever seen at open-source data and intelligence collection. We'd both been part of the team that had

58

helped stand up the CCD and had worked together for several years, doing some very interesting work. While Tex had been out messing around doing buy-busts with crackheads in Dorchester, we'd been doing some of the first real work going after the emerging crews of Russians, Ukrainians and Brazilians that were running identity theft scams, putting together monster botnets and generally finding as many ways as possible to raise hell on the Internet. While I'd spent most of my time in CCD doing straight investigative work and honing my technical skills, Harris had found his niche mining the Web and public databases for information on targets. He'd become the go-to guy not just in our agency, but also for the local FBI guys and other agencies around New England. He had an uncanny ability to pull together little bits of data from dozens of different sources and weave them into a comprehensive picture of a specific person or group. It was kind of terrifying.

"Yeah man. Go ahead," I said.

"So you were right about him not having much of a jacket. He's clean, man. All we have on him is a couple of speeding tickets and a harassment complaint from a former tenant a few years back that was eventually dropped. Came here from Brazil in 1997 with his wife, 10-year-old son and six-year-old daughter. Became a citizen a couple of years ago. He's listed as the owner and sole proprietor of a grocery store in Plymouth."

"Yeah, we saw the store. He's not even pretending to do any business there."

"Apparently not. He had revenue of $3,133.70 last year from that place. But he also has another business that's doing slightly better. DeSilva runs a travel business that caters exclusively to Brazilians."

"So he puts together tours for other immigrants?"

"Actually, no. He's on the other side, helping Brazilians come up here. You know how tight the immigration situation has gotten in the last couple of years. A lot of citizens from South American countries that are ostensibly our allies can't even get a visa for legit business trips or vacations, so there's a lot of money to be made for people who know how to work the system. And there's even more cash flowing to guys who can get you into the U.S. and find you a way to stay here for good."

"Did you say 'ostensibly'?"

"I did."

"Just checking. Carry on."

"So I dug around on the site for this travel company, Rio All-American Tours, and there wasn't a whole lot there. It was in Portuguese so I was using a translated page, but mostly it seems to consist of a brochure-ware front end with clip art photos of the Statue of Liberty, Grand Canyon, shit like that, and a contact email address and 800 number. One interesting thing though?"

"Do tell."

"When I was messing around trying to find a directory or any hidden pages they might have, I got a database error message on one of the internal pages. SQL Server version number, etc. Just thought you'd like to know."

"Ah ha. Doesn't he know that there are bad guys out there who might want to take advantage of such a mistake?"

"Apparently not. Anyway, the other sort of odd thing about this company is it seems to be targeting pretty much only women. There's all this stuff about package tours for groups of women, shopping excursions, special female escorts once they're here to help them out, all that."

While I was talking to Harris, Tex had taken Reggie and wandered across the road and was now standing on top of the dunes, talking to a pair of girls in bikinis. The two girls, who looked to about 20 at the most, were fawning over Reggie, alternately giggling and tucking their hair behind their ears. Tex looked over and gave me a thumbs-up. I gave him the finger.

"So he's making some money with the travel thing?" I asked Harris.

"Uh, yeah. Shows revenue of just under two million last year."

"Damn. We're in the wrong business."

"For many, many reasons. And, that two mill is just what he reported. A lot of these businesses deal in cash or electronic payments through PayPal or whatever, so it wouldn't be hard for DeSilva to hide a significant chunk of income."

"So, OK. That's something," I said. "We're talking to his lawyer in a bit and I get the feeling we're going to need all the leverage we can get. DeSilva's got all the markings of a pro. I don't care what his record says.

61

Can you do me a favor? Keep digging on this guy, see what else turns up."

"Yup, will do."

"And send me the link to that error page you found. I should warn Mr. DeSilva about that."

"Of course. We wouldn't want him getting hacked."

"OK, thanks man. Talk to you."

I stood up and waved Tex back over. I filled him in on my conversation with Harris.

"This guy's a shithead, for sure," Tex said. "But that doesn't necessarily mean he dropped a bunch of bodies in that pond or even that he knows who did."

"All true. And I'd imagine that's what Santos is gonna try to sell us, too. Minus the part about him being a shithead."

"Eh, Santos is a lawyer. He knows a shithead when he sees one."

Six

"He's a shithead," Santos said, shrugging.

We were sitting at a table in the bar area at the British Beer Company, waiting for the waitress to come around for our drink orders. The small space was filling up quickly and in an hour or so it would be shoulder-to-shoulder in here, jammed with people watching the Sox game, bitching about what a hump J.D. Drew was. The BBC was a small chain on the Cape and this one was the northern outpost. It was only about a dozen steps off Court Street in the middle of downtown, but it was hidden away on a one-way side street, next to a dance academy and a storefront church, so it had the feel of an out-of-the-way spot.

Our waitress finally made her way through the crowd to our table. Tex and Santos ordered Sam Summer drafts and I asked for a pint of Ipswich Ale. She waded back into the crowd in the direction of the bar to collect our beers.

"DeSilva is mean and nasty and I've heard about some ugliness with his wife. But that doesn't mean he's part of this thing. I've spent a lot of time in court with him in the last few years. Civil crap, mostly," Santos said. "He took a couple falls in Brazil, some petty drug stuff. I'm sure you guys already know all this."

We both nodded. We hadn't gotten as far as checking with the authorities in Brazil yet, but that now moved to the top of the list.

"Even though he's been a citizen for a while and Brazil is not generally considered a terrorist state, anyone with brown skin who talks funny gets harassed these days. It doesn't take much for Immigration or someone to decide they want to crawl up your ass with a flashlight."

"No doubt," Tex said. "And him running a business bringing lots of other people into the country probably makes him a target of opportunity for enterprising ICE guys. Especially if some of those people happen to forget to go home again."

Santos shook his head. "As far as I know, he runs a legit travel business. He's been at it for years and it does quite well for him, from what I gather."

Our waitress returned with our drinks and set them on the table. Her name was Caroline and I knew her slightly from seeing her in here and at a lot of local road races in the last few months. She was about 25, blond and very fit. She was mostly a 5K specialist and she was always at or near the front of the women's pack.

"Thanks darlin'," Tex said, laying the southern accent on extra thick. It came out sounding like a bad imitation of Foghorn Leghorn.

She smiled politely and looked over at me. "You doing the BAA half marathon next month by any chance?"

"I think so. I'm registered and should be in decent shape," I said. "We'll see how things go. You?"

"My girlfriend talked me into signing up, but I'm still going back and forth on it. I don't usually race past 10 miles, but I want to do Boston sometime soon, so this would be a good test."

"It's a good race, tough course though. Plenty of hills going out and coming back. Let me know if you want some company for a long run some weekend. I'm always around."

She smiled, a real one this time, which was something to see. Her eyes were what carried it, the green irises sparkling and turning almost luminescent. "I might take you up on that. Thanks. It gets boring out there after an hour or so."

She moved off to another table, but threw a glance over her shoulder on the way. Huh.

"She's twelve," Tex said.

"She's at least fifteen," I said, taking a sip of my beer. "And that didn't stop you from going into full-on Matthew McConnaughey mode."

Tex winked. "Just keeping my skills sharp, my friend."

I turned back to Santos. "So, he's got this bullshit storefront down the street here, selling dust bunnies, and a travel business that's bringing in, what, a couple of million bucks a year. That we know about. A lot of that is coming in as cash. Seems like a nice setup for laundering money, you ask me. Our intel guys say they've been looking at him as a possible banker for some of the gangs on the South Shore."

That last bit was a straight bluff, but it wasn't a bad guess.

Santos shrugged again and drank some beer. He was somewhere in his late fifties and built like a pile of wet sand, all lumps and clumps. Tex had told me on the ride over that Santos had once been a minor star in the

65

semi-pro soccer league down New Bedford and Fall River. The teams were sponsored by local bars and ethnic social clubs and the competition was brutal. Apparently Santos had been a tough, Wayne Rooney-style striker. It was tough to picture.

"Like I said, as far as I know, it's a legitimate business. I'm not his accountant. I don't have a clue what he's doing or not doing with his money. And frankly, I don't give a shit. He could be funding a search for life on Uranus for all I care. He pays my bills on time. Sure, I've heard the rumblings about him being tied in with some of the Brazilian crews around here. The Plymouth cops have made it a point to let him know they're watching. But I'm telling you that he hasn't had a bit of criminal trouble that's stuck since I've represented him, and that's been almost five years now."

"That's all fine," Tex said. "Nothing wrong with making some money. Hell, I'd like to make some myself one of these days. But there are some pieces here that don't fit, so we're gonna be taking a hard look at him. Just so you know. If there's nothing there, so be it. But the guy owns a piece of land that looks like it's been used as a human dumpster. Nine bodies, man. Nine. In his pond. And, just to give you a picture of what we're dealing with, two of them were executed. One round each in the back of the head. And someone took the extra step of hacking off the hands of those two with a machete. I'd say the younger one was maybe eighteen, nineteen years old. Not much older than your girls, Mario. But it was sort of hard to tell since they'd been in the water so long. The others all got shotgun blasts in the chest. So, it's great that DeSilva pays his bills and all that, but if he's in this, we're gonna figure it out and then we're gonna fucking bury him."

Santos drained the last of his beer and took a twenty out of his wallet, put it on the table and set his empty glass on top of it. "You definitely inherited your old man's gift for bullshit. Look, I told you what I know. I understand that you guys need to do your jobs, and that's fine. Do it. But I need to do mine, too, so don't get the idea that I'm going to hand my client over to you because I used to play spades with your dad, Frank. Fuck that. Find something or get out of his face."

He stood to go. "The beers are on me. Enjoy."

Santos weaved his way through the crowd and walked out onto Middle Street.

"I think that went well," I said. "So far we've managed to piss off just about everyone associated with this case. And it's only the first day."

Tex nodded and signaled to Caroline for two more beers. "Batting a thousand," he said, glancing up at the TV hanging on the wall behind the bar. "Which is about 750 points higher than J.D. Fucking Drew."

Caroline brought our beers and handed me a folded slip of paper. "Call me about that run," she said. "Or whatever."

"OK. I will."

She walked over to the corner and went up the steel spiral staircase to the top floor, which held a few more tables and a service bar. I couldn't help but watch, which I hoped was the point. It was not disappointing. I sat back in my chair and had a long swallow of beer, looking up at the spot where Caroline had disappeared at the top of the staircase.

"Or whatever," I repeated to myself.

Seven

I woke up early Sunday morning with the sun streaming through the windows on the top floor of the house. I'd left the windows open overnight and I could hear the small waves lapping at the shore. I put out some food for Reggie, who would sleep for another hour at least, pulled on my wetsuit, grabbed my goggles and headed over the dunes to the beach. It was close to low tide and the beach was wide and flat and clean. It was barely 7 a.m., but the temperature already was in the high 70s. Even with the brutally hot summer we'd had, I knew the water would only be in the mid-60s. The Gulf Stream warmed the waters all along the East Coast on its way to the North Atlantic and eventually the west coast of England. All of the East Coast, that is, except the beaches in northern New England, thanks to Cape Cod sticking its fat forearm in the way and absorbing all of that warmth. It was great for Buffy and Chip at the resorts in Chatham and Dennis, but for the rest of us, it sucked out loud.

I waded in up to my knees and stood for a minute while the shock wore off and then plunged in. After I got past the small breakers, the water was nearly dead calm. I settled into an easy rhythm and began turning over the events of the past 24 hours in my mind. I wanted to focus on the few things that we knew for sure and ignore our suspicions for now. We knew that all of the bodies hadn't been dumped at the same time, based on their level of decomposition. We knew two of the girls had been shot once in the back of the head and had their hands cut off, likely with a machete. We knew that the other seven had been shot with a shotgun. We knew that the guy who owned the property had a couple of busts in the homeland that we needed to check up on. And that was the list. Most murder investigations started out with a little more data than that: a name for the victim, a crime scene that we could process for usable evidence, some neighbors or co-workers or friends we could talk to, something. But this one had none of that. Normally we'd be focusing on trying to ID the victims as the first order of business, but the way things were shaping up, we may never be able to put names on them. If this was what I thought it was, those bodies would likely stay Jane and John Doe forever.

Even as I worked through the long stream of things we didn't know about this mess, my mind kept wandering back to the bar and Caroline. There was something unique about her, and it wasn't just her looks, although she was pretty exceptional in that respect. It was more the combination of her looks and the fact that she'd noticed *me*. Of course I'd known who she was, but, especially with women of her caliber, I never expected them to remember me from one day to the next. But she sought me out, which made it much more intriguing. That was a new one for me, and I wasn't exactly sure what to do with it. Still, what could a weekend run hurt?

I looked at my watch: almost thirty minutes. I made a wide loop and headed back for shore. As I neared the beach, I stood up and waded through the shallows to the tidal pools, where the trapped hermit crabs and minnows scattered underfoot. I climbed over the dunes and walked across to my house. My cell phone was ringing as I came in the door and Reggie was standing with his front paws up on the counter, barking at the phone. I looked at the screen and saw it was Tex calling.

"What's happening?" I said.

"You're up. Good. Meet me at the scene. They're pumping the water out of the pond, just in case there's something--or someone--else in there. Captain is up there and wants an update from us."

"Damn. And here I thought you were calling to tell me you'd solved the case in a dream last night."

"Not unless the killer is Mila Kunis."

"And who would press charges if she was?"

"Not me. Listen, can you get up there in a half hour?"

"Sure. See you there."

I sprinted through the shit-shower-shave routine and was out the door in 20 minutes flat. I went out to the driveway and climbed into my CJ-7. I'd had it since college and had spent a lot of nights and weekends working on it, getting it back to its former glory. I'd combed salvage yards and eBay obsessively, looking for original parts for it and had finally gotten it where I wanted it about a year ago. It was a 1985, white-on-white with blue sport stripes on the hood. Straight six with a four-speed manual. A real Jeep, not like the shit they were turning out now, named after movies and video games.

I slid The Cult's *Electric* into the CD player as I turned out of the beach lot onto 3A, and was pulling onto the dirt access road at the pond 15 minutes later. I sat in the Jeep for a minute while Astbury tore through the last bit of "Love Removal Machine" and then hopped out and walked over to where Tex was standing with Winthrop.

"Detective Tobin. Nice of you to make it," Winthrop said.

"I was in the neighborhood."

"Yes. Well, Detective Teixeira was just filling me in on the, ah, progress you made yesterday. It sounds like you're at a bit of a standstill."

"Not at all, sir," I said. "We're just getting our feet under us. This guy DeSilva who owns this place? He's in this somehow. He may not be the one who dumped the bodies, but he's involved one way or another. We just need to find out how. His lawyer said he's got a record back in Brazil, which we're checking on now, and we're going to go talk to the Plymouth cops today and see what they know about him. The lawyer said they've been jocking DeSilva hard lately for some reason."

"OK. That's a decent start, but as I said yesterday, there is a distinct sense of urgency on this case."

I started to protest, but Winthrop held up a hand. "I'm aware that it's a complex case and that you're dealing with a lot of disadvantages, detective. But the fact remains that Superintendent Cooper is personally interested in seeing this investigation resolved quickly. She was kind enough to call me this morning to remind me of that. Just in case I'd forgotten overnight. And so I'm reminding you two."

"Yes, sir," Tex said, sensing that I was on the verge of saying something unwise. "We're aware, sir."

Tex nodded at the crew of men pumping the water out of the pond. "Have they found anything else in there?"

"They drained half of it so far and came up with a bunch of cinder blocks and lengths of chain, which I'd guess were used to weigh the bodies down," Winthrop said.

"No more bodies though?" Tex asked. "That's a win."

As they talked, I glanced over Tex's shoulder at the treeline where I'd seen the man standing yesterday. I didn't know whether I was hoping to see him or hoping for nothing, but he wasn't there. I felt a twinge of disappointment.

"I wonder why the bodies came up now, though. And all at once," Winthrop was saying.

"My bet is the storm," I said. "That was a major blow the other night, and it could have stirred things up enough to cut them loose."

Tex nodded. "I thought the same thing. It's as good an answer as any. But the real question isn't why they came up, but who put them down."

"Indeed it is, detective," Winthrop said. "And I'll let you two get back to the business of figuring that out."

He nodded and walked back to his car, stepping carefully around the mud puddles. Tex and I walked over to the pond and watched for a few minutes as the pumping operation continued. There wasn't much to see, so we headed back to the access road and our cars. A uniformed Duxbury cop was standing in front of the crime scene tape that was still set up at the head of the access road, and standing next to him was the man I'd seen at the treeline yesterday. He was dressed in the same clothes he'd worn the day before and was speaking quietly with the Duxbury officer. They both looked up as we approached. The cop, who'd been at the scene yesterday too, said something to the man and then ducked under the crime scene tape and walked over to us.

"Who's that guy?" I asked. "I saw him here yesterday too."

The cop gave a short laugh. "Local nutbag. We get a call from him at least once a week, talking about ghosts and goblins and shit like that. Lives about half a mile from here in a small place back in the woods a ways. He's harmless. Crazy as a shithouse rat, but harmless."

I looked over my shoulder toward the access road and saw that the man was gone. I turned around and walked a few steps toward the tape and caught sight of him, walking down the dirt lane, zig-zagging from side to side. There was no reason to go after him now that we knew where he lived and who he was. Sort of.

"What did he want here?" Tex asked the cop.

"Nothing, really. We were over to his place a few nights ago. He called about seeing a flying saucer or

UFO or something in the trees. Flashing lights. He was just asking me whether we'd found anything on that."

"Flashing lights?" I said. "Where did you say this guy lived?"

The cop pointed into the woods on the far side of the pond. "That way, roughly," he said. "Maybe a ten-minute walk through the woods if you go that way."

"You said this was when, that you guys were over there?"

"Would've been Thursday, I guess."

"Christ, and none of you guys thought to mention that to us?" I said.

The cop looked confused. "Um, I guess not. But why would you care? He's just a loon."

"Come on, man," Tex said. "Think about it. This guy calls you out here Thursday night to check on some flashing lights and shit in the woods, and the next morning we're all out here looking at a pond full of bodies. In pretty much the same location. You think maybe there's some sort of connection?"

The cop cleared his throat and looked out across the pond toward the trees, which were pretty sparse on that side. "I guess from his place over there, lights coming down the dirt road here might look sort of weird, bouncing up and down and all that."

"Ya think?" I said, my voice rising now as I thought about the chance that they'd missed. "Probably a better bet than a fucking UFO. Shit, man."

"Hey, listen, we didn't know," the cop said. "We figured the guy'd been eating paint chips again or something."

He was no more than 24 or 25 and had probably been on the job for a year or two at most. He may not have ever seen a dead body before yesterday and he was right, there was really no way for him or anyone else to have known what was going on back here. But still, if they'd taken five minutes to look around the other night, we might have been sitting in an interrogation room with the killer instead of out here with nothing. I didn't want to think about it much longer.

Tex put his hand on the cop's shoulder. "We know, man, take it easy. We're just a little anxious to get something going here. We're running into brick walls all over the place."

The cop nodded, but he still looked a little wounded. No one likes to be told he screwed up, especially when he might have saved a life, or at least given us a good shot at the bad guys. Well, fuck it. He was in the deep end now, and his feelings would have to mend themselves. I didn't have time to hold his hand.

"How do we get to this guy's house?" I asked.

"It's pretty easy," the cop said. "When you get back out onto East Street, take your first right and then go down about a quarter mile or so and you'll see a dirt road on the right. His place is maybe a third of a mile down there. It's the only house back there, so you can't miss it."

"OK. Tex, why don't you drive over there. I'm gonna walk from here. I want to see what's between here and there," I said.

Tex nodded. "Sounds good. What's this guy's name?"

"Joao Alves," the cop said. "You want me to ride over with you? He's kinda squirrelly, like I said, so it might help if he saw me with you guys."

I shook my head. "No, thanks. You've got a job to do here and I want to see what this guy is really like, not a watered-down version of him."

"Sure. Well, happy hunting, I guess," the cop said and walked back to his spot on the other side of the yellow tape.

Tex walked after him and went down the road to where his car was parked. I started walking through the field, skirting the western edge of the pond. The heat and winds of the last couple of days had dried the ground out and I could see how badly damaged the area around the pond was. It was completely scorched, with all of the grass and other vegetation having been burned away for a radius of about 50 or 60 yards around the pond. The soil looked bleak and poisoned. I doubted anything would ever grow here again. Most of the trees that had once been near the pond were gone, either burned to cinders or knocked flat, their branches stripped and their trunks rotting into the ground. It reminded me of the black-and-white photos I'd seen of the battlefields at Gettysburg and Manassas, with mangled corpses littering the ground everywhere as one or two medics stood by, overwhelmed at the magnitude of the destruction.

As I walked through the clearing, stepping around the fallen trees, I thought about the dead girls and how they had just been discarded, tossed aside like so many empty fast food containers. They'd been chained to cinder blocks at the bottom of a shallow pond, expertly killed, but inexpertly hidden, with their families presumably left to wonder what had become of them. It was hard to think of a worse state of being for a parent than the limbo of having no idea what's happened to your child. Death, even the hideous, violent death visited upon the people we found in that pond, at least offered the comfort of finality. There was no possibility that any one of those girls would walk through the door of her parents' house on a crisp fall afternoon, hug her little brother and go back to her life. But with no body to identify, the families of our victims would always reserve that small pocket of hope in their minds, imagining that their daughter or son had simply gone away camping with friends for a week or two and forgotten to call. Of course it was an irrational idea, but hope and fear produce our most irrational thoughts, and who wanted to take away a parent's hope for their child? I'd done it before, and if we did our jobs on this case and identified the bodies, I'd be doing it again soon.

I stepped out of the clearing and into the trees and saw a small house off in the distance, perhaps 200 yards away. As I got closer, what I saw made it clear that the word house shouldn't really be applied to this structure. It was about the size of a large RV and was made out of logs, or, more accurately, trees. The little rectangular building was set in a tiny clearing, surrounded by old-growth pines and there was a smaller outbuilding off to one side, maybe twenty yards from the house.

The trees that made up the walls of the main building were roughly cut and of irregular size, but the structure itself looked like it had been built with great care. The walls were probably 10 feet tall and the logs were cemented expertly. I couldn't see any flaws in the outside of the house at all, and it was clear that someone had taken quite a lot of time building it. I stopped about 10 yards away from the house and turned around to look back toward the pond. Even through the trees, I could clearly see the activity around the pond and even make out some of the people.

This was in the middle of the day, but I'd guess at night it would be fairly easy to see headlights pointing this direction from the access road. There was a small window on the house that faced the pond, so Alves would have a clear view of any activity at the pond or in the clearing from inside the house. I walked around the front of the house and saw Tex's car sitting in the dirt driveway. He got out of the car as I came around.

"He's in there," Tex said. "He looked out the window when I pulled up, but didn't come out. Guess he isn't in any hurry to talk."

"Not his choice," I said. I stepped up to the door and was about to knock when the door swung open.

"Hello. Come in, please."

Alves stood aside to let us in. We walked past him and he closed the door behind us. Inside, the tiny house was even more cramped than I would have guessed from the outside. It was one open room, with a small stone fireplace set into the left wall and a single bed standing along the righthand wall. An armchair sat at the foot of the bed, with a small pedestal table next to it. A pair of binoculars sat on the table, next to a framed photo and a hardback copy of *Every Dead Thing*. The photo was of a woman and a teenage girl, who was obviously her daughter. They both had long black hair and fine, delicate features. They were standing on a beach, arm-in-arm with the ocean in the background, the sunlight dancing off the waves. It was the only personal touch I could see in the room. Much of the rest of the space was taken up by stack after stack of books. A large oak dining table stood by the fireplace, flanked by a pair of low benches. The set looked to be handmade and the top of the table was easily four inches thick. And all of it--the tabletop and benches alike--were covered by books. I wandered over to the table and twisted my head sideways to have a look at the books. The titles were all over the map. I saw a lot of biographies and history, a few woodworking manuals, a handful of technical and math texts, a number of cookbooks and dozens of novels: William Gibson, Cormac McCarthy, Hiassen, John MacDonald, Neal Stephenson. An odd mix, but I couldn't argue with his taste.

Tex gave Alves our names and showed him his creds. He said we were working on the case at the pond and would like to ask him a few questions.

"You've read all of these?" I asked, turning to Alves.

"Yes. Some of them many times."

His English was heavily accented, but grammatically perfect. It had the sound of someone who had spent a long time learning the precise way one was supposed to speak the language. He looked to be about 40 or 45 years old, but it was difficult to tell. His skin was deeply lined and was the color of polished oak. He seemed perfectly at ease having us in his house and appeared to be in no rush to find out what we wanted. Then again, he was the one who'd been hanging around the crime scene, so maybe he had something to tell us.

"Would either of you like a drink? Some water or lemonade, perhaps? It's quite warm outside," Alves said.

"Sure," Tex said. "Water would be great."

"Same. Thanks," I said.

Alves nodded and walked to a small dorm-size refrigerator near the rear wall and pulled out two bottles of water and handed them to us. I twisted the cap off mine and drank about half of it down. I hadn't realized how thirsty I was until then and the water felt cold and perfect going down. I looked at Alves and waited for him to speak, but he simply stood still in the center of the room, waiting for us to make the opening move. Silence is the oldest conversational and interrogation gambit there is, but I'm an impatient man and didn't have the time to play the waiting game with this guy.

"So I've seen you hanging around over at the pond the last couple of days. What do you know about what's going on there?"

"Nothing at all. The pond is in my back yard and so I am naturally interested in what is happening there," he said. "I'm simply an observer."

I nodded. "Sure. Lots of excitement over there. How long have you lived here?"

"Four years and one month. I built this house myself, as you might have guessed, and it took me quite some time," Alves said. "I worked on it every day until it was to my liking and then I moved in."

"Do you lease this land from DeSilva?" Tex asked.

Alves formed what could have been taken for a smile with his lips, but it was an expression that was unmistakably bitter and hateful. He turned toward Tex, regarding him slowly and seemingly for the first time. "You are Portuguese," he said. A statement, not a question.

"I am."

"Then you will understand some of what I am about to say, but not all. DeSilva is a parasite, a human maggot. He presents himself as a businessman, as a man who helps his countrymen who have come here, offering them jobs and housing and other services. He and his helpers go to the new immigrants, whom they know have no connections here and know no English, the weakest and most vulnerable among us, and offer them a hand. Come, he says, I will help you up. I was once like you: poor, confused, lost in this new country without friends or family to help me, he says. But I have made my way and become a success and so can you. Let me show you the way. I will give you a place to live and a good wage and soon, you too will be like me: an American success story." Alves paused and shook his head. "But it is all bullshit. Vile lies and half-truths. He makes us all...what is the word? *Escravos*?"

"Slaves," Tex said.

"Yes, slaves. He promises fair pay and good work and instead gives us criminal wages for the most menial work. Collecting garbage, cleaning toilets, scraping dead, rotting animals from the roadways. DeSilva is a piece of shit, a predator. So no, I do not lease this land from him. I live here at his pleasure. As I said, I built this house myself, but it is his land. If I anger him or somehow fall out of his favor, I will be out on the street within an hour."

"Or in the pond?" I said.

Alves cut his eyes at me, but said nothing. I saw something in the look that made me think that whatever else might happen, this man would not allow himself to end up as a nameless corpse at the bottom of a cranberry pond. Not ever.

"Were you in the store yesterday when we came in?" I asked.

"No. I was across the street, watching."

"What do you do for DeSilva?" Tex asked.

"Whatever he wishes. Mostly, I am his driver. I take him here, I take him there."

"That doesn't sound so bad," I said, and as soon as I finished the sentence, I knew I'd made a mistake. Alves stared at me for a full 30 seconds before answering.

"No, it doesn't, does it? It sounds like a nice, easy job. I sit in a nice air-conditioned car all day, no toilets to clean, no trash to pick up. But the garbage-pickers have it better, detective. In Brazil, before I came here, do you know what my job was?"

I shook my head.

"I was an engineer. I helped design bridges and buildings. I am an educated man, detective," he made a sweeping gesture with his arm, indicating the mass of books. "I was a respected man in my country, at the top of my profession. I turned away work that others would beg for. And now? Now I am the servant of a man who I would have spit on in Brazil."

I looked at Tex, hoping he'd pull me out of the hole I'd dug for myself.

"What do you owe him? Why do you continue working for him?" Tex asked.

"He helped me immigrate. Even though I was a professional, I could not get a visa. So DeSilva made it happen. I did not ask how, but I assume it involved some bribes or threats or both. I have a valid work visa now, but he can make that disappear any time he chooses. So I work and I wait."

"For what?" Tex asked.

Alves just stared at Tex without answering. The silence lingered, and not comfortably. Tex finally looked away. It was time to move on to why we were here.

"Let me ask you something," I said. "The local police told us that they are out here pretty often talking to you. Something about, ah, flashing lights and strange sounds."

"Yes. I have called them a few times. They think I'm a crazy man, living here in the woods by myself with no TV. So they dismiss whatever I tell them as foolishness. But I saw you walking over here from the pond and turning around to look back. You know what I can see from here. There's activity over there sometimes, but no one cares."

"When was the last time you saw something over there?" I asked.

"If you talked to the Duxbury police, then I'm sure they told you I called them on Thursday night. I saw lights over there and could hear voices. I had my windows open and sounds carry quite well out here."

"What do you think was happening?"

"I don't know. Is that not your job, to figure that out?"

"It is," I said. "And it's a lot easier for us to do that when people cooperate and don't give us a load of shit instead of answering our questions."

"I'm not being rude, detective. But let me ask you this: You found a bunch of dead bodies in that pond, correct?"

I nodded.

"And you know that DeSilva owns that land, correct?"

"Yes."

"Then there's nothing else I can tell you that you don't already know. *Lex parsimoniae*," he said.

"Well, in my experience, the simplest answer isn't always the correct one. Just the easiest one," I said. Alves looked surprised by my response. "I'm not as dumb as I look, Mr. Alves. I've read a few books in my time, too."

He nodded. Tex and I moved toward the door and Alves opened it for us. I went out and Tex followed, but turned around before Alves closed the door. "One thing I meant to ask," Tex said. "How did you get hooked up with DeSilva in the first place? Did you go through his travel company?"

"No. It was much simpler than that," Alves said. "He's my uncle."

"Aren't you the lucky one," Tex said.

Something passed across Alves's face then, just for a moment, a flicker of wistfulness or regret, I couldn't be sure which. Maybe both.

"I am indeed," he said, and closed the door.

Eight

I rode back to the pond with Tex and neither one of us spoke on the way. When he pulled into the dirt access road and killed the engine, we sat in the car for a minute longer in silence. He was stewing about something, but I knew him well enough to know that he'd come out with it when he was ready. I had a feeling we'd missed something back there with Alves, but I wasn't sure what it was. The idea of this guy, who was clearly not the head case that the locals made him out to be, working for a man he despised day after day, eating heaping spoonfuls of shit all the while, made no sense to me. Even if he was here illegally initially, if he had legit status now, he should be able to find a real job with no trouble. If the craftsmanship on the Big Dig was any indication, there must be plenty of work out there for non-idiot engineers.

"There was something wrong about that guy," Tex said at last.

"You mean apart from the fact that he lives in Abe Lincoln's childhood home?"

"He was pushing us pretty hard down the road toward DeSilva. I mean, I get the fact that he hates this guy and all that, but he is still Alves's boss, not to mention his uncle. That's not something that they take lightly, the family connection. You remember my cousin Brian? Fucking guy was running a meth lab in my aunt's garage for what, a year and a half? And when the cops knocked on the door with the warrant, she went out the back door and torched her own garage.

87

Damn near cratered half of Fall River in the process, but they didn't find any evidence they could use on Brian."

"Not that time," I said.

"Good point. Anyway, I'm sayin', it takes a lot for us to turn on our own family. And yeah, I'm saying 'us' even though these guys are Brazilians. They may be our bastard children, but the culture is pretty much the same, as far as that stuff goes. Blood is blood and everyone else can go screw. But Alves isn't on that program, at least not with DeSilva."

"You think he's got some ambitions, maybe gunning for the old man's seat?"

Tex considered that for a minute, but finally shook his head. "I didn't get that vibe from him. I guess it's possible, but it felt to me more like straight-up hatred. Like Alves would gladly sleep on a park bench and feed the pigeons for the rest of his life, as long as DeSilva was off the board. No, I think there's something more basic there. I can't speak on what it is, but it's there."

"That's something we could use, I think," I said. "Hatred tends to make people irrational. Even educated, otherwise intelligent people. And it sounds to me like our man Alves has had about enough of DeSilva at this point."

"It does, doesn't it? Why don't we see what we can find out about Alves while we're checking up on DeSilva with the guys in Brazil. It's Sunday, so we're probably not going to have much luck on that today, though."

"I asked Harris in CCD to check with a guy he knows down there. We worked on a case right before I left with a couple of their federal guys. Some d-bags down there selling banker Trojans that ended up being used against Citibank customers up here. He's supposed to forward me what he gets from them, but I don't know when that's gonna be. Could be two or three days."

"OK, so I'll put in a request on Alves and see what we get. Probably nothing, but it can't hurt. I'm going to see if I can salvage what's left of the weekend with the kids and Kim. I've seen enough of you for the time being."

"I've seen enough of me, too. Let's regroup tomorrow and see where we stand."

"Sounds good."

"Give Kim a hug for me, or maybe even a grope."

"Done and done. Later, man."

I climbed out of Tex's car and hopped into my Jeep, not even glancing over at the pond. They could do it without me for the rest of the day. I'd had enough filth for one weekend. I glanced at my watch: It was barely noon, so I still could salvage a good portion of the day. I grabbed my phone and dialed Caroline's number. She answered on the second ring.

"Hey," I said, "it's, ah, Dan, the guy from last night at the BBC? We talked about running?"

"Took you long enough," she said. I could hear the smile in her voice.

I laughed. "Sorry about that. I figured you were still sleeping. I know how you kids like your sleep."

"Please. I've been up since seven and already did twelve miles this morning. You missed your chance."

"Damn. Well, I have a better idea anyway. How about an afternoon at the beach and then dinner? I'll cook."

"You had me right up till the part about you cooking. You sure you're up for that? I mean, I don't know too many bachelors who can cook anything more than mac and cheese."

"I think I can swing it, don't worry. As long as you're not allergic to seafood or good beer, we're set."

"Only thing I'm allergic to is boredom," she said.

Mmmm. Like. "None of that here," I said. "So it's a little after noon now. You want to meet me at my place at two? I live down by the beach."

"You're on."

I stopped at Wood's Seafood on the way home and picked up the stuff I'd need for dinner and then dropped by the liquor store and grabbed a couple six packs and a bottle of rum. By the time I got back to my house is was past one. I had enough time to shower quickly, change and get the coolers out before I had to head down to pick Caroline up. I left the house open and brought Reggie with me. He scrambled into the front passenger seat and put his front paws on the dashboard. We got down to the parking lot and found Caroline just getting out of her car, a late-80s 300ZX that would have made it about nine feet down the dirt road before it either got irretrievably stuck or she hit a rock and dumped all of the oil on the sand.

Caroline waved as she pulled her beach bag from the car and locked it down. She was wearing a bright yellow bikini top and a white sarong and had her hair tied up in a long ponytail. Her skin was a healthy golden brown and she turned the heads of a car full of teenage boys as she walked past. I smiled and waved back and chased Reggie into the tiny rear seat to make room for her.

"Hey," she said, as she dropped her tote bag into the back and swung up into the front seat. She gave me a smile that warmed damn near every inch of me and then touched my knee.

"Hey. Ready to go?"

"You bet. Who's this in the back?" she said, turning around and giving Reggie her hand. He took one sniff and then wiggled his way in between the front seats and plopped his head in her lap. Caroline laughed and began scratching his ears.

"That's Reggie. He's very shy."

"I see that. Well, Reggie, it's nice meeting you."

I dropped the Jeep into gear and swung back onto the dirt road. The road was lined on the ocean side with SUVs and trucks, people pulling chairs and coolers and hibachis out and scrambling over the rocks and dunes to the beach below. Caroline had her face turned upward toward the sun, still scratching Reggie behind his ears as we drove.

"Love the Jeep," she said, her eyes half open as she took in the sea air. "CJ-7?"

I looked over at her and she gave me a satisfied smile.

"My older brother had one when I was in high school," she said. "It was a junker, but it was so bad-ass. It was red with black seats, just an AM radio. He took the doors off one summer and could never figure out how to get them back on. Somehow that made it even cooler."

"It takes me two hours to get the doors back on this thing. Did you inherit his?"

"I wish. He took it to college and it never came back. I think he might have sold it one year when he needed money for spring break. Can you imagine?"

"Nope. I'd sell one of my kidneys before I sold this Jeep."

"Always have another kidney," she said.

"Exactly."

By the time we got to my house, Reggie had abandoned all pretense of civility and was sprawled across Caroline's lap, his head stuck out the side of the Jeep with his tongue hanging out. Reggie was usually a pretty good judge of character, although he'd happily lick the hand of Brendan Vick if he thought there was a piece of steak in it. Still, his affection for Caroline was a good sign. I parked in the driveway and Reggie leaped out and ran up the stairs to the door while I grabbed Caroline's bag and we trailed along behind.

"I always wondered who lived in these houses," she said as we walked inside. "You live here all year?"

"Yeah, for the last couple of years. It was my family's summer house for a long time before that. We'd come up here for a few weeks every summer, sit on the beach, go sailing and pretend we were Kennedys," I said.

"I love the view."

"It's a great spot, for sure. So, you ready? I've got chairs and some sandwiches and drinks in the coolers, but we can always walk back over here if you need something else."

"All I need is a patch of sand, some sun and a towel and I'm set. I'm pretty low maintenance."

I smiled. "Let's hit it, then."

I put a leash on Reggie and grabbed the cooler and we walked across the road and over the dunes to the beach. The tide was on its way out and there already was a lot of beach available. The public section of the beach had been packed when we drove in, but you couldn't get to this part without a resident's pass, so it was always less crowded, even on a holiday weekend. We found a flat spot about 15 yards from the high-water mark on the sand and dropped our stuff. Reggie immediately spotted a seagull and was straining at the leash. I let him off and he got within a few feet of the bird before it took off. He barely broke stride as he adjusted course and headed straight for the water, splashing right in up to his chest. Dogs were supposed to be leashed out here, but no one really cared as long as he wasn't attacking their kids or shitting on their picnic blankets, so I usually let him run. He'd be back when he got hungry. I set up the chairs and we sat down, the cooler between us on the sand and the sun slightly behind us. Caroline let out a long, satisfied sigh as she dug her feet into the sand, burrowing her toes down to get to the cooler layers beneath.

"So how do you like being a cop," she said, glancing over at me.

"How'd you know I'm police?"

"Come on. I've seen you around town and in the bar plenty of times, sometimes with other cops. The other day you were in there and I could see the gun on your hip, under your shirt. You're never in uniform, so I'm guessing you're either a detective or some kind of boss. But you don't look like the desk-and-chair type to me," she said.

"OK, nicely done. Yeah, I'm a homicide detective. State police. I guess I'm not as slick as I thought I was."

"They never are," she said, laughing.

"Ouch," I said.

"Also, my dad is a cop, so I can spot one a mile away."

"Ahhh, I see how it is. Where's he work?"

"Boston. He's on the gang squad right now. Scott Nelson."

"Whew. Don't know him."

She laughed.

"Being police is all I ever really wanted to do. I didn't even consider the idea that it wouldn't work, to be honest. I have no idea what I'd be doing if I hadn't gotten into the academy. A lot of guys get into it because they come out of the military or college or whatever and can't think of anything better to do, and they think they'll just drive around and hand out speeding tickets and then retire to Palm Beach after twenty-five years. And you can get away with that in a lot of places, honestly."

"That's not you."

"That is most definitely not me," I said.

"So what's it about for you? Being the good guy, cops and robbers and all that?"

"Not really. It's all about the puzzle, the challenge of figuring out how the pieces fit together to form a complete picture. Most of what we do is about trying to crawl inside the minds of the guys we're up against, figuring out why they do what they do, what their weaknesses are and how we can force them into mistakes, or how we can capitalize on the mistakes they've already made."

"And they always make mistakes?"

"No, not always. There are a lot of absolute morons who kill people, and trust me, I've met a lot of them. Killing someone is usually not the result of a reasoned, well-conceived plan. It's usually a spur-of-the-moment thing that leaves the killer with a big mess to clean up. Those are boring. They may take some time to tie up, but you know they're going down. But, we also come up against some really, really smart and careful guys for whom killing is just a part of their business, a consequence of someone doing something he shouldn't have or owing the wrong person money. They're not doing it out of passion or hatred or any other emotion that makes people dumb and careless. For them, it's just a way to solve a problem. So those guys know what they're doing and how to do it, and that makes them very tough to catch."

"Those are the ones you enjoy, I'm guessing."

"That's a fact," I said. I reached into the cooler and took out two bottles of Pacifico and held one up to her. She nodded and I opened it and handed it across, then opened my own..

"If you had pulled a Bud Light out of there, I would've walked home," she said as she shifted lower in her chair and stretched her legs out along the sand. It was a lovely sight.

"Who could blame you?"

A couple with a young boy of maybe six or seven came over the dunes behind us and set up camp about ten yards away. They spread out a blanket and I watched as the father, a guy maybe a year or two younger than I was, struggled with a pop-up sun tent. He finally wrestled it into submission and plopped himself in a chair, exhausted from getting his butt kicked by a twelve dollar beach shelter. The mother was busy trying to convince the boy to let her put on sunscreen, and he was running laps around the tent trying to keep away from her. After a bit of that, she stopped and hid behind the tent and then sprang out and grabbed the kid as he came around the side. She caught him by the arm and dropped him to the sand and began spraying on the sunscreen while he continued to squirm.

"Mom! Stop being mean! You're hurting me," the kid squealed. His mother paid him no mind, continuing to hose him down with the sunblock.

Caroline watched all of this with a look of amusement.

"I remember calling my mother mean once when I was about that age," she said. "She was trying to get me to clean up my room and I wasn't listening. I was pulling clothes out of my dresser and throwing them all over the place. She was furious. She finally said that if I didn't clean up, any toy that she had to pick up for me was going in the trash. I told her she was being mean, just like that kid did."

"How did that go?"

"My mom's the nicest woman, but she's a proper Southern lady and she was *not* going to have me talking to her like that. So she told me very calmly to go play outside. An hour or so later I came back in and she had taken every single thing in my room--clothes, toys, furniture, pictures, everything--and locked it all in the spare room. All of it. When I saw it, I didn't know what to do. I just stood there. So my mom looks at me and says, You want to know what mean is? *This* is mean."

"You ever call her mean again?"

"I don't think I've called *anyone* mean since then."

Reggie came running back up from the water and stopped a few feet in front of us. He seemed to consider his options for a second and then plopped down on the sand between us, next to the cooler. He probably figured it was a good idea to keep the guy who fed him happy, while at the same time sticking close to the pretty girl. He might have been ugly, but you couldn't say he was dumb. Caroline reached down and patted his head and he let out a contented groan.

97

"He's an...interesting looking dog," she said, glancing sideways at me.

"It's OK, you can say it. He knows he's ugly. It's taken years of therapy and image consulting, but he's come to grips with it."

"That's a big step."

"It really is. From what I can tell through his, ah, interactions with the ladies at the park, he might have some other assets that make up for his looks."

She giggled at that and snuck a look down at Reggie, who had rolled over on to his back and was wiggling around, trying to get at something that was itching back there.

I drained the last of my beer and put the empty bottle back in the cooler and pulled out a fresh one. I held one up for Caroline and she nodded, handing me her empty. "So what about you?" I asked. "How long have you been at the BBC?"

"Like you don't know," she said, winking at me from behind her sunglasses. "About six months I guess. I wanted to live at the beach for the summer and the bar is an easy way to make good money. But now that the summer is over, it's back to reality."

"Which is what?"

"School. I'm working on my Ph.D. in contemporary art at BU. I'm pretty much finished, except for my thesis, which is about half done right now."

"No shit? Art. And here I thought you were just a pretty girl who worked in a bar," I said. "Now I have to deal with brains too? I don't know if this is gonna work out."

"I really should wear a pin or something that warns guys about that. It would save me a lot of trouble."

"That assumes that they can read, though."

A smile then.

"So what are you going to do once you're finished? Teach?"

"No idea. Not teach, though. I'm not trying to live in Northampton or Iowa, or wherever preaching about the beauty and purity of art to freshmen who couldn't care less and just want to pass so they can move on to something that will make them money. And who can blame them? I'll probably end up waiting tables again," she said. "The most over-educated waitress on earth."

"Who cares? As long as you're doing something you like, that's the secret."

"Amen. Once I find out what that is, I'll be all set," she said. "Until then, sitting on the beach drinking beer seems like a pretty good way to pass the time."

"That it does," I said. "That it does."

It went like that, the afternoon slipping away easily until dusk started to gather and we got our things together and went back to the house. Caroline went upstairs to shower while I got started on dinner. I shelled a quarter-pound of shrimp and put them in a bowl with some lemon juice, garlic and a pinch of salt to marinate. Then I got the meat for the burgers out of the refrigerator, along with some veggies and a block of habanero-laced cheese I'd slice up to melt on the burgers. I'd bought some ground bison and I mixed that in a bowl with some ground Kobe beef, just to add a little more fat content to the bison, and little bit of dried onion and oregano. I formed the meat into four patties and set them aside while I started cutting up some honeydew, cantaloupe and watermelon for a fruit salad.

By the time I was finished with that, Caroline was coming down the stairs from the shower. She was wearing a pale pink tank top and light tan shorts that did absolutely nothing to hide her terrific legs. She came over to the counter where I was working and surveyed the lineup.

"I'm mildly impressed," she said.

"Don't get ahead of yourself. You haven't tasted any of it yet," I said. "I hope you're not offended by the lack of a salad with sprouts and watercress and whatever. I have an aversion to the vegetable aisle."

"I'm all carnivore, my friend. I like some veggies, but salad is what food eats."

I laughed as I caught the playful smile she threw me. I pointed to the bar set up in the living room. "Help yourself. There should be anything you need over there. Or there's plenty of beer in the fridge and I have some good pinot noir my dad brought back from Napa last year, if you'd rather have that."

"I better stick with the beer at this point or I might get a little too friendly," she said as she walked to the refrigerator.

"We can't have that."

Caroline took two bottles of Sierra Nevada from the refrigerator, opened them and handed one to me. "Can I help with anything?" she asked. "It looks like you have this pretty well under control."

"I'm good, thanks. Just about to start the grill and get the shrimp on the skewers."

I walked out to the back deck and got the fire going on the Weber. By the time I was done, Caroline had found the skewers and was nearly finished loading them with the marinated shrimp. I put them on a platter and carried them out to the deck and she followed, Reggie trailing along after her. We ate outside, finishing up as the sun was dropping below the trees in the Eel River marsh. The insects were buzzing in the marsh but the mosquitoes had gone away for the year. The dinner conversation had been pleasant, mostly focused on Caroline's thesis and how much she was dreading the prospect of finding a full-time job when she was done. I'd told her a bit about the case we were working on and she'd grown quiet and a look of disgust passed across her face as she listened. I'd left out the nastier bits, but she'd gotten enough of the picture to understand what was going on. Reggie had spent the entire meal curled up on the deck next to Caroline. He hadn't even bothered to lift his head when a bird landed on the railing, practically begging him to chase it. I was pretty sure I'd lost him.

"Can I ask you something?" she said after listening to the rundown of the case.

"Sure."

"How much does being a cop mean to you?"

"Ah, well..."

"Just listening to you talk about the case and the victims...I can tell that it's already getting to you."

I stayed quiet, wondering where this was going.

She scooted forward in her chair and rested her elbows on the table. "It's just...well, I grew up seeing how my dad's work affected him, how much the garbage he had to walk through every day bothered him. He's a good man, but little by little, it just sort of...it changed him."

"How so?" I asked.

She shrugged and began pushing the leftovers on her plate around with her fork, avoiding eye contact. She picked up a stray piece of burger and dropped it on the deck for Reggie, who caught it on the bounce. She looked up after a minute, her eyes narrow and tight.

"Not in a good way, I'll just say that," she said, her voice small. "He was a great dad, but the stress was really tough on my mom. She didn't do well with it. None of us did. They're still together, my parents, but not in any real way. It's been hard, especially after..."

She cleared her throat, looking away toward the marsh.

"I can understand that," I said. "It's not a job that you just do for eight hours and then leave it at the office. It's your life. And it's a challenge, and sometimes it's actually fun, but it's hard as hell on marriages and families. Divorce lawyers make a fortune off cops. I know all that, trust me. But, for me, at least right now, it's what I do."

"I guess what I'm asking is, is it who you are?" she said, and I got the sense that this was not an idle question.

My answer should've been automatic. And as recently as a year ago, it would've been. But things had changed and so had I. Now, I wasn't so sure. But I was even less sure about how I was supposed to answer here.

"Honestly? I guess it is," I said. "Well, let me say this: I love the work, but I don't like the job, if that makes any sense. But it's all I've ever really known, so I wouldn't even know what to do without it. I'd probably just wander around giving random people polygraphs and asking them their whereabouts on the night in question."

She gave me a tight, nervous smile and I knew the joke had failed. And maybe I had, as well.

As we carried the dishes back inside and began cleaning up, Caroline glanced at her watch a couple of times. It was after ten o'clock by the time we finished putting things away. "It's late, so you're more than welcome to stay here," I said. "But I'm happy to drive you back to your car if you want. Well, maybe not happy, but I'll do it."

She laughed. "It's not you I'm worried about. What's going to happen to Reggie if I leave?"

"It could get ugly, I'm not gonna lie. We might be looking at a hunger strike situation."

"Mmmm. There's nothing worse than dog guilt," she said. "I'm not sure I want that on my conscience. Tell you what: I'll take the couch with Reggie as long as you promise we can go for that run in the morning."

"Sold. It's gonna have to be early, because I have to work by 8 or so. Is that cool?" I said.

"You got it."

I got some pillows and blankets and made up the couch for her, which put Reggie into a near fit of excitement. Caroline gave me a demure kiss good-night.

"Thanks," she said. "This was a really good day. I needed one of those."

"You and me both," I said.

In the morning, we were out the door by 6:30 and did about six miles at an easy pace and I was pleased with myself for not struggling to keep up with her. Although she wasn't pushing it, so I wasn't getting too excited. When we got back to the house, Caroline headed upstairs for a shower and I called Tex to check in and see what the plan was for the day.

"I was just gonna call you," he said by way of greeting. "There's not much new right now, but we've got a two-man team sitting on DeSilva as of six a.m. today. They're at the store right now. He got there about an hour ago."

"Good. I want to know immediately if he moves. We don't know a lot about this guy yet and if he goes and meets someone or goes to lunch or whatever, I want to know. We need some data on who he's with and what else he's doing."

"Yup, they have instructions to call me as soon as he walks out the door."

"OK. What else? I'm sort of at a loss for where to start pushing right now. I feel like we have a bunch of little pieces that might not even belong to the same puzzle."

104

"I know it. What about the Brazilian connection? Have you heard anything from your boy on that?"

"Shit, I forgot about that. Lemme see if he emailed me anything overnight. Hang on."

I put the call on hold and switched over to my email and found a message waiting from Harris. I scanned it quickly and saw that he'd gotten a file from the Brazilian federal police on DeSilva. I forwarded it to Tex and switched back to the call.

"I just forwarded you the file from the federales that Harris sent me. I only glanced at it, but it looks to me like he was a little more active down there than Santos led us to believe. I saw a list of charges that were dropped along with the ones that stuck."

"You don't say."

"I do. But it's not the drug shit I expected. I saw at least two kidnapping charges on there. Maybe more. So I think maybe we need to get on the phone with someone down in Brazil and see what we can see about our boy. I think there's a lot here that we're not seeing. If the guys down there have something that we can use to push on with him, all the better."

"Yep, agreed. OK, so why don't you get a name from Harris and see if he can maybe get us on the phone with the right guys. In the meantime, I'm gonna get with Mitchell and see if he has anything for us. He said he might have some early returns by today, right?"

"Yeah. So you do that, I'll talk to Harris and maybe we should check back in around midday and see where we stand."

"Sounds like a plan."

I went back and opened up the file Harris had sent me and looked through it more carefully. DeSilva had been charged three separate times with kidnapping during his time in Brazil, all within a period of less than nine months. All of them had been dropped before DeSilva ever saw the inside of a courtroom. That smelled a lot like payoffs, which were a way of life in a lot of South American countries, especially if you wanted to do the kind of business that DeSilva appeared to be doing. Aside from the kidnappings, there were also a couple of battery charges that had been dropped, along with the minor drug charges that Santos had mentioned. It didn't add up to the sheet of a career criminal, but it had the look of someone who was a bad guy and knew his way around the system.

I called Harris and got his voicemail. I left a message asking him to put me in touch with someone in Brazil who could give us the rundown on DeSilva as soon as possible. When I hung up, Caroline was coming down the stairs with her stuff, ready to go.

"All set?" I said.

"Yeah. Whenever you're ready."

As we headed for the door, Reggie planted himself in front of it and turned his head to the side, as if to say, I don't think so. Caroline laughed and bent down and let Reggie slobber all over her face while I slipped past him and opened the door. She gradually extricated herself from Reggie's clutch and backed out the door after me while he started whining like a two-year-old in dire need of a nap. I drove Caroline out to her car and asked if I could call her later.

She hesitated a beat, but it was long enough to make my stomach drop and remind me that I may not have had the right answers to her questions last night.

"Yeah," she said. "I'm working, but give me a call this afternoon if you want."

"I will."

She nodded and got out. She drove out of the parking lot and I hopped back in my Jeep and headed home. On the short ride back I could feel the happiness of the last 18 hours already draining out of my system, replaced by a creeping sense of dread about what we were getting into with DeSilva, Alves and the rest of this case.

Nine

Harris called as I was finishing up breakfast.

"Hey Danny. I got a name for you. Grab a pen."

"Go. I'm ready."

"Carlos Pena. He's a captain in the federal police down there. I haven't worked with him directly, but my guy down there vouches for him. That's about the best I can do at this distance." He read off Pena's phone number.

"Better than I could do. I know the police forces down there can be kind of a disaster, so I'll take anything I can get. Thanks."

"Yeah. Listen: I was digging around a little more on DeSilva last night and his name popped up in some interesting places. I was searching through some of the forums that immigrants and illegals use and the name of his travel company was in a number of posts. It seems to be pretty well-known in that community for being able to get people into the country. One way or another."

"Ah. Lot of demand for that kind of service these days."

"Sure. And there are plenty of people willing to provide it, but most of them are bad at it. ICE and Border Patrol do a booming business taking those guys down and sending their customers back down south. Mainly they're just guys who get lucky bringing over a few people once or twice and then they figure they can make a business out of it. But that doesn't usually end very well. DeSilva seems to be on another level, though. From what I could glean from the forum posts, his fees are higher than most, but he delivers. He doesn't just leave you stranded once you're across the border either."

"Yeah, I get the feeling he has some good people working with him on this end, too," I said.

"Not just good. It looks to me like he may have some connections in pretty high places. The way that these people were talking on the boards, if you were working with DeSilva's company, you were hooked up. Green card, legit papers and a job once you're here. It's a package deal. That kind of shit is not easy to arrange. The job, sure. But a green card and the rest of it? No."

"No doubt. He'd need some help at Immigration, maybe some people at Border Patrol to look the other way when he's bringing them in. That's probably not that hard, though, honestly. Those guys don't make that much money, so you give them some extra just to wave a couple of trucks a month through and it's easy pickings."

"Probably so," Harris said. "Anyway, I pulled down a bunch of the relevant messages, so I'll send them over to you this morning. Most of it was in Portuguese or Spanish, so I ran it through Google Translate."

"OK, thanks. Lemme know if anything else pops up."

"Yup, will do."

I ended the call and headed upstairs to shower and change. When I was ready, I sat down on the couch with my laptop and opened the email that had come through from Harris. I had a pretty good idea what I'd see, and it was mostly what I expected: essentially a running conversation among a bunch of people using pseudonyms. The handles were a primitive, but highly effective, form of protection for the posters. The chances of unmasking any of the people on the board without a subpoena were virtually nil, and even with that authority, the ISP or owner of the forum would likely delay and fight it long enough that it wouldn't matter by the time we got the data. I didn't give a shit about any of these people, specifically, but if one of them could give us some insights on DeSilva, I'd like to have that conversation.

The translated posts that Harris had sent me were mostly seemingly innocuous messages about trips people had taken with DeSilva's company to Miami or New York or Boston or wherever. People talking about who they'd visited and what they'd seen. There were a couple of names that came up in messages from different people who should have had no reason to know one another, as they'd allegedly gone on trips to different cities at different times. Ten or twelve individuals mentioned that they'd seen their "Uncle Sal" and "cousin Jesus" during their trips. Unless all of these people were related--which I guess was always possible--Sal and Jesus were getting around. Maybe delivering new IDs and green cards. Or maybe everyone really had a cousin named Jesus. I'd like to be Jesus's cousin. It would be a great icebreaker.

The name of the forum that Harris had pulled these messages from didn't mean anything to me, but if it was like most forums, all you needed was an email address and a username to register and then you could post and read whatever messages you liked. I looked it up online and found it quickly, part of a larger site that looked like it catered to recent immigrants and potential émigrés. Sure enough, the forum simply required a username and email to sign up. I used a disposable email address and within a minute I had the confirmation message from the forum and I was in. Unfortunately, like Harris had said, just about all of the traffic was in Spanish or Portuguese. But I used the search function to look for messages that referenced DeSilva's company, and there were several dozen, including a few that had been posted since Harris had grabbed the last post. I'd have Tex take a look at those later.

The amazing thing about Web forums and message boards like this, even ones that discuss illegal activity like smuggling in illegal immigrants, is that people are constantly giving up information about themselves, intentionally and unintentionally. They put their email addresses or cell numbers in their signatures, talked about the name of their kids' schools, mentioned where they worked and even used their real names in some cases. A quick Google or Maltego search and you could have their home address, employer, dog's name and whatever else you wanted on them. People like to talk, and unsophisticated criminals are no different. The Internet might have been a gift from God for smart criminals, but for police who knew how to use and abuse it, it was the equivalent of a unicorn shitting chocolate ice cream. A little luck and we'd find a nice big hot fudge sundae in some of these posts.

I closed my laptop and was getting set to leave when my cell rang.

"Tobin."

"Detective Tobin. Happy Labor Day." Winthrop.

"And to you, sir."

"Yes. I'm hoping it will be. To that end, I have a meeting with our commissioner in an hour and I'd like to have something positive to tell her regarding our nine bodies. Will I have to lie to her?"

"Ah, no. No, sir. Let me just update you on where we are."

"Please do."

"It turns out that this guy DeSilva runs a travel company that supposedly runs tours in the U.S. for South Americans, mainly Brazilians apparently, but not all. But there's nothing to the company, it's just a shell it looks like. And this store that he runs in Plymouth is a total front. The stuff on the shelves is older than I am and he's not even pretending to do any business there. Tex and I jacked him up at the store and he didn't even blink when we told him about the bodies. He knew and he didn't care."

"That doesn't make him a killer."

"No, it doesn't. It doesn't even mean he's involved. But we think he is. We spoke with a guy who works for DeSilva, his driver he says, and he did not have a lot of nice things to say about his boss. Called the guy a predator, said he's making all of his money off the backs of poor people he helps get into the country and

113

he's exploiting his countrymen to do all of this. Harris in CCD did some digging and it looks like DeSilva is probably running illegal aliens into the country through this travel company, which would help explain the cash he's pulling in from this thing."

"That's all very nice, detective, but what about the bodies? How does any of that tie DeSilva or anyone else to the bodies?"

"We don't know yet, captain. That's what we're trying to get at right now. But if DeSilva is a bad guy, and I think it's pretty clear that he is, and he's the owner of the land where the bodies were hidden, then he's someone we need to focus on, at least until we find a good reason not to. We have a surveillance team watching him now because we need to see who he moves with and where he goes. As far as the victims themselves go, the ME said he may have some preliminary results for us today and Tex is following up on that. But we already have the cause of death, so I'm not sure how much more we're going to find out there."

"Probably very little."

"Right. So, with what we know about DeSilva and his background, I think we need to pull him in for questioning and I'd also like to get started on a search warrant for his store and any computers that he has in there," I said. "He's doing all of his business online we think, so there's bound to be a lot of good data on his PCs. We can show that he's running an online business that makes use of those computers and we believe that the business is supporting illegal activities and may be relevant in a multiple murder investigation."

Winthrop sighed. "That's pretty thin, detective. If you want to bring him in for a talk, that's fine. Do it. But I don't hear enough probable cause there for a search warrant. Not even from a friendly judge."

"Yeah, I understand captain, but we need to find out what cards he's holding and I don't think we're going to get that by putting him in a room with his lawyer for an hour. He won't say shit and we'll just end up letting him know how hard we're looking at him. If we can get the search warrant and get into those computers before we talk to him, then we're on solid ground."

"But you need to be on solid ground with the probable cause before you even try that. And you're not. Try again."

"Christ, captain. We *are* trying. That's what I'm telling you here," I said, my voice getting a little too loud now. "As you keep reminding us, Cooper is watching this and we don't have a lot else to go on here. The bodies aren't going to tell us anything, so DeSilva is the best option we have right now. We need to find a crack there."

"OK, settle down, detective. I'm trying to prevent you from wasting more time with a search warrant affidavit that's gonna get kicked back. If you two think that this DeSilva guy is somehow involved and maybe at the center of it, then fine. Push on him and see what happens. But you better push hard and do it now, because Cooper is giving us a little rope with this being a holiday weekend and all of that, but that's not going to last."

"I get that, sir. Can I ask you why we're on this case in the first place? I mean, why didn't the Duxbury guys give it a shot first and then call us if they hit a wall?"

"They didn't call us. We called them."

"What? Why?"

"It's an election year, detective. I know that doesn't mean much to you, but it does to those of us in the upper reaches of the department. Superintendent Cooper wanted this case, and now we've got it. Or, more accurately, you've got it. A big, splashy case like this? We take this down, Cooper gets to take credit and, using the transitive property, so does her boss."

"The governor."

"Correct. So as I said, go at DeSilva if that's the best option you have right now, but you better hope it's the right one, because you won't have time for a U-turn on this."

"Yes, sir. We're doing our best," I said, but he had already hung up. Awesome. Good way to start the day. I walked out onto the front deck and stared out at the ocean. Reggie came out behind me and I bent down and scratched his head while I thought about where we were on the case. I wasn't sure at all that DeSilva was good for the murders himself, but I was pretty sure he was in it up to his eyes. We didn't really have much supporting that conclusion, as Winthrop had pointed out, but I'd learned to trust my instincts on these things. State attorneys and judges, on the other hand, tended to like actual evidence. Which we had none of at this point. That would have to change, and quickly.

I went back inside and called Tex to fill him in on my conversation with Winthrop. He came to the same conclusion as I did.

"We need to see what we have with DeSilva. If he's involved, however remotely, we need to find out how and get to work on him," he said. "For some reason, I feel like he's the key to this thing, regardless of whether he or his people killed them. We can worry about the warrant later."

"I agree. I say we take another run at him, let him know what we know about his bullshit travel company and the illegal immigrants and all of that and see what he does. You never know."

"I like it. OK, lemme call the surveillance guys and see where they are and then let's see if we can't make life a little less comfortable for him."

We met the surveillance team--two guys from intel named Moore and Davis--in the parking lot of a small Brazilian restaurant in North Plymouth. It was just before noon and DeSilva and his crew had been inside for 20 minutes. We were sitting in the surveillance van, a white Econoline with a cable company logo on the side, and Moore was giving us the rundown on their morning.

"Pretty tame," he said. "Two guys showed up around 10:30 carrying a duffel bag, went inside, came back out about five minutes later minus the duffel. That was pretty much it until they left for lunch."

"So who's in there exactly?" Tex asked.

"DeSilva, two meatheads who I'd guess are bodyguards of some kind, a younger guy of about 20 or 22 and another Latino-looking guy who drove them over here," Moore said. "But I don't know whether they're meeting anyone in there."

"Was DeSilva's crew inside the store all morning?"

"Yup. They showed up around 9:30 in that Mercedes over there," Davis said, pointing through the windshield at a black S-Class parked in a handicapped spot. There were a half-dozen other cars scattered around the parking lot.

"OK. We're going to go in and jack DeSilva up, see if we can't shake something loose. I don't anticipate him doing anything dumb in there, but who knows. So you guys stay loose out here."

We went out the back of the van and walked into the restaurant. Inside, it was relatively small, with about 15 tables scattered around the center of the floor and a handful of booths on either side. I spotted DeSilva and his people at a long table near the back wall, close to the kitchen. He was facing the door, with his back to the kitchen. Alves sat to his left and the two juiceheads were in chairs away from the table, leaning against the back wall, sunglasses in place. Alves saw us first. He caught my eye, held it for a moment, and then looked down at the table, shaking his head slightly. One of the juiceheads noticed us walking toward the table and simply brought his chair down onto four legs and stood up. His partner looked up, saw us, and followed suit. We stopped in front of the table and no one spoke. DeSilva simply continued eating without looking up

118

and in no way acknowledged our presence. I pulled out a chair across from DeSilva and sat down. Tex remained standing, looking blankly at the two goons behind DeSilva.

"What's for lunch today?" I said.

DeSilva put down his fork and for the first time looked up from his plate. He wiped his mouth with a napkin and looked at me with complete impassivity. He didn't seem annoyed or upset or even vaguely bothered that we were interrupting his lunch. He simply waited for us to get on with it.

"I know you speak English, so I'm not going to bother with that bullshit this time around. We just thought you'd like to know that we've spent the weekend doing a little homework on you and your operation here," I said. "It's a nice little set-up you have, with the travel company and all of that. I can't imagine why the owner of a tour operator would need muscle like these two apes, but maybe it's because you're running illegals into the country from Brazil and the rest of South America and maybe not everyone is a satisfied customer. Or maybe it's because you've turned some of those customers into indentured servants, chaining them to shitty jobs and shitty living conditions and telling them if they make any noise you'll get them deported by morning. Or, better yet, maybe it's because you were a low-rent drug runner and extortionist in Brazil and you're worried that some of your victims down there might have friends up here. I don't know. But what I do know is that we're onto you and your little bullshit crew here and we're going

119

to stay on you. There are nine bodies in the morgue right now and we found them on your property and I'm pretty sure you know who put them there. Maybe it was even you. Either way, we're going to find out and it's probably not going to be much fun for you."

As I was speaking, DeSilva just sat and listened. I watched him closely and saw his face tighten at the mention of the drugs and kidnappings, but otherwise he was as calm as could be. I glanced over at Alves, who, by contrast, looked as if he would rather be sitting in a dentist's chair getting a double root canal. He was sweating and kept fidgeting with the knife on the table in front of him. I waited for DeSilva to respond, but instead it was the younger man to his right who broke the silence.

"What do you know of our business? You come in here and disturb my father's lunch and call him a criminal? He's a businessman. All we do is help people get into the..."

"Andres." DeSilva grabbed the younger man's arm, cutting him off. He released his grip after a few seconds and patted his son's arm softly, almost tenderly. I stared at the younger man for a few seconds and saw a fierceness in his eyes and his demeanor that I recognized. It was something I'd seen often in guys who thought they were invincible, talking shit on the street corner or the back of a cruiser. It never lasted. Either the fire and the hatred died, or he did.

"Please, excuse my son," DeSilva said. "He is very protective of me and gets upset when he thinks someone is being disrespectful. He is young, so he doesn't understand the way things work sometimes. But I know that you're not being disrespectful to me. You just don't know very much about me, so you've drawn incorrect conclusions. I, however, know a great deal about you, Detective Tobin."

"Is that so?" I said. He had the same polished, accented English that Alves did.

He nodded. "It is. For example, I know you've been in homicide for two years. I know that you were in computer crimes before that and I know that you have a reputation for bringing in big cases. But you also are known as a stone in the shoe of your superiors, not playing ball when they ask you to."

I shrugged. "So you can read the newspaper. Congratulations."

DeSilva smiled. "I'm also aware that you have a brother named Brendan who lives in Palo Alto, California, and is a priest in St. Bonaventure parish. He lives in the rectory and usually says the Saturday evening Mass and hears confessions beforehand. Your mother died some years ago and your father is retired and lives in Virginia, outside Washington. He worked for the government. I know you had a sister named Erin. You live in the house on Long Beach that he owned until recently and you drive a Jeep. Shall I continue?"

I'd tried to resist the impulse, but I'd flinched when DeSilva mentioned Brendan. Even though he was my older brother, I had always been protective of him. He was a good and gentle person, in ways that few people I knew were. Yet he also could be very naive and trusting, traits that were not assets in today's world. Finding him would have been difficult but not impossible. Getting info on Erin and what happened to her would have been much, much harder. DeSilva was pleased with the speech and had a small smile on his face. I felt Tex's hand on my shoulder and I took several slow breaths, trying to push down the bile that was rising in my throat. I could feel the heat building in my face and I knew DeSilva could see that he'd gotten to me. I hated myself for letting him do it so easily.

"Not so tough now, huh?" It was DeSilva's son, smiling, arms crossed. "Doesn't feel so good to be on the other end of this right?"

"Shut up junior, the men are talking now," I said. I held his gaze for a few seconds, then looked back at the older man.

"Be very careful, Mr. DeSilva," I said, my voice rising. A few of the other customers had taken notice and were looking at us now. "Very careful. You might think you know something about me, but you'd be wrong. I know what you are and I know what you're doing. So go ahead and smile and enjoy your lunch. Just know that your little bullshit empire here is crumbling. And I know you've got a family of your own, your son here, a wife and daughter. So don't think you're invincible either."

DeSilva blinked at the mention of his wife and daughter. "Now who's being foolish, detective? I expected more from you, to be honest. I'd been told you were a serious man, a man to be respected. Perhaps I was misinformed."

"I don't give a fuck what you expected or who you talked to. You can respect me or not, I couldn't care less. I've seen dozens of tougher guys than you and they all have one thing in common. They're all in jail." I pointed at him "I'm gonna drop you" then his son "and you" and Alves "and you, and anyone else who was in this."

I stood up and gave the table a little bump, sloshing some of the water in DeSilva's glass into his lap. He nodded slightly and mopped it up with his napkin. I shoved the chair back in and turned to go. Tex stood staring at the two goons for a second, then smiled and said, "See y'all again soon."

We made it about ten feet. "Detective Tobin," DeSilva called. "I hope you had a nice time last night with Ms. Nelson. She's a lovely young woman."

I slowed my pace for a second and turned around, but Tex put his hand on my chest and kept me moving and we went out the door into the parking lot. We went back to the van and climbed in the back. I dropped onto one of the benches and pulled a bottle of water from the cooler they had stocked for their surveillance. I drank half of it down and let out a sigh.

"I gotta get to Caroline," I said to Tex. "I gotta go. If he knows where I live and who she is, he sure as hell knows where she works and probably where she lives. I gotta go."

My words sounded tinny in my ears and my voice was raspy. My heart was racing and I was having a hard time focusing my vision. This was craziness. I'd known her for all of 24 hours and I was sick to my stomach about bringing her into this thing. My chest was tight, my scalp tingling. I wanted to walk back into the restaurant and shoot DeSilva in the stomach and watch him bleed out. Instead, I drank the rest of the water and stood up to go. Tex moved between me and the door.

"Hang on, man. Hang on."

"No, not again. This is *not* happening again, Tex. He knows about Erin? What the *fuck*?"

"Slow down, slow down. Nothing is happening. He's just pushing buttons. Why don't you give Caroline a call first? Is she at the bar?"

I nodded.

"OK, so she's in a public place with lots of other people around. No one's going in and pulling her out of there," he said. "She's safe right now. Give her a call and just check in. If you go charging in there like a crazy person, you're going to spook her and you're going to give DeSilva what he wants. He's trying to freak you out."

I took a deep breath and let it out slowly. I dialed Caroline's number and held my breath. It rang once, twice, three times. Come *on*.

"Hey," she said. "You actually called."

I felt all of the tension drain out of me and I stumbled to the side a bit. Tex caught my arm and lowered me onto the bench.

"I told you I would," I said, willing the words to sound normal. "See? I'm not that guy."

She laughed, a musical, lilting laugh that helped calm me. "All right, all right. Definite points for you," she said. I could hear the noise of the bar in the background. "I can't talk long, it's jammed in here today. But I should be out of here by eleven or so. Is that too late for us to get together? I know you old guys need your rest."

"Settle down there, young lady. I make it through Johnny Carson's monologue most nights still."

The laugh came again and I relaxed a little more. Maybe I wouldn't get to shoot anyone today after all.

"That's quite a feat," she said.

"It is. Anyway, I was thinking I'd come by there this afternoon, grab a couple beers with Tex, if that's OK."

"Sure, that sounds great. Like I said, it's tight in here, but I'll throw a couple of the rummies out and save you some seats at the bar."

"Perfect. We'll see you in twenty then."

"I'll be here."

I ended the call and leaned back against the side of the van. Tex looked at me. "Don't say it," I said.

"No need. Happy she's OK."

I nodded and looked at Moore and Davis. They were clearly waiting for us to fill them in on what happened in the restaurant.

"OK, so it seems like DeSilva was expecting us to do something like this. He was ready for it. I told him we knew about his immigrant operation and that he was a minor league douchebag in Brazil and all of that and he just ate it."

"No reaction?"

"Oh, he had a reaction," I said. "He basically laid out my life's story for me, named my parents, my

125

brother, told me he knew where I lived, all of it. He did his research."

"Christ. How the fuck does he have your home address? Did he threaten you?"

"Not directly. My family's owned that house for a long time and a lot of people in town know us, so it's probably not that hard to figure out," I said. "It was just him pipe swinging, letting me know that he wasn't going to be bullied."

"Sort of what you were trying to do to him," Moore said.

"Yeah. Thanks for that."

"You want us to stay on him?" Davis asked.

"For sure," Tex said. "I'm not fucking around with this guy. He's a pro. In fact, I want one of you guys on DeSilva and one on his kid. We hadn't seen him before and he rose up a little bit in there. I want to know what his story is."

"OK. You got it. By the way, we ran the plates on that Mercedes while you guys were inside. Must be the kid's. It comes back to an Andres DeSilva, age twenty-three, address down in the Pinehills," Davis said. He read off the address for us and Tex took it down.

"Fancy address for a kid that age," Tex said.

"Yup. He also has three other vehicles registered under his name: an Escalade, a Lexus and a 1967 Corvette."

Tex whistled. "I hate this kid."

"OK, thanks guys," I said. "Let us know if he bolts for Canada or something."

We climbed out of the van and went back to our cars. I had something I wanted to check on, so I told Tex I'd meet him at the BBC. I drove south on 3A into downtown and parked across the street and a block down from DeSilva's store. Since they were all at lunch for at least a little while longer, it gave me a chance to check something I'd been thinking about since our visit the other day. When we were inside the store, I'd noticed a wireless router sitting on the shelf behind the counter. It was an older model and since DeSilva didn't strike me as the most technologically astute guy around, I was hoping he'd made a mistake setting it up. I got out of the Jeep and walked across the street. I opened up the WiFi settings on my iPhone and walked up the block slowly. I picked up three hotspots right away, none of which looked right. When I was within about ten yards of DeSilva's store, another access point popped up on the list and I was pretty sure it was his: The network name was Pele1970.

I touched the name on the screen and waited. A box popped up asking me for the network password. Damn. OK, so he wasn't a complete idiot, he'd at least managed to enable the encryption. But that still wasn't much of an obstacle if I was right about the age of his router. The older ones only gave you one option for encryption: WEP, which had been broken for years. There were dozens of tools out there that could crack the password for the router and then let you see all of the traffic going through the router and the victim wouldn't have a clue. If I was right, I'd need to make a phone call.

127

By the time I got home it was mid-afternoon and the beach was overflowing. The weather had remained hot and humid over the weekend and it was in the low 90s now. I tried not to look over the dunes at the people enjoying themselves on what was essentially the last day of summer. Once this case was over, I told myself, I'd spend some quality time with the new Brendan Connelly book on the beach. But I knew it wasn't true. By then, the warm weather would be gone and I'd likely be in no mood for relaxation. I'd be black-assed, in a trough on the other side of the adrenaline high from the chase--and hopefully the catch.

A lot of cops I knew had the same problem, this infuriating inability to let go of cases, regardless of whether they put them down or whiffed completely. It's one of the reasons so many cops drank themselves stupid and ended up divorced and miserable. Nice thoughts on a sunny summer day.

I let myself into the house and found Reggie napping on the couch in the living room, his head hanging halfway off the cushions. He didn't move a muscle when I came in. Hell of a guard dog he was. I went upstairs and showered and changed quickly and drove back toward downtown. On the way, I dialed from memory a number I hadn't called in probably three years. It was not one that I ever kept in my phone or anywhere else someone might come across it. The phone rang once on the other end.

"Danny."

"Hey JD. How are things?" I asked. "It's been a long time."

"Things are good, man. I'm on the boat, feet up on the rail, about to crack the first beer of the day. How's by you?"

"Good. Protecting, serving, violating civil rights, whatever the situation calls for."

"Excellent. So is this a social call, or do I get to break something for you?"

"Depends. Are you near the Internet?"

"Not even close."

"You got some free time to come to Boston for a couple of days?" I knew better than to ask where he was or what he was doing.

"I can make time. How soon?"

"Soon as you can get here. I'm in the middle of a thing that could benefit from your expertise. It's almost a waste of your talent, honestly, but I can't do it myself, so..."

"Shit, man, you know I got you. Lemme think. Today's what, Thursday? I can probably be there by tomorrow afternoon."

"Today's Monday, JD."

"Really? Wow. OK, I can still be there tomorrow afternoon. I'll hook it up and send you the info in email. Your Hushmail address still good?"

"Yup. Listen man, I really appreciate it. This thing is, ah, sort of off the books, so I can't get the department to cover your expenses or anything, but I'll take care of them on my own. Cool?"

129

He laughed. "I ain't charging you and you couldn't afford it if I did. Just send a car to get me at Logan tomorrow and buy me a big fucking lobster dinner and we're straight."

"Done. Thanks, man. Send me your flight info and I'm gonna send you a little rundown of what I have in mind."

"Nah, hang onto that. Tell me when I see you. I hear the cops can subpoena email records now."

I had to laugh. "I'm slippin' today, man. Sorry. This is a layup for you anyway. See you tomorrow. I'll have some Lone Star in the fridge for you."

"Perfect. Tomorrow, man."

I pulled out onto Main Street, heading for the bar. I parked a block short of the British Beer Company and walked down, thinking about a cold beer and Caroline. Definitely not in that order. The place was just as crowded as she had said, but she'd blocked off two stools for us at the bar, as promised. Tex was already planted in one of them, sipping a beer and chatting with her. I grabbed the stool next to him and Caroline leaned across the bar and gave me a quick kiss. A jolt of electricity ran through me as I realized how quickly I'd become attached to her.

It had been a long time since I'd felt that. Too long.

"Where you been?" Tex asked.

"Had to make a quick stop and then I got caught up on a phone call. What did I miss?"

"Tex and I have been having a nice talk. I'm learning quite a bit about you."

130

"Fantastic. Just what I need is you getting my life's story from him. So I guess he's told you all about my extensive charity work with crippled kids and all the times I've been on Oprah to talk about the research I do on a cure for blindness."

"Absolutely," she said, setting an Ipswich draft down in front of me. "That, and your deep love of Coldplay and the Twilight books. It's been quite revealing."

"I can imagine. So, it's been busy all afternoon?" I asked. I swiveled my stool around and scanned the bar. I didn't know what I was looking for, and if DeSilva had someone in here, it was likely someone I'd never seen before, so it was a waste of time. But as much as it pissed me off, he'd gotten to me with that comment about Caroline and I felt like I needed to be doing something. Sitting here in the bar with her was the best I could do at the moment. The room was fairly full and I saw some familiar faces, but nothing or no one that struck me as out of place.

"Yeah, we've been slammed," Caroline said. "Nonstop. Speaking of which, let me go seat this group. Back in a minute."

I didn't tell Tex what I'd been up to since we left the restaurant. If it worked out, I'd tell him then, but if not, there was no need for him to be exposed too if things went south.

"So while you were napping or whatever, I was doing some actual police work," he said.

"About time."

"Yeah. I was talking to Moore and Davis for a little while after you left and they said they'd been helping out on a case down in New Bedford the last couple of weeks. It looks like some remnants of the mob still hanging on, operating out of a club down there, running girls, selling dope, whatever. But the interesting part is that these guys have been flush with girls and dope for the last year or so, and then all of a sudden things dry up. No more dope, no more fresh girls, just the same tired ones."

"And?"

"And these guys were well-known for having the best South American girls. Teenagers, mostly. And mostly Brazilian."

"No shit."

"Nope. And it gets curiouser. They've had a wiretap on one of the Italians' phones for about a month now and they got him screaming at some guy for like five minutes about a shipment that got lost, calling the guy a thieving Mexican and a stupid wetback and all kinds of other pleasantries."

"When was that?" I asked.

He smiled. "Three weeks ago."

"So right after that, all of the product and girls disappear for the Italians, and then a couple of weeks later we're finding a bunch of bodies in a cranberry pond," I said.

"Correct."

I drank some beer and glanced down the bar at Caroline, who was drawing a pint of Guinness and laughing at something one of the customers had said. I caught her eye and she winked. It occurred to me that she was roughly the same age as some of the girls we'd found in that pond, maybe a year or two older. But life had been kind to her. She'd grown up healthy and happy, knowing she was loved and that if she worked hard, she would succeed. The picture of this case that was forming in my mind now made me think that the girls in that pond had never had that chance. It was an ugly, blackened picture and I couldn't bring myself to hold the image in my mind for long. I looked at Tex, unsure if I wanted to give voice to what I was thinking. His look told me he had already gotten there.

"Jesus," I said.

"Yeah," Tex said. "Yeah. So here's what I was thinking: We lay off DeSilva for the time being. Let him think that he got to us today, that we're going to back off. In the meantime, we go at these guys in New Bedford and see where that takes us. Moore said they have a pretty good CI that's connected to the Italians who will sit down with us and at least answer a couple questions. I don't know whether we'll get anything from him, but it's worth a shot."

"OK, yeah. That makes sense. DeSilva got the last word in today, so maybe he's feeling a little cocky. If we lay back for a day or two, he might think we've moved on to someone else."

"Right. Maybe he lets his guard down a little, who knows."

Caroline came back down to our end of the bar and replaced our empty beers with fresh ones. I could get used to this.

"Have you guys finished breaking down last night's episode of Desperate Housewives yet?" she asked.

"Just about," Tex said. "We can't agree on whether Bree is a Madonna figure or a whore or both."

"My opinion? She's just a manipulative twat," Caroline said.

Tex had to cover his mouth and turn away to keep from spitting his beer all over the bar. I nearly choked to death on the Chex mix I was chewing. And the fifty-something woman to my right turned a shade of red normally seen only on boiled lobsters. If I wasn't already taken with Caroline, that line alone would've sealed the deal.

I cleared my throat and tried to compose myself. "We'll defer to your expert opinion on that," I said.

Tex was wiping tears from his eyes. "Man, she's a winner, Tobin. A fucking winner," he said. "Listen, I had an idea. How about if you two come over for dinner with me and Kim and the boys one of these nights? Maybe tomorrow or Wednesday?"

I looked at Caroline. She looked a little hesitant, not sure of what to say. I smiled, mouthing *please*.

"Sure," she said. "Why not? I'm off tomorrow night, actually."

"Done. Kim will love it. She gets pretty tired of just having guys around. Even Danny is too manly for her."

"Wow. Should I bring the Sex and the City box set and some chamomile tea?"

"Oh God, if you did, she wouldn't be functional again for about six weeks. How about just a bottle of wine?"

"You're on," she said, and looked at me. "Pick me up at six?"

I nodded and she walked back toward the end of the bar. Man. I was pretty sure I was in trouble here.

"One other thing," I said to Tex. "I want someone on her. If she's with me, even at my place, that's fine. I can handle things there. But I don't want her alone for the time being, whether it's here or at home or wherever."

"Yeah, I had the same thought. Should we put someone from intel with her, someone non-obvious? Or do we want a uniform, to make it clear that we're watching her?"

"Her dad's a cop, so she's tough. I think she'd resist pretty hard on having a uniformed trooper escorting her around, and we probably couldn't get that approved anyway."

"Her dad's police? Where?"

"Boston gang unit. Scott Nelson."

"Oh shit, I know him," Tex said. "Remember last summer when those two crews in Mattapan were battling it out for like three weeks? I got pulled in for three or four days to work the narco connection. They dropped like six or seven bodies and one of them was a six-year-old girl who caught a stray bullet while she was playing on her porch."

"Sure."

"Well, the thing that ended it is that Nelson and a minister brokered a meeting between the heads of these two crews. They show up at the meeting at a park and one of the bangers just walks in with his gun drawn and pops off a couple of shots, trying to show how hard he is. Everyone is hitting the deck, scrambling around, and Nelson pulls his weapon and shoots the guy square in the face. Game over."

I wondered if that was the thing that had tripped Caroline up last night.

"I guess we probably shouldn't get his daughter killed then, huh?"

"I'd think not," Tex said.

"So let's get one of the guys from intel to handle the babysitting."

"OK then. I'll talk to Davis and get that set up."

"Thanks."

"She's a keeper, my friend. Hundred percent."

Before we left, I took Caroline aside and gave her the bare bones of what was going on with DeSilva and told her I'd be back to pick her up around eleven when she was finished working. If she was upset or scared, the only sign was that she chewed on her lower lip as I talked. When I was finished, she just nodded and said she'd see me later.

I went home and ate dinner and then took Reggie out to the beach and let him run around for a while. The beach was pretty much empty by then and he happily terrorized a small, bewildered flock of seagulls for twenty minutes. I killed some time when we got back to the house by doing some paper work on the case and prepping for what me and JD were going to get up to tomorrow. It was a warm night, so I hooked Reggie up to his running line in the back to let him burn off some more energy. He'd be passed out by the time I got home.

I headed back to the bar just past eleven and texted Caroline when I got there that I was outside waiting. She came out five minutes later and we headed out of town to the beach. She was quiet for most of the ride, lost in thought, her head tilted upward as she gazed up at the nearly full moon through the Jeep's open top. As we neared the turn for the beach, she turned her head and looked out her window.

"I don't need protection, you know," she said firmly. "I can handle myself just fine. I learned to shoot when I was thirteen and I'm probably better with a handgun than most cops are."

"I don't doubt that," I said as I turned into the beach parking lot. "I really don't. But this isn't some stalker or stick-up kid we're talking about. These are professional bad guys who maybe killed a bunch of women about your age and then threw them in a pond. They're fucking nuts. One of them basically threatened me in front of Tex and a restaurant full of people today. That was a first for me."

"So do you honestly think they're going to come after you? Or me?" There was a note of genuine concern in her voice. And maybe something else underneath that.

"Look, I'm not saying that. But what I am saying is I'm not going to make the mistake of taking them lightly. You're safe when you're with me, and when you're not, we'll have someone with you," I said. "You won't even notice him. His whole job is to stay out of the way unless something goes wrong."

We pulled up to the house and I parked the Jeep in the driveway. I went into the house and asked Caroline if she could go around and wake Reggie up and bring him in. It would be the highlight of his day. I was coming out of the bathroom when I heard her scream. I pulled my gun and ran out the front door and leaped down the four stairs from the deck. I sprinted around the side of the house, my feet struggling to get traction in the soft sand. I found Caroline kneeling on the ground, hunched over, her back to me. My pace slowed as I got closer and I realized there was no one else there. She was lit up brightly by the floodlight on the side of the house and as I got to her she turned her face up to me and I saw the tears on her cheeks.

"What is it? What's wrong?" I asked.

Then I saw it. Reggie was laying on his side, his body half in the shadows and his head thrown back at an odd angle. I thought for a moment he was just sleeping, but then I saw the dark pool of blood and the pile of entrails next to him on the sand. I squatted down next to Caroline and looked more closely. There was a large bullet hole in the side of his head and his stomach had been sliced open, his organs spilling out in a black, foul-smelling heap.

I dropped my head as a wave of rage and nausea built. I put my hand on Caroline's shoulder and brought her up. She was sobbing silently and pressed her face into my chest, wrapping her arms around my waist. I led her toward the house and was about to take her in when it dawned on me that someone could still be here. I left her on the porch and quickly made a circuit of the outside of the house and then checked inside, as well.

Nothing.

We went in and I locked the door behind us. Caroline was still shaking as I sat her on the couch. I waited for her to regain her composure and after a minute she wiped her eyes and looked at me.

"Who does that?" she said. "I mean..."

"It's what I was telling you: These guys are on another level."

"But a dog? It's just..." her voice faded and she sank back into the couch cushions as the tears came again. She pounded the cushions a couple of times and then sat forward again, looking at me. "This is...I don't know if I'm ready to deal with this. I didn't think any of this was going to end up touching me. I came down here to get away from"--she waved her hand around in a circle--"all this shit, and now here it is. Again."

I sighed. "I get it. Look, Caroline, if you're not ready to get into this, I understand. It's probably going to be messy, messier than this. But you probably know that."

She nodded, keeping her eyes on the floor.

"But I think there's something here for us, and I'm not interested in letting this bunch of clowns derail that. I'm in," I said. I reached over and lifted her chin. "Are you?"

She kept her eyes down a second longer, then looked at me, her pupils dilated, her eyes red.

"I don't know," she said. "I just don't know."

Ten

I called Tex after Caroline had finally fallen asleep, around one A.M., and told him what had happened.

"They must have had someone watching the house," I said. "I wasn't gone for more than about twenty-five or thirty minutes. And I didn't see any vehicles on the road on the way in or out, so I'm wondering if maybe someone was just hanging out on the beach."

"Could be, or maybe even across the inlet or in a kayak or something, who knows. Your place is not hard to find. Whatever the case, they got their point across. So what's the move now?"

"We stay the course, do what we were planning and lay off of them for a bit. This actually helps with that scenario a little, making them think that this scared us off along with him fronting me in the restaurant," I said. "Fuck him. We go talk to Moore's CI and see where that takes us."

"I'm with that. OK man, get some sleep."

"Yeah."

I went back outside and walked over to where Reggie was lying on the sand. I unhooked him from the line that was still attached to his collar, trying to avoid looking down at the oily mess on the ground next to him. I noticed that whoever had killed him had also taken his name tag. Nice touch.

I grabbed a shovel from the shed and carried it and Reggie's body around the back of the house toward the inlet where the ground was more dirt than sand. I laid

141

his body down and dug a small, rectangular hole. I carefully lowered Reggie's limp form into the hole and covered it quickly with the sand and dirt. I stood for a moment looking down at the freshly turned earth, again feeling the nausea filling my stomach, rising into my throat.

DeSilva had made it clear in the restaurant today that he wasn't intimidated by us or even particularly worried by our interest in him. That kind of bravado or genuine courage, if it was that, was essentially a job requirement in DeSilva's world. You don't get to where he was without climbing over a huge number of obstacles and people on the way up. And you don't do that without being able to use violence and the threat of it effectively. He'd known that taking a run at me or Tex directly was a career-limiting move of the highest order, so he'd done the next best thing: come at me indirectly, both with the remark about Caroline and by killing Reggie. OK, fine. At least I knew where we stood now.

Caroline slept in my bed, while I spent the night on the couch, alternating between restless sleep and laps around the house to check on her. Around three, unable to get any decent rest, I called my brother. I knew he'd still be up because he liked to begin each day by praying the rosary at midnight. He'd be up again at five, prepping for the early Mass. More discipline than I'd ever have.

I filled him in on the last couple of days: Caroline, the DeSilvas, Caroline, Alves, Caroline...

"Sounds like you have two problems there," he said. "First, I think you're in trouble with this girl. She sounds great and you sound like you're totally gone already."

"Yeah, it feels like that too."

"Well, I can't help you with that one. Not my department."

"I think I got it covered. Thanks."

"The other part...you're saying that these guys threatened me?"

"Sort of. They let me know that they knew who you were and where you lived and all of that," I said.

"And that's supposed to show you that they're powerful and they can get to me if they want to?"

"Something like that."

"And this worries you why?" he said.

"Uh, because you're my brother and I'm not interested in you getting hurt."

"Danny, they can't. Whatever it is they think they can do to me doesn't matter. You know this."

"No, Brendan, this is not a metaphysical discussion here. These are real-life guys, not theoretical evil forces. I'm not trying to scare you, but they know everything they need to know to find you and then it's game over, man. If they get angry enough--which is likely if we continue messing up their business--then there's every chance that they'll do just that. And I can't have that."

He gave a long sigh. "So this is about Erin."

"No. It's about you and me and I'm just trying to get across the point that I'm taking these guys seriously

143

and I think you should, too," I said. My voice was getting a little loud and I knew I must have sounded angry and unreasonable to Brendan. "Until we have a good handle on where all of this going, I just want you to be careful. I can make a call to the cops out there and have them send a guy over if I have to."

"Danny, your concern is coming through quite clearly. And so is your anger, I might add. I'm concerned that you're reacting emotionally and not rationally here. Remember: Erin may be gone, but she's with God. You can't forget that. And He will take care of the man who killed her, as well. Believe that."

I sighed and sat back against the couch. Brendan and I differed on so many things, and religion was just one of them, but to his credit he never let it get in the way of our relationship. He didn't preach and he didn't lay on the guilt. He didn't need to. I had more than enough to carry already.

We talked it through for a few minutes and we ended up back in the same place. He was unimpressed by my concerns.

"Dan, look. I get where you're coming from and I understand how much guilt you're carrying around because of what happened to Erin. It was a totally different thing for you than it was for me. You feel like you could have done something about it or maybe *should* have done something. And to be totally honest, maybe I sort of wish you had. I don't know. But the point is that nothing is going to change any of that now," he said. "I'm totally at peace with where I am and what I'm doing and I know that whenever my life ends, I'll be in a better place. It is assured. And I know that you don't have that same conviction, and that's fine. But I pray for you constantly. I pray for your safety, yes, but I also pray that you keep your head on straight. That worries me."

I looked down at the case file spread out on the table in front of me, running my eyes over the photos of DeSilva, Alves and the others.

"It worries me too," I said.

In the morning, Caroline was still shaken and she resisted any attempts I made to talk about what had happened the night before. Her eyes were still red and looking at her then, I wondered if this thing was already over before it had ever had a chance to get going.

I drove her to the bar to meet up with the guy that Davis had sent over from intel. His name was Ahearn and he looked as if he'd just come off a three-day bender. He was wearing a ragged blue t-shirt that said "Masshole" on the front in red block letters, tan cargo shorts and a pair of red-on-white original Nike Air Max running shoes. His brownish hair was longer than Caroline's and was tied back with a red rubber band. I was half expecting him to ask me if I had any weed.

Caroline looked at him for a minute and shook her head. "No one's going to peg you as a cop," she said. "You look like the bass player in my brother's band."

"I'll take that as a compliment," he said, bowing slightly from the waist.

I gave him a quick rundown on what I wanted from him, gave him my cell number and told him where I'd be the rest of the day. While Caroline walked down the block to get her car, I made things a little plainer for him.

"She's important to me and to this case. And her dad's a Boston cop, so we're not having any fuck-ups on this, clear?"

He nodded. "Sure. Not to get out of line here, but I'm good at my job. I know I look like shit, but I've been doing this for five years, so I get it. Davis wouldn't have sent me down here if I was some flunky. He gave me the lay of the land. I'm on it. She's in good hands, man."

"Yeah, sorry. I'm just...sorry. Bad weekend."

"I'll check in with you around noon and let you know what's happening," he said. "Have fun with the guidos."

I walked down to Caroline's car and said goodbye and told her I'd still be by her place tonight at six to pick her up for dinner. After she drove off, with Ahearn following in a ten-year-old Honda Accord, I got in my Jeep and headed toward Route 3. I called Tex on the way and we agreed to meet at the barracks in Middleboro. Davis had talked to his CI yesterday and Davis was going to bring him to the barracks at eleven for a chat with us. I don't think Davis had told the guy exactly what we were working on, but he knew we needed some info on the situation in New Bedford. Davis had told Tex that the guy was a bouncer at the club the Italians owned and did some low-end muscle work for them, too.

I pulled into the parking lot at the Middleboro barracks and saw Tex's car was already there. I walked in and went back to the homicide unit and dropped my laptop bag on my desk and saw Tex and Davis talking with Winthrop in his office. I wanted to avoid him for the time being, at least until we had some solid information on the thing in New Bedford and whether it was related to our case. I didn't want him to think we were wasting more time chasing leads that were going nowhere, so I ducked into the break room and waited for them to finish. Ten minutes later, Tex found me.

"We all set?" I asked.

"Yup. The CI is named Sal Delia and he's in interrogation one and Davis is going to come in with us," Tex said. "He said the guy is pretty reliable with his info, but isn't the most stable individual on earth. So we may need to be a little careful."

"Excellent," I said. "Because what we need on this case is some more crazy people."

"No doubt. Let's go see what's what."

We found Davis near the interrogation rooms.

"What's the weight on this guy? Why is he helping you, or us for that matter?" I asked.

"He was selling steroids and HGH out of a gym in Dartmouth and the Feebs pulled him in as part of a haul they made back in the spring," Davis said. "They were after someone much higher up the chain and didn't have any use for him. He took a fall a few years ago for beating the shit out of a clerk at a Store 24 during a stickup, so he was facing some actual time if he went back in. When he offered to talk about some other local drug shit, the feds turned him over to us. He's pretty low-level, but he's in the club all the time and he sees everything and knows all of the players, such as they are now. "

"Roids, huh? Wonder if he knows David Ortiz."

"Fuck you, Ripken," Davis said.

"Watch it. Don't you take the Iron Man's name in vain, not in my presence. He is a god, and you know it."

"No one plays in that many games in a row without some help. Maybe it was some of those B-vitamin shots that Palmeiro used to get."

He popped the door on the box and we all went in.

Delia sat at the stainless steel table, his hands folded in front of him. The interrogation rooms are purposely claustrophobic, designed to give the subject a sense that there was nowhere to go. But this one felt like an overcrowded elevator with the four of us in there. Actually, it would've been crowded with just Delia in there. It was hard to tell for sure, as he was sitting down, but he looked to be at least six-and-a-half feet tall and was probably 275 pounds. He was wearing enormous black sunglasses and had a diamond stud the size of a small onion in his left ear. His hair was slicked straight back, Gordon Gecko style, and had enough product in it to qualify it as a federal Superfund site. Davis and Tex sat down at the table across from Delia, while I stood behind them against the wall.

"So Sal, as I told you, these two detectives are working on a case that they think you might be able to help them with," Davis said. "I told them that you would be able to give them some perspective on what's happening with the situation down in New Bedford right now."

Delia just took a gulp from the huge can of energy drink sitting on the table in front of him.

"Tex, it's all yours," Davis said, sighing.

"OK. I don't know whether Davis told you anything about our case, but the short version is that we're trying to figure out who killed eight women and one man and then left them in a cranberry pond up in Duxbury. Our investigation has sort of led us in the direction of the, ah, gentlemen you're working with at the club," Tex said. "We know that they've had some trouble getting the supplies that they need for their business lately, and we know that they had a dispute with some Brazilians recently. Seems like those two things might be connected."

Delia drank some more poison from the can.

"So here's what we want to know from you: What happened to the dope and the girls? Why did your supply dry up?"

Delia sat silent for another fifteen seconds or so and then removed his sunglasses and set them on the steel table. It was immediately obvious why he wore them: his left eye was badly damaged, milky pink fluid having flooded the formerly white sclera. The skin around the socket was puckered and scarred, with a jagged white line running at a sharp angle from between his eyebrows to below his wrecked eye. It was difficult to look at him without staring at the damage. The wound looked pretty fresh.

Delia looked at Davis. "I could trust them?" he asked. Davis nodded.

"I don't know the whole thing, but what I hear is we had a truck coming in a few weeks ago. We went to the meet, the truck never showed. So we call the guys, see what the fuck happened. They tell us they don't know what happened, they'll check it out. They come back and tell us the truck got stopped on the way up here in fucking Delaware or whatever and it's a loss. Everything gone."

"What was in the truck?" Tex asked.

Delia just blinked.

"Girls?"

He nodded.

"Dope?"

A shake of his head.

"So how much did that cost you guys? What was the damage?"

"Don't know for sure. But that was about a month's supply of girls, so a lot." He shrugged. "A hundred grand, maybe? One fifty?"

"Lot of money. And your bosses did what when they got word of this?"

He snorted. "They went insane. Lot of talk about going at them right away, blowing up their shit and figuring out a new supplier later. Always somebody else to get whores from. That ain't the problem."

"Why didn't that happen?"

"Cuz they're a bunch of fucking humps," Delia said. "This ain't the 1960s or whatever with Carlos Bambino and whoever else running the show."

"Gambino," I said. "Carlo Gambino."

"Huh?"

"Forget it."

"Yeah. I was sayin', the guy running our crew is fucking legit retarded. I'm not even joking. He needs someone to help him order dinner, he's so fucking stupid. Forget about ordering anything else. But he's got the right last name, so he's the boss."

Tex glanced sideways at Davis, who nodded.

"OK," Tex said. "So they just ate it? No retaliation at all?"

"Nothing that matters," Delia said, shaking his head. "There were some angry phone calls and a car might've been blown up, but that's it. The fucking spics are laughing their asses off at us. It's weak as shit, man."

"So things must be pretty slow at the club then," I said. "No girls. Hard to make money in a club like that just selling Gansett drafts and hard-boiled eggs."

"No shit. Place is fucking deserted. Me and a couple of guys were thinking about riding up to Plymouth, maybe tuning somebody up, just to see what shakes loose. We're bored out of our titties, man."

"What's in Plymouth?" I asked. Delia sat back in his chair and folded his arms, knowing he'd made a mistake.

"You know a guy named DeSilva?" Tex asked.

"I live in New Bedford, man. I know a hundred guys named DeSilva."

"How about Paolo DeSilva?"

151

Delia's eyes flicked sideways for a second. "Nah, man. Don't know him."

"What about Andres DeSilva? Know him?"

He shook his head. "Nope."

Tex looked back at me and I shrugged. Seemed like we'd gotten about all we were going to get.

"Sure," Tex said.

"OK, listen, thanks," Davis said to Delia as they all stood up. "I'll talk to you."

Delia didn't respond, just walked out and left the door open behind him. "OK then," I said. "No doubt now that DeSilva's guys are in on this. But I still don't get why they pulled back from the Italians. Money is money."

"It is, so there has to be something else there," Tex said. "Maybe there really was just some screw-up with the one shipment, like they said, and then when the Italians went ballistic, DeSilva decided he didn't need them anymore. Always someone else to buy dope and hookers."

"Could be. I'll run down the shipment and see whether the Delaware cops or someone else actually stopped the truck somewhere. But I'm pretty sure we know where those girls are already."

We spent the rest of the morning in the office returning phone calls and trying to pull together the limited information we could find on the Italians in New Bedford. Delia wasn't kidding when he said it was a goat rodeo down there. The FBI had systematically dismantled the New England mob over the course of

152

the last fifteen years, pulling it apart from the inside with the help of a parade of high-level informants who had grown tired of the Boston winters and decided that a government-sponsored relocation to Arizona or Florida sounded nice. A couple of crews--one in Boston and one down in Providence--had been hanging on, scraping by on old-school protection rackets and prostitution mostly. They'd missed the boat on the really profitable stuff--heroin and club drugs--leaving the door open for the newer immigrant gangs to rush in.

The Italians had tried to make a belated move into the ecstasy and heroin markets a couple of years back; it hadn't gone well for them. The older guys didn't have the stomach for the rough stuff anymore and the newer generation, who were willing to mix it up, had far more balls than brains. So four of the younger guys had tried moving in on a couple of the spots the Mexicans controlled in Fall River, a pool hall and a rundown bar, pushing their own low-quality junk and waving guns in the Mexicans' faces. That lasted about three days, until one of the Italians came home one afternoon and found the headless body of his seventy-eight-year-old father in a fifty-five gallon drum of acid on his front lawn. The next afternoon, the Mexicans had just set up shop in their old spots as if nothing had happened.

A little before noon, I got a call from JD saying he was on his way down from Logan and would be at my place by one or so. I called Ahearn to check in and he assured me that Caroline was still alive and he would let me know if that changed. I'd had enough sitting and

153

reading for the day, so I found Tex and told him I was going to call the cop down in Brazil and see what he could tell us about DeSilva.

"You feel like we should make a trip down New Bedford soon?" he said.

"Yeah. Do you know this place where the Italians are, the club?"

He laughed. "Yeah. It's the place that used to be The Narwhal, the fishermen's bar? The one with the unisex crapper in back, down a hall with the curtained-off rub-and-tug rooms. Now it's some sort of shitty dance club, I guess. I haven't been past there in a while, but I remember when they bought it, must be two years ago now."

"OK, so maybe we should run down there one day this week. See if we can figure out what the story is," I said.

"OK, I'll see you tonight. Six-thirty, yeah?"

"See you then."

I dialed the number for the cop in Brazil that Harris had given me. I dialed and then started the car and backed out, heading for home. Pena answered after a couple of rings. I identified myself and got straight to the point.

"I'm working on a case that involves a man named Paolo DeSilva. He's an American now, but he was born in Brazil and we understand he had some run-ins with the police down there before he moved. I'm sure you don't remember him offhand, so I was hoping..."

"I know this man. I remember him very much," Pena said. His voice was soft and melodious, a deep tenor that was not diminished by the 5,000-mile phone connection. "He was terrible man. A man who like girls. No women. Girls. You understand?"

"Yes."

"He like girls young, before they can be pregnant. Is a disgrace, this man."

"He doesn't have much of a record down there, though."

Pena made a dismissive pfffft sound. "Arrest record means nothing here. DeSilva was a tool for the *traficantes*, the gangs. You see? He would get the women for the *traficantes* and they would let him keep the *meninas*. The little ones."

A chill ran up my back as I pictured DeSilva, a shriveled, polluted old man rotting from the inside, satisfying his hideous appetites with pre-teen girls. Girls who, if they were fortunate, would be killed after DeSilva had finished with them. And if they were horribly unlucky, they would be freed, perhaps finding their way home days or weeks later, their parents, tears on their cheeks, hugging and kissing them and thanking God for their safe return. Until they saw the hollowness and hatred in their daughters' eyes, and then they would know. They would know what happened and know, too, that their daughters' were ruined, their lives over. Then their fathers and brothers would lie awake in bed and beg God for the chance to meet the man who had done this, to just give them five minutes with this man, to make him feel a tiny piece of the pain and shame and despair that now consumed them.

"And so the gangs would protect him from the police and look the other way on his habits as long as he kept them supplied with women?" I asked.

"That is it. Yes."

"He has his own family, right? A wife, son and daughter?"

"Yes. His wife, I knew her some. She is very nice person. I do not know why she is with this man. Maybe it is because of her damage. I do not know."

"Damage?"

"Si. Her face, it is, um, I don't know right word. It was cut."

I felt my pulse jump. "She has a scar?"

"Yes, a scar. Her face was cut when she was a girl, it has a big scar on the cheek and the nose, a little. Long, pink scar. She is very pretty woman, but she was damaged, you know?"

If Pena was correct in his description, which I had no reason to doubt, then DeSilva's wife was laying on a table in the Plymouth County medical examiner's office. I couldn't wrap my head around what that meant. The cars in the other lane seemed to be coming at me in slow motion, with shimmering halos of white bending around them. Even though the top was off my Jeep, the only sound I could hear was Pena's voice.

"Could you send me a picture of DeSilva's wife, if you have one? Even if it's old, that's OK. And maybe the daughter, too."

"Of course. I have of the wife, but the girl, she was very young here. We didn't have one for her."

I gave him my email address and he said he'd send it as soon as we got off the phone. "What's his wife's name?" I asked.

"Sofia. Is she part of this?" Pena asked. "She was clean here, much as I know."

"I don't know yet. I'm just trying to figure out what's happening right now. It seems like DeSilva might be on the other end of that business with the girls up here now," I said. "He's got himself a fake travel business that brings women into the U.S. and then he hands them off to his customers here. He's doing very well, it looks like."

"But he make a mistake, you say."

"He made a big mistake, yeah. A bunch of his women turned up dead and it looks like he's the reason. Now we're on him."

"Good luck, my friend," Pena said. "Call me when he is fall. I will make a party."

Eleven

I was running low on beer and food at my place, and with JD coming to town for a few days, I needed to restock. He lived on a boat and God knows when his last real meal was, so I was preparing as if a swarm of hungry locusts was about to descend on my place. I stopped off at a supermarket near downtown and cruised through the aisles, putting pretty much one of everything in my cart, figuring I'd worry about the particulars of what I was going to make later.

A hundred and fifty dollars later, I checked out, dropped the bags in my Jeep and then walked across the parking lot to the liquor store.

I snagged a couple racks of Lone Star and a bottle of wine for Tex and Kim. As I turned the corner to head for the checkout, I nearly ran head-on into Andres DeSilva coming the other way. I stopped short and the wine slipped out of my hand and shattered, spraying both me and Andres with glass and shiraz. He looked at me and smirked, pleased.

"Oops," he said. "Shame."

"That was a twenty-five dollar bottle."

"My apologies," he said. "That was probably a month's salary for you."

"Clever," I said, moving to step around him and the broken glass. He slid a half step to his left, blocking my path.

I stepped back and looked down at him. I was several inches taller than he was and was wearing my gun in plain sight on my hip and yet he was smiling and acting as if he had the upper hand here somehow. He had the cocky, superior air of the star high school quarterback for whom the crowd always parted as he walked down the hall. I hated that kid in school and seeing an adult version of it now was even less appealing. I looked down at the bottle in his hand: Ketel One vodka. Figures.

"Get the fuck out of my way," I said, shouldering him aside. He lost his balance and reached out for the shelf to steady himself and knocked several bottles of cheap gin to the floor. He yelled and the commotion brought a young female clerk into the aisle. She looked at the mess on the floor and then at me and Andres standing toe-to-toe and walked back to the checkout counter. I stared at Andres for a few seconds, my face inches from his. He smelled of expensive cologne, and underneath, whiskey. We stood that way for a minute or so and eventually he smiled and backed away a couple of feet.

"Are you confused?" I asked.

"About what?"

"About what's going on here. I just don't want you walking around with the wrong idea in your head about the situation. Because it seems like you think you're somehow in the driver's seat. I can straighten that out for you right now: you're not. In fact, from the way things look right now, you're going to be lucky if you don't go to jail for a long time," I said. "And I don't really think you're the lucky type. You think you have this town wired and that you and your old man are big time? Good for you. Keep thinking that. Just know that I'm not going anywhere."

"Good. I'd be disappointed if you did. I've been bored lately and things are starting to get interesting around here," he said. "I like interesting."

"Yeah? That's funny, because I heard some interesting things about your father today. I knew he was a dirtbag, but I didn't really imagine he was a child molester and a rapist too. You know, picking little kids up on the street and forcing yourself on them is about as bad as it gets. I've seen some ugly, foul shit in my career, but I'd have to put your father in the top five all-time assholes I've come across. Maybe even top three. I'd have to think about it. He's a hall of famer, for sure. It probably shouldn't have surprised me, though. Guy like him, nothing is too low."

Andres's eyes flashed and he clenched his jaw, the muscles flexing. He opened his mouth to say something and then thought better of it and took a deep breath, letting it out slowly. His face reddened and his expression was a mask of shame and anger. He tried to hold my gaze but broke after a couple of seconds and looked down at the floor, shifting his weight from one foot to the other.

"Don't like hearing that? Hurts, right? Too bad. This is big-boy baseball now. Next time you think it might be funny to talk about me or my family, think again. You keep my name out of your mouth. Understand me?"

He said nothing and walked toward the counter, his head bowed.

161

I got back to my place a few minutes before one and put the groceries away and the threw a couple of the leftover bison burgers on the grill. I was sitting on the back deck, drinking a diet Coke and watching a pair of swans paddle around the Eel River inlet when I heard the front screen door bang. I pulled my gun and eased the back door open, creeping into the house on bare feet. I came around behind the stairs and saw JD standing in the living room, a North Face backpack and a small black duffel his only luggage. He was wearing baggy shorts, Tevas and a black t-shirt that said "I'm an advanced persistent threat" on the front. He dropped the duffel and put his hands up in mock surrender when he saw me. I holstered my gun and walked over, feeling a relieved smile on my face.

"Hey man, I was worried I had the wrong place," he said. "I was pretty hammered the last time I was out here."

I shook his outstretched hand. "Ho shit, that's right. You borrowed that girl's truck to go get more beer and somehow went the wrong way on the beach road and ended up getting stuck out on the crossover when the tide came in. I believe I was able to console the young lady."

"Right. While I swam back to the beach. You were consoling the hell out of her by the time I got back here, as I recall. Good times."

"It was. Here, let me get your stuff and I'll tell you what's happening." I grabbed his duffel and took it into the living room and set it by the couch, then went to the fridge and grabbed two Lone Stars and carried them out to the back deck. The burgers were just about ready. I handed JD one of the bottles.

"Thanks brother," he said, drinking it down to the bottom of the neck. "Long trip. So. What's the word?"

I gave him the barest bones of the case, just the bits he needed to know. He wouldn't want any more data than was necessary and telling him about the girls and the rest of it wouldn't do any good. He didn't need any motivation. All he needed was a target and I had that for him.

"Doesn't sound like a problem," he said when I had finished. "Getting in is going to be cake, but once I'm in, what are we looking for?"

"Database. The guy is running a travel business that specializes in bringing people up from Brazil and other Latin American countries. Even a bullshit operation like his must have some sort of records. I don't know what we'd find in there, but I'm really looking for some names that might help us. We need to ID some victims and there's a chance that their names are in that database somewhere."

"Why not just subpoena them or get a warrant or whatever?"

"Tried that. No dice."

"My way is easier and quicker anyway." He grinned. "If you don't know exactly what you want from the database, you want me to dump the whole thing if I can get to it?"

"I guess you'll have to. It's kind of a shot in the dark anyway. He might keep everything in a shoebox in his closet for all I know."

"Well, if he does, that's your domain. But if he's got it on his network somewhere, I'll find it."

"That's what I figured," I said. "All right, enough of this shit. Let's eat."

"Hell yes. I'm so hungry I could eat a bowl of lard with a hair in it."

"I finished all the lard for breakfast, but I got some bison burgers for your country ass. That work?"

"I guess it'll have to do."

We sat on the deck and ate, drinking beer and watching as two kayakers spent twenty minutes trying in vain to maneuver their boats into position to get a good picture of the pair of egrets that had taken up residence in the Eel River grasslands this summer. The egrets seemed to know exactly what the couple was doing and kept flying between the tall grass and an overturned jon boat that was on the lawn of one of the houses across the inlet from mine, playing hide-and-seek with the bewildered kayakers. The man had what looked like about $8,000 worth of camera equipment in his $2,000 boat and couldn't believe that he was being outsmarted by birds with brains the size of walnuts. The couple eventually gave up and paddled out into the sea, defeated.

"God, we're a stupid species," JD said after the kayakers had slunk away. "How the hell did we make it this far?"

"It's one of the great mysteries of science. My theory is that's why we haven't had any alien visitors yet. They probably took one look at the reruns of King of Queens and Two and Half Men that we've been beaming out to space and said, fuck that, those people clearly have nothing to offer us. Let's stay on Hoth instead."

"What do you mean no alien visits? How else do you explain Sarah Palin and Tom Cruise? Or the entire state of Florida, for that matter."

"Fair points."

My phone buzzed on the table: Tex.

"What's up?" I said.

"I'm on my way to your place. I got a couple of the early autopsy reports from Mitchell and there's a couple things in there I want you to see. Sort of interesting."

"Yeah, come on over. I got a surprise for you when you get here."

"Yeah? You wearing that mesh half shirt again? I don't need to see that more than once in my life."

"Kim loves it, so you might want to pick one up for yourself," I said. I could hear Tex stifle a laugh on the other end of the line. "Actually, JD is here. He's in town for a job this week, came by for a bit."

Smallest of pauses. "You worried that I'm gonna come in there and start shooting?"

"Just letting you know."

"Relax, I'll behave. See ya in a few," he said.

"Tex is coming by," I said to JD after I'd ended the call.

"Cool. Haven't seen him in forever."

"Everything's OK with you guys?"

"OK on my end. You know I'm not trying to stay mad at anyone. Especially him."

"Sure. But then again, you were the one who left *his* sister standing at the altar, not the other way around."

"She wasn't actually standing at the altar," JD said, finishing his beer. "I believe she was sitting in the apartment with the caterer and the cake maker or whatever you call her."

"Baker," I said.

"Yeah, thanks for that. Baker. They were sitting there trying to decide whether we should have bacon-wrapped scallops and lamb kebabs or little tiny quesadillas and some sort of puff pastries as the passed appetizers," JD said. "I was standing in the kitchen, listening to this, and I got lightheaded. I seriously thought I was going to faint. My ears started ringing and all I could think of was go, run, get the fuck out. You know as well as anyone how I felt about Amy. I loved her so much I couldn't stand it. And that was the problem in the end, I think. I got to the point where I spent all of my time with her, all of it. You remember. You guys were killing me for being such a lap dog, not hanging out anymore."

"Dude, you went away to a B&B in Vermont on Super Bowl weekend. Fucking Super Bowl!"

"That's my point. I loved every minute of it. She was exactly the kind of girl I wanted to be with and then all of a sudden, I realized that once I walked down the aisle and said I do and everyone clapped and we raised our glasses and went on the honeymoon and all of that, I'd be dead. I don't mean I'd be unhappy. I'd be with Amy and I loved her like hell, but I saw myself ten years later, mowing the lawn, going to PTA meetings, making potato salad for a block party, whatever, and I just couldn't fucking handle it. I thought that's all the stuff I wanted, but it wasn't. I just couldn't do it. It killed me to know what it would do to Amy, and Tex too, but I had to go. Had to."

He stood up and walked into the kitchen and came back with two more beers, handing one to me. He sat down heavily in his chair, clearly feeling all the emotions of that day, more than five years ago now, coming back to him. He sighed.

JD and Tex had met during their freshman year in college and had been as tight as brothers for ten years. It had been an odd friendship from the start and from what I knew of both of them, they hadn't ever had much in common. JD was a focused, self-taught programmer who would sometimes disappear for days at a time when he was working on a project and then resurface at the end, having not eaten or slept and surviving on Mountain Dew and Miller Lite. He wasn't exactly anti-social then, but he had a hard time relating to people whose IQs were south of 170 and he'd often just wander away in the middle of a conversation if he got bored or distracted by something. He talked as fast as a meth-head on a two-day binge and God help you if you couldn't keep up.

During his senior year of high school JD had developed a Web security scanner as a weekend project and sold it to a big software company for nearly $5 million. He only went to college to meet girls, which wasn't exactly his specialty at the time considering the low number of available women hanging out in his parents' basement. So when Tex introduced him to Amy over Christmas break that first year, JD was done. Done with school and done with pretty much everything that didn't involve Amy or computers. Tex was a little hesitant about the relationship for a while, but once he saw that JD was serious, he bought in. JD moved up to Boston and he and Amy were the golden couple for a long time. And then...

"I knew exactly what I was losing. I knew Tex would want to kill me, like actually kill me," JD was saying now. "I knew Amy would be destroyed, I knew you'd have to stay on their side, which I never faulted you for. Never did. You had to do it. I was the asshole, not Tex or Amy."

"And yet you still walked away."

"Had to. I would've lost my shit eventually, and as bad as it was when I took off, it would've been a thousand times worse later. Say we had a kid and a house in Braintree and all that happy shit, and then I went out to pick up lunch one afternoon and just never went back. Amy would have been suicidal."

"And Tex may have actually killed you then."

He nodded. "Yup. And with justification. Not that I didn't deserve it for what I did anyway. But I truly believe that it was harder on me than it was on Amy or you or anyone else. Y'all still had each other. I was alone and fucking miserable. As much as I knew I'd made the right move, it didn't help a damn bit when I'd wake up at two in the morning and stretch my arm out to touch Amy and she wasn't there. Nothing was worse than those few seconds after I remembered why and what I'd lost. It hurt so bad I'd have to get up and puke sometimes. Run to the bathroom and hurl like a fucking fifteen-year-old who found his daddy's gin stash. That didn't stop till about a year and a half after I left. So, yeah, I fucked up. But I paid a price too, man."

"I'm not the one you have to convince," I said.

"Oh, I know. I figured there was a good chance I'd see Tex when I agreed to come, so I'm ready. It's time."

"Cool. You know I hate it when mom and dad are fighting."

I stood up and started gathering the plates and beer bottles. JD took an armful as well and we went into the kitchen and got everything put away. I checked my watch. Tex should be here any minute.

"I gotta hit the head," JD said. "Upstairs, right?"

"Yup, unless you want to water my plants outside for me. We've had kind of a dry summer."

"Couple more beers and I'll take you up on that," he said, heading up the stairs.

I finished cleaning up the lunch debris and was contemplating a third beer when Tex walked in. He had a tense, expectant look on his face and glanced around the kitchen and living room hesitantly.

"Where's JD?" he asked, a note of hopefulness in his voice, maybe thinking that I'd just been messing with him on the phone.

169

"Taking his talents to South Beach," I said, nodding upstairs.

Tex nodded absently and dropped onto the couch. He looked like he'd rather be at a Baptist revival meeting or a quilting bee. He reached for a magazine on the end table, flipped through it quickly, dropped it back on the table, pulled out his cell phone, scrolled through his email, then moved on to chewing his nails. He stood up and paced around the living room for a few minutes and then wandered out onto the back deck. He stood at the rail looking out at the inlet. I decided against going out and talking to him and after a while he came back in and sat down again. A minute later, I heard the toilet flush upstairs and a second later JD came down the stairs. He saw Tex on the couch and hesitated for just a moment before he walked over and offered his hand.

"Hey man, been a long time," JD said.

Tex looked at JD's hand, and for a painfully long second I thought he was going to just punch JD in the groin. Instead, he stood up slowly and wrapped JD in a huge, tight embrace. Tex was a good six inches taller than JD and I lost sight of JD for a second, half thinking that Tex was going to squeeze him to death like a python. But they broke the hug a few seconds later and I could see the relief and gratitude on JD's face. Tex, too, looked as if a small car had been lifted off his chest. He looked at JD for a long beat and still didn't seem like he knew what to say. JD saved him the trouble.

"Shit man, I came down those steps, I figured it was fifty-fifty on whether you were gonna shoot me."

"It was probably closer to seventy-thirty, but me and Tobin might have to shoot some people later, so I didn't want to waste any rounds," Tex said.

JD laughed, a mixture of relief at the break in the tension and true joy at having his friend back. "Damn, man. You don't know what--I mean, I've been thinking about all this for years and I just..." JD's voice broke and he shook his head, waiting for the moment to pass. Tex stayed quiet and waited, too. "I need to kind of get this out, so just lemme go for a sec here. I know how badly I hurt Amy and you with what I did and I don't have any excuses for it. It was a purely selfish move and I knew it then and I still did it. I loved Amy like hell, like I know I'll never love anyone else again, and it killed me to walk away from her. But I just wasn't going to be good at being tied up forever, no matter who it was with, and when I figured that out, I had to go. The timing sucked, and I'm sorry for that. I really, really am. But if I had waited and gone through with it and walked out somewhere down the road, it would have been a train wreck. I know it all seems totally gutless and pathetic, and I guess it was."

He paused for a breath, running his hands over his short, spiky hair. "Anyway, it's just fuckin' good to see you."

Tex nodded. "Yeah, it is. It is."

"Lemme ask you: Why didn't you or Danny come and find me? I'm sure you could have done it pretty easily."

171

"Honestly? The only thing that stopped me from coming after you back then was Amy. She understood it better than either of us did, even though she was broken in a million pieces. She said she always knew that you might do something like that. Not like that exactly, but something flaky and unpredictable."

"She did? Shit, I didn't even know until I knew. So why did she stick with me then, and go through the wedding plans and all of that?"

"I asked her the same thing. She said that whatever time you two had together was worth the pain that might come if you did take off one day."

JD walked a few paces away and looked out the front door toward the ocean, the late afternoon sun turning the water a bright orange. "Ah, man," he said after a minute. "How dumb am I?"

"Scale of one to ten?" Tex said. "Eleventy."

"Yeah," JD said, sighing. "Yeah."

"If you two are done with your little tea party here, maybe we can move along to the business at hand," I said.

"Don't be jealous. We could get married in this state now," JD said.

"Let's not talk about marriage, huh?" Tex said.

JD laughed. "Good point, good point."

"So what are you doing in town?" Tex asked. "Do I even want to know?"

JD chin-nodded at me. "Danny called me couple days ago, said he had some work for me, so here I am."

Tex glanced at me. "Yeah? What kind of work is that, Tobin?"

His tone wasn't quite annoyed, but I could tell he wasn't happy to have been left out of the loop on this. He was technically my superior, so I still needed to tread a little carefully here. "Just some home repairs, little painting, stuff like that," I said.

"That's what you're doing these days, JD? I sort of remember you being more into the email machines and all that."

"Yeah, you know how it goes. Gotta make a buck however I can in this economy," JD said, smiling and trying to keep from laughing.

Tex nodded. "Good. Like I said, I don't think I want to know anyway. So, Tobin, let's sit down for a minute. I want you to have a look at these reports."

"Sure."

"I'm gonna go wander around the beach a bit," JD said. "See if I can get into some trouble. Be back in a while."

We watched him go out the front door and I waited for Tex to say something, wondering what was coming. But he didn't. He just started flipping through the autopsies, looking for whatever page he wanted to show me.

"You handled that well," I said finally.

He nodded, still thumbing through the pages. I realized now he wasn't actually looking for anything, but just trying to keep himself busy for the moment. My phone dinged and I suddenly remembered the email I was expecting from Pena. I quickly scrolled through my recent messages and found the one from him. I opened the attachment and found a picture of DeSilva

173

and a smiling woman standing in the foreground, the famous Rio mountaintop statue of Jesus, arms extended, in the background. DeSilva had the same smugly placid look on his face that he always had when I'd interacted with him. Not bored, but sort of mildly amused by the silliness of the world around him. I studied the woman next to him, looking for any evidence that I was wrong about who she was, but there was none. The scar, the facial features. It was all there. She was younger and perhaps a bit thinner, but it was her, without a doubt.

I slumped back against the couch cushions and stared up at the ceiling, trying for what felt like the hundredth time to figure out what the hell was going on with this case. Every new piece of information we got seemed to stack another brick of uncertainty and weirdness on the last. It was getting to be very frustrating, and yet I still felt like we were on the right path with DeSilva and his crew. There were no real indications that anyone else was in this, at least not at the level he was. But if that was so, how did his wife end up in a pond in Kingston?

I looked over and saw that Tex still had his head down in the autopsy reports, oblivious. Whatever he'd wanted to show me in those reports probably was going to pale in comparison to what I was about to spring on him.

"So, I talked to Pena, the cop in Brazil, this afternoon," I said.

"Yeah?" Not raising his head, still focused on what had happened with JD.

"Yeah. He had some interesting info on our boy DeSilva. Apparently he has a taste for young girls, like *really* young. Twelve, thirteen, like that."

He looked up now, engaged.

"Pena said DeSilva was tied into a couple of the stronger drug gangs down there and would keep them supplied with fresh women for their personal use or for prostitution or whatever. In return, they let him hold onto the youngest ones and ran interference with the local cops and the federales, which doesn't sound like it took much doing."

"That would explain his lack of any real record down there," Tex said, into it now.

"Right. But that's just one piece of it." I reached over and shuffled through the autopsy reports. I found the one I was looking for and then put down my phone, the picture of Sofia DeSilva on the screen, next to the headshot of the lifeless, bloated Jane Doe with the scarred face. Tex glanced at the two photos, getting it and not getting it at the same time. He looked at me, eyebrows raised.

"That's Sofia DeSilva. Paolo's wife."

He sat back in his chair, arms folded, thinking. He kept his eyes focused on the middle distance for a minute and then looked over at me. "Damn," he said finally. "I mean...damn."

"Yeah. That was my first thought too."

"What was your second one? Cause I don't have one."

"I'm not real sure. I was kicking it around a little bit and the only thing I can think of right now is that

DeSilva must not know. He can't. I don't care how fucked up he is, he couldn't be as calm and collected as he's acting if he knew his wife was in that pond. Or even suspected that she might be. She'd been in there for a while when we found her, so she's obviously been missing for what, a month or two at least."

"Do we know that they're still married or living together?"

"I guess we don't, but even if they're not, a guy like that is going to keep tabs on his wife or ex-wife or whatever. He'd know if she hadn't been seen for weeks."

"OK, so let's assume that he knows she's gone. Does he seem like the kind of guy that's going to just sit back and wait for her to come home? Not to me he doesn't. To me, he's the guy who sends out three or four guys and tells them not to come back till they find her."

"Yup."

"And as far as we know, he hasn't been doing that. Davis and Moore have been on him for a couple of days and haven't seen any signs of panic or distress, even with the pressure we've been putting on him," Tex said. "If we call the Plymouth cops, we're gonna find out that he didn't file a missing persons report. So that leaves us where?"

"I think it leaves us with the conclusion that DeSilva knows that his wife is missing, and has been for some time. He knows that a bunch of bodies were found in a pond on his property and he knows that he

176

has a shit ton of enemies. And he doesn't seem to care about any of it."

Tex sighed and stood up. He began walking in circles, doing laps around the kitchen island. On the fourth or fifth circuit, he stopped and looked at me.

"Do we think he killed his own wife?" he asked.

"I think we might," I said. "But why? I mean, why do we think that, not why would he do it? I'm assuming he'd do it because he's a fucking pyscho and he had some reason for it, at least in his mind. But are we jumping a couple of steps too far here?"

"Yeah, I don't know. In fact, I don't know a thing about this case right now. Nothing."

"You know we have nine bodies."

"*That* I know. And we've ID'd one of them, which has somehow fucked the case up even more. We're bad at this."

"Not me. I got us a picture, all the way from Brazil."

"True. And look how much that's helped us," Tex said, producing a weary smile. He snapped his fingers. "Reminds me, I actually did come here to show you something."

He sat down and quickly pulled out one of the autopsy reports. He spun it around on the coffee table so I could read it and pointed to a paragraph halfway down the page. The report was for the one man that had been in the pond and the section Tex had highlighted was the analysis of what had been in his stomach and digestive system. Along with the assorted sludge from whatever he'd eaten last, there were two latex bags--

probably either condoms or surgical gloves--filled with heroin lodged in his large intestine. Mitchell's report said that one of the bags had ruptured, spilling the uncut drugs into the man's digestive tract, leading to acute toxicity and a quick, and likely very painful, death. Cause of death: massive heroin overdose.

"Um, didn't this guy get one in the back of the head, like the rest of them?" I asked.

"He did. Report says the gunshot wound was post-mortem."

"OK, so I'm no expert on drugs, but this is a pretty standard smuggling technique, no?"

"Yeah, sure. In fact it's a pretty old one. It goes back to the cocaine cowboy days in Miami in the '80s. The customs guys will get a tip about a suspected courier on a flight or a cruise ship and pull them in the back room and make them take a dump in a Plexiglas cube while they watch," Tex said. "They can't hold on for long, because they know the latex will deteriorate pretty quickly in there and then it's game over. But this doesn't make much sense to me as a smuggling job."

"Why?"

"There isn't enough product in there to make it worthwhile. I mean, if you're going to go through the effort of shoving some heroin-packed rubbers down someone's throat, you're not going to stop at two. Most of the time, it's more like eight or ten, sometimes as many as fifteen. Two's a waste of time."

"Maybe he was part of a bigger operation and somehow got separated," I said, knowing how weak the idea was even as I said it.

178

"Mmm, even then it would be kind of useless. If you're sending a guy across the border from Mexico or wherever with a stomach full of dope, wouldn't you want him to be as full as possible? If he gets caught, he gets caught. He's fucked either way."

"Yeah. You're right. So then what's the story? Maybe he was just the guard or guide or whatever they call it and he decided to make some extra coin by bringing in some dope and selling it on this side."

"That's not terrible," Tex said. "What was it that Delia said today, about the shipment getting lost?"

"Yeah, they had a shipment of girls that went missing and the Italians lost their shit and blew up on DeSilva's crew. So we have the girls, or at least we think we do."

"Right, so here's the thing: We know that at least a couple of the girls went into the pond a few weeks earlier than the rest of them, right?"

I nodded, unsure where he was going.

"We need to know when this guy went in. Mitchell should be able to give us a good idea of whether it was with the first group or the second group."

"Sure, but so what?"

"Maybe our boy here was the one who messed this whole thing up. Let's assume for a second that he's their security. His only job is to make sure that those girls get to their destination intact. You have to assume that DeSilva has greased the skids for them ahead of time, paid off some cops, customs, whatever needs to be done. He's in this for the long haul. Knowing what we do about DeSilva, this guy's end of the deal is

179

probably not cash but a green card and a soft landing up here," he was pacing back and forth between the front door and the kitchen, warming to his theory now. "So if this guy somehow screws things up, maybe he takes a different route in the truck than he was supposed to or he decides to sell off a couple of the girls himself to a local contact, and DeSilva finds out, he's totally screwed. Not only is DeSilva super pissed, but so are the Italians, who are the ultimate customers here and the ones who lose out on the product. So now DeSilva somehow has to make good with the Italians--or in his case, tell them to go fuck themselves--which is going to cost him money either way."

"OK, I'm with you so far, but I'm still not clear on why we care when this guy was killed," I said.

"Think about it. If he went into the water around the same time as the majority of those girls, then we're right, he's the guide for them and he screwed up somehow and got them all killed. That makes it even more likely that DeSilva's crew killed them or let them die. Because if they had actually made it to New Bedford, even with some sort of fuck-up, I don't think the Italians kill them all and then drag them up to Kingston to dump them on DeSilva's land."

"OK. That all makes sense," I said. "But then, what about DeSilva's wife and the other girl? How do they factor in?"

"The hell do I know? It's your turn, man," Tex said. "I just pushed out that giant food baby of a theory. What you got?"

180

"Fuck all. That's what I got," I said. I stood and stretched, cracking my neck. "Maybe DeSilva was just ready for a new wife so he had his boys take her out while they were busy killing a can full of girls anyway. I mean, what's the difference at that point?"

"That's some dirt, even for that guy." He looked at his watch. "Ah shit, I gotta run. We still have dinner tonight and I'm supposed to be picking up the crabs and lobsters at Wood's."

"You best get on. I need to get all prettied up, anyway."

"You heard from the guy who's with Caroline, what's his name?"

"Yeah, Ahearn. Talked to him a little while ago. He said she's good. I'm picking her up on the way to your place."

"OK, good," Tex said, gathering the autopsy reports and heading for the door. "Ah, not to be rude here, but you're not bringing JD, are you?"

"No, relax. He's on assignment tonight, anyway."

"Not listening," Tex said on his way out the door. "See you in an hour."

I watched him go and saw JD walking up the driveway as Tex was climbing into his car. Tex stopped and they talked for a few seconds and then shook hands before Tex got in the car and backed out. JD trooped into the house, knocking the sand off his Tevas as he came up the stairs.

"You good for tonight?" I said.

"Sure. It shouldn't take me much more than an hour or so. Depending on what I find when I'm in there."

I nodded. "OK. There's a park across the street, always plenty of people hanging around, doing whatever people do in parks. I'll drop you there."

"I'm set then. No better way to spend a nice summer night than owning up some citizen."

Twelve

Half an hour later, JD stepped out of the Jeep on the far side of the street from DeSilva's store, his backpack draped casually on one shoulder. I watched him take a seat on a bench near the courthouse lawn, then I drove off. I called Ahearn on the way and let him know I was ten minutes out.

"How's our girl?" I asked.

"Still in one piece. And sick of me."

"Already? You work fast."

"She wanted to go for a run through downtown this afternoon, and I nixed that. You can imagine how that went."

"Well, she can be pissed all she wants, as long as she's safe," I said.

"What I told her."

"K, see you in a few minutes."

Caroline lived in a three-decker on a quiet side street a mile or so north of downtown. She had the bottom floor and the owners, a retired army captain and his wife, had the top two. The neighborhood was neat and populated mainly with young families and older couples. I cruised the street once, seeing nothing, then banged a U-turn at the end of the block and parked across from her house. She was already coming down the steps, dressed casually but carefully in a yellow sundress with blue flowers on it and sandals. Ahearn was sitting on the hood of his car and nodded once at me. When we were on the road, she reached over and put her hand on my thigh. I glanced over, and saw a tight smile on her face. I waited.

"I've been thinking about this all day and I've decided that I'll let you do this, this protection thing, but not for long," she said. "I'm an adult and I don't like being treated like this. It's embarrassing and demeaning and it just sucks. I want to do what I want, when I want. I'm not used to letting anyone tell me what to do. Not my boyfriends, not my teachers, not my parents and not *this* guy."

She was looking straight ahead, sitting very still.

"But I know this is important to what you're doing and if it'll help you, I'll suck it up for a few days or whatever, but that's about it," she said. "After that, I'm done."

"By done, you mean?"

"I mean done with playing possum."

I nodded. "That's fair. The good news is, if they're going to come at you, I think it'll be soon. We're making some progress and things are moving. These guys know we're on them and they also have other problems they need to solve. So that's why we're being so careful right now. I think in a few days, things will have shaken out one way or another."

"That's comforting," she said.

"I thought you'd like that. Point is, I understand how hard this is on you, but it's also necessary. I'm not just doing this because we've gone out a couple times and I like you," I said, catching a quick sideways glance from her. "I'd be doing this for any witness or citizen that was threatened like that. It's the reasonable thing to do. But I know it's a pain in the ass."

She shrugged. I looked over at her and saw the tension in her jaw and shoulders. Something else was on her mind, but I figured she'd bring it up when she was ready. I was hoping tonight would be a respite from the stress and intensity of the last couple of days. For all of us. And I didn't want to put a pall over that with an argument or deep philosophical conversation.

Caroline seemed to be having the same thoughts. She reached over and flicked on the radio, fiddling with the buttons until she found the Red Sox game. We listened quietly for ten minutes, winding our way south and west to Tex's place while Tim Wakefield walked three consecutive Orioles and then gave up a bases-clearing double. As I pulled into Tex's driveway, Caroline squeezed my hand.

"Look. I don't want to ruin this."

"Tonight? You're not."

"Tonight, yeah, but I mean *this*, me and you," she said, turning halfway in the seat to face me. "I don't know what this is going to be, but I don't want to let this other stuff get in our way. I know it's serious and I know it could go bad, but I also know that it's temporary. So let's have fun tonight and forget about the rest. I want to have one too many beers--maybe three too many--laugh, tell dirty stories and relax. Can we do that?"

I leaned over and kissed her, holding it for as long as I dared and then looked up at her. "So you're in?"

She smiled. "I'm in."

Two hours later, we were sitting on the deck behind Tex's house, the long glass-topped table covered with newspaper strewn with lobster carcasses, shards of crab claws and corn cobs. We had successfully avoided any mention of DeSilva or anything having to do with the case, which hadn't been hard. Tex and Kim virtually never talked about his work, especially when there was an outsider around, so we'd stayed on neutral ground, talking about how Caroline and I had met, her PhD work, Tex and Kim's three boys, like that. Caroline and Kim had hit it off, and Caroline was now pressing her for stories about me. This could go downhill quickly.

"I just need one," Caroline said, smiling. "I don't have anything on him yet. I need some leverage here."

Kim cleared her throat and sat forward in her chair, giving me a quick glance. "Well here's one, and it's probably my favorite story about him."

I shook my head slightly at Kim, knowing what was coming, but she was working on her third glass of wine, rolling.

"Excellent," Caroline said, rubbing her hands together like a Bond villain. She took a long swallow of her Harpoon IPA and gave me a little kick under the table. "Let's have it."

"So a couple of summers ago we all went out on the boat for the day. It was us, Danny, the boys and a couple of their friends and Danny's sister, Erin. We spent the morning fishing off Cutty Hunk, not catching much of anything. Around lunch time, we decide to run over to the Vineyard, get something to eat, let the boys

186

ride the carousel, whatever. We get over there, tie up in Oak Bluffs and go over to this little dockside seafood place to eat. I don't even remember the name of it now, but--"

"The Sand Bar," I said quietly.

"Right, Sand Bar. Anyway, we have a nice lunch, couple of cocktails. The boys are getting restless, so Tex takes them to go ride the carousel and get ice cream. Danny stays at the bar with me and Erin. We get another round and settle in, watching the boats and people go by on the dock. A little while later, this group of guys comes in, three or four of them, maybe a year or two out of college. They sit at a table right behind us and you can tell right away that they're in the middle of a long afternoon. Being all loud, harassing the waitress, all that stuff. We ignore them, and you can tell everyone else is trying to, but a couple of families got up and left and the manager came over to ask them to calm down. They were too deep at that point."

I took my beer and walked over to the deck railing, not wanting to hear the rest of the story, but at the same time anxious to see Caroline's reaction. She was into it now, leaning forward, elbows on the table.

"So at some point Danny goes to the bathroom, and it's on the other side of the place, and we can see the line, must be ten, twelve deep. As soon as he disappears around the bar, these guys are standing next to me and Erin, talking about, hey let's get some shots, blah blah. We shake them off and ignore them, but this keeps going on. They're putting their arms around our shoulders, all over us and just won't back off. The

187

whole time we're looking around the corner, wondering where Danny is."

Tex came over and stood at the railing with me, slapped me lightly on the shoulder. He knew the story, of course, but had never heard his wife tell it. The version he knew came from me and the Oak Bluffs police. Caroline looked over at me, smiling, loving this. Not for long, I thought.

"Must have been fifteen minutes later when he comes back. By that time, one of the guys is draped all over Erin, and the others are surrounding me, not letting me get off my stool. So Danny walks up in the middle of this, looks around, says nice and evenly, OK, kids, recess is over. Time to move along. They all sort of look at him, look at each other, and laugh. The guy sitting with Erin hops down, grabs her wrists and sort of pushes her against the bar. A couple of them are pretty good size and they didn't get what was going to happen. Danny sort of nods to himself, separates Erin from the guy who's attached to her, moves her to a side table, then comes back toward me. The guys still don't see it, still think they have the upper hand here. So the one who is with Erin steps toward Danny, throws this wild punch and Danny just sort of moved aside and gave him a shove in the back on the way by, putting him face down in the sand. The other three start shouting and one of them comes at Danny while the other two grab hold of my arms."

"What? They were holding you down?" Caroline said.

"Sort of. So, anyway, Danny hits the second guy, blood flies everywhere. He goes down. By this time, the other two guys have let go of me and are putting their hands in front of them, saying, no no no, backing away. Danny walks over to the guy on my right, grabs his face and bounces it off the bar. I mean *hard*. Guy doesn't make a sound, just falls backward on the sand. He's totally dazed, but still conscious, I guess. He's kind of scrambling around on his hands and knees, completely lost. Danny turns to look at the last guy, and he's gone. Took off. So Danny looks down at the guy on the ground, then he's on top of the kid. I'm frozen, have no idea what's going on. I can't move. I look at Erin and she's got this glassy look in her eyes."

"Make her stop," I said to Tex, quietly, still not really sure if I wanted her to.

"Too late," he said.

"Don't know how long all of this took, but at some point Tex and the boys came back and Tex grabbed Danny, pulled him off this kid, who by then was out. Gone. Tex is screaming at him to calm down and get out of there, go get on the boat. But the cops were already coming in, grabbing everyone and herding us into the back room. I thought for sure we were all going to jail. No doubt in my mind. So Tex takes the lead cop aside, talks to him for twenty minutes or something, explains who they were, what happened, all that. The cops all huddle up, go talk to the one kid who is still coherent, figure out they don't want any part of pressing charges. Finally, the guy comes over and says, Get the fuck out of here. Get on your boat and go home and don't ever come back. I even hear about you getting on the damn ferry or getting as far as Hyannis, I'll arrest all of you, your kids too. Just fucking go. So we went. Ran to the boat and never looked back."

I had been watching Caroline's face, half lit by the flickering hurricane lamps and tiki torches, waiting for her reaction. She sat back slowly in her chair, drained the rest of her beer, then nodded quickly.

"Wow. Crazy story," she said, her voice not betraying any real emotion. Then she stood and began clearing plates and bowls from the table. "Come on Kim, let me help you with all of this."

Kim looked at me, a question on her face. I shrugged, not sure what was happening myself. We all pitched in and had the place cleaned up in twenty minutes or so. Caroline had hooked her fingers through my belt loop while we stood at the sink rinsing dishes, and gave me a short, hard kiss. Her eyes were dancing, flicking back and forth between mine. A few minutes later, she went to the bathroom as we were getting ready to leave. As I was gathering her purse and the leftovers, Kim caught me alone in the kitchen.

"Danny, look, I'm sorry. I shouldn't have told that story. I guess I'm just used to talking to cops' wives," she said. "For us, that's a *good* story, you know?"

"It's fine. Don't worry about it. I don't think she's under any illusions about me being an altar boy."

"No, I know. Still." She looked down, shaking her head. "Listen, I've been reading in the Globe about this case and Tex told me what happened to Reggie. I'm so sorry. That's awful. It makes me ill. But Danny, this whole thing is making me sick to my stomach. You know I'm not a worrier and I don't get spooked, but something about all of this just feels off to me. I mean, I know anyone who's killing people and dumping them in a pond is totally wacked, but beyond that. I have a really bad feeling. I've never asked Tex to take himself off of a case, and I never would. And I wouldn't ask you either, but I'm just, I don't know. I don't know what I'm doing."

I hugged her. "I understand, kid. I do. Don't sweat it. We're on a good track with these guys, we have people watching them. We're not being reckless. You know we're careful."

"I know that, Danny. It's just, I guess maybe that's part of the reason I told that story tonight. Maybe I wanted her to know that this isn't a picnic, this life. It's fucking *hard*. And it gets harder as you get older, not easier. Things that don't seem like a big deal when you're twenty-five or even thirty suddenly feel like a *very* big deal when you're closer to forty than thirty and you have kids and you have a life and all you want is for your husband to come home every night, no matter what he has to do to get here."

"And that's all we're focused on, every day. Getting home. Sometimes that's easy and sometimes it's not," I said. "But it's always in the front of our minds. Trust me."

I looked at Kim and saw, maybe for the first time since I'd known her, real fear in her face. Her features were pinched, her eyes red and liquid. I squeezed her tight and kissed her on the forehead.

191

"Just..."

I nodded. "I know. I know."

She walked back outside and busied herself blowing out the torches and wiping down the table. Caroline came back in from the bathroom and we went out and said goodbye to Tex and Kim. Caroline got hugs from both of them and Kim whispered something as they separated. Caroline smiled and nodded.

"Thanks guys," I said as we walked to the door. "Tex, I'll call you in the morning, we can figure out the plan for tomorrow night."

"Not too early," Caroline said, pressing her hip into mine. I could see the flush in her face and feel the vibration in her touch.

Thirteen

We were back to my place thirty minutes later. I'd set JD up at the hotel at the other end of the beach for the night and he'd said he'd just grab a taxi back there when he was done with his job. As soon as we were in the door, Caroline turned and kissed me hard, pinning me back against the door. She held the embrace for twenty or thirty seconds, then broke and backed away a couple of steps, a curious look on her face, somewhere between excitement and anxiety. Before I could say anything, she kicked off her sandals, slipped out of her sundress and turned and walked toward the stairs. By the time she got to the bottom step, her bra was gone. And so was I.

We made it upstairs, but just barely, going at each other desperately right on the hardwood floor, not bothering with the bed sitting ten feet away. There was a sense of urgency to Caroline's movements that was a little unsettling, almost forceful. I had the feeling that I didn't have much choice about this. It wasn't really about me. We moved from the floor to the bed for round two, taking our time a bit, enjoying it and exploring each other.

An hour later, we lay side-by-side on a towel on the deck outside my bedroom, looking up at a slivered yellow moon. I was exhausted, both from the last hour and from the events of the last few days, and felt completely drained. My limbs felt rubbery, disconnected from the rest of my body, useless. I tried to figure out what had just happened, where that had come from, but I couldn't focus my thoughts long enough and I found I really didn't care much.

"Well," Caroline said after a while, a tired smile lighting up her face in the dark.

"That about sums it up. Even better than I'd imagined," I said. "Not that I've, you know, been sitting around thinking about this for like five days or anything."

She laughed, a wonderful, contented giggle.

"You were, um, pretty eager tonight," I said, glancing over.

She raised up on one elbow, looking down at me, searching my face. "Is that a complaint?"

"Not even. Just an observation. I guess I'm just used to having to deploy some of my considerable charm before I get to this point in the proceedings."

"And how does that usually go for you?"

"Eh, win some, lose some. I'm not in the Tom Brady-Derek Jeter super platinum club, but I haven't been sitting around chewing my fingernails either."

"I didn't think so. That wasn't an amateur performance."

I gave her an exaggerated head bow. "I aims to please."

Another laugh. "So, that was fun tonight, with Tex and Kim. They're cool."

"Two of my favorite people," I said, waiting for what was coming next.

"I'm sorry I prodded her into telling that story. You looked really uncomfortable."

I sighed, wondering how far down this road I wanted to go. Too far and this might end before it even really started. Not far enough and she'd end up finding out eventually and be hurt that I hadn't come clean earlier. Thanks Kim.

"Look, there are a lot of things I've done and said over the years that I regret and wish I could take back. That night is not one of them."

She raised her eyebrows, sitting up now, leaning back against the deck railing.

"That fight didn't just come out of nowhere. There was a lot of background there that Kim didn't know. She just saw me defending her and my sister and thought that was great, which I guess it is. There were a lot of other emotions involved though. I'd been dealing with this situation with my sister for like six months and it was just...it was eating me up. I couldn't sleep, I was drinking way the hell too much. I was a mess. Fucking disaster. You have to understand: Erin and I are eleven months apart. We were as close you could be growing up, did everything together. Brendan is three years older than me, and we were close, just because we're boys. But me and Erin, I don't know, we were just always together. It sounds like it would annoy the hell out of a kid to have his sister around all the time, but it wasn't like that. We had a great time together growing up, and even as adults, before I moved up here, we hung out a lot."

"I wish I'd had that," Caroline said. "My brother is nine years older, so we didn't even know each other till we were grown."

195

"It was great. She was my best friend. And so when I moved up here a few years ago, it was hard on her. Hard on me too, honestly. She was in law school, busting her ass, working at night, completely flat out all the time. And after I left she started going out with this guy from the restaurant where she worked, a bartender. She said he was a good guy, but my dad met him and said he didn't like him right away. I went down to visit, and the guy was a disease. Totally leaching off of Erin, crashing at her place, probably selling coke out of there too. Erin admitted to me that he did coke from time to time and dealt some on the side to the waiters and kitchen help. And I notice that he treats her like shit, talks to her like an idiot. I ask her if he's hit her and she said no, but I knew she was lying. I knew."

Caroline looked down at her hands.

"Around this time she came up for the weekend and we went out on the boat with Tex and Kim. It was supposed to be a break for her, some time to think about what was going on, make some decisions. So, the night before we went to the Vineyard, she breaks down in tears, hysterical, tells me she's pregnant and doesn't know what to do. She's sure this guy, Donald, is gonna freak out when she tells him, so she's delayed it for months. She's already six months at this point and starting to really show. So she has to tell him soon. I tell her that if he's an asshole about it, like I figure he will be, tell him to go screw and we'll figure it out. She can come live with me, whatever. We'll make it work."

I stopped and gathered myself, took a deep breath. Caroline stood and led me back into the bedroom, where we dressed and then sat cross-legged on the bed facing each other. A sliver of moonlight filtered through the screen door, casting an eerie crosshatched pattern on the floor.

"Tell me," she said softly.

I rubbed my palms together, trying to dry them. "I'm not sure I've said all of this out loud before. So, anyway, what happened on the Vineyard had a lot more to do with what was going on with Erin and all of that than it did with those barneys in the bar. They were just collateral damage. The next day, Erin flew back to Virginia and was planning to tell the guy about the baby in the next couple of days. I talked to her that night, and she was really relaxed, happy to be getting it out in the open. I called her the next day, couldn't get her. Next day, same thing. Call my dad, he hasn't heard from her for two days either. So he calls the police, they go to her apartment, get the manager to open it and...ah Jesus."

I closed my eyes, seeing it in my mind even though I'd been 500 miles away. I could envision the crime scene better than most I'd actually worked. Caroline stayed silent, just waiting.

I breathed deeply, opened my eyes, reminded myself that Caroline was here, here for me. "She was lying on the kitchen floor, blood all over the linoleum, the walls, the countertop. The ME said later that she'd probably been dead about thirty or forty hours when they found her. The way the cops pieced it together, she'd taken a pretty savage beating, bruises all over her face, arms, chest. She had a massive crush wound to the

197

back of her head, which she probably got from hitting it on the granite counter. Probably died before she hit the floor."

"Oh, Jesus, Danny. I didn't..I mean..."

I shook my head. "So she took my advice, told this asshole she was pregnant, he takes it like a little bitch, loses his mind and starts beating her and she ends up dead. Alone in her apartment, no one to comfort her, no one to defend her."

"Danny, oh my god. You didn't have anything to do with what--"

"I know. Look, I'm way past the self-indulgent trip of blaming myself for this. Believe me, I did that. For a long time. If I had walked into your bar two years ago, you would've called the cops to come drag me out. I was a train wreck. But I let that shit go. It was literally killing me, chewing me up. I see it for it what it is now: Erin made a bad choice with this guy and he made her pay for it. With her life."

Caroline was looking at me expectantly, waiting for something more. I knew what it was, but couldn't do it. "The baby. Danny?"

I just shook my head, looking past her out the window to the houses and condos across the inlet. She nodded, sank back into the pillows, running her hands through her hair.

"My God," she said after a minute. "I just...I don't understand how people do these things and then go on with their lives. How does that work? I mean, here we are sitting on a beach, safe and happy and somewhere

198

there are people walking around thinking about doing things like that."

"Right. So when you hear that story about me and those kids in the bar, I don't want you to think that I'm just running around beating the shit out of dudes for sport. It's not who I am."

"It never occurred to me that it was," she said.

"That story didn't scare you."

She shook her head. "I mean, my dad's a cop. I didn't know all of the stories of what he did when I was a kid, but I know a lot of them now. I know he's killed two people and he was shot once when I was really young. So, I get that part of the job. It's dangerous and people get hurt. If the people who get hurt are thieves and killers, too bad."

"The problem with that is, it's not always the shitheads who get hurt. A lot of times it's the bystanders and the bad guys' families and their friends and their babies and their parents. Or us. Your dad got shot, you said. I've been lucky, but there's no guarantee that's going to continue. None of the people I deal with on a daily basis is a good person. They're all garbage and they'd all hurt me or Tex or you or Kim or anyone else in a second if they thought it would give them an advantage."

"Are you trying to scare me now?"

"No, of course not. All I'm trying to do is explain where I'm coming from. Like I told you tonight, even if we weren't...whatever we are, I'd still have put the protective detail on you. It's the smart thing to do. But that impulse also scares me."

"Because it means this, whatever it is, has some meaning to you, some value," she said, nodding.

"And it does. But it's more than that." I sighed. "That story about Erin, what happened to her? There's no beautiful redemptive ending or silver lining to it. My baby sister and her child were killed, through no fault of hers or anyone else's except the douchebag who killed her. Good people get hurt all the time, and there's no way for me to say with a hundred percent certainty that won't happen to you. I just can't."

She sat upright, put her hand on my chest. "Danny, I get it. And I'm fine with that. Whatever we have here is a good thing. I like you and if I understood your grunts earlier, you sort of like me too."

That got my first smile in an hour.

"We'll see where things go," she continued. "But I'm not going to run scared because some asshole thinks he knows something about me. Please. I'm with you, and I'm staying."

I pulled her in, hugging her tight and feeling the soft warmth of her, letting it chase away the chill that the last hour had brought on. She held the embrace for a minute, then pulled back and looked up at me.

"What happened to the guy? Donald? When the cops got him."

"Cops never got him," I said.

"Wait. He's still out there?"

I shook my head. She stared at me for several long beats, her face impassive. "Then what?" she asked.

I shrugged. "I have a lot of friends in Virginia."

I waited for the next question, the pull-back, the tears.

They didn't come.

Instead, she wrapped her arms back around my waist and laid her head on my chest. A few minutes later, she began snoring softly.

Fourteen

That night I dreamt that I was at a house party in some blurry suburb, with Kid 'n' Play, Biz Markie and the kids from Zoom. We were all playing quarters while Biz DJ'd and handed out copies of his new mixtape to everyone who came in. In the middle of "Just a Friend" Biz suddenly freestyled into "Hip Hop Junkies" and was just killing it. I couldn't believe how much he sounded like Greg Nice. It was uncanny. Then I felt someone kicking me and realized it was my ringtone and not Biz. Really disappointing on several levels.

I looked at the clock: 5:17. Not good. I grabbed my phone from the bedside table and saw it was Tex. *Really* not good.

"Unless you've been hijacked by Somali pirates or you're stuck in London and need me to send you money, I'm going to kill you when I see you," I said.

"DeSilva's kid is dead," Tex said. "Andres."

"Oh, for God's sake," I said, sitting up. "Please tell me it was a car accident or heart attack. Please."

"Well, he might have had a heart attack at some point, but I think it was probably the shotgun blast to the head that killed him. Just guessing, though."

I slipped out of bed and walked out onto the deck, closing the door behind me. "Jesus. Shotgun?"

"Tells you something right there."

"Wait. Didn't we have someone on him?"

"Yeah, Davis was on him. I haven't talked to him yet, though. No idea what happened."

"Fuck. *Fuck*! Why do we have surveillance teams if they can't track one guy? How fucking hard can this be? I mean, we're talking about one dude, we know where he lives, where he works, who he moves with and someone still manages to kill him while an alleged professional is tailing him? Come on!"

"Settle down, man. We don't have a clue what happened here. We need to talk to Davis first, before we make any decisions," Tex said. "Maybe Davis was right there, who knows."

"Where is he now? I want to talk to him, like *now*."

"Easy, Danny. Easy. He's at the scene, near DeSilva's store."

"Where was he found?"

"In his car. He was parked a block down from the store, near the cleaners. Just sitting in the driver's seat, like he was waiting for someone to come out of the store," Tex said.

"Who called it in?"

"Citizen. Some guy out walking his dog. Car was still running."

"Four in the morning? Who walks their dog then?"

"Meth addicts?"

"OK, look, give me a half hour to get ready and I'll meet you down there," I said, glancing inside at Caroline. Still sleeping. "By the way, do we know where DeSilva is or did we lose him too?"

"We know exactly where he is. He'll be waiting for you at the scene."

"Good."

I went back inside as quietly as possible and went in to shower and shave. By the time I finished, Caroline was up and getting dressed. Her body had looked terrific in the moonlight last night, and it didn't look any less spectacular in the daylight. Youth was not wasted on her.

"Sorry I woke you," I said. "I really wish we could get all the killers together at a meeting sometime and just all agree that that they'll only kill people between like eight a.m. and eight p.m. It would be a lot more humane."

"Who wouldn't agree to that? It would leave them more time for glue-sniffing and Xbox. Everybody wins."

"Someday, someday. In the meantime, I have to go to work. Fresh new body for me this morning, so I can drop you by your place on my way out. That work?"

"Sure. I need to get started on packing my stuff today. Miserable."

"About that," I said. "Is there anything preventing you from staying down here? I mean, if you're just finishing up your thesis, we do have the Internet here now. You could probably extend your lease for a while, right?"

She cocked her head to the side and looked at me. "Well now. That sounds a lot like an invitation," she said.

"Does it? It was more of an observation and a question, I thought."

"Well, the short answer is, no, there really isn't any good reason why I couldn't stay down here. I haven't thought about it, but I don't think my landlord would mind. The longer answer is, I don't know. This already feels like it's going pretty quickly. Not that it's a bad thing, it's just...fast. But it's something we should think about it."

"Let's do that."

"OK," she said, and kissed me lightly on the mouth.

We finished getting dressed and were out the door in about fifteen minutes. I called Ahearn on the way and let him know that we were on the way back to Caroline's place. When we pulled up, he was sitting in the same position on the hood of his car as he'd been in when we left last night. I was happy to see he'd at least changed clothes. He was now wearing slightly browner cargo shorts and a t-shirt with a giant mug shot of a cornrowed Randy Moss with a speech bubble that said "Straight cash, homey."

I kissed Caroline goodbye and told her I'd call her later in the day. After she went inside, I called Ahearn over and filled him on the situation with Andres DeSilva.

"I thought you guys were supposed to be solving murders, not making more of them," he said.

"Eh. No one's gonna miss him, except maybe his dad, and even that I'm not so sure about."

"Nice family."

"You bet. Anyway, just keep your head up. If they're starting to eat their young, things might be coming apart a little bit over there. So you never know what's going to come flying out."

"I'm with you," he said.

"Lemme ask you something," I said. "Davis was on this kid when he was killed, or he was supposed to be. You ever know him to lose someone or screw up like that?"

"Not ever," he said, shaking his head. "You get in there and start talking to people, I'll bet you'll find out he didn't this time either. Something else must've happened."

"Kind of what I thought. OK, thanks."

I made the short drive down to the crime scene near DeSilva's store and by the time I got there, it was a zoo. Plymouth cops, troopers and EMTs were all standing around and all of the activity had attracted a pretty sizable crowd of onlookers for six in the morning. As I walked up, I saw Mitchell leaning into the driver's side of a black Escalade. Tex was standing on the sidewalk on the passenger side, talking to a Plymouth cop I didn't recognize. I nodded to him and went over to Mitchell's side of the car. He was checking Andres's wrists and fingers for the level of stiffness, trying to get a read on the time of death. After a minute, he pulled his head out of the car and stood up, noticing me for the first time.

"You know this one?" he asked.

"Yeah, he's the asshole son of our asshole suspect on the pond thing. We only met him a couple days ago, but once was plenty for me."

"Doesn't look like you were alone in that sentiment," he said, nodding to the body. "First glance, looks like one shotgun blast, fired from fairly close range. hard to tell for sure though, since most of his head is on the windshield."

I stepped around Mitchell and took a look at Andres. There wasn't much to see. The left side of his head was completely taken apart, with a large portion of his skull gone, his brain exposed. Most of his lower jaw had been blown off and his ear was gone, as well. I didn't see any glass on the floor or on him, so it looked like his window had been down. The passenger side window was blown out, though, and there was a dark red stain with some pink chunky material on the inside of the windshield.

"Got the job done," I said when I'd stood up again.

"Surely did. Am I going to find *his* stomach full of dope?"

"At this point, nothing would surprise me. Have you gotten the cuts done on any of the rest of them yet?"

"We finished up two more of them last night," he said. "Want to hazard a guess?"

"Dope."

"Both of them. One had twelve packages in her, the other had fifteen. They both had at least one package that had ruptured, same cause of death as the male. Essentially a massive overdose. It's a fairly bad way to go, from what I hear."

"How long till we know about the others?"

"Close of business today," he said.

"Ok. Give me a call as soon as you're finished, if you can."

"Sure thing. But I'd bet we're going to find the same thing in the rest of them. Just a matter of how much."

I nodded. "I'd bet your salary on it."

I left Mitchell to his work and walked over to where Tex was, still talking with the Plymouth uniform. I looked past the cop and saw Paolo DeSilva on the brick steps of an antiques store, arms crossed on his knees. Alves was standing on the landing behind Paolo and his two bodyguards stood a few feet to one side, sunglasses on, arms folded. A plainclothes detective was standing in front of DeSilva, trying to ask him questions and DeSilva was looking right through him, hearing none of it. I still hadn't seen Davis anywhere. The Plymouth uniform started to walk away as I came up.

"Hang on a sec," I said. He turned back and I nodded at DeSilva. "You guys ever had any trouble with that guy?"

"Nothing we could make stick. We had a twelve-year-old girl go missing from the middle school about two years ago. A teacher got the tag number and it turns out to be one of DeSilva's cars. So we bring him in, he says shit, but we charge him anyway, going on the teacher's say-so. Next day, the girl turns up at home and the parents come in and say they want the charges dropped. End of story."

"Were the parents Brazilian by any chance?" Tex asked.

"Yup. Worked for DeSilva cleaning houses or something."

"You guys get much trouble from the Brazilians around here?" I asked.

"God, no. Gimme a whole town of Brazilians, we wouldn't need but about two cops."

"OK, thanks," I said.

"Where we at?" I asked Tex when the cop had moved off.

"You saw it," Tex said. "Locals have been trying to get the old man to talk for an hour now and he hasn't said a word. Nothing. I haven't talked to Davis yet, but he's hanging around here somewhere. I think that's our first move, then we have a go at DeSilva and see what we can do."

"OK. We need to talk to him about his wife, too, don't forget."

Tex nodded. "He wants to play dumb on this, we hit him with that. We'll get a reaction one way or another on that."

"I sure hope so. Let's go find Davis."

We found him standing in a knot of cops, including Winthrop, who, even at this hour, looked like he'd just come from Sunday dinner. Davis saw us coming and looked relieved, which was slightly odd. Or more than slightly. Winthrop, on the other hand, was red-faced and had a large vein pulsating on his temple.

"Detectives. Which of you would like to tell me what the fuck happened here? I don't care which one it is, but one of you should start talking. Now."

"Captain, we are just figuring that out for ourselves right now," I said. "We just got here and we haven't had a chance to interview anyone yet. We need to talk to DeSilva, at least, before we have anything to tell you."

"That's interesting, because Davis here has already told me plenty."

I looked at Davis, who was making a diligent study of his shoes. "Has he?"

"Indeed. Among the things I've learned so far is that Davis and his friend Moore had gotten a little tired of following the DeSilvas, so they decided to tag their cars with GPS beacons. Which seems like a perfectly logical idea, right? Sure it does. Put the tags on, fire up your receiver and watch their movements from the comfort of your office or house. No need to sit in a hot car all day, right Davis? I mean, who does that these days?"

Davis looked like he might vomit. A lot. And soon.

"They did overlook one detail in all of this, though," Winthrop continued, his voice never rising past the conversational tone he always used, no matter how angry he was. It was like when your parents stopped yelling and started speaking very quietly. Bad things followed. "Davis, why don't you take it from there."

At the mention of his name, Davis's head jerked and he took two small steps backward and sat against the hood of a Plymouth cruiser. He wiped his hands on his jeans a few times and looked around anxiously, as if he was hoping for an asteroid strike or D.B. Cooper to ride by on Secretariat. Didn't happen.

"So, we tagged their cars yesterday. With two subjects like that, who are together a lot, it doesn't make a lot of sense for two of us to sit there and watch them all day, so we just put the transponders on their cars and that way if something happens, we know where they are at least. It's pretty standard."

"Sure, for subjects that have one known car," I said. "Andres has at least three that we knew about."

Davis looked down and nodded. "Yeah. We tagged the S-Class."

"God*dammit,* man," I said.

I looked at Winthrop and Tex, both of whom were just staring at Davis. Tex looked like if we hadn't been standing in the middle of the street with our boss next to us, he might simply beat Davis to death. His bald head was turning bright red and he was flexing his forearms, making the tattoos that covered them ripple and contort. It wasn't a comforting sight. I rubbed my face and walked in a tight circle a couple of times. I was furious, both with Davis and Moore, but also with myself for having trusted someone else to handle a key part of our investigation. I hardly ever did that, and now I remembered why.

"He wasn't just some guy, Davis," I said. "He was the number two guy here and we were just starting to figure out what he did and how he fit in all of this. Now he's a grease spot and we're screwed."

"Look, it was a mistake, man. I get it. And I'm sorry. You know we take this seriously. We just made an honest mistake."

"Yeah, I know, I know. OK. Take me through it last night," I said. "What happened?"

"OK, so we were with them pretty much all day yesterday, even after we tagged them, we still stayed with them. After they went to dinner, the kid went back down to the Pinehills. I went with him, watched him go in and stay there. I waited forty minutes or so, and then figured he was in for the night."

"What time was that?"

"A little after twelve. I came back up here and checked in with Moore, and he was still with the old man at his place over in west Plymouth. The driver had just dropped him off and left. Moore stayed at DeSilva's place till quarter of one or so, watched all the lights go out, then took off. We had the receivers set to alert us if the cars moved during the night, and around three-fifteen or so the alert goes off for the old man's Cadillac. I looked at it for a bit and watched it roll out from Duxbury and head down Route 3 toward Plymouth. Once I was sure where it was going, I was out the door a couple minutes later."

"Duxbury?" Tex said.

"The driver, Alves. He takes the Caddy home at night and parks it as his place and then picks DeSilva up again in the morning. So I took off and headed down to DeSilva's place, figuring I'd be a few minutes behind Alves. I had the receiver with me, but after I saw him going down here, I didn't check it again until I got off the highway and was headed for DeSilva's house. I was only a couple of blocks from his house when I checked and realized he wasn't going there."

"He was coming here," I said.

"He was already here," Davis said, nodding. "By the time I turned around and got here, the 911 call had already come in and the Plymouth cops and the EMTs were rolling. When I got here, the Plymouth guys had just pulled up and Alves was here."

"Pretty quick 911 call," Tex said.

"There were two, actually. The first guy said he'd heard the gunshot and knew what it was because he'd been in the marines. He was up on Pleasant Street on the other side of the park. Told the 911 operator that he didn't see anything but he definitely heard one gunshot and it wasn't far away. Second call was a couple of minutes later from a different cell phone, guy didn't give his name, just said there was a dead guy in a car on Sandwich Street."

"The number returns to a Tracfone," Winthrop said. "Disposable."

"Great," Tex said. "Davis, you talk to Alves when you got here?"

He shook his head. "Nope, I stayed in my car. Wasn't worth me being seen. Guy was already dead and I didn't even know whether it involved us at that point."

"Good."

"So I sat and watched the Plymouth guys working and then about twenty minutes later DeSilva shows up, with one of the goons driving him. I see him go over to the truck and that's when I kind of put it together. The Escalade and all. I checked the plates and then got out and pulled one of the Plymouth guys aside and got the story. That's when I called you, Tex."

"Alves see you at that point?"

"I don't think so. It was still pretty dark and he was half a block away with DeSilva. But he's seen me now, over here with all of you guys."

"Yeah, but I don't mind him knowing we have surveillance on DeSilva. In fact, I kind of want him to know. I just didn't want him figuring out the bit with the transponders. He's no dummy, and the tags should still be useful as long as he hasn't put that together."

I looked across the street at Alves, who was openly watching us. He was leaning back against the wrought iron railing, taking it all in calmly. DeSilva still sat on the step, in much the same position he'd been in when I got here. He was obviously in pain, having just seen what was left of his son sprayed across the front seat and windshield of his SUV. And if I was right about what happened to his wife, his day was going to get much, much worse. Even from this distance I could see the anguish, his tiny, wizened face twisted and contorted. It was the lowest point a parent could ever reach, and yet I felt not one ounce of sympathy or compassion for him. None.

I tapped Tex on the elbow and tilted my head toward DeSilva and Alves. "Let's go," I said. "If DeSilva is ever going to have his guard down, now's the time."

Tex nodded. "Captain, we're gonna go have a talk with DeSilva and Alves. We'll check back in with you before we head out of here."

"Glad to hear someone around here is doing some police work," Winthrop said, cutting his eyes at Davis, who just shook his head and walked down the block toward the park. Tex and I followed and found a relatively quiet spot and sat on the low granite wall that fronted the street side of the park. I twisted the cap on a twenty ounce diet Coke I'd brought, taking a deep gulp. Tex was on his second Red Bull already, and it was barely seven a.m.

"Any strategery here?" he asked. "Who are we talking to first?"

"Alves. I need to hear a good reason why he was here at that hour. I can't think of too many."

"Sudden urge for a nine-month-old can of refried beans?"

"Right, and some Ho-Hos from the Nixon administration," I said. "So let's see what he has to say, then we talk to DeSilva. I want to see his face when we tell him about his wife."

"That sounded a little sadistic."

I shrugged and stood up, began walking across the street toward the stoop where Alves and DeSilva were. Tex followed and the two goons saw us coming and moved between us and DeSilva. He stood up and pushed his way between them, expecting us to confront him. I moved around him and pointed to Alves.

"Come on," I said. "Time to talk."

Alves looked at DeSilva. "Don't look at him," I said. "Look at me. Let's *go*."

He walked down the stairs and DeSilva made to follow him. Tex put a hand in DeSilva's chest and shook his head. "You're staying here. You'll get your turn."

DeSilva simply sat down on the step again and we took Alves back across the street to the park. Most of the onlookers and police activity were on the other side of the street, closest to the Escalade and the store, so we walked up into the middle of the park and sat on a stone bench, looking down the street toward the crowd and the flashing lights and yellow tape.

"Some scene," I said.

Alves said nothing, and the three of us watched as the attendants from Mitchell's office lifted Andres DeSilva's body out of the SUV and placed it onto a waiting gurney and zipped it into a black body bag. They wheeled the gurney down the hill to the waiting ambulance and pushed it into the open rear compartment and slammed the doors shut. The ambulance pulled off and, with the body gone, many of the rubberneckers began to drift away, off to call their friends and tell them about the excitement of seeing an actual murder scene. I waited and watched Alves and his expression never shifted.

"Any thoughts on what happened here?" I asked.

Alves shrugged and shook his head. "You are the police, not me."

"Yeah, we are, and so far what we've found out is that Andres is dead and you were maybe the first person here after it happened. What were you doing here at four in the morning?"

"The alarm company called me. They got a signal that someone had broken into the store and they are instructed to call me when the alarm goes off."

"Not the cops?" Tex asked.

217

"No. DeSilva has it set up so that I am called at home and the police are not notified."

"So the alarm company called you and you just came over here? Did you call DeSilva or anyone else when that happened?"

"No. This happens sometimes. It's usually nothing, as it was this time. I got here and there was nothing wrong in the store."

"And then what happened?"

"While I was in the store checking on everything, I heard a loud bang," he said. "I didn't know what it was, but I didn't think much about it, either. After I was done a few minutes later, I locked up and got back in the car. When I pulled out from behind the building, I saw Andres's truck on the street with a police car parked nearby."

"Did you call DeSilva right then?"

"Who told you I called him?"

I just stared at him. He shrugged and waited. He'd clearly been through this process a time or two.

"So who called him?" Tex said at last.

"I don't know. Perhaps the police. What does it matter? He's here."

"What matters is the timeline and what happened when. That's what we're trying to figure out here and it would be nice if you could help us."

Another shrug.

"OK, look," I said. "Enough with the ambivalent bullshit. I get that you're not a big fan of DeSilva, so you're probably not going to mourn Andres for long. I don't know who will, honestly. But that's not the point here. We still have a bunch of unsolved murders that look like they're going to land pretty close to you and now we have another one that is pretty much in your lap. The shadows are starting to get pretty close to your doorway, Alves."

"I've told you what happened. If you're interested in talking with me any further, you'll have to either charge me or talk to my attorney."

"Fuck your attorney and fuck *you*," Tex said, standing up and putting himself right in front of Alves. He was a full foot taller than Alves when they were on even footing and with Alves sitting down, Tex was looking down on him as he would one of his kids. "We'll talk to you whenever we want and if you want to be charged, say the word. I'll think up something and we'll plant your ass in MCI Plymouth for a few weeks. This ain't a game, jackass. We have ten fucking murders on our hands here and you're in the middle of all of them. *Ten.* We might not take suspects out in the country and bury them up to their necks here, but we still take murder pretty seriously. And ten? If we find out you're even remotely connected to one of them, we'll tie you to all of them and you'll fucking die in prison. You'll be begging the guards to shoot you after a few years. So don't sit here and act like you're doing us a favor by talking to us. You're in this up to your ears, Alves, and if you'd like to get out of it with any sort of deal, you'd better stop fucking with us and start telling us something useful. *Now*, motherfucker. Now."

Alves gave a small nod and glanced quickly across the street at where DeSilva sat. A pair of Plymouth cops were now standing next to him, talking and taking notes and DeSilva didn't appear to be paying any attention to us.

"You do not understand the position I'm in," Alves said. "I am tied to DeSilva in ways that make it impossible for me to speak freely, even if I wanted to."

"Yeah yeah yeah. We got the tragic story the last time," Tex said.

"Oh, did my story bore you, detective? I'm so sorry. Let's see whether you were paying attention. Do you recall when I told you I was just working for him because I was waiting for something?"

"Yeah."

"What I'm waiting for are my wife and daughter. They stayed behind in Brazil when I came here and I haven't seen them since. It's been seven years. My daughter was a child when I left, twelve years old, and now she is a woman. DeSilva has promised me for years that he would bring them to America, but he has never delivered."

"He knows that as soon as they're here, you're gone," I said.

"Perhaps. But he told me a few weeks ago that everything was set and that they would be on their way very soon. He showed me the paperwork. And when I talked to my wife, she said that they were to leave a few days later."

"And that was when?" I asked.

"Three weeks ago. I have not heard from them since."

I looked at Tex, who dropped his head and then sat back down on the bench, rubbing his hands over his cleanly shaved head. Alves sat impassively, as he always seemed to do.

"What does DeSilva say?" I said after a minute.

"What does he say. He says nothing. He will not speak to me about it. He refuses," Alves said. "But he has his own problems."

"Death seems to follow him around," Tex said.

Alves said nothing. After a time, he stood up and looked at both of us carefully. "May I go now?" he asked, and began walking down the path toward the sidewalk.

"Before you do, tell me about DeSilva's wife. How well do you know her?" I asked.

Alves stopped and turned around, but didn't walk back toward us. He considered the question for a few seconds. "Not well. I don't socialize with them and she's not involved in the business, so she is not around very often."

"What we hear, she hasn't been around at all lately."

A shrug. "As I said, I do not associate with them, so I wouldn't know if she's been on vacation or gone home for a while or something else. Nor do I care. I'm sick of all of this, of all of them."

I gestured across the street to the Escalade. "Looks like some other people are, too. Do you think your Italian friends did this?"

"I don't pay much attention to who he does business with these days. It's not interesting to me. The only thing that interests me now is getting away from all of this."

"How do you plan on doing that?"

"Sometimes these things take care of themselves," he said as he walked away, back to the street and DeSilva.

We watched him go and as he crossed the street and got within a few feet of DeSilva, he seemed to draw within himself, his back slumping over and his shoulders slouching. He slipped past his uncle and walked back up the stairs and resumed his spot, leaning against the brick facade. DeSilva was still standing with the Plymouth cops, but was paying them little attention and instead was staring down the street at the Escalade. The crime scene crew was crawling all over the truck, pulling whatever they could from it.

As we watched them work, my phone buzzed. It was a text from JD: ALL SET. I hit reply. OK. WILL CALL YOU LATER.

"Let's go take a run at the boss man," Tex said, standing up and cracking his neck.

"For sure. We going to spring the news about his wife?"

"I've got the autopsy photo. We talk to him about the kid first, see where he goes with that, if anywhere. If it looks like he's vulnerable, we show him the photo."

"And watch the fireworks."

"That's the plan," he said.

We walked across Sandwich Street, which was still blocked off at Lincoln and Water streets, on either side of the crime scene. The Plymouth guys had apparently tired of talking to each other and being ignored by DeSilva and had walked over to watch the crime scene techs process the SUV. As we neared DeSilva, he separated himself from the rest of his crew and stepped off the curb, meeting us in the middle of the street. There was something off about him. His air of superiority and authority wasn't gone, but it was diminished somehow, dented. A small man to begin with, he seemed to have collapsed in on himself and shrunk even further. He was kneading his hands, turning them over and over on each other and the skin looked red and worn.

"Mr. DeSilva, let me start by saying we're sorry for your loss. We know this is a terrible day for you and your family," Tex said, selling it.

DeSilva looked up, nodded. His eyes were rimmed with red and there was no trace of the cocky smile we'd seen in our previous encounters with him. "Do I need my lawyer here?"

"We do need to ask you some questions about your son and who might have wanted to hurt him. If you want to have your lawyer here, that's certainly your right, but this is about your son, not you."

"Then let's go." He led us back across the street to the low wall near the park. He sat and we both stood. "What do you need to know?"

"First, who would want to harm Andres?" I asked.

He shook his head slowly. "I don't know. He is not a violent man. I cannot make sense of this."

"Maybe it wasn't about him."

223

"You mean it was meant to be me in that truck?"

"No. I was thinking more along the lines of it being a message to you."

"What message?"

"You tell me. You're the one involved in all of this, not me. Way I hear it, there are some Italian guys not too far down the road that aren't real happy with you right now. They might have some guns, I'm not sure."

DeSilva waved dismissively. "You are talking nonsense. The people you're talking about are gnats. They are of no concern to me. They don't have the balls for something like this."

"They might not be a concern to you, but maybe the feeling isn't mutual. They tend to take things very personally and they don't usually forget," I said. "But you're telling me that doesn't matter. Makes sense."

"I don't care what you think or whether it makes sense to you," he said. "That is *my* son they killed, *my* son who was blown apart in that car. It's your job to find out who did that, not to stand here and tell me what I should think."

"And that's what we're trying to do here, figure out who killed him. So if you think that the Italians aren't responsible, give us another idea."

"I don't have any!" he said, throwing up his hands. "I'm just a businessman. I run a store and a travel company. I try to help people and be good to them and I am given this as a reward. This is the way America treats its people? I work hard, I provide jobs for people, I provide a place for them to live. How am I different from other business owners? I am not a gangster. I am a man with a business and a family. Or I was. Now, I don't know what I am."

"Have you talked to the rest of your family about this yet?" Tex asked.

"No," he said, keeping his head down, eyes on the sidewalk. I looked at Tex and nodded.

"We'd like to talk to your wife about this as well, see if she has any information that might help us," Tex said.

I watched DeSilva carefully as Tex spoke, and he tensed at the mention of his wife but he didn't meet Tex's gaze. He continued to look down, playing the distraught parent to the hilt. I had no doubt that his grief was real and there had to be a large pile of guilt pressing down on him as well. Even with all that, and knowing what we were about to tell him, I felt nothing but contempt for him. I couldn't rid myself of the image of him driving around small towns in Brazil, luring young girls into his car with the promise of work or money or food and then blithely destroying them. Standing three feet away from him made me itchy and I found myself looking forward to his reaction when we told him wife was dead.

"No, that's not possible," DeSilva said.

"Why not? We can make her come talk to us if we need to, but I'd rather not go through all that."

DeSilva simply shook his head.

"Do you know where your wife is, Paolo?" I asked. More silence.

"Paolo. Look at me. Where is your wife?"

A shrug. "I cannot say."

225

"You can't or you don't know?"

"I have not seen her in several weeks. I don't know when I'll see her again."

"Did you two have a fight? Did she leave?"

"What does any of this have to do with my son's murder? I can assure you that my wife did not kill him."

"Answer the question please, Paolo. Did she leave you?"

"She's not here, so you can draw your own conclusions. She went to Boston on a shopping trip one day and did not return. She was to be there overnight, making a weekend trip. She called me the day she was to return and said that she needed some time to herself. She said she would call me in a few days to talk. That was the last I heard from her."

"Have you tried calling her? I assume she has a cell phone," I said.

"Of course. She does not answer. Neither does my daughter. I have called every day and neither of them will answer."

I glanced at Tex and saw the surprise register on his face. The daughter was gone too? "Your daughter went to Boston?" I asked.

DeSilva nodded. "As I said, a weekend shopping trip, just the two of them. They have always been very close and they do this once in a while. Andres and I spent most of our time together, and that often leaves Sofia and Gabriela on their own."

"OK, listen," Tex said. "This is going to be difficult for you, but I want you to look at a picture right now."

Tex pulled out the autopsy photo, which had been cropped to show just the face. He hesitated for just a second and then handed it to DeSilva. The effect on him was immediate and startling. DeSilva's face crumbled, his mouth hung open and he seemed to collapse in on himself. He began to moan in a low, aching tone and started to rock back and forth on the wall. He then bent over, his head between his knees, and began weeping softly. Tex began looking around and shifting his weight from foot to foot uncomfortably. I kept my eyes on DeSilva, waiting. After a few minutes, he began to gather himself and sat upright again, wiping his eyes and nose on his sleeve.

It was a display of raw emotion and I had no doubt it was genuine, profound sadness. DeSilva was a smuggler and a rapist and probably a murderer, and yet here he was crying openly in front of two cops on what likely was the worst day he'd ever have. The day that he'd had to identify the nearly headless body of his son, the kid's grey matter smeared on the inside of the windshield, and now he was holding an autopsy photo of his wife in his hands. It was about as bad as it could get for DeSilva and I fucking *loved* it. I wanted to freeze-frame this moment and remember it forever, to make him live in this moment for the rest of his life. I wanted him to feel the pain and anguish and guilt and self-loathing that was consuming him right now until it was all he could remember, until he couldn't recall ever feeling good or happy or content.

Tex wasn't enjoying it as much as I was and finally had enough. "Paolo, that photo is of one of the bodies that we found in the pond last weekend. Is that your wife?"

"You know it is," he said, his voice already back to its normal tone. "You knew that before you gave it to me."

"That's right, we did," I said.

"But you showed it to me anyway. Did you enjoy that? Did you like seeing my pain?"

"We needed to see your reaction. We needed to know whether you knew your wife was dead."

"Well, now you have your answer."

"Yeah, we do. And that's fine. That's one small piece of this. The more important thing is trying to figure out who killed her and the rest of those women."

DeSilva's head snapped up. "And you still are standing here thinking it is me?" he said. "My wife. My *wife* was in there and you think I did this. Get away from me."

"No, I don't think so, Paolo. I don't think so. There are a lot of details about this that you don't know, so the fact that your wife is one of the victims doesn't disqualify you as a suspect. We've worked a lot of cases where a husband or wife or son or father is the killer. Happens all the time, actually. So, that's not going to work."

"Work? What do you mean, work? This is not some plan that I constructed! I didn't put my wife's body in the pond to take myself out of the investigation. Who thinks like this?"

"Cops. And that's what we are and it doesn't much matter to us whether you like our methods or our thinking. The way it looks from here is that you or someone in your organization fucked up in a big way and a whole bunch of girls ended up dead," I said. "Someone is bound to be pissed about that, and whether it's the guys in New Bedford or someone else, I don't know. But the bottom line is that now your family members are starting to show up dead and you're telling us that your daughter is missing, too. This is a bad week for you, Paolo, and if you'd like it to get any better, you might want to stop fucking around here and start helping us out. Because we're the ones who are trying to figure out who killed your wife and your son. And maybe your daughter."

DeSilva sighed and rubbed his hands across his face several times, stroking his goatee, thinking. After a minute, he stood up and looked down the street to where a tow truck driver was loading the Escalade onto a flatbed wrecker. He watched for a few seconds and then turned to me.

"Talk to Santos," he said. "I'm done with you."

He stepped off the curb and walked back toward his crew, the headshot of his dead wife still dangling from his hand.

Fifteen

Tex went to find Winthrop and update him on where things stood while I called JD.

"My man," he said when he answered.

"Did you win?"

"I sure did. No problems."

"Nice. OK, I'm gonna be a while longer here but I should be home by early afternoon. Meet me over there around two and we can sort it out."

"You got it. From what I can see so far, there's some pretty interesting stuff."

"Good. See you in a while."

I found Tex standing near where the Escalade had been a few minutes before. There was a blue latex exam glove laying on the ground where one of the crime scene techs must have dropped it. The fingers were stained dark red with Andres's dried blood. Tex dropped down and sat on the curb, watching the Plymouth cops wind up the crime scene tape and begin the process of disassembling the crime scene and turning this back into a public street.

"So this one is ours too. Just in case you were wondering," he said.

"Excellent. Might as well make it an even ten, right?"

"Sure. Could be eleven soon if we don't find his daughter wandering around somewhere."

"What are the chances we'll just find her hanging out at the food court at South Shore Plaza? It could happen."

"Oh, absolutely. I'm sure she's either there or at a really long slumber party," Tex said. "No chance she's dead. Don't sweat it."

"Phew. So, on the off chance that we do have to figure out what happened to her, we may want to gather up the photos of the rest of the vics from the pond and show them to DeSilva. Unless we want to take him down to the morgue and let him have a look at the bodies himself."

"I know which one you'd prefer."

"Damn skippy."

"You were a little rough on him back there," Tex said carefully.

"You know what, I don't give a fuck. The guy's wife is dead, and probably his daughter too, and that sucks. If it was anyone else--*anyone* else--I'd care and I'd have some empathy for him. But not him. He doesn't get that courtesy."

"Danny, we don't know whether he actually did anything wrong here. For all we know, someone killed his wife, along with nine other people, backed up a truck and dumped them all in his pond. From the evidence we have, that scenario is exactly as likely as any other one."

"I say again: I. Don't. Give. A. Fuck. Even if we find out he's a hundred percent clear on this whole thing--which is not going to happen--DeSilva is a tier one asshole. Remember: This is the guy who drove around the countryside in Brazil, picking up little girls-- and I mean *little* girls here--and taking them home for his pleasure. To satisfy his foul, twisted appetites. We don't know how many girls or what happened to them or how badly these girls are damaged now. I'm guessing pretty badly. So, for that, he gets every bit of shit and misery and pain I can possibly heap on him. All of it. He can't take it? Too fucking bad. That's life."

"Look man, I get all that and you know if anything like that ever happened to one of the boys, I'd hand in my badge and go and burn down anyone I thought I was involved. And I'd never give it a second thought. Never. But this isn't that, man. These aren't our people. I know he took a shot at Caroline the other day, and I know you were losing your mind, but you gotta separate that from the reality of what we're doing here."

I shook my head. "There is no separation," I said. "Not in this. He's the one who made it personal and brought this into it. So fuck him. Fuck him all day long. His wife is dead? Sorry. His son's brain is sitting in the passenger seat of his SUV? Sorry again. His daughter is missing and probably dead? Really sorry."

I walked a few feet away, trying to puzzle out exactly how I felt about all of this. What I knew was that this case was generating a lot of feelings that I wasn't used to anymore. It had been a long time since this kind of anger and bitterness and spite had come up to the surface. The odd thing was, they weren't entirely unpleasant feelings. I found myself searching for them, hoping that the rage hadn't disappeared somehow.

Because it was focusing me.

I turned back toward Tex.

"No. Actually, I'm not sorry," I said. "Not about any of it. The world is a shitty, mean, capricious place and you know what, bad things happen. They happen to all of us and a lot of the bad things that go down are by chance or accident. You're coming up to a crosswalk and you slip on some ice and slide into the street and get hit by a car. Boom, game over. But a lot of other stuff is not by accident. People wake up in the morning and consciously set out to do heinous, miserable shit. DeSilva is one of those people, man. He's a fucking disease and he preys on people who have no defense against him. And he got away with that stuff in Brazil and he's been getting away with it here for a long time, too. That needs to end. However it happens, it needs to stop."

Tex was still sitting on the curb and was picking up small handfuls of gravel and sifting them, letting the stones and sand and tiny bits of auto glass trickle between his fingers. I wasn't even sure he'd heard what I'd said until he tossed away the final handful and stood up, dusting his hands off on his jeans.

"That sounded a lot like a guy who isn't real interested in actually figuring out who killed all these people," he said. "It sounded like you're much more interested in blowing DeSilva up. I can't believe I need to explain this to you at this point in your life, but we're not in the revenge business here, Tobin. We're in the business of making cases and taking down bad guys. That might sound pretty corny and hollow to you, but that's what this job is, man. That's it. It's tedious and it's hard and a lot of times we lose, but we don't just

234

get to arbitrarily decide who's going down. The right guy goes down or no one does. That's how it works."

I shrugged. "He's the right guy. And he's going down. You with me on this?"

"I'm with you if he's the guy. And I think he probably is, regardless of how little solid evidence we have here. He probably didn't pull the trigger on any of them, but I'd say it's 80-20 that he's the one behind the killings. His wife and his kid are a different story, though. I don't know what to do with them."

"Yeah, me neither. As much as I hate to say it, I don't think he put his wife down. And clearly not the kid. From what we have right now, standing here today, I'd say we have two killers on our hands. At least."

"One guy killed the man and most of the girls in the pond. The second one killed DeSilva's wife and the other Jane Doe with the head wound."

"I think so. And maybe Andres."

"Different weapon on Andres, though. Shotgun fits with the other girls and the guy, not Sofia and the Jane Doe. And that other Jane Doe is..."

"DeSilva's daughter, I'd guess."

"Yeah. Well, I guess the good news is that we've solved her disappearance and we only found out about it a half hour ago."

"I'm sure that will satisfy Winthrop. For at least fifteen seconds."

"Yeah. Well, in the meantime, how about if we see what kind of actual evidence we can find that ties DeSilva to this thing? If he's involved, there must be something out there that points to him."

"Something, or someone," I said, looking up the block at the stoop where Alves stood with DeSilva and the others. He turned toward me and met my gaze, not blinking, refusing to look away. I nodded once and turned back toward Tex, who was watching me with a curious look. I stooped down and came up with a handful of the road dust, sand and windshield glass that had collected in the gutter. I sifted it through my fingers until all that remained was the pebbled safety glass. I pocketed the glass and walked back down the block.

I found Davis still standing near the Plymouth cruiser. Actually, he may not have moved in the hour or so that we'd spent talking to Alves and DeSilva. He definitely didn't look happy to see me coming back over.

"Look Danny, I'm sorry," he said.

I held up my hand. "I know, man, I know. I've soiled myself plenty of times on this job. It happens. We're past it."

He sighed and shook his head. "I don't know. I mean, that kid is in pieces because I made a basic, rookie mistake. I didn't just blow the tail or lose him for an hour. I got him killed."

"No, you didn't. I think he'd be dead either way. Whoever killed him walked right up on him, like they were having a conversation about the weather, and blew him apart. So that's probably someone he knew pretty well. Maybe you'd have been able to chase the guy down or get his plate number, but I don't think you would've been close enough to stop it."

Davis shrugged.

"Hey, look at this way," I said. "If you're gonna get someone killed on a tail, it might as well be a douchebag like that."

He gave a short laugh and looked past me at Alves, DeSilva and the others across the street. "So what do you want us to do now? I mean, assuming you still need us."

"We definitely do. I think there's a good chance we're going to see some action from DeSilva in the next couple of days. What it will be, I don't know. But we need you guys to stick on him. Tight. I'm sure he knows we're watching him now, so don't worry about being too subtle. Just stay on him."

"Both of us?"

"Yeah, for now. He's just lost his son and his wife in one morning, and he looks like he's starting to come apart at the seams a little bit," I said, looking over my shoulder at DeSilva, who was talking animatedly with Alves now, swinging his arms and pointing at Alves. "That was me? I'd be going batshit, running wild Sonny Corleone style, fixing to shoot everyone. So who knows what he might be thinking about doing."

"Got it. What about the guy he's with over there, his driver?"

"Alves. Yeah, I don't know what to make of him yet, honestly. He's got a serious problem with his boss, who is also his uncle. The guy's been promising to bring Alves's family up here from Brazil for years and it's never happened. Now, his wife and daughter are missing after DeSilva tells him that they're finally on their way up here."

237

"Oof. This guy DeSilva's bad juju, man."

I nodded. "He's the real thing."

An hour later Tex and I were sitting at a table by the front windows at T-Bone's, plowing through two pounds of buffalo wings and trying to work out a plan for the afternoon. They had the windows--which were more pocket doors than actual windows--wide open and we had a nice view of the foot traffic going by on Court Street. It was a warm, cloudless day and a non-trivial number of women were taking one of the last opportunities of the year to show off their tans. God bless them. Within a few weeks it would be all sweaters and long coats and another six or seven months until the female population of New England was brave enough to bare its arms and legs again.

"I think when this case is over I'm going to sell my house and move to Anguilla," I said. "Just thinking about another winter here makes me want to curl up in a ball and cry."

"You do, and I'm loading Kim and the boys on the boat and going with you," Tex said through a mouthful of wings. "This whole thing is starting to grind me down."

"The case?"

"The case, the people we have to deal with, the bosses, all of it. I spend all day wallowing in this garbage, talking to some of the worst people in the world and trying to convince a bunch of flat-assed bureaucrats to support us and give us what we need. And then I get home at night and try to turn all of that off and sit down and have a normal dinner with my family and it just doesn't work. How am I supposed to listen to Kim talk about her book club or the boys tell me about baseball practice or what girl they like? After I've spent the afternoon at a crime scene where some piece of shit stabbed his cousin in the throat because he turned off the Xbox in the middle of a game."

"No idea. I don't know how you do it at all. I get home at night, all I want to do is drink a couple of beers and watch a baseball game and think about anything other than this. I can't even think straight most of the time."

I spun my glass idly on the table for a minute, watching the people go by outside.

"You know what I keep thinking about?" I said after a bit. Tex shook his head, waiting. "Matty Ebert."

Tex spat a piece of gristle onto his side plate, tossed a mauled wing on top of it. "Why would you think about that guy? He's not even worth the energy it takes to say his name."

"What if this one turns out like that case?" I said.

Tex looked at me for a beat, a curious look on his face. "What makes you think it would?" he asked.

"I don't know, I just have a feeling that it's slipping away from us a little. That there's something we don't know."

"I'm sure there's a lot we don't know," Tex said. "There always is. But I can't see this ending up like Ebert."

Matty Ebert had been a prosecutor in Plymouth County for more than twenty-five years. He had a reputation for being a strict law-and-order guy who would never consider plea deals, no matter what the circumstances were. He'd put away a lot of people in his career, pimps, drug dealers, killers, whatever came his way. But he also had a tendency to make simple and sometimes baffling mistakes in court. He'd introduce an exhibit that the judge had warned him not to try and end up in a mistrial. Or he'd forget to ask a key question of a witness, leaving the defense attorney an easy opening. It didn't happen often, maybe once every couple of years or so. But it was enough that cops and lawyers and judges and reporters would talk about in the bars and the hallways. No one ever thought much of it, and it never really turned into an issue.

Until Matty's wife decided she'd had enough of him banging every young clerk and secretary who came through his office and filed for divorce. His wife was a regular on the charity and cocktail circuit and had never worked a day in her life, but she was determined to get half of poor Matty's assets, which turned out to be quite considerable. Far more extensive, in fact, than what one would expect a civil servant to be able to afford legitimately.

Mrs. Ebert's divorce attorney had the foresight to hire a forensic accountant, who had eventually discovered that Matty owned not just the big house on Warren Avenue and the summer place in Maine, but also had three separate offshore accounts that, it was revealed, contained more than a million dollars in total. Much to the dismay of Mrs. Ebert--and Matty--it was further revealed that the cash was the result of bribes paid to Matty over the last two decades by various and sundry criminals whom he had prosecuted but had somehow managed to win acquittals. It seemed that Matty Ebert's brain farts and oversights were in fact tactical errors that had been bought and paid for by the same people he was meant to be putting in jail.

When Mrs. Ebert's attorney made this information known to Matty's bosses, he'd been fired immediately and his former colleagues had begun investigating him. When the Plymouth police eventually showed up at his house with a warrant a few weeks later, Matty didn't answer. No one did, in fact. After one of the uniforms looked through the front window and saw a pair of legs underneath the coffee table, they called for backup and eventually broke down the door.

What they found was Mrs. Ebert sprawled on the Oriental carpet in the formal living room, her severed head balanced on her stomach. Her eyes were wide open and her mouth was agape. It wasn't empty, however. Someone had stuffed it full of dollar bills. Quite a lot of them, actually.

Tex and I had gotten the case, just the second one we'd worked together. It didn't take much in the way of clever police work to settle on Matty as the main suspect. But when we tried to find Matty, we hit a brick wall. He was just...gone. All of the cars registered in his name were accounted for, as was his boat. The house in Maine was empty, and none of the neighbors there had seen him for months.

So we fed his name to the FBI, put traces on all of his credit cards and then we waited. Nothing happened for a few months, and then about six months after the murder, one of Matty's former lovers in the prosecutor's office got an envelope in the mail, with a postmark from Havana. Inside was a picture of Matty standing next to a diminutive old man who was holding the reigns of a burro. Old town Havana was plainly visible in the background, and Matty was smiling, a sweating bottle of Tecate in his hand.

We had tried a few tricks with the feds and Winthrop had even gotten a friend in Washington to call in a favor with Kennedy and get some pressure applied in the right places. But none of it worked. Matty's mother had come over from Cuba in the '70s and that was enough to get him a soft landing.

Matty won and we lost.

Everything about that case bothered me and every time I passed the Eberts' house, it still burned me that Matty was able to slip away so easily. And now I had the feeling that DeSilva would end up doing the same thing somehow. I wasn't sure I could handle it. Actually, I was sure that I couldn't.

I shrugged. "I don't know, man. It wouldn't be a stretch. DeSilva has a network down there, he knows his way around the borders and all that. Who knows."

I wiped my hands on a paper napkin and sighed, my shoulders slumping.

"So what if that does happen?" Tex said, a little edge to his voice now. "What if we knock on his door one day and he's gone. Poof. Or if he beats us in court or we never even get that far. What then?"

I shook my head, not looking up. "I don't want to find out. I'm just a little fried right now, I guess. I need some sort of clean start, a break. Dealing with these guys every day is wearing me out. I need some time with normal people. People who don't shoot each other for sport."

"Well, Caroline seems like she probably hasn't killed too many people," he said.

I nodded vaguely.

"I'm not saying you guys need to run off to the chapel, I'm just saying that she seems like she gets it."

"Yeah. She's great. I mean, she's smart, funny..."

"Not hard to look at, either."

"Not at all. Not at all," I said. I polished off the last wing in a couple of bites and sat back in my chair, looking out at the couples walking past, just a few feet away. "You know, after we left your place the other night, I told her about Erin."

Tex's features hardened and he picked up a dead chicken wing and began tearing it apart, snapping the joints and picking it clean of cartilage. He and Erin had been very close and he'd always treated her like his own sister, even helping out with her law school tuition on a couple of occasions. When things had started going bad with her, he'd taken it just as hard as I had, and when she'd been killed, it was only Kim who had stopped the two of us from flying to Virginia that night. It had taken a lot of screaming and tears from all of us, but Tex and I had finally given in and spent that night emptying a bottle of Woodford Reserve and talking things out.

243

The next morning, I'd made some calls.

"I'm really sorry that Kim brought that up. It wasn't the best time for that," Tex said.

"It's fine, man. It's one of those things that would've come up pretty soon anyway if things keep going. We just hadn't had the Big Talk yet, comparing childhoods and families and figuring out whether we're second cousins or something."

"Yeah, I know. It still pissed me off, though. That whole situation just never should have gone down the way it did and it makes me ill just thinking about it. Sick."

I nodded.

"Anyway. How did Caroline react? Did you give her the whole story?"

"Pretty much. I only gave her the shape and size of the box at the end, but she figured out what was inside. It's funny, her reaction was a lot like yours and mine were at the time. I got the feeling that if she had been with me then, she would've driven us to Logan, bought three tickets and gone with us. The look on her face was pure fury, man. Once she realized what all happened, with the baby and everything, something changed."

"It's that maternal instinct. If something starts to threaten a child, even if it's not theirs, a switch flips and they turn into aggressors. I've seen it happen with Kim and some of her friends. It's an interesting thing, but not something I'd want to mess with. They do *not* hesitate to go straight after someone if they think they're a threat and they don't care who it is."

"No, you're right. That was the kind of vibe I was getting," I said. "She never met my sister and she barely knows me, to be totally honest about it, but the look on her face? She was ready to tear someone's throat out."

"Maybe we should turn her loose on DeSilva and his band of circus freaks."

"Why not? She couldn't do any worse than we have. So far all we've managed to do is get my dog killed."

"And DeSilva's kid, let's not forget that," Tex said.

"True, but he's slightly less important to me than Reggie was. Plus, Reggie was smarter."

"Not to speak ill of the dead, but Andres probably had him in the looks department."

"How dare you? On his worst day Reggie got more ass than that guy dreamed of getting in his whole pathetic life. And, *and*, he could lick his balls while he was asleep."

Tex picked up his glass and raised it. "To Reggie: He might have been as ugly as a hat full of assholes, but by God, he could lick his own nuts."

"While sleeping," I said, clinking my glass against his. "Respect."

"Respect."

"So, Winthrop was kind enough to remind me-- again--that the clock is ticking on this. I politely explained to him that we had identified at least one of the victims from the pond and that we'd likely be identifying another one later today once we get DeSilva to look at the rest of the pictures."

"And he said something like, 'Well detective, does that put you any closer to figuring out who actually killed any of these young women?'"

"Actually, he said exactly that. So I assured him that we had several promising leads and that we'd probably have some significant progress to report in the next day or so."

"We do? We will?"

"The hell do I know? I just needed to shut him up. What I do know is that we need to take a closer look at your boy Alves. There's more to him than what he's showing us," Tex said. "I get the feeling that he thinks he's smarter than we are, and that pisses me off."

"If that's what he thinks, that's fine. Let him. Maybe we can use that to our advantage at some point. But I think you're right--there's something about him that's bugging me. He's a weird dude, sure, but there's more than that to it, I think."

"What do we make of his story about his wife and daughter? You buying that?"

"You know, I'm not sure," I said, turning it over in my head for the first time. "I think I probably do believe it, or some version of it. He's got some serious hate for DeSilva and I don't think that comes from just him being a shitty boss. That's some major, deep down hate, and that usually comes from something personal."

"I'm with you. Nothing about these people would surprise me at this point, and so the idea that DeSilva might have killed Alves's family, whether it was intentional or otherwise, doesn't strike me as unlikely at all."

"But why? What's the motive?"

"I'm telling you, you're worse than my kids with all the questions, man," he said. "Christ. Don't you watch Law & Order? I don't need a motive if I have means and opportunity. Two out of three is plenty."

"I like the way you think."

Tex's phone rang and he looked down at the screen and then turned it so I could see the name. Davis.

"I wonder who's dead now," Tex said. While he answered the call, I ducked outside and called Caroline and let her know I was done at the scene and would probably be home in a half hour or so. She said she was going for a run and Ahearn was going to trail her in his car.

"Whatever you do, don't make him get out and run," I said. "I can't deal with another dead body today."

"I'll be gentle," she said.

When I went back in, Tex was still on the phone and was scribbling in his notebook. I waited for him to finish and after a minute he closed the notebook and smiled at me.

"Our luck may be changing," he said.

"Did Davis shoot DeSilva for us?"

"Sadly, no. But he got a call from Delia after we left. Sounds like there's another truck full of girls on the way."

"When?"

"Friday sometime, probably late night. Davis said Delia was a little hesitant on the details, trying to hold out on him. But he'll get it. Point is, Delia said that he

247

thinks this might be sort of a make-good for the last time."

"Oh that's nice of them."

"You know what they say: The customer is always right. It's hard to argue that DeSilva delivered the product he promised. I think people generally like their hookers to be alive."

"There you go, generalizing," I said. "Maybe some people aren't as picky as you are."

"I guess the question is, what do we do with this information?"

"I do believe we go and fuck up their program, no?"

"Well, sure. But how? I mean, snatching up some guys who are running girls into the country would be nice and all, but aren't we more interested in DeSilva and Alves and putting these murders on them?"

"You mean if they're guilty, that is."

"Of course. Didn't I say that? Sorry."

"Well, I think we get them on whatever we can and worry about the rest of it later," I said. "Obviously I'd be much happier to pin the bodies on them, but if we can take them down for trafficking or prostitution or something else, then fine. As long as they're inside, I'll be happy."

"Inside? Or elsewhere?" Tex asked.

"Look man, please don't start feeding me the self-righteous crap. Just don't. You want these guys as badly as I do."

"Yeah, I do. But the difference maybe is that I want them the right way. I'm not interested in doing it any other way. That's not going to change, no matter how many times we talk about this," Tex said.

"Fine, whatever. I don't feel like going into this again. All I'm trying to say here is that this shipment gives us a chance to make some headway on this thing."

"I'm with you. What we know so far is that the truck is coming Friday night, there are going to be roughly fifteen women in it and that Delia is meeting the truck with two other guys. I don't imagine that DeSilva is going to be there himself, but someone from their side should be, especially since they screwed it up so badly the last time," Tex said.

"Could be Alves or the two meatheads. But it doesn't really matter. As long as someone from that crew is there, we have the connection we need. We need something to push these guys with."

"Do we want to let the tactical guys in on this? Never know what's going to happen with these dopes. They seem to have a thing for killing people."

"Nah, I think we can handle a bust like this. I thought you narco guys knew how to do it," I said.

"Yeah, you know how we do it? We bring a lot of guys with big guns and helicopters and body armor and we take any thoughts of violence out of their heads. That's how you stay alive."

"OK, so maybe we think about it. But before we get that far, we need to figure out what's actually going down. Can Davis push Delia some more for the details?"

"Yeah, I think so. But just in case, why don't we have a talk with him and see if we can't get access to their wire? Can't hurt to have a little extra information."

"Shouldn't be a problem," I said. "God knows they owe us after today."

"No doubt."

My phone buzzed and I looked down and saw a text from JD: WHERE YOU IS?

"Ah, damn, I gotta run," I said.

"Booty call?"

"Not unless JD has gotten a lot lonelier than I thought living on that boat. Gotta talk a couple things over with him."

"You're going to let me in on this at some point, right?"

"If it turns out to be anything, I will. But I don't know anything right now. Just looking for a way to get us some of that extra information we need."

"OK, just keep me posted. Or don't. Shit, I don't know."

I laughed. "Sure, I can do that. Or not."

Sixteen

When I got home, I found JD sitting on the front porch, feet up on the rail, eyes closed. There was a large paperback book with the title "The Shellcoder's Handbook" spread on his lap. I dropped into a chair next to him and pulled a bottle of Sierra Nevada from the cooler on the deck. I took a long pull on the beer and looked over at JD, who might have been asleep for all I could tell.

"Hi honey, how was your day?" he said, eyes still shut.

"Oh, the usual. A dead guy in a car, brain all over the dashboard. Bunch of guys standing around, no one knows anything. Captain up our asses for not solving it before we got to the scene. You know."

"Man, I sure do wish I had joined the po-lice," he said. "It sounds like a lot more fun than what I've been doing. I don't hardly have anyone to yell at me or tell me what to do anymore."

"I can fix that for you, if you want. I'll just give Amy your phone number, fix that right up."

"Come to think of it, maybe I'm good the way I am."

"Ya think?"

"I do. I also think you should be a little nicer to me if you want me to tell you what I got up to last night. Pretty interesting stuff."

"So now you're going to play hard to get? How many more beers do I have to give you before you'll put out?"

"One more should do it. I'm a cheap date," JD said, setting his empty on the deck and grabbing a full one from the cooler. He settled back in his chair, propped his feet back on the rail. "So the setup was the way you described it with the wireless network. But I took a look at it and decided that it was probably easier to just go in through the Web."

"Why?"

"Well, a few reasons, but mostly because the site was so poorly protected it didn't make any sense to jump through extra hoops. Like you said, it had a sweet SQL injection hole, and I found a bunch of other bugs too, without even really trying."

I nodded. "Yeah, I don't get the impression that he was doing too many pen tests on it."

"No. So, after a couple of tries, I got in and dumped the database. I have it on an encrypted thumb drive for you. I haven't really looked at it, mostly because I didn't know what I was looking for."

"I'm not sure I do either, but I just want to see what names are in there and whether any of them mean anything to us," I said.

"Any chance they'll figure out you were in there?"

JD smiled. "Always a chance. I'm not Mark Dowd. But I was pretty careful. One thing, though."

"Yeah?"

"While I was there, I banged on the Web server a little bit..."

"Ah, shit, JD..."

"It was sort of asking for it, man. Anyway, I found an old Apache bug that worked and so then I started looking around the network a little. I got on to an XP machine that looked like they use for office stuff and while I was on there, I noticed that there was a shitload of Skype traffic going through there. Like, a lot. I was only in there for about forty-five minutes or so and I saw ten or twelve different calls come in. I don't know what that means, if anything, but I figured you might want to know."

"Huh. I'm not sure what it means either. But I do know that a lot of the Brazilians and Cape Verdeans and other immigrants around here use Skype to call back home."

"Yeah, but how many calls can a couple of guys make in forty-five minutes? That's a lot of calls."

"True. I need to think about this some more."

"Probably nothing, but there it is," JD said.

I thought it over for a minute. "Sure would be nice to have a way to know what's going on with that."

He smiled again and looked sideways at me.

"What?" I said.

"Well, I sort of thought you might say something like that. So I left a something behind. Tiny little program that I can connect to remotely. No sweat."

"I didn't want that. What if one of them gets bored and decides to scan that machine or something? Then they'll know someone was in there."

"Look, it's a modified version of something I wrote like a year ago. No one else has a copy of it, so none of the antivirus scanners would find it and even if they did it would just look like a random file to them. It just sits and waits and does nothing unless I tell it to. Relax, man."

"You're the one who said there's always a chance they'll figure out someone hit them. What then?"

"If they ever got that far, it would be a dead end anyway. Worst case is that they find the tool and remove it. So what? Even if they're logging the activity on that machine, which I seriously doubt, that gets them nowhere. I was using Tor when I went in and I used a machine that I bought two days ago after you called me. I wiped it, installed a new OS and then did the job and wiped it again. They'll get exactly nowhere."

I sighed. "OK. Let's say I'm hypothetically interested in seeing what is going on with the Skype calls. Can we do that? I mean, doesn't Skype traffic just look like regular HTTP traffic?"

"Well, sort of. But the real problem is that Skype calls are encrypted. We'd be able to tell when Skype is initiating outbound connections, but it would be useless to us anyway."

"Well, but wait a second. The session has to be decrypted at some point on the client side, right? So if you're on the machine, you should be able to see that."

"Should I?" he asked mockingly. "Hey! You're right!"

"OK smartass. How can we do that?"

"That's pretty straightforward, really. If a Skype call comes in while I'm in there, I can monitor it and record it. But the weird thing about what I was seeing is that it seemed like someone was not only answering calls on that box, but also then initiating multi-party calls. So I think whoever is using that PC is sort of acting like an operator almost."

"I wonder what the point of that is."

"Not sure. But one thing you should think about is that Skype isn't just on PCs these days. You can have it on your iPhone or iPad or just about anything."

"All these guys carry cell phones, but I don't know what they are."

"If they're iPhones or something like that, some kind of smartphone, you're onto something. The newest iPhones can make Skype calls over 3G. They don't even need to be on WiFi anymore," JD said. "So they could be using Skype as their default communications method."

"You know what's funny, I think you're right. We subpoenaed DeSilva's cell phone records a few days ago--he does have an iPhone, by the way. And when we got the records there was nothing there. Nothing. He makes like two calls a month, and they're to his home number. He doesn't make any other calls on that phone at all. We figured he was probably using Tracfones for business, but now...shit."

"I had to bet, I'd say they're doing Skype-to-Skype calls on their phones or from their PCs to communicate. The encryption makes it impractical to eavesdrop on in real time and I'm not even sure that you could intercept it anyway, because Skype uses a decentralized architecture so calls are routed through random nodes depending on geography and traffic and all that."

"So if they're mainly using it on their phones, then we're screwed anyway. We don't have any visibility on there and there's no chance we're getting a wiretap order for those phones. We'd never be able to show cause."

"You're definitely screwed on the mobiles, but think about it this way: I'm on one of the machines that is part of the Skype network, assuming this is what they're doing. As long as I'm on there, I can see incoming and outgoing calls on that machine. So at a minimum, I'll have one side of the conversations and we'll also have a look at who is talking to who and when."

I thought about that for a bit and the more I kicked it around, the more I liked it. Obviously, what JD had done was six kinds of illegal and monitoring the calls was another level up from that. Me having asked him to do it put me very deep in the shit if anything ever came out of this.

But I knew JD was good and I also knew that if it ever came to it, he'd just leave the country and not come back. End of story.

"OK, thanks man," I said after a minute. "That's nice work. Not that I thought you'd come up short or anything."

"Not a problem," he said. "Happy to help. And getting paid in beer ain't so bad either. Not so healthy for my bank account, though."

"On the other hand, beer isn't taxable."

"Not that I pay taxes anyway. But it's the principle of the thing."

"Sure."

Seventeen

We shot the shit for another twenty minutes or so and then JD went inside to take a nap. I told him I'd wake him if I left for the night and he gave me the thumb drive with the dump of DeSilva's database on it. I checked my watch and decided I had time for a quick five miles. It would give me a chance to work out in my head what Tex and I wanted to do tonight and also chew over what JD had given me.

I called Davis quickly and asked him about the wire. He thought about it for a second.

"I think we can do that," he said.

"All we're looking for is some info on a meet on Friday. Need a time and location."

"I'm on it. I'll let you know."

I went upstairs and changed and headed out the door. I ran south on 3A for a couple of blocks and then hung a right on Clifford, pushing it pretty hard, working out the kinks from the last few days. This was one of my favorite routes. Nice rolling hills, great scenery along the Eel River and virtually no traffic along the back roads. It was a residential area with big, but not showy, homes on secluded wooded lots. It gave me a lot of options in terms of mileage and I could easily do five, eight or ten miles back here without seeing a car or person for an hour.

I had just come around the bend on Clifford and was coming up on the little bridge over the Eel when I heard a car coming up behind me. The road was narrowing and there's no sidewalks, so I moved a bit more to my left toward the shoulder to let the car pass. But as it came up beside me, the driver slowed to match my speed and stayed next to me.

I glanced over quickly to see what the deal was and saw that the driver's window sliding down. Alves was peeking over the blacked out window of DeSilva's Cadillac, alternating glances between me and the road ahead of him. I was almost relieved to see it was him until I saw the odd, somewhat manic look on his face. His eyes were pegged wide open, and there was a patina of sweat shining on his face. He looked pallid and hungry, almost feral, a complete change from the man we'd interviewed just a couple of hours earlier downtown. His skin had a grayish pallor to it and his hair was soaked with sweat. I barely recognized him, but I'd seen the look and the desperation before on other men.

I slowed my pace a bit and began to call out to him, but as I did, Alves raised his hand to the window and the sunlight glinted off something metal in his grasp. My mind flashed and I dove left off the road into the brush and reeds, covering my face as I rolled through the undergrowth, thick with brambles and thorns.

I tumbled two or three times, rolling down the short, steep bank toward the marsh. Coming to a stop on the edge of the wetland, I held my breath and waited for the sound of the gunshot, but instead heard a small tinkling sound on the pavement and the engine of the big Cadillac winding up as Alves accelerated away.

I pulled myself up slowly, my shirt and shorts snagged and torn by the stickers in the brush, small dots

258

of blood emerging up and down my limbs. I high-stepped my way out of the weeds and looked up the road and saw the Cadillac cresting the hill on the far side of the bridge, heading toward Jordan Road. Standing on the road, I breathed deeply several times, waiting for my heart rate to recover and the blood to stop pounding in my ears.

What the hell?

I looked around on the road, trying to figure out what the sound had been. I walked a few yards up the road and saw a small rectangle of metal on the blacktop, the sun shining off its polished surface. I stopped and stared at the trinket, recognizing it at once, bending down to pick it up, my hand trembling with adrenaline, fury and hatred.

I saw my name and address engraved on one side and then turned it over, seeing Reggie's name and license number on the reverse. I rubbed my thumb across the letters forming his name, feeling the anger and pain surge through me, welcoming it. The tag was spattered with dried dark blood droplets and I instinctively wet my thumb and forefinger on my tongue and made to wipe them off before thinking better of it.

I wanted the blood on there as a reminder of what DeSilva, Alves and the others had done, what they were capable of doing, not just to Reggie, but to the girls and women and men that they had maimed and killed and damaged beyond repair. I felt a chill ripple through me, unsure whether it was from the sweat drying on my skin or the disgust at what was happening around me.

I twisted apart the soft metal ring on the top of the tag and hooked it onto the silver chain I wore around my neck, right next to my St. Patrick medal. I started running again, following Alves's route and banging a right on Sandwich Road, gradually increasing my pace until I was breathing one-and-one, my lungs telling me I was on the edge of trouble.

I let the pain wash over me, embracing it, reaching for it, pushing for more, driving myself up the hills and hammering down the other side. Within a mile and a half or so, my legs felt numb, disconnected from my body, a feeling I knew well from the final stages of races. It was a signal that lactic acid was flooding my muscles and overwhelming their capacity to do work, the last warning sign from my distressed and exhausted body that the end was near.

I ignored it, throwing the last remaining bits of focus and energy I had into maintaining the ruinous pace. I saw the opening to the beach road ahead, perhaps four hundred yards away, the cars going in and out blurring into one another as my vision began to narrow and soften with the effort. Traffic rushed by me, yet I heard nothing. The entrance was only a few dozen yards away now and I wondered idly whether I'd pass out before I reached it.

I hit the parking lot at a dead sprint, darting in front of a yellow Hummer, the driver standing on his brakes to avoid hitting me. I staggered through the line of cars waiting to get on to Long Beach and made it to the sea wall.

I sagged against the weathered stones, trying to steady myself, waiting for my heart rate and breathing to return to normal. Looking around at the people queuing up for a late afternoon on the beach, I felt no connection to any of them. The smiles, the laughs, the carefree attitudes. I couldn't imagine where the joy behind that was coming from.

Didn't they know what was happening around them?

Couldn't they smell the stench of the poisonous, befouled people walking among them?

How could they sit on the beach, reading crappy Dan Brown novels or baking in the sun when two miles away there were people planning new ways to ruin the lives of dozens of girls?

How could this be?

I didn't want to think about it for long because I already knew the answer: No one cared.

No one.

If it wasn't their kid or their sister, then it didn't register. Not their problem.

Fine. I wasn't doing this for them anyway. It was for me.

DeSilva and Alves and the rest of them were going to fall and I wanted to be the one who pushed them.

Eighteen

It was after six by the time I got home and JD was already up, rummaging through my fridge. He came out with some leftover sesame noodles and shrimp spring rolls. I couldn't remember ordering them, which didn't bode well for JD's digestive health.

"Careful there," I said. "That stuff is probably older than my last date."

"Listen, from what I hear, I have belly button lint older than her."

"I know that's right."

"I live on a boat, dude. I bathe when I feel like it and I eat what I find. I'll survive."

"Don't say I didn't warn you."

"Noted," he said, looking me up and down. "How far did you run? You look like you did 20."

"Just five, but it was eventful." I told him what happened with Alves. He listened to all of it then was quiet for a minute while he took it in.

"How did he know where you'd be?" he asked.

I looked at him.

"They're watching you," he said. "What is that, dude? They're watching *you*. Since when does it work that way?"

"It doesn't," I said.

"So what do you do about that?"

"Not sure. It was kind of dumb if you think about it. I mean, I sort of suspected that they might have been doing something, but now I know for sure."

"So you have the advantage on them again."

"I have no idea. I really don't know much of anything these days. But I'm not even sure whether DeSilva knows Alves did that. I'd bet he did it on his own," I said. "Like I said, it was pretty stupid and that doesn't seem like DeSilva's M.O."

"Maybe this guy Alves was just trying to rattle your cage, get you off your game somehow."

I shrugged. "Yeah, could be. But he looked like he was kind of out of his mind. Sort of crazed."

"What about Tex?" JD asked. "You think they're watching him too?"

I smacked my palm on the counter. "Where's my phone?" I said, looking around the kitchen.

"Here." JD slid it down the counter to me. As I went to dial, I noticed I had two missed calls and voice mails. All from Tex. I quickly punched the speed dial button for him, silently counting the rings. Two, three, four. Come on Tex. Answer. *Answer*.

He picked up on the sixth ring. I could hear a lot of noise in the background.

"Tobin. Where you been? I've been trying to--"

"Listen listen listen. Are you OK? Are the kids OK?"

"Wait, what?"

"I was out running and Alves came up on me in his car and threw Reggie's tag out the window at me and then I ran home and I was talking to JD and I figured out they're watching us and--"

"Slow down, man. Slooooow down. What are you talking about, they're watching us? Who?"

"Alves, DeSilva, all of them. He knew where I was and knew I'd be out there by myself so he waited till I was in the middle of nowhere."

Tex was quiet on the other end of the line, but I could still here a lot of commotion wherever he was. It sounded like a mall or a restaurant, but I couldn't be sure.

"You didn't answer my question," I said. "Is everyone OK on your end?"

"Well, define everyone," he said after a pause. "Kim and the boys are fine, yeah. They're up in Hingham at her parents' place for the night."

I let out a long breath. "OK. OK. Good," I said. JD looked over at me and I nodded. He smiled.

"I can't say the same for Delia though," Tex said.

"Who?"

"Delia. The CI from the other day?" Tex said.

"Oh yeah. Sorry, yeah. Why, what happened?"

"Car accident. He's got a broken pelvis, compound fracture of one of his femurs and a bunch of broken ribs," Tex said. "He's seriously banged up, man."

"Ah, jeez," I said, sitting down for the first time since I'd gotten home. "How did it happen?"

"Don't know. I'm at St. Luke's right now, waiting to talk to the docs. I did talk to one of the EMTs for a minute and he said that Delia told them someone ran him off the road. Guy said Delia's Vette was completely totaled, just shredded. He was sort of delirious by the time the EMTs got to him, so that was about all they got from him. He's sedated right now."

"It was DeSilva, man. For sure. Think about it: They were watching me and probably you too. They see us go to the office, maybe someone sits there and sees Delia come in, they wonder what the hell he's doing at a state police barracks. Two plus two is four."

"I don't know about that. From what Davis said, this guy's been in trouble with his own people anyway, agitating for more money and juice. Could easily have been them."

"Maybe, but even if it was, I'd bet DeSilva's the one who tipped them off to what he was doing. It saves him from having to do the dirty work and takes care of the problem of Delia talking to us."

"Danny, look. It's starting to feel a lot like you're ready to pin everything from the kidnapping of the Lindbergh baby to the Gardner Museum heist on this guy. I'll grant you that he's a major-league asshole and I would love to get him out of circulation, but you gotta stop looking at everything through the prism of DeSilva and his crew," Tex said.

"What other conclusion is there to draw from the facts that we have right now? It's the most logical explanation."

"Maybe so, but it's not the only possible one. And we don't have all of the facts, just a small subset of them. We need to step back a little bit and see what else could have happened here. I mean, a guy like that probably has his share of enemies, right? He could have cut someone off in traffic or something. Who knows?"

"Come on, man. I don't believe in coincidences and neither do you."

He sighed. "All I'm trying to say here is that we need to find some facts before we crucify DeSilva for this. In the meantime, we need to figure out what happened to Andres."

"No, you're right. I know," I said.

"So I'm going to call Santos and let him know that we need to have DeSilva come down and officially identify his wife's body in the morning. Let's start there. We can have him look at the other body too, see whether it's his daughter," Tex said.

"I'm almost certain it is at this point."

"Me too."

"But how does that help us with Andres?"

"Doesn't necessarily, but we get him in there, it finally sinks in that he's all alone now and everyone is gone, his whole family, and maybe we get somewhere with him. He's got to know at this point that the walls are closing in on him."

"Are they, though?" I said. "A lot of people are dead and half of them are his family members, but maybe our best chance of getting any real information on this guy is sitting in that hospital with you now. Delia was the only guy that was giving us anything decent on DeSilva, and he's in pieces."

"So we find someone else. Or we wait a day or two and see if he comes around. If anything, he'll probably be more motivated to help us now."

"Yeah," I said, thinking of the database and JD's rootkit sitting on DeSilva's PC. "OK, so what's your plan for tonight?"

"I'm gonna hang around here until I have a chance to talk to the doc and then I'm going home, I'm putting my feet up and I'm watching the Sox game. And I'm forgetting about this shit for a while. What about you?"

"I'm about to call Mitchell and get the results of the rest of the autopsies. I think we're going to find out the rest of them were full of dope, too. Which means I think we're going to need to figure out why all these girls were carrying dope when Delia said they weren't and what that means. After that, I'm gonna pick up Caroline, we're gonna drink some wine and watch a movie and then maybe have some sex."

"You win," Tex said.

"I usually do."

Mitchell was still in his office when I called a little before seven.

"Hiya Danny. You calling for the COD on the guy from this morning?"

Morgue humor, nothing better. "Yeah. I figured it was either Bari-Bari or hair cancer."

"Close. Turns out he had some lead in his brain, which can be somewhat detrimental to your health. Just so you know."

"Good to know. Thanks. So, tell me about my floaters. Dope?"

"Easy with the name-calling, my friend. I'm a respected man in my profession."

"Let me rephrase: Did my floaters all have stomachs full of illegal narcotics?"

"They did indeed," he said.

268

I sighed. "Guess that's that then. OK, thanks."

"Don't you want to know what killed them?"

"I'm guessing it was the presence of a half a kilo of heroin in their stomachs."

"No sir, it wasn't. The latex containers in the stomachs of these women were still intact. None of them died of an overdose. They were all killed by the gunshot wounds to their heads. Probably a .22. No exit wounds, so the slugs are still in there."

"Huh. That doesn't help me at all," I said.

"Sorry about that. I could go back and double-check for you, see if I can find a way to break some of those latex bags for you."

"Yeah, I'd appreciate that. The way things stand now, I'm going to have to do some damn investigating here. You're messing up the program."

"Glad to help," he said with a laugh.

"Yeah, thanks."

"Listen, you want my opinion?"

"Why not?"

"Seems to me that you have more than one guy working here. Got a couple of bodies blown apart with shotguns and without hands. Got a couple more that died of heroin toxicity but have gunshot wounds to the head, too. And you got the rest that are full of dope too but were killed before the dope could get to them," he said. "And let's not forget the one from this morning, if you think that one is connected. You're the cop here, but that doesn't add up to one person to me."

"Yeah, we're thinking along the same lines. The thing that bothers me though, is the two bodies without

269

hands. Even the drug guys hadn't seen it before around here. It doesn't really fit with the rest of what we have, either."

"I can't really help you with that. But I will tell you that the hands definitely were removed post-mortem. Both women were dead when their hands were amputated."

"We knew that, didn't we?" I asked.

"It's what I thought when I first saw them, but I'm certain now. I looked at them carefully during the autopsies and I don't think there's any way that could've been done while they were alive. Like I said, there's no real tearing or indication of struggling."

"They probably would have bled out pretty quickly after that if they'd been alive, right?"

"Within a few minutes. Lots of blood flows in and out of the hands," Mitchell said. "One other thing I should mention, though."

"Yeah?"

"Taking those hands off would not have been an easy thing. Even if the victims were dead, which we think they were, and the guy had as much time to figure it out as he needed, the force you'd need to go cleanly through the muscle and tendons and bone would be pretty significant. That's not a trivial task. In fact, I'm not really sure how he did it."

"Tex talked to a guy down in Miami who said they'd seen that kind of thing from time to time with drug gangs. Said it was done with a machete usually."

"No way, Danny. Uh uh. I've seen pictures of that sort of thing before, and those wounds are messy and ugly and you can usually see hack marks on the bones. I don't think many people are getting through on the first swing, no matter how hard they try," he said. "It's not happening."

"OK, so if it wasn't a machete, what then?"

"I can't say for sure, but I'd guess something mechanical, not manual."

"There goes my theory about it being William Wallace."

"See, I'm helping to narrow down the suspect list."

"Sure. So, you think it could be like a band saw or something along those lines?"

"Could be. Something very sharp and very powerful, in any case. I were you, I'd be looking for someone with some skills in that area. Whoever did those two knew what he was doing. It wasn't a sloppy job."

I told Mitchell that we'd probably be by in the morning with DeSilva to look at the Jane Does without hands and make positive IDs. He promised to have them ready. JD had graciously agreed to bunk at the motel again and he gathered up his gear and said he'd check in with me around midday tomorrow.

Thirty minutes later Caroline and I were sitting on the couch, making our way through a large extra cheese pie from Mamma Mia's and a good bottle of Malbec. It was sort of overkill for the pizza, but what the hell.

I caved on the movie choice and we ended up with one of those terrible romantic comedies with Dermot Mulroney or Patrick Dempsey or Ryan Reynolds or some other himbo. It was brutal, but I couldn't have cared less as long as she was there.

"So let me get this straight: They're best friends, but he's pretending to be her gay boss at her half-sister's wedding?"

"Shhhh! This is the good part," she said.

"Ohhh, *this* is the good part. Does it involve some hilarious misunderstanding about her fake boss and some zany antics?"

"Shut it or I'll put it back on 'Say Yes to the Dress'."

"Are you threatening me? I'm police, you know."

"You sure?" she said, a little fleck of something in her eye. "How's that whole thing working out for ya?"

"Shitty, thanks for asking. Those crab fishing and swamp logging shows on TV are starting to look pretty good about now."

"Oh I could see that," she said, tucking her hair behind her ear as she looked over at me. "You cruising around some swamp in Arkansas."

"I could do it."

"Sure," she said, scooping up the last slice of pizza. For a girl who weighed all of maybe 125 pounds, she could put it away like a pubescent teenager.

"The good news for you is, people up here keep getting themselves killed, so I'm probably sticking around."

"How did things go today with the new dead guy?"

"Still dead. Which is probably good for the rest of us. Except me."

"Is it connected to what's happening with the rest of this stuff?" Caroline asked, a little concern in her voice. "Cause I thought you guys were winding that up, and now there are more people turning up dead."

"Yeah, it is. But it's not anything you need to worry about. If anything, this guy being dead is probably a good thing for you," I said. "It's one less asshole to worry about."

She nodded and looked back at the TV, unconvinced.

I'd spent a lot of time in the last week worrying about this case and what it might mean for me and my career, and whether Caroline was in any real danger. But what I hadn't really thought about was the toll that the stress of all this might be taking on her. She didn't sign up for this and I really wouldn't have blamed her if she just looked at the situation and said, Screw it, I don't need this, so I'll just go back to school, finish up and move on.

Probably what I would've done under the circumstances. But I didn't think she'd do that. Not sure why, but I just didn't see it.

I was also still turning things over in my head, trying to figure out why she'd gotten such a hold on me. She had a lot of things going for her, but so did a lot of other women I'd dated and they hadn't stuck. Maybe it was the timing.

Maybe I just needed something to lose right now.

She slouched back on the couch, holding her wine glass by the stem, balancing it on her stomach. "Can I ask you something? Without you getting upset?"

"Sure. I'm not that fragile."

"Were you serious this morning about me staying down here instead of going back to the city?"

"Absolutely."

"Why?"

I looked over. "Why what?"

"I mean, why do you want me here?"

I sat forward on the couch and half turned to face her. "Not to be crude," I said, "but have you seen you?"

A short laugh. If I accomplished nothing else for the rest of my life, I could live with making her laugh and be pretty satisfied.

"I'm serious, Danny. I'm asking because the answer is important."

"Ok, look. I asked you to stay in town because I really like you and we're having a good time together and I'd like that to continue. I thought all of that was obvious."

"It is, but I'm just wondering if that's all there is to it."

"Meaning what?" I said.

"Well, it's a pretty quick move--and I'm mostly OK with that. But I want to be sure that we're doing it because there's something here and not because you're feeling a need to...protect me." She hesitated on the last bit, unsure of her footing.

"As in, am I making you a proxy for Erin, trying to do some sort of penance."

"Well..."

I took her wine glass and placed it on the coffee table and then held her hand in both of mine. "Look,

I'm not going to tell you that stuff hasn't crossed my mind recently. Because it has. Talking about Erin the other night with you, dealing with all of these murdered women...it's brought a lot of that back up. And it hurts. A lot. I miss her every day, constantly. I can't tell you how many times I'll think of something that I want to tell her and be halfway through dialing the phone when I realize what I'm doing. Like this, us. That first night after we hung out at the beach, I wanted to call Erin and tell her all about you, what you look like, how your laugh sounds, how great your smile is. All of it. She would have loved you."

Caroline smiled, her cheeks reddening.

"Am I projecting some of that on to you? Yeah, probably. But is that my motivation for all of this? Not a chance. I've been in love twice, and this feels a whole lot like that. At least to me it does. Now does that mean we're going to live happily ever after and be sliding down rainbows into piles of marshmallows from now on? Probably not, but I'd sure like to find out."

She smiled again, this time without the embarrassment. But I still saw the hesitation and tension in her eyes.

"Am I asking myself rhetorical questions like Rickey Henderson? Yes I am."

I got the full laugh this time and it was great. I couldn't imagine ever tiring of it. I handed her wine back to her and then picked mine up.

"I understand if you have some doubts. I do too. But I'd really like to give this a legitimate shot. I mean, worst case scenario is you get to live down here near

275

the beach for a few weeks and write and finish your dissertation. How bad could it be?"

"Will you cook for me?" she asked.

"Sure. Will you do that, um, thing you did for me the other night?"

She touched her wine glass to mine.

"I'm in," she said.

Nineteen

I was up and out the door by seven the next morning. I wanted to get in a quick five or six miles while Caroline was still sleeping, but with what had happened the day before with Alves, I wasn't taking any chances. I called Ahearn and had him come out and sit in the driveway till I got back. My legs were pretty sore from the beating I'd given them, so I cruised through an easy forty-five minute run and was in the kitchen making breakfast and going through my email by the time Caroline came down. She kissed me quickly, wrinkling her nose at the post-run stank, grabbed a bagel and some OJ and went back upstairs to shower and dress. Ahearn was waiting outside to take her to work.

I had a message from Tex saying that Santos and DeSilva had agreed to meet us at the morgue at nine. I hated going to that place most of the time, not because of the presence of ten or fifteen dead bodies in refrigerated drawers. Not because of the smell, which was a mix of various chemicals, bodily fluids and three-day-old takeout food. None of that really bothered me.

What got to me was the forced casualness that the docs and cops who spent any time in the morgue affected. It was like some sort of contest to see who could act the least bothered by all of the death around them. Showing any kind of emotion about the situation was seen as not just uncool but as a sign of weakness. As if being surrounded by dead bodies was a normal thing and letting it get to you was abnormal.

I was interested to see how DeSilva would react. I was sure he'd seen a body or two in his time, but it's a different story when you walk in and see someone you love lying on a steel table. You try and prepare yourself for it, telling yourself it's just the body and that the person you remember, the one you'd had lunch with the day before or talked to on the phone that morning, was somewhere else, someplace better. But then the ME pulls the sheet back and you see the grey, waxy skin and the slack jaw and everything changed. I'd seen a marine throw up in the trash can at the sight of his daughter's body and I'd once been punched in the side of the head by a mother who snapped and eventually had to be sedated after seeing her murdered seven-year-old son on the table.

I had no idea how DeSilva would react, but nothing was out of the question.

I pulled into the parking lot of the morgue and saw Tex's car already there. He was sitting in the driver's seat, talking on his cell phone. I rapped on the window and pointed to the building. He gave me the finger, so I took a seat on the hood of the Outback and waited. He finished the call a few minutes later and came out.

"Any time, man. One more minute sitting on this car and I would've been searching for Oprah clips on YouTube and ordering yoga pants from J.Jill," I said.

"Just a normal morning for you."

"Also, I think I may have gotten a yeast infection."

"You know what they say about sitting on strange car hoods."

"You expecting any fireworks from Santos or DeSilva on this?" I asked.

"No idea. That was Santos I was talking to just now. They're five minutes away. When I talked to him yesterday he sounded pretty freaked out. I'm not sure why, but I think the fact that his client's entire family is now dead might have something to do with it."

I nodded. We walked into the building, a nondescript brown brick cube, and went down one flight of stairs to the basement where Mitchell's office and the morgue were. The smell of antiseptic and ammonia hit us as we were halfway down the steps and we both hesitated for a second before we went through the stainless steel door. Tex took a deep breath and pulled it open. The cool air rushed out and the full force of the smell inside the room came with it.

The combination of cleaning and preservative chemicals made my eyes water and burned the inside of my nose. I stood inside the door for a second, letting my eyes adjust to the bright lights and trying not to pass out. Tex had somehow been born with an immunity to the unique pleasures of the morgue, and he just charged on in, heading across the wide, open room to where Mitchell was standing between a pair of exam tables. He waved us over.

"Morning guys. I went ahead and pulled these two out for you," he said, nodding at the two tables, both of which were occupied. "You gonna need me in here for anything, or is this it?"

"Should be it," Tex said. "Just an ID."

279

He nodded. "OK. Well, lemme know if you need anything else from me." He walked to the back of the room where his office was.

I looked down at the tables, thinking about what it would be like to have to come into a room like this and know that you were about to see your wife and daughter lying there. I wasn't sure that I'd be able to do it, to walk through the door and see the lifeless shapes under those sheets. My dad had done it after Erin was killed and I knew it had almost been too much for him. I'd gone down to Virginia a few days later and he was a wreck, physically and emotionally. He barely spoke for the first day I was there. And although I'd never asked him about it, I knew what it cost him to go in and see Erin's body lying there, to nod at the ME and say yes, that's my daughter.

I felt Tex tap me on the arm and I looked up to see DeSilva and Santos crossing the room. I hadn't heard the door open, and they were already most of the way to us. Santos shook hands with both of us, stealing a glance at the tables as he did so. DeSilva hung back a couple of steps, head down, body half-turned toward the door, as if he was considering bolting.

"OK. Let's get this done," Santos said.

Tex looked past Santos at DeSilva, waiting for him to move. But he gave no indication that he was planning to get anywhere near the tables. Tex shrugged and pulled back the sheet on the first body and then stepped back a few feet.

Santos winced, recognizing the face of Sofia DeSilva. He turned and took DeSilva gently by the arm and led him to the table. DeSilva kept his head down as he approached, hoping to delay the inevitable just a few more seconds. Finally, he looked up, taking a quick look at his dead wife's face before looking over at Tex.

"This is Sofia, this is my wife," he said, his voice as soft as a paint brush on canvas.

Tex nodded and slid the white sheet back over Sofia's face. He then moved to the other table, pausing to look down at the body and then over at DeSilva. The old man was still standing near his wife's head, his back to the other table. His shoulders were slumped and his head hanging low. He was crying softly, breathing deeply as he tried to regain control of his emotions.

After a minute or so, DeSilva wiped his eyes with a white handkerchief and turned to face Tex. He gestured toward the other table and nodded. Tex uncovered the face of the other body and DeSilva fell completely apart. He began wailing loudly and covered his face with his hands, rocking from side to side as he muttered something over and over that I couldn't quite make out. He began to shake, shivering as if he were caught outside the Kremlin in January, and then suddenly turned to face me and pointed his finger at me, wagging it as if I were a misbehaving child.

DeSilva stepped closer to me and poked his finger into my chest, still repeating whatever it was he was saying and crying. I grabbed his wrist and twisted his arm, spinning him around and pushing him toward the wall a few steps away.

Santos started yelling, "Whoa, whoa, whoa!", and grabbed my sleeve. I shoved him away with my free hand and Tex held onto him as I got DeSilva to the wall and pushed him up against it face-first. DeSilva grunted, but didn't resist. Instead he went limp and I let him slump down to the floor, turning him around so he was sitting with his back to the wall. He dropped his head into his hands and drew his knees up so that he was folded into a tight ball the way a four-year-old sent to the corner would. I wasn't really sure what to do, so I just stood there looking down at him, waiting.

Nothing. Just more sobbing and muttering.

Santos walked over and tried to pull DeSilva up, with no success. He looked at me and shrugged.

"So is that a positive ID on the daughter?" I asked Santos.

"Christ, you really are an asshole, you know?" Santos said. "Yeah, that's her. Did you enjoy the show? Did it work out the way you hoped?"

I turned to face him.

"Don't talk to me like I'm one of your psychopath clients. We're not friends. Or even acquaintances, for that matter," I said. "He's a material witness in an investigation that involves about a dozen murders at this point. Some of them are his family members, and that's a shame, but don't think that I'm going to listen to a raft of shit from you or him about the way that we're doing things."

"Easy, easy. No one's telling you how to do your job. I'm just saying that you could show a little compassion while you're doing it. My client has lost his entire family in the last twenty-four hours. That's not an easy thing for anyone to deal with under the best of circumstances. And these are less than ideal circumstances, I'd say."

"Probably so. But that's not my problem. I'm here for one reason, and that's to figure out who killed those women. Whatever else happens is irrelevant, honestly."

"Nice. That's really nice, Tobin. And what about Andres? You planning to figure out who killed him at some point?" Santos asked.

I stared at Santos for several seconds, then looked down at DeSilva, who was still sitting on the floor, shaking.

"Ask your client," I said. "Maybe he has an answer for you."

We stood in the parking lot and watched as Santos and DeSilva drove away. DeSilva had regained his composure by the time they got to the car and tried hard to give me the dead-eyed stare. He failed.

"I'm starting to like him," Tex said. "He's got some heart."

"I don't think the feeling's mutual."

"Yeah, probably not."

"What's on tap for the rest of the day?" I asked.

"I'm open to suggestions. Any ideas?"

"I want to talk to the guys down in New Bedford. Delia's crew. I want to see what the story is with them and maybe get a sense for why they're suddenly willing to go back into business with DeSilva after the last time."

"You think we're going to get anything out of them? I mean, Delia talked to us only because he had to and even then we didn't get a hell of a lot," Tex said. "Now we don't have him and we don't really have any leverage on them."

"All true, but I think we still need to do it. They're part of this and we don't know how, other than buying hookers from DeSilva. There's more to it than that and I want to know what it is."

"OK then, let's go. I'm always happy to see my people."

Twenty

We left Tex's car at the morgue and headed south on 495, picking up 24 down to I-195. I called Davis on the way and got a quick rundown on Delia's crew.

"Guy you want to talk to is Vin Maglia, nephew of the man in charge. Runs most of their stuff and is the guy behind the club," Davis said.

"What's he like?"

"Asian girls and meth, far as I can tell."

"Don't we all."

"He's the one we caught on the wire screaming at the DeSilva kid, if that gives you an idea."

We cruised into New Bedford twenty minutes later. The city was in the middle of one of its periodic comeback attempts, a cycle that had recurred every fifteen years or so since the decline of the whaling and commercial fishing industries that had dominated the South Coast town for hundreds of years. Once the most lucrative fishing port in the world, New Bedford had been on a long, ugly slide for the better part of fifty years now as the big fishing operations had moved on to more productive grounds, taking with them the high-paying jobs that generations of Portuguese and Cape Verdeans had come to think of as their birthright.

For the better part of two hundred years, New Bedford boys had gone to sea as soon as they were old enough to hold their liquor and pull a line. It was miserable, brutal work and the number of ways that you could die on a commercial fishing boat were limited only by your imagination. But, if you were lucky and careful and the fishing gods were with you, you could pull down a hundred grand or even a bit more in a good year. In the same way that five or six generations of Detroit men had depended upon GM, Ford and Chrysler for a livelihood they had no hopes of finding anywhere else, New Bedford boys had pinned their futures on the sea.

And for a long time it didn't disappoint. But then came the federal regulations and the rise of the factory boats where the processing and storage was done on board. That advancement eliminated a whole sector of jobs at the on-shore processing houses and took with it other smaller businesses that fed off the processors. The disappearance of the fishing jobs was the third major betrayal New Bedford had suffered, following the end of the whaling industry and the decline and fall of the textile industry that had risen up to take its place during the early years of the twentieth century. Now, the city was once again trying to shake off the bitterness and pain to remake itself.

The latest effort was centered on the Charlestown-ization of downtown by a new group of civic leaders who had no real ties to the city or its past. Historic buildings that once had housed the components of the city's economic engine had been carved up into lofts and condos and filled with young professionals hoping to ride the latest renaissance to a quick profit. Bars that had catered to fishermen and their legendary appetites for decades had been transformed into dance clubs and tapas restaurants and coffee houses.

Where many people saw progress and evolution, Tex just saw change. And he did not like change. As we stood on Union Street looking across the way at the drab granite building where The Narwhal had been for so long, he spat on the cobblestones in disgust.

"Xploits. So clever. You see what they did there, dropping the E?" he said. "I hate these guys already."

"Imagine your dad and your uncles walking in there? They'd have to call a hazmat team after they got finished."

We walked across the street and went into the club, which, in the middle of the day on a Thursday, was exactly as empty as you'd expect. There was a chrome and black-tile bar along the right side of the room and a handful of tables scattered around the rest of the space. A long low stage edged by lights ran along the left side, with the requisite stainless steel pole set in the middle of it. A hideously thin Latin American girl, who might have been seventeen at the most, danced listlessly around the pole. A pair of guys sat a table near the stage, nursing beers and not paying much attention to the dancer.

A red velvet curtain in the back hid the hallway that led to series of small rooms that used to be known as the fishermen's friends. The name was probably different now, but their purpose was likely the same.

Tex sighed. "God, this is douchey."

"And what the hell is that music?" I asked. "It sounds like the guy just keeps saying the system is down over and over. It's making my ears bleed."

A conspicuously muscled guy about my height came toward us from the bar area. He was wearing oversized dark sunglasses, a lot like the ones Delia had worn, and a gold extra-medium t-shirt with some sort of abstract skull design on it. He walked with a forced nonchalance, letting us know that he was doing us a major favor by even getting up to come over.

"Help you officers?" he said.

"Need to see Vin," Tex said, showing his credentials, somewhat unnecessarily.

"Got an appointment?"

"Don't need one. Go get him or we go get a warrant and pull this place apart. Slowly. I'm guessing we might find something interesting around here. Go."

The guy considered that for a second, shrugged, and slouched back toward the bar. A minute later, a horribly thin, angry looking guy came out to the front to meet us. He wore black jeans and a white silk t-shirt with dark, stringy hair pulled back into a long ponytail. I was a full foot taller than he was and Tex towered over him like a bald, tattooed oak.

"You Vin Maglia?" I asked.

"Fuck you two want?" he said.

"Easy, little man," Tex said. "Need to talk to you about Andres DeSilva."

Maglia snorted and turned to leave. "Got nothing to say. That guy's dead to me."

"He's dead to everybody," I said. "Someone blew him apart in his car, two nights ago."

He stopped and turned back to us. "Who got him?"

"Don't know. You?"

288

"Not me. I'm an entrepreneur," he said, making a grand sweep of the club with his arm.

"Yeah. How's that working out for you?" Tex said. "Hear things have been a little slow lately."

Maglia shrugged. "We're in a double-dip recession. Discretionary spending is down. Things are tough all over."

"Even tougher if you're a DeSilva, I'd guess," I said. "Seems to be open season on them right now."

"Yeah. Well."

"You heard about all of the women that were found in that pond up in Duxbury?" Tex asked. "Messy shit, man. Bunch of pretty, young women floating around naked in that pond, some of them hit with a shotgun. We hear they were on their way down here. Might just be a rumor, though, I don't know."

"The fuck I care about Duxbury?" Maglia said.

"Listen, we're not all that interested in what you're doing here," I said. "We're homicide, not narco or vice. You're running whores or meth or whatever out of here, I don't really care. People are gonna get that stuff somewhere. What I care about is trying to figure who wiped out DeSilva's family and the rest of these people. We know you had some dealings with DeSilva's people and we know that he is bringing girls into the country through his travel company. It follows that you're probably taking some of those girls off his hands. Again, we don't necessarily give a fat crap about that. Unless it turns out that you were in on the killings. Then we care a lot."

"So what's your question?"

"My question is: Do you have any thoughts on who might have killed these girls? Or Andres DeSilva?"

Maglia jerked his head to the side, indicating a booth on the left side of the club and led us over to it. We sat on one side, and he slid into the bench on the other. He looked hard at Tex for a minute, as if seeing him for the first time.

"Do I know you?" Maglia asked. "Where you from?"

"From here. Lived on Rockdale, near the park for most of my life. Still have a lot of people over there."

Maglia snapped his fingers and pointed at Tex. "I got it now. You played tight end at New Bedford, like mid-90s."

Tex nodded.

"That's it. My cousin was on that team with you, you guys beat Fall River by twenty-four that year. Tony Antonelli. You caught that little screen pass, took it up the sideline like sixty yards for a score."

"Tony was kind of a hump, I remember right."

"Kind of? Fucking kid got so drunk at my eighteenth birthday party that he crawled into my sister's bed and started feeling her up. My dad put him in the shower, turned it on full cold and made him stay there for an hour. Thought he was gonna die of hypothermia."

"That's the guy I remember," Tex said.

"You play in college? You were pretty good."

"Nope. Ripped my knee up playing pick-up hoops the summer after I graduated and that was the end of it.

I would've been a tackling dummy in college anyway. No big loss."

"Shame," Maglia said.

"So, like I asked before, we're looking into what happened to DeSilva and those women. You have any thoughts on that?"

"I might. But I need to know my name's not gonna show up on some report or get whispered in the ear of one of those Mexicans up there," Maglia said.

Tex looked at me. I nodded.

"Fine by me," I said. "But you do know they're Brazilian, right?"

"And I'm half Greek. Who gives a fuck?"

"Fair enough," I said. "So what do you know?"

"I know that they have some major problems over there," Maglia said. "The old man is a creep. Guys have avoided doing business with him for a long time because he's not...right."

"So why do you deal with him?" Tex asked.

"If I do anything with him, it's because we never had a problem. Product is product and money is money. Where it comes from and where it goes ain't my concern. Long as I get mine."

"But you did have a problem with him," I said.

"There was a mixup, yeah. Mailman didn't deliver, and it wasn't no holiday. We got caught short and our customers weren't real happy. Made us look bad."

"And that's a problem for you," I said.

"Course it is. We might not be what we was, but whatever rep we still have is what makes us money. People start fucking with that..."

"Things start going bad. For everyone," Tex finished.

"Something like that," Maglia said. He picked up a cardboard table tent that advertised the upcoming appearance of a dancer named Big Sloppy and began spinning it in his hands. "But I'm telling you straight: Wasn't us put those girls in the pond."

"You had to bet, who would you put your money on?" Tex asked.

Maglia made a show of thinking about that for a second, then shrugged. "Coulda been anyone. Best I can tell, that kid didn't have a lot of friends. He was a head case, always yelling and screaming, even about little stuff. Always threatening to shoot this guy or beat up that guy, for no reason. His old man makes my skin crawl, but at least I know what's what with him. He understands how things work."

"What about the kid?" Tex asked

"It's like he was playing a role, trying to show everyone how hard he was all the time. Didn't go so well with some of the guys here. Or up there."

"But his father trusted him. Or seemed to," I said.

"Don't know about all that. I can tell you that my uncle did business with the old man for years and never had a single problem. Still talks to him from time to time, in fact," Maglia said. "The kid comes in, all of a sudden things start going sideways."

"How long had you been working with Andres?" I asked.

"Not long. The...mixup was only the third deal with him."

292

"Other two went ok?"

"The product was ok. But he started trying to raise the price right away on us, for no reason. Wasn't going to work for me. We got plenty of other options."

"And you told him that," I said.

Maglia nodded. "Sure. He started screaming and yelling, talking about how he was in charge now and things were going to be different, all this shit."

"Lemme ask you: How much business did you do with him?" Tex asked.

He shrugged. "On average, about eight or ten a month."

"Girls."

Maglia nodded.

"How much dope?"

"None."

"Right. How much?"

"I'm telling you. None. We didn't deal with them on that. Never did," Maglia said.

"Why not?" I asked. "If you're already working with them, why go somewhere else for dope?"

"Far as I know, they aren't involved in it."

"Just girls then?"

"That's all I use them for. Rest of it ain't my concern. But whoever put that kid down, I'd say he did us all a favor. He was young, but he'd made a name for himself among a lot of the wrong people."

"Some of them are down here, right?" I said.

He shrugged. "What I hear is that the kid might have been doing some things that his dad didn't know about. Maybe moving a girl here or there on the side, something like that. The old man has always kept his head down, gone about his business and been quiet about it. Andres, he'd be in here acting like a hot shot, throwing money around, being a douche. Even with the crowd we get in here, he stood out."

"OK. Safe to say none of your guys is gonna miss him?"

"None of the girls either," Maglia said.

"So are you done with the DeSilvas?" I asked. "Or have you guys patched things up?"

Maglia looked at me carefully, a small joyless smile on his face. "What makes you think there's anything to patch up?"

I knew I'd made a mistake, but it was too late to back up, so I tried to deflect. "The fact that they didn't deliver the last time."

"Like I said, business is business," Maglia said. "Gotta make money somehow."

"How's your uncle these days?" Tex asked.

Maglia shook his head. "Not so good. He ain't around much now."

"I knew him a little bit, few years ago when he was still working. I was in narco. He still wearing that seersucker suit?"

"Every damn day."

Twenty-One

I dropped Tex back at the morgue and told him I would catch up with him later in the day. I wanted to check out that database JD had found, see if there was anything useful in it. I dialed Caroline on the way home and caught her in the mid-afternoon lull.

"Did you see dead people?" she asked.

"Dead people, mobsters, strippers."

"The New Bedford trifecta. What's going on now?"

"Headed home for a bit, do some paperwork. Listen: I was thinking maybe you oughta head back up to the city for a while till this thing calms down. Maybe stay with your folks. I just don't like the way things are going with these guys right now."

"Well. Last night you were all excited to have me stay down here for a while, and now you want me to go back to Boston? Should I be offended?"

"No. Look, I told you some of what these guys are about, but there's more to it than that and I'd just feel better about things if you were in a safe spot that they didn't know about for now," I said.

"Danny: Did something else happen? I mean besides the thing with Reggie?"

"Ah hell."

I told her what happened while I was running the day before and she eventually agreed that maybe staying at her place in Plymouth wasn't the best idea right now.

"I'll call my dad," she said.

"Whatever you do, don't tell him the truth. I don't need him coming down here and shooting me."

"Thanks for that," she said.

I was just pulling into the beach parking lot when Davis called. I pulled to the side near the sea wall and watched the small rollers hitting the shore.

"We're striking out on the meeting details," he said. "In fact, there hasn't been much talk at all on there in the last couple days. Really quiet."

"Shit. We're running out of time on this."

"Sorry man, I don't know what to tell you. Do you have any other moves you can make?"

I thought about that for a minute as I watched a couple of teenagers skim boarding in the slop as the tide went out. One of them dug the nose of his board in and took a header, doing a couple of barrel rolls before hopping up and looking around to see whether anyone had noticed. No one had.

"I don't know, man," I said. "Might be one other way to go at it. Guess I'll find out. Thanks anyway."

"Sure thing. I'll stay on it and let you know if anything bubbles up."

At home, I got out my personal laptop and plugged in the flash drive JD had given me. Didn't want any traces of this data on my department-issued machine. I knew just how easy it was to find remnants of files buried on a hard drive, regardless of how thoroughly someone thought they'd cleaned it.

The database was smaller than I expected, only a few megs, and as soon as I opened it I knew something was wrong. Almost none of the names were Brazilian or even Latin American. Just a bunch of whitebread New Englanders: Sullivans and Connollys and Millers. Not at all what I was expecting. DeSilva's business was bringing people up here from South America and getting them settled. But none of these people fit that description.

Damn. Had we been wrong about his business or what he was doing with these people? I didn't think so. I went through what I knew for sure about DeSilva: He was a native of Brazil. He'd moved here a few years back with his wife and children. He owned a travel business that catered to other Brazilians. He had a bullshit store in Plymouth that was a front for...something. And his wife and daughter were dead. That was about it.

None of that gave me any ideas about why he'd have a database of like, what, a hundred and twenty first initials and last names and phone numbers of people who clearly weren't illegal immigrants. Unless they were aliases, which was a possibility. But not likely. If you were going to assign aliases to a bunch of South Americans, you probably wouldn't use names that came from the passenger list of *The Mayflower*. I thought about it for a few minutes, couldn't come up with a good answer. Called JD and told him what I'd found.

"Lemme come over," he said. "I'm just at the hotel."

Fifteen minutes later he was staring at my laptop screen, shaking his head.

"I didn't really look at the data," he said.

"Did you see more than one database or was this it?"

"Well, once I found that one I didn't keep looking. I figured that was it."

"OK. It just doesn't make a lot of sense," I said. "I don't know what this is, but it's not the data set I was expecting."

"So maybe it's his bridge partners or the customers from the store. Who knows."

"Yeah," I said, chewing it over. "Wait."

I scanned the data again, looking for any sort of pattern or flag. Nothing popped up right away, but then I saw a name I recognized: S. Delia. And another: V. Maglia. Oh man. And then a third: S. LaFontaine. Uhh...

"Danny? Danny. Whatcha got?" JD was saying.

"A giant fucking problem."

I went back through the list a couple more times, saw a handful of other names I knew, none that mattered.

"Hell am I gonna do with this now?" I said, turning it over in my head.

"Sorry man," JD said. "I just grabbed what I saw."

"Not your fault. You didn't know what I was looking for really. What do you think it is?"

I thought about it a bit more. "I think it might be a list of DeSilva's clients here. Not the people he's bringing in."

"That could be useful, right?"

"Ah, man. This is gonna get me so fired," I said.

"Hey, were you guys down in New Bedford today?" JD asked.

"Yeah. How'd you know that?"

"Well, I was a little bored this afternoon so I thought I'd see what was going on with the Skype thing. You know, just see if anyone was talking."

"OK..."

"So I was sort of poking around, just listening in on a couple of calls here and there to make sure that I had things set up correctly."

"Get to the point, man," I said.

"OK, OK. So I heard a couple calls come in, nothing interesting, and then a guy calls and asks to be connected to someone named Alves. They talk for a minute or so and then one of them mentions you."

"By name?"

"No, but I'm pretty sure they were talking about you guys. The first guy asked where this guy Alves was, and he says, 'I'm in New Bedford waiting for them to leave the club. They left Plymouth about an hour ago and they've been in here for about fifteen minutes.' The other guy says ok, let him know when they leave. Few minutes later, the Alves guy calls back in and is connected to the other guy."

"You get his name?"

"Rodrigues. No first name."

I'd have to check, but I was pretty sure that was one of the two goons that DeSilva kept around.

"So Alves says the guys are leaving the bar and wants to know what he should do," JD said. "Rodrigues tells him, 'Follow him until he gets back to the beach and then check in at the house.'"

"The beach."

"Yup. I wasn't sure what you guys were doing and it didn't sound like anything you needed to know about right away, so I didn't call you. I figured you already knew they were watching you."

"No, you're right." I thought about what it might mean for DeSilva to know that we were talking to Maglia and his people. I wasn't that excited about it, but I couldn't think of how it could mess things up for us. At least not yet. DeSilva would have to assume that we'd be talking to the people he does business with, and that would include Maglia's crew. And if they'd been watching us since this thing started, then they probably already knew that we'd talked to Delia, or at least that he'd talked to someone on the state police, because they could have seen him at the barracks that day.

"It seems sort of careless of them to be using names on these calls," I said.

"Not really, if you think about it. Like I said, Skype calls are encrypted, which is probably the main reason they're using that instead of disposable phones or something else. So they're probably thinking that they're safe with that, and rightly so. No reason for them to think otherwise."

"That's true. And they're also taking the extra step of not calling each other directly, so even if one of them somehow got compromised, all the cops would see is a bunch of calls to the store."

"Funny thing is, that's what gave us our way in," JD said.

"And at least now we know that your rootkit works."

"Oh, ye of little faith."

"Hey, did you hear anything from any of these guys about a meeting tomorrow sometime? Any mentions of a delivery or a shipment or anything like that?"

JD sat back and looked up at the ceiling, replaying the conversations in his mind. His memory was remarkably odd--he couldn't tell you what he'd had for lunch the day before, but he could recall in minute detail conversations he'd had months or years earlier and could reproduce huge chunks of code that he had written ten years ago, line by line. It was a weird thing to see in action.

After three or four minutes he sat forward again.

"Maybe," he said. "Before the bit about you guys and the beach, there was a separate conversation, two other guys. They were talking about where they were going to meet for dinner tomorrow night. I came in in the middle of it and it didn't seem that interesting, so I honestly wasn't paying that much attention at the time. I was just happy my shit was working."

"Do you remember any of it?" I asked.

301

He looked at me the way a disappointed parent looks at a misbehaving child. "Dude."

I held up my hands. "OK, OK."

"They were talking about dinner, like I said. When I came in, one of them was asking where they were meeting Friday night. He said, 'Are we still on for tomorrow night?' The second guys says, 'Yup. We're getting together at ten at that place you like in Duxbury. The place Myles owns, with the nice view.' The first guy says, 'That's a good spot. How many people are coming?' Other guy says, 'Fifteen. Big group this time.'"

"That's a pretty late dinner reservation," I said.

"Yeah."

"And a lot of people."

"Yup."

"They say anything else?" I asked.

He shook his head. "That was it. Is it any help?"

"Just might be," I said.

I asked JD to have another look around in DeSilva's system and see if he could enumerate all of the regular users of the Skype network, just so we knew who was who. He took off, saying he was going to hang on the beach with his laptop and he'd check in later. With Caroline gone, he was going to be crashing with me again for the time being.

I ran through everything with Cooper one more time, trying to make some sense of it. But the pieces only fit together one way, and when they were assembled the picture was not a pretty one. What I kept coming back to was that the superintendent of the state police was somehow tied up with DeSilva's operation. In a big way. And the people she was, ah, in bed with, were following two of her homicide detectives and seemed to know every move we were making before we made it.

I thought about the pressure that Cooper had been putting on us from the beginning of this thing, how Winthrop had put it down to her being worried about the upcoming election. It was a facile answer, but it had the advantage of being completely plausible, especially for a political animal like Cooper. She would forever be worried about her job and the next election, and so it would make sense for her to use that as an excuse to get up Winthrop's ass about DeSilva.

But the possibility of being exposed as a client of a low-rent prostitution ring would be an even better motivator. Add in the fact that she was a woman, and one who had just gotten married and you had a pretty powerful cocktail. Even in the People's Republic of Massachusetts, the idea of a high-ranking state police official using call girls to satisfy herself wouldn't sit very well.

Cooper. Jesus.

Twenty-Two

I wandered out to the back deck and looked across the inlet, thinking. I watched the two egrets chase each other around the inlet for a while and then walked down to the edge of the water, near the spot where I'd buried Reggie. It had only been a couple of days since he'd been killed, but it felt like months, given everything that had happened since.

I bent down and scooped up a bit of the dirt from the top of his grave, let it filter through my hands. As I stood up, I caught a flash of color across the inlet. I thought maybe it had been in one of the condos on the other side, but they were empty yet, having just been finished a couple of weeks ago. I stood still, watching the egrets for a long minute, waiting.

The darkness was beginning to gather, and it was getting hard to see across the inlet. After another minute, I went back inside, up the stairs, grabbed my binoculars off the dresser. I went into the bathroom, kept the light off and carefully moved the blinds aside an inch or two. I scanned the windows the of the four condos with the glasses, slowly looking from side to side.

On the third pass, I saw it again: a quick movement, a glint of metal and short glimpse of something yellow in the top floor of the building on the right. I let the shade fall back into place slowly, and sat down on the hardwood.

Those buildings would be a perfect vantage point for someone wanting to keep an eye on my house.

Secluded, empty and with a direct view of the beach and several of the houses on it. I thought about what Harris had told me about DeSilva owning some condos in town somewhere, but I couldn't remember exactly where they were. Easy to check, though.

I went downstairs and grabbed my work PC and connected to our VPN and then the case file system. I found the file for DeSilva and paged through until I got to the property records. Yup: Those were his buildings. I should've checked that before, but knowing it now made me feel even better about getting Caroline out of here. If they were that close, there wasn't much I could do here without them seeing it. And I didn't want her anywhere near that.

I was already thinking of ways that I could use it, though. And maybe the Cooper information too...

I called Tex, ran it down for him.

"Davis came through with the info on the drop," I said. "That was a good call."

"Nice. Glad they could get something right," he said.

"Uh, yeah, me too."

It was driving me a little nuts piling all these lies up with him, but it couldn't be helped. At least not right now.

"So where is it?" he asked.

I told him where I thought it was, based in the information that I had. I was pretty sure of the general area, but I couldn't work out the precise meeting spot.

"We're going to need surveillance on all of these guys then," Tex said. "Problem is, we don't know exactly who's going to be there, so we're gonna have to cover them all."

"We can probably narrow it down on DeSilva's end. We're already watching him, and those two bodyguards are always with him and Alves usually is too."

"So we leave Davis and Moore on that group and then put some extra eyes on Maglia I guess, and maybe a guy watching the club itself, just to see whether there's a big exodus from there."

"I'll talk to Davis and get that going."

We agreed that we should brief Winthrop on everything we knew before the delivery to Maglia tomorrow night. If we were going to have the chance to take DeSilva's guys down, I wanted to make sure that everything was lined up ahead of time, so we didn't have any loose threads.

"I'll call Winthrop and set it up for the morning at the barracks," Tex said.

"Not too early," I said, "I have a couple of things to do beforehand."

"OK, say nine?"

"Good."

I walked back out to the rear deck and called Caroline to see what she'd figured out with her dad. It was almost full dark now, and there weren't any lights on in the condos, but I had a feeling someone was still in there. Good.

307

"You're in luck," she said when she picked up, "my dad agreed to take me in off the streets, no questions asked."

"None?"

"Well...maybe one," she said.

"Aw hell."

"I just told him that there was a guy who'd sort of been stalking me at work and I wanted to check out for a little while till he forgot about me. It's mostly true."

"Not bad."

"I'm a cop's daughter. You think I don't know how to lie when I need to?" she said.

"Good point. So when are you heading up there?"

"In about a half hour. Ahearn's gonna drive me up in my car and have someone meet him at the house later."

"OK. Lemme talk to him real quick."

"Hang on."

Ahearn came on the line and I told him that there might be some serious movement tomorrow. I didn't give him everything, because I wasn't sure what was going on with Cooper and DeSilva's guys just yet and I couldn't be positive who was clean.

"Listen man, these guys have been following me and probably Tex for several days and they have a good idea what we're doing, so if you have even the slightest indication that someone's tailing you guys tonight, you put the hammer down on that 300 and drive straight to the closest barracks," I said. "Anywhere but her parents' place. No one gets near her."

"I got it, man," he said. "I've been watching, and I haven't seen any signs that they're keeping tabs on her, at least not up close."

"OK, thanks for doing this, man. I appreciate it."

"Sure thing. I'll buzz you when she's tucked in at her parents' house."

"Thanks. Put Caroline back on for a sec."

"Allright, I think you're set," I said when she was back on. "Ahearn knows what he's doing, and once you get to your dad's, I'll feel a lot better."

"I won't," she said. "Things are just getting interesting."

"You mean with you and me or with the case?"

"Well, both I guess. I want to see how things turn out."

"I have a feeling the case is coming to a head soon," I said. "I don't know how it's going to work out, but it could be messy. And me and you...we'll have plenty of time to see how that turns out once this is done. All the time in the world."

"It just feels like a crappy time for an intermission," she said.

"I know it. Look, hang out with your folks for a few days, let your mom make you pancakes and bacon in the morning, read a trashy novel, relax. When it's over, maybe we'll head over to Nantucket for the weekend, play tourist."

She sighed. "OK. You watch yourself. Please."

"Yes ma'am. You too."

After I hung up with Caroline, I went back to my laptop and spent some quality time with the case file, trying to work out the chain of events that got us where we were. Best I could tell, when we walked up to the pond that day, we stepped into the middle of not just a pissing match between DeSilva's crew and Maglia's people, but also some sort of problem between Alves and DeSilva.

The explanation from Alves that he hated his uncle simply because he gave his fellow immigrants shitty jobs and crummy apartments to live in just didn't ring true. Why would Alves care what happened to a bunch of people he didn't know? He wouldn't. He had his little cabin in the woods, with his books and his tools and whatever else, and all he had to do was drive DeSilva around. That wasn't a bad deal in any country, no matter how much he hated DeSilva. It's not like it was his family out there mopping floors and mucking out toilets.

His family...

That had to be it. Alves said that DeSilva had been promising him for years that he'd bring his wife and daughter up from Brazil. So he'd waited and worked and waited some more, and nothing had happened. I imagined him sitting in that tiny cabin, night after night, waiting for some indication that they were on their way, growing more bitter as each day passes.

And then DeSilva finally went to him with the news that the women were on their way. Alves would've been ecstatic, busying himself with getting the house ready for their arrival, planning outings to the beach, up

310

to Boston. And then the days began to leak away with no word from them and nothing but stonewalling from DeSilva. The realization that they weren't ever coming might not have hit him all at once, it may have crept up little by little, each passing day adding another layer.

At some point, he would have simply known. He would have woken one morning, not with the hope of seeing his wife's face or hearing his daughter's laughter, but rather with the certainty that he would never do those things again.

And then he would have gone looking for DeSilva.

I glanced at my watch: 10:40. Called Tex back, ran through it again while I waited. It made sense.

"Tobin, shouldn't you be snuggling Caroline about now?"

"I should. But I sent her up to her parents today. Get her away from this for a while."

"Good. So what's up?"

"So I've been going over the paperwork on this thing and thinking about a few things. What if Alves is the key to the whole deal?"

"How do you mean?"

"Well, I mean what if we've been looking at this from the wrong angle? We've been focusing on DeSilva and trying to figure out what he was up to that resulted in all of these girls getting killed. It didn't make any sense from the beginning. His business relies on him being able to supply live women to his customers. If he can't do that, he can't make money."

"Right..."

311

"So then let's say he gets the call from someone in his group telling him that there was a problem with that one shipment. One of them died in transit or something else went wrong, whatever it was, what sense does it make for his response to be, kill them all?"

"None."

"Exactly. Delivering a few less girls is better than none, and killing them creates a lot more problems than it solves. It pisses off Maglia, it brings in the possibility of us showing up, it puts the rest of his operation in jeopardy, all of that. So I think whoever killed them did it on his own."

"OK, I'm with you on all of that," Tex said. "But haven't we been over this ground? Why would any of his guys do that? Their main motivation is money too, and if one of them jumps the tracks and does something like that, he'd need a really good reason."

"I was thinking about that, and the two things that I came up with were that either someone was running some sort of inside game on DeSilva or they were trying to stick it to him for some reason."

"And which of those is the more plausible explanation to you?"

"The latter. I could think up some scenarios where that guy who was with them making some kind of move, screwed it up somehow and ended up having to kill the girls. And then he tries to explain it to DeSilva and gets killed for his trouble," I said. "But it seems more likely to me that DeSilva made someone mad enough that they came back at him and took out his product, which just happens to be women."

Tex was quiet for a minute. "Man, that's an ugly train of thought."

"It is."

"But not crazy," he said. "Lemme think about this for a second. OK, so...you started this off by suggesting that Alves might be the real key here. Does that mean you're putting him down for all of the murders?"

"I'm not totally sure on that, but yeah, it's possible."

"Why? The drugs?"

"His family. His wife and daughter. They were supposed to be on their way here and they never showed up. He waits and waits and waits and they never come. And he can't get in contact with them in Brazil either, so he finally has enough and goes after DeSilva in the one way that he knows will hurt him."

"But from what we know, Alves is just his driver. He's not really involved in the shipments or mechanics of the business. How would he have gotten to the girls in the first place?"

"I don't know, but how hard could it be? He's worked for DeSilva forever, knows the operation, knows all of the people," I said, trying to work it out on the fly. "He finds someone else who's unhappy or underpaid or whatever, promises them some money or dope and he's on his way. Has the truck diverted to his place, lines them up and does it."

"Possible. So then the guy in the pond makes more sense. Alves makes the deal with him, he delivers on his end and then Alves kills him too, just for good measure," Tex said. "No one to talk, no one to get greedy and ask for more money."

"So what do you think?"

"I think it's mostly plausible. And it makes as much sense as anything else we've heard. Also, I think we need to pick up Alves as soon as possible."

"And get him talking," I said.

"Yeah. Before DeSilva figures it out too and puts him in the ground."

Twenty-Three

It was after eleven by the time I hung up with Tex. I thought about checking in with Davis to see what was happening with DeSilva, but I figured I'd fill him in on everything in the morning once we'd talked things through with Winthrop. We were going to need Davis and Moore to be all over DeSilva tomorrow.

I texted Caroline, made sure she was safely at her parents. She was. Dialed Ahearn to see whether he'd seen anyone on the trip up.

"Nothing," he said. "We were clean."

"Good. Listen, hang loose for the night at her place. Just park your car outside like you've been doing, let anyone who might be looking see that it's still there."

"You got it."

"I'll call you tomorrow. Some things are probably going to shake loose and I may end up needing your help at some point."

"All right, I'll be around."

I spent another half hour or so going through the case file and trying to poke holes in the Alves theory, but I couldn't come up with much. The one thing that bugged me though was how DeSilva's wife and daughter fit in. How had they ended up in the pond with the others? They'd been killed with a different weapon--a shotgun--and had been dumped later. I couldn't work out why and how that had happened. But I figured if we could get the rest of it nailed down, that piece would fall into place.

Just as I was ready to trudge up to bed, JD came in.

"Any luck with the Skype recon?" I asked.

"I saw a total of seven users. Only six of them seem to be active," he said. "Just a bunch of chatter right now, nothing going on."

"OK. I got a couple more chores for you in the morning if you're up for it..."

"That's what I'm here for, man."

I talked over my ideas with him quickly, he made a couple of small suggestions. I still hadn't let Tex in on what we'd been up to, and if things went well, I might not have to. I'm sure he had some idea what was going on but wasn't going to get himself involved if he didn't have to. That was fine with me.

"So first thing tomorrow, we'll go pick up a new phone for you and then you should be set," I said.

"See ya in the morning."

Upstairs, I kept the lights off and went out on the deck, looking across at the condos. I felt that we were on pretty solid ground with the thinking on Alves, but I also couldn't shake the feeling that DeSilva was part of it. Guys like him usually didn't change. They were who they were. He was a pedophile and probably a killer and those instincts and appetites don't disappear. If anything, they intensify over time. Where once he could satisfy himself by picking up a girl every few weeks, soon enough that would become every week and then it would become almost a daily habit, DeSilva hungering for more and more until nothing could satiate his foul cravings.

And yet, he had somehow managed to stay above the fray here. Maybe it was as simple as him being more discreet here, learning his trade as he went along. But maybe it wasn't. Maybe he'd had some help over the years. Most crews like his couldn't get by for long without some sort of assist from a cop on the take or a politician with some skin in the game. If they were operating on any kind of large scale, which DeSilva was, it was just too hard to stay off the radar. Cooper had been on the job for a year and a half, and from what I'd seen, DeSilva hadn't had a bit of trouble since then.

Until now.

And now we were getting pressure from Cooper to make this thing go away as quickly as possible.

No such thing as a coincidence.

I pulled out my personal laptop again and started looking through the recent messages in the chat room that Harris had pointed me to earlier. I hadn't been back in since that first visit and there were dozens of new posts. Most of them were crap, just people going back and forth about where to find cheap health insurance or day cares that didn't ask too many questions.

But after a few minutes, I found a thread with five or six people discussing the fact that their various relatives were on their way into the country in the next few days. The most recent message was from a woman who said that her daughter had just finished high school in Brazil and was moving up here to join her and her husband. She was clearly excited about seeing her daughter for the first time in four years and said that she had a party planned for her on Saturday afternoon. Earlier on in the thread, a man had posted a question about whether anyone had been told where to pick up their relatives on Friday night. No one had, but I already knew where they'd be.

And I knew that none of these people would be seeing their relatives any time soon.

At 7:30 the next morning I was sitting outside the Walmart in west Plymouth, waiting for JD to reappear. He'd gone in ten minutes earlier, and I'd been turning things over in my mind, trying to figure a different way to handle things. I didn't see one.

It had been a long time since I'd had anyone around to ask me the kind of questions that Caroline was now bringing up. I had never been much for sitting around thinking about my motivations or moral framework, but some of the things she'd been asking had pushed me down that path. I had sort of known for a while that the way I thought about things didn't necessarily line up with how most people did, especially when it came to stuff like what constituted justice. That concept is an elemental part of a cop's life, not just on the job, but all the time. It's drilled into us from the beginning of our time in the academy, all the way up through the ranks, every day, that justice is a concrete thing. Black and white. And it's defined by the law, not by circumstance or nuance or anything else. Judges, jurors and lawmakers, who are far removed from the actual reality of what's happening, are the ones who decide who's wrong and who's right.

And to me, that was fucked.

Right and wrong as pre-defined concepts that could be applied evenly across every situation was a fairy tale. It was the chupacabra of law enforcement. People loved to talk about it, but it was a waste of time because it just didn't exist. And I had no time for it.

My own thoughts on how justice worked had evolved over the years, but ultimately it came down to winning. I *needed* to win. I didn't give a shit whether the justice system got its desired outcome. It was about me making sure that the target knew that I got him. *Me*, not the police as an abstract entity.

What I'd told Caroline originally was true: I loved my work. But I'd gradually realized over the last few months that my sense of justice was probably incompatible with my job. How I won didn't matter to me, only that I won. And for police, the how was the most important part of the process, even more so than the result.

I had never thought about not being a cop, but something had to give in this equation, and I could feel the pressure building.

When JD finally strolled back out at quarter of eight, I was could feel the adrenaline rising. Something was coming.

"What took so long?" I asked as JD climbed in.

He pointed to the bag in the footwell, which was roughly the size of a large wombat

"That place is ridiculous. It took me ten minutes just to find the aisle where the phones were, and by that time I'd already gone through the meat department and the frozen foods. You're all set with bacon and frozen

319

buffalo wings for the next six months, by the way," he said.

"Awesome."

"Oh, and Pampers, too. You're good there."

"Those could come in handy on stakeouts," I said. "It's a drag having to fill up Big Gulp cups all the time."

"You're welcome."

"Did you happen to get the phones while you were in there?"

"Yeah. We're set. One for each of us."

I drove back east on 44 and hooked Route 3 north. We talked about the plan for the rest of the day and the night's festivities, making sure that we were on the same wavelength about what needed to be done and when. I pulled off the highway in Pembroke and drove a couple of miles into Marshfield to a car rental agency. I stayed in the Jeep again while JD went in and this time he was back out in under ten minutes, keys in hand. He got into a bland white Nissan Pathfinder and followed as I pulled out and headed back to the highway.

We were back at my house by 8:30 and I just had time to grab a bottle of apple juice and a Clif bar and head back out for Middleborough.

"Just leave the car in the driveway," I said on the way out. "I'll be back later and we can finalize the rest of it then."

"Got it. Nap time for me."

A half hour later I was sitting in a conference room at the barracks, looking across the table at Winthrop as he slowly tapped his Mont Blanc on the table. Tex was sitting next to me, nervously glancing back and forth between me and Winthrop, who hadn't spoken since we sat down and handed him our case file. After about five minutes, he set the pen down and looked up.

"So. There's some good solid work in here," he said. "Plenty of detail and a solid foundation for your thoughts on DeSilva and Alves."

"Thank you, sir," Tex said.

"But there's also a lot of supposition and leaps of faith. I'm in no way convinced that these two killed all of those women. I believe that they were involved and that their operation, whatever it is, was probably responsible in some way for the murders. But I can't understand what their motives would be and I also don't see how the murder of DeSilva's son, Andres is it? How that fits in."

"You're right, sir," I said, "there are a lot of rough spots in there. We know that. But we've been working this from every angle and the only way that it adds up is the way that we put it down in the report. We believe that DeSilva is the head of an ongoing criminal enterprise that is involved in, among other things, human trafficking, drug smuggling, prostitution, money laundering and probably murder for hire. We know for sure that he's been supplying women and perhaps drugs to a prostitution ring operating on the South Coast for the last several years. We also know that he is hiding some major cash income from his travel business and that he's probably helping other crews on the South Shore clean their dirty money, too."

"All of which is great and none of which adds up to him killing those women," Winthrop said.

"No it doesn't. So let's look at Alves," I said. "We think he's the key to the whole thing."

Winthrop looked at Tex. "That right?"

Tex nodded, a little hesitantly. "It is."

"Proceed, detective," Winthrop said.

"As I said, Alves is really the most important piece of this thing. He has a major problem with DeSilva, despises him, to hear him tell it. DeSilva is his uncle and has helped him get into the U.S. and to prosper here. But Alves hates what DeSilva stands for and who he is. We know that DeSilva is a pedophile and was known to kidnap young girls in Brazil and probably killed --or had killed--many of them. He's continued that here, keeping some of the younger girls that he brings into the country," I said. "We don't know what's happened to them, but we can guess. Alves told us that DeSilva has been promising for several years to help get Alves's wife and daughter into the country, but has never delivered. So Alves has had to just eat it and wait. Then finally Alves finds out that his family is on the way here, everything is set. And then...just when he thinks everything is coming together, the wife and daughter go down the rabbit hole. They're gone. No word from them for weeks, DeSilva says he doesn't know what happened. They're just gone."

Winthrop nodded, waiting for the rest of it. All of this was in the report, but sometimes it's more convincing when you hear it out loud.

"So what we have is a guy who already hates DeSilva, then he finds out that his family is gone and may well be dead," I said. "He's deeply involved in DeSilva's organization, knows what's happening when and where. Alves understands who his uncle is and what he loves: money. So when Alves figures out that his wife and daughter probably aren't walking through that door anytime soon, he goes looking for a way to hurt DeSilva."

"And the best way to do that is to disrupt his business," Winthrop said.

"Right. And the easiest way to do *that* is by pissing off customers and destroying the product."

Winthrop looked at us. "And their product is women."

"It is," Tex said.

Winthrop said forward in his chair and started flipping through the report again. He read for a minute, then looked up. "I see the line of reasoning and I understand it, but I don't buy it. Alves clearly has the motive to do something to DeSilva, but going at him directly makes more sense. Why bother with all of this mess when he could just as easily have killed DeSilva outright or stolen a pile of his money?"

"He could have, but Alves is...an odd duck," Tex said. "On a practical level, he's DeSilva's driver, so he could kill him any day he chooses. Simple. But I think on some sort of emotional or psychological level, he can't do that. DeSilva *is* still his uncle and family is everything to these people. It's somehow more acceptable to do it this way, so that DeSilva might know in the back of his mind what happened but he can't be certain."

"I'm not interested in your amateur analysis of his psyche," Winthrop said. "We deal in facts and evidence, not guesswork."

"I understand that, sir. What we're trying to tell you is that there aren't a ton of known facts here. These guys are good at what they do and they've been ahead of us the whole time. They're not remotely bothered by us getting in their business and poking around. It seems a lot like they think they're immune, like they aren't even worried about what we're doing. Maybe they know something we don't."

I sat as still as I could and just waited for Tex to continue.

"But the point is, we know we're on solid ground here. We have good information from the CI on the botched delivery last month and we know about the conflict inside DeSilva's organization. The most logical conclusion we can draw is that Alves snapped when he found out about his wife and daughter, knew about the shipment coming for the Italians, saw his opportunity to get at DeSilva, and took it."

"I follow you on that," Winthrop said. "But what about the drugs? How does that fit?"

Tex nodded at me. "We're still trying to figure that part out, to be honest, " I said. "Our working theory right now, as we said in the report, is that either Alves or Andres DeSilva, or maybe both, were using the women as mules as a way to make some side money for themselves. The CI said that they don't buy dope from DeSilva. Maglia confirmed that when we talked to him. So unless all of the women got together and decided to swallow a bunch of heroin on their own, it looks like someone in the crew was running a side business."

Winthrop flipped through the file for a second. "But, not all of the women had drugs in their stomachs at the time of death."

"That's right. The two who were clean were DeSilva's wife and daughter."

"And they were the two who appear to have been dumped at a later time," Winthrop said.

"Right," I said.

"OK. So then...you like Maglia and his crew for those two?"

I nodded. "It fits. Once they found out that the shipment had been lost, there was a lot of talk that they were going to go after DeSilva directly. Our CI said that in the end the bosses were too soft to do it, but he didn't know about the wife and daughter, either. Maglia is seriously struggling without those girls, and he'd had some issues with the DeSilvas in the past, so it makes sense."

Winthrop nodded. That seemed to be enough for him. I'd been through a dozen of these meetings with him in the last couple of years and the funny thing was, once he was satisfied that the investigators had done the work and weren't just taking the first off-ramp that they came across, he was done. He'd put that part of it behind him and just move on. The hard part was getting him to that point.

Inside the homicide unit, these meetings were known as "Winthrop's War" and they could sometimes last several hours. They were the equivalent of a Ph.D. defense--at least for a bunch of cops. Winthrop expected the detectives to come in, present their case in detail and have bulletproof reasoning and support for every damn bit of it. Once you'd said your piece, you'd better be prepared for Winthrop to take it apart bit by bit, word by word. Guys would sometimes come out of the room soaked in sweat, their case shot to pieces by Winthrop, months of work blown up.

But if you survived and your evidence and reasoning passed muster in that room, you could walk into the DA's office, drop it on his desk and know you had a great chance at a conviction. Winthrop was smarter than any defense attorney I'd ever come across and he knew that the fewer opportunities we gave the DA to screw up our work, the better his clearance rate would be. And that's what got him promoted and what would eventually get him into Cooper's chair, which was what he cared about. Which mean that's what we cared about. At least right now.

"Tell me about tonight," Winthrop said. "What, when and where."

We ran through it for him, telling him what we knew about the delivery and our thinking on who would be there and what the opportunity was for us. Told him how Delia had painted it as a make-good from DeSilva's people and also what had happened to

Delia. I didn't get into how we knew where and when the meet was and he didn't ask.

"Tactical is going with you," he said when we were done.

"Captain, I think if we have a bunch of guys with helmets and AR-15s there..."

"It wasn't a question, Tobin. That was a statement. They're going. Get with Murray and figure it out," he said. "There's a lot of dead people already and I'm not interested in having you two join the parade. They're going."

I shrugged. "Fine. But they're going to do it the way we tell them. This is probably the one chance we're going to have with these guys and I don't need a bunch of rodeo clowns screwing that up."

"It's your investigation, so you run it," he said. "Next thing. Right after I leave this meeting, I have to call Cooper and update her on this. As you know, she's very anxious to have this case resolved, and in particular, she's quite interested in Mr. DeSilva. She told me she's been getting questions from people around town about this guy and why he's still walking around when it looks like he killed a dozen people. I'm not sure I believe that, but that's the way it is. She doesn't enjoy looking foolish, and I don't blame her. She wants this case down, but more importantly, she wants DeSilva out. I don't think you two have enough here to go for arrest warrants on either Alves or DeSilva for the murders. It would be a mistake for you to try. So what you need is either more evidence, and I mean direct evidence, witnesses, people talking, or you need to get them on something else."

"We hope to do that tonight," I said.

"Hope isn't gonna get you very far. Am I on solid ground telling Cooper that DeSilva will be off the board tonight?"

I looked at Tex. He shook his head.

"We have no way of knowing whether he'll be there tonight," I said. "He may be, but we don't know. If he is, we'll get him. But who knows."

"Davis and Moore are still running surveillance on him, so we'll have a handle on where he is the whole time," Tex said.

"Any thoughts of picking him up tonight before this starts?" Winthrop asked.

"We kicked that around, but I don't think he's going anywhere. He's old as shit and I think he knows it's the bottom of the ninth for him," Tex said. "And I think if we did that it would put everyone else on edge and they might scatter."

"Well, then I leave it to you two to hammer out the details," Winthrop said as he stood up.

"Was that a win?" Tex said after the captain had left.

"I'd call it a draw."

I stopped by the tac team's cube farm on the way out of the meeting, looking for Murray. He wasn't around, so I left word with one of his guys to have him call me as soon as he got back in. By the time I was done there, Tex was nowhere to be found. I wandered back out to the parking lot and was about to take off when I saw him standing outside the side entrance talking with Davis. I banged my head on the Jeep's steering wheel a couple of times and then climbed out and walked over. They saw me coming and Davis gave me a thumbs-up and a smile I didn't like so much and went back into the barracks.

"You're an asshole," Tex said, walking away from me as I approached. "Ass. Hole."

"Whoa, hang on, hang on. Listen to me for a second here."

"Why? So you can try and explain why you've been lying to me for a fucking week now?"

"Well, technically I've only been lying for a day or so," I said.

"Come on, man! This isn't a joke. You made me look like a total dope just now with Davis. He had no idea what I was talking about when I thanked him for the info on the meeting," Tex said. "None. So now I have to wonder where it came from, and the only thing I can figure is that you and JD somehow figured out a way to tap DeSilva's phone or Alves's phone. Tell me I'm wrong."

"You're wrong."

"Really, Danny? Really? So then you tell me how you found out where the meet is, because I can't think of another way. Unless you went into Delia's hospital room and pinched off his IV. Tell me."

"OK, look, you're sort of right," I said.

"Shit!" he said, walking a few feet away before turning back to face me. "Tell me. And I mean all of it."

"I was basically trying to get us back onto an even footing with these guys. They were killing us, like you told Winthrop, always ahead of us, and we didn't have a good way to fix that."

"So you two fixed it."

"Well..."

I gave him the story, from the beginning when I called JD to the specifics of what he did on the network to what I found in the database. By the time I'd finished, he'd gone from red-faced angry to apoplectic. But the mention of Cooper's name in the database stopped him cold.

"Cooper? You're sure?" he said.

"Yep. No doubt."

He thought about that for a minute. Walked across to his car, came back. Looked at me for another twenty seconds or so.

"You fucked up, man. Seriously. I'm sure you know this already, but I'm not sure how much you care at this point," Tex said. "It seems like you were looking for a way to kick a hole in this thing from the beginning. Man, I should've known when JD showed up."

"Look, calm down for a second and listen. I was just looking for something that would help us track down the victims and figure out who they were and where they came from. All I asked JD to do was dump the customer database so I could look through it.

330

Winthrop shot us down on a warrant for DeSilva's computers, so this was the only way we could get it."

"He shot us down for a good reason. We didn't have cause."

"Maybe not, but we still needed the data."

"None of which actually helped us identify any of the victims, Danny. We did that with actual investigation, if you'll recall. All this BS has done is put us in a position to get fired. There's a win."

"Stop it. You know how good JD is and you also know that there's no way he'd say a word to anyone about any of this," I said.

"Whatever. That's not even the point. The real problem is that you have this great information that's completely useless to us. The fact that Cooper is one of DeSilva's customers doesn't help us at all. Yeah, it explains her motives in wanting this thing sewn up as quickly as possible, but the evidence of her involvement is unusable. What are we going to do, confront her with a spreadsheet from a database we shouldn't have access to? We're fired on the spot and probably in jail ten minutes after that."

"Like I said, this was not my plan. I was--"

"What plan?! There was no plan, clearly. Instead of just doing the work, you jumped ahead and had to have a look at the answers. You might not give a shit about how this affects your career or your reputation, but I do, man. I don't live on the beach, banging 25-year-olds and drinking beer. I live in the real world, with kids and a wife and a metric ton of bills and other shit to worry about. And my five-year plan does not involve being busted down to traffic detail on the Mass Pike. I like my job and I'd like to keep doing it, and having you and that asshole JD get in the way of that *really* pisses me off."

I held up my hands. "I know, I know. And I'm sorry. But none of this is going to come back on you. It's not."

"Danny, there's no way you can guarantee that. You don't even believe that yourself. If someone finds out about this, it won't matter one bit that I didn't know about it. I'm the lead investigator and it's my case. So I take the fall."

"OK, look man, let's get past the assignment of blame here. I know it's on me and believe me when I tell you that if it ever comes down to it, I'll eat it all. Every bit of it. JD is out of here tomorrow and no one will have any luck finding him once he's gone."

"You know what really bugs me? You're not even acting like a cop anymore. I don't know what's happening here, but it's getting to the point where I don't know what to expect from you. You're sort of losing it here, man."

I knew he was right, but I also had no idea how to stop it. I could feel the change in my thinking over the last few days and weeks and I also could feel a shift in the way that I felt. Not only about the job and this case in particular, but just life in general. Things were changing, pieces were moving and shifting, and I was trying to figure out what all of those changes meant on the fly. It was hard, and right now it wasn't working very well.

The dressing down from Tex should have shaken me out of this, but it didn't. It was having the opposite effect, in some ways.

I was more sure than ever that what I'd done and what JD had done was the right thing. Maybe it hadn't been legal or even maybe that smart at the time, but it was going to be important, I was pretty sure.

But I was also worried that bringing JD into this may have done some permanent damage to my friendship with Tex. Even though the two of them had kind of squashed their issues a couple of days ago, I didn't think that was going to be the end of it. I had underestimated the effect that JD's actions had on Tex back then and how much it was still bothering him even now. We had talked about it a few times over the years, but it had been in the abstract. Now that JD was here, right in Tex's face, and had helped me with the database hack...now it was real life again.

And I could tell that, as much as anything, was what had Tex riled up. He was pissed at me, no doubt. But if JD hadn't been involved, it wouldn't have been like this. At least not yet.

"OK, look," I said, "why don't we concentrate on what we can do now to make sure we get these guys and button everything up? Us standing here screaming at each other isn't getting us any closer to solving this thing. And that's all I want."

"Really? You sure about that?"

"Yeah. I'm sure."

Tex looked at me for a long moment, then let out a deep sigh and clapped his hands.

"OK. But we're not done with this," he said.

Twenty-Four

We went back inside and spent a half hour going over what we expected to happen tonight, who would be where and the contingency plans if things went south on us. Tex was keeping his answers short, strictly business. His face was tight, his eyes narrow and his shoulders hunched. He was drawing inward, trying to shut out all of the stuff we'd just talked about and focusing on the operation.

As we were wrapping up, Murray stuck his head over the cube wall.

"Heard you were looking for me," he said. "You boys need some adult supervision tonight?"

"That's what we were told," Tex said.

"Might be tough for me. Friday is usually the night I meet Kim at the Days Inn on 24, but we can postpone that. It's getting a little stale anyway, to be honest," Murray said.

He ducked down below the metal divider as Tex hummed a blue racquetball at his head, just missing.

"Good thing you can shoot better than you throw," Murray said, slowly coming back up.

"I shoot better than *anyone* throws," Tex said.

"And we're all very impressed," I said. "Murray, this should be a picnic for your all-stars. We've got a meet set up between two crews tonight and there's some pretty bad blood between them. Lots of bodies."

"This the thing from up in Duxbury?"

335

"Yup. We're not necessarily expecting any fireworks, but it's certainly possible. Lemme run through it..."

Murray scribbled down notes while I talked and when I was finished, he was quiet for a few seconds.

"I don't like this location so much," he said. "It's going to be a pain in the ass for us."

"Will be for them, too," I said.

"True, but all they're interested in is moving some people from one truck to another and getting out of there. We're trying to keep track of an unknown number of assholes, some of whom will be armed, and to stop them from getting out of there."

"That's why you got the fancy night time goggles and scary face paint," Tex said.

"Can we just shoot them all and call it a training exercise?"

"Sure. But only if I get to play, too," Tex said. "Can't let your goons have all the fun."

"How many guys you gonna bring?" I asked.

"Not sure, but off the top, I'd think at least six," Murray said. "If you figure they're going to have a minimum of two guys on each side, assume they're all armed, we'll be in good shape with six plus you two."

"OK. We are going to try and get a better handle on exactly who will be there later today, so I'll update you on that," Tex said. "What else?"

"Nothing else. Lemme get with my team and work it out and we'll reconvene late afternoon with you guys. Good?"

"Good."

Murray walked away and five seconds later the racquetball bounced against the side of Tex's cube, a couple of inches from his ear, and pinged off his temple.

"I'm still a better shot!" he yelled to no one.

"What was the bit about us getting more info on the meeting?" I asked once Murray had gone. "How is that happening?"

"Davis said that Delia is awake. I guess he came around sometime overnight," Tex said.

"Is he...lucid?"

"How would we know? I mean, how lucid was he to begin with?"

"Good point. I guess it's worth a ride down there."

A half hour later we were sitting in plastic, egg-shaped chairs in Delia's room at St. Luke's, watching a male nurse draw vials of blood from his arm. There was a New Bedford cop standing outside the room. I'd only met Delia the one time, but even if I had known him since kindergarten, I don't think I would have recognized him. His face was a disaster, all jagged edges and unnatural angles. His ruined eye, previously an awful, pitiable wound, now looked like his best feature. His left leg was in an air cast from ankle to hip and I could see ugly purple and black bruising on both of his arms. He had an IV drip in his right arm and I could see a larger bag filled with dark yellowish-brown urine next to him.

The nurse finished what he was doing. "I just gave him two Percocets, so I don't know how long he'll be able to talk."

"OK, thanks," Tex said. The nurse threw him a quick smile on his way out.

"He must have seen your Outback in the parking lot," I said.

Tex opened his mouth to say something, thought better of it, and instead slapped me in the back of the head as he stood up and walked over to Delia's bed. He looked down at Delia, who was clearly in significant pain, squirming in the bed, trying to find some level of comfort.

"You remember me?" Tex said.

Delia winced as he pushed himself up a bit, trying to get a better look at Tex. He stared for a few seconds and then nodded. "Cop."

"State trooper," Tex said. "We talked to you a couple of days ago about DeSilva and his crew from Plymouth. You with me?"

Another nod.

"Good. Can you tell me what happened to you? How you got here?"

Delia swallowed hard, wincing with the effort. "You," he said. His voice was weak and broken, like he'd been chewing on rusty nails.

"Me. How's that?"

"Was fine one day. Next day, I talk to you fuckers. Now I'm here," he said between short, sharp breaths. "Get it?"

Tex looked back at me. I nodded, made a "get on with it" gesture with my hands.

"Who hit you?" Tex asked.

Delia turned his head toward the window. No answer.

"Look, I don't really give a shit. It's not my deal," Tex said. "But if you want some help, we can do that."

Delia turned back toward Tex, snorted. "I fell."

"Off what, the Zakim?"

A shrug.

"Whatever. That's your problem," Tex said. "Our problem is that we need to know who's going to be at the meeting tonight. You remember this meeting, right? You told Davis about it before your, uh, fall."

Delia nodded. He shifted his weight slightly to take some pressure off his bad leg and he bumped the leg against the guardrail on the bed. Even with the air cast, he was in trouble. He gritted his teeth and sweat beads popped on his forehead. Tex poured him a cup of water from the pink plastic pitcher on the side table and handed it over. Delia gulped it down and handed it back, nodding his thanks.

"How many people will be at this thing?" Tex asked.

"Not sure," Delia said. "Eight? Ten?"

"How many will be armed?"

"Most."

Tex nodded. "OK. How about I give you some names and you can just say yea or nay? Tell me whether you think they'll be there."

339

"K." He was starting to fade. I could see the sweat running down his face, and the sheets were wet.

"Maglia." A nod.

"His uncle?" Nod.

"DeSilva." Nod.

"Alves." A shrug, not sure.

"OK. Listen, that's good. You did good," Tex said. "One thing: How do you guys contact them? No one uses cell phones, right?"

"Hell no. Those guys think they're tapped. Watch too much HBO," he said. He was breathing heavily now. "Never cells. Don't have to talk to them but once a month or so. Just send a guy...to Plymouth...tell them to meet at the club."

"Like I said before, if you want us to help you with this, we can."

"Heh. I'm dead. In here, out there. Don't matter," he said. His eyes were starting to close, bouncing up and down like a child fighting to stay awake on Christmas Eve.

Tex sighed. I stood up and walked over to the bed.

"Sal, we can protect you, get you to a safe place, talk to the DA about the help you've given us," I said. "There are things we can do. It doesn't have to go this way."

"Help? You want to help?" he asked. His eyes were closed now, his breathing slowing down.

"I said we would."

"Kill them all."

And he was out.

We stopped to talk with the New Bedford uniform on the way out.

"Anyone else been in here to visit him?" Tex asked.

"Just his lawyer."

"When was that?"

"About an hour ago, I guess. Not too long after he woke up."

"You know the lawyer?" Tex said.

"Guy named Santos. Ambulance-chaser, represents lots of the assholes down here, over in Fall River. Whoever will pay him."

"Mario Santos?" I asked.

"That's him."

"Ah, shit," I said. Why would Delia and DeSilva be sharing an attorney? There were plenty of lawyers around who weren't that picky about their clients. Curioser and curioser...

"Did you used to work narco?" the cop, whose name tag said Corrao, asked Tex.

"Yeah..."

"You ran my little cousin in a few years ago, holding like sixty tabs of X," he said. "Over in Marion. He was carrying a super soaker full of piss he used to squirt on people at stoplights?"

"I remember. He got my partner with it. Caught a pretty good beating too, I think."

"Nothing like the one I gave him after he bonded out. Little fucker."

"He straighten out?"

"Not even. Caught his third strike last year, doing three to five in Bridgewater now."

341

"Sorry about that."

"I'm not," Corrao said.

Twenty-Five

Outside, starting to see it coming together.

"I was thinking...where are Kim and the boys?" I asked.

"Sent them to Maine for the weekend. They're seeing the sights in Portland, coming back Sunday night."

"Good."

"Caroline is still at her parents' place?"

"Till further notice."

"How is that? Things seem pretty serious there, at least for you."

"It's...great. There's something there, for sure," I said. "I feel like I'm throwing a no-hitter here, though, and we shouldn't jinx it."

"OK. Let's do this: It's...one-fifteen now. Let's grab some lunch and then take a drive up and see Alves. I had a thought..."

We took my Jeep and drove back to Plymouth, stopped at Wood's for lobster rolls and Cokes and ate on the way up to Duxbury. I made a phone call to Brazil on the way, talked to Pena for a couple of minutes and got what I needed. I waved at Moore sitting in his shitbox Corolla as we turned off the road into the woods toward Alves's place. We pulled into the dirt drive and parked behind DeSilva's car. There was no answer though when we knocked on the door.

We walked around the side and found Alves in the back, splitting wood. He stopped when he saw us, stuck the ax in a log and sat down on a stump in the shade of a big pine. It was in the mid eighties and felt ripe for thunderstorms later.

"Detectives," Alves said as we walked over. I glanced at the tool shed off to the side and saw that the doors stood open. I could see several floor-standing apparatuses in there, but couldn't tell what they were.

"What can I help you two with today?"

"We thought maybe we could help you, actually," Tex said. "We have some information about your wife and daughter."

Alves didn't say anything or move or even blink. After a few seconds, five or ten, he stood up, took a rag from his back pocket and wiped the sweat from his face and neck. Judging by the pile of cord wood stacked between two trees nearby, he'd been at it for several hours. And he still had four or five large trunks lying to the side, promising a long afternoon's worth of work. He walked into the house and came out with three plastic tumblers of lemonade, handing one each to me and Tex. We nodded our thanks and Alves went back and sat on the stump in the shade while we stood in the sun like dopes. I hadn't figured much out in the last week, but I did know that Alves moved at his own pace and trying to change that was a waste of time. So we waited.

"Do you know why I enjoy working with wood?" he said after what seemed like five minutes of silence and lemonade drinking.

"Nope," I said.

It made me ill to stand there and talk to him, knowing what he'd done to those women and to

Reggie. I had a brief fantasy about walking over and punching him in the throat and kicking him in the head for a while, but I stood there and listened like a sap instead.

"There are many reasons, actually, but the most important one, the one that matters most to me, is that it's unpredictable. When I start a project, I never know how it's going to turn out. No matter how precise the measurements and how well-planned it is, there is always some quirk, a small knot in a board, something that changes the outcome," he said. "It's those elements of chance that I love. It's the exact opposite of engineering and math, my fields. If I start a design or a problem, I always know how what the result will be. It's pre-determined. A squared plus B squared is always going to equal C squared. There's nothing I can do to change that. But the outcome of a woodworking project is always in flux. And the way that these logs split and fall is totally dependent on where I strike them, and that's different every time."

None of that seemed to require a response, so we waited some more.

"You say you have news of my wife and daughter. I know you owe me no favors, and I wouldn't presume to ask you for any, but whatever it is you know or think you know, please don't tell me," Alves said. "Right now, I can still sit here on a warm day and picture them lying on the beach at home, or walking through the hills outside our town, oblivious to all that is happening here and elsewhere. I can imagine that Ellie, my wife, and Antonia, my daughter, are happily preparing for their trip here, talking excitedly about what America and Boston will be like. How different everything will seem, how big and grand. But if you tell me, that ends. That all goes away. There is no potential scenario in which things end well."

Tex looked at me, with something like empathy in his eyes. I felt it too, but we'd decided to go down this path and there wasn't much we could do about it now. If Alves was the key, as we thought, we needed to know.

"Look, that's not our problem. This isn't a choose your own adventure book or something. We can't change what's happened. We're only interested in getting at the truth, and we have to do that any way we can," I said. "You're part of that, and so are your wife and daughter. I understand what you're saying, but we can't worry about that."

Alves gave a short laugh. "I saw how you did that with my uncle. I saw how you used his grief and his pain for your own purposes. That's a wonderful investigative method you have, detective."

"Since when do you care how he feels?" I said. "All we've heard from you for the last week is what a parasite he is and how he uses other people for *his* own gain and then discards them when they're no longer useful to him. When did that change?"

"It didn't. My feelings about Paolo are irrelevant. I'm talking about what you did. You took advantage of him, knowing that he'd be weak. And now you're trying to do the same to me. No, thank you."

As we talked, Tex was wandering aimlessly around the property, looking idly at planting beds and flowers, like a bored fourth-grader on a field trip. He was working his way toward the shed that held Alves's tools. Alves wasn't paying him any attention and was focused on me.

"I'll say it one more time: I'm not your priest or your rabbi. We have some information you need to hear and that's the way it's going to go," I said. "We're not positive, but we think there's a very good chance that your wife and daughter were among the victims from the pond over here. The timing of your description of when they left Brazil and when those women were dumped seems to fit and so does the fact that you said DeSilva was bringing them in. We talked to the police in Brazil and they confirmed that your family left the country when you said they did. It all goes together. Now, like I said, it's not a hundred percent, but it's what we think happened at this point."

Alves just nodded. I glanced over at Tex, who was now pretending to inspect the begonias in the window boxes on the shed.

"I know this is hard for you to hear, but we need you to come and have a look at the bodies and see whether they're in there," I said. "It will go a long way toward helping us finish this case."

Another nod. He walked slowly over to the stand of trees that separated his property from the clearing around the pond. He stood with his back to me and stared out across the clearing for a long while. I wondered whether he was crying and trying to compose

347

himself. I looked back and saw Tex inside the shed, making a quick tour of it. After a couple of minutes Alves turned and walked back and his face showed no signs that he'd been crying or was even mildly upset. Instead, he looked relaxed and it seemed that something--resolve, maybe, or resignation--had settled on him.

"Tell me when. I will come," he said flatly.

"Good. Let's plan on tomorrow, probably in the late morning," I said. "It won't take long."

"Fine," he said, as Tex came up beside me.

"Let me ask you something: DeSilva told us that you drove his wife and daughter up to Boston a few weeks back. Why didn't you bring them back? What happened?"

"Just that. I took them to the city, waited a couple of hours while they shopped, and then they called and said they were going to stay overnight. So I called Paolo and he told me to come back. That's it."

"When did you find out that they decided to stay indefinitely?" Tex asked.

"I didn't. Not until the day that Paolo had to go to the morgue."

"Really? You're as close to him as anyone, and he never mentioned or you never noticed that they hadn't come back? Paolo told us that he talked to you about this in detail when you came back."

Alves shrugged. "I don't care what he said."

"You have any thoughts on how they might have ended up in that pond over there?" Tex said.

A blank stare.

"Yeah," I said. "Why didn't you go to the morgue with him? You being his driver and all."

"His attorney went with him. He didn't need me, so I didn't go."

"It wouldn't have anything to do with you not wanting to be around when he saw their bodies, would it?" I asked. "That could be a little awkward."

Alves shook his head and picked up the ax again. I saw Tex's hand go to his gun, but Alves just began splitting logs, methodically breaking each one into four pieces. We watched him stack the logs for a minute.

"We'll let Santos know what time to meet us at the morgue tomorrow," I said. "Enjoy the day."

He continued his work, never looking up.

Back in the Jeep, heading back to the barracks, talking it over. I could feel the pressure starting to mount, the hours slipping away. I needed to get back home and lock everything down with JD still.

"Shed was full of tools, all kinds. Right in the back corner was a big-ass Jet band saw. Probably a sixteen or eighteen-inch," Tex said. "Had a few other things too, drill press, table saw, stuff like that. All nice stuff."

"You get a look at the band saw at all?"

"Not really. I just had time to take a quick look around. But one thing I noticed is that he has one of those big central vac systems set up in there, collecting the sawdust and all that," he said. "Depending on how often he gets around to emptying that..."

"We need to get in there with a warrant."

"Let's talk to Winthrop when we get to the barracks," Tex said. "Another thing that will help: There were three or four guns hanging in a rack in the ceiling. Couple of hunting rifles, couldn't see what."

"Shotgun?"

"I think so. It was quick and it's kinda dark up there, but pretty sure I saw a pump-action."

"We're right there, man. Right there," I said. Glanced at the clock: almost three. "If we can get Winthrop to agree and find a friendly judge right quick, we could get back there with the warrant before six or so, maybe we get Alves out of the way before things happen tonight. Can you call Davis and see what's going on? I want to know where everyone is for the next few hours until we get this straightened out."

"Yup."

By the time he got off the phone with Davis, we were pulling into the barracks in Middleborough. I heard him tell Davis that we might be making some moves even before the thing tonight, so they'd need to be ready.

"DeSilva is holed up at home. Davis said he hasn't really moved in the last day or so, just moping around there," Tex said.

"Fine. Let him stay his ass there for a few hours more, then we're set."

"Davis is staying on him and Moore is gonna break off from Alves for a minute and come over here for the briefing tonight."

We found Winthrop in his office, on the phone. He waved us in and we waited while he finished. He was doing a lot of listening and not much talking. He hung up after a minute and sank back in his chair, looking across the desk at us.

"When this case is over, remind me to quit," he said. "You know we just arrested the daughter of a Harvard divinity professor for murder? That wouldn't be so much of a problem if it wasn't for the fact that she's a special needs student in sixth grade who just happens to have the same name as the fifty-seven-year-old woman we meant to arrest. Jesus. We're going to be so sued."

He gave us a fake smile. "Now, how can I help you two?"

"All we need is a search warrant, sir. Nice and easy," I said.

"Tell me."

We did, putting special emphasis on the guns and the possibility of there being some forensic evidence in the vacuum system. He listened, thought about it for a minute, and said, "Write it up. I'll call Rourke and clear the way. Don't put any BS in there. What you have is good enough."

"Yes sir," I said.

"I'll handle the writing," Tex said when we were out in the hall. "Last time, you spelled 'suspect' k-i-l-l-e-r."

"So picky. I'm gonna go track down Murray and see what he's cooked up for tonight. Think we have any use for him when we execute this warrant?"

"Christ, I hope not," Tex said.

"K. Be back in twenty minutes."

I went to Murray's desk and one of his guys pointed me toward the gym. I found him getting dressed in the locker room, having just finished his workout.

"Get decent and lemme buy you a grape Nehi," I said.

He walked into the cafeteria five minutes later and looked at the bottle of diet Coke on the table in front of his chair with pure disgust.

"Where's my Nehi?"

"I forgot we were in New England."

"Fuckin' homicide. Full of liars," he said. He dropped his gym bag and sat down. "You run today?"

"Is today a day? Then I ran."

"Nobody was chasing you, right?"

"Just old age. Can't end up looking like you."

"You should be so lucky," he said. He pushed the diet Coke aside and leaned forward on his elbows. "So I think we're set. I talked with the guys and we're gonna bring six plus me."

"OK. Tell me about it."

"There isn't but one way in and out of that spot. Just a big loop. We'll have that covered and we'll also have a couple of guys in the trees near the meeting place itself to support you and Tex," he said. "Once they come in, it's all yours. We wait for you to move and we come in right behind you."

"What about the water?" I said. "Do we need to worry about anyone coming in from that way?"

"I don't think so. I grew up in Duxbury and I know that area pretty well. Most of the land around there is private property, a bunch of giant trophy houses.

352

Anyone coming up from the water would have a long hike up and they'd have to wind their way through a bunch of yards and fences and crap like that. Could happen, but it seems like a long shot."

"I'll take your word for it. One thing that worries me is having some of these assholes running around loose in the trees out there. I know it's gonna be late, but there are probably people in there all the time, kids drinking beer, playing grab-ass, whatever."

"'Playing grab-ass?' Is this nineteen sixty-two?"

"What do the kids do now?"

"Make sex tapes," Murray said.

"It'll be too dark for that, I hope. Anyway, you see any harm in sending a couple of guys in there earlier, wander around and make sure the place is as clear as we can make it?"

"Nope, we can do that. I'll get two guys in there by seven or so. You figure these guys will be doing the same thing, scouting it out in advance?"

"I do. Both of these crews are a little bit on edge right now and I'd bet they're both anticipating trouble, one way or another," I said.

"OK. I'll let them know. I'll have to catch them up after the briefing, too. Anything else?"

"Don't think so. See you here at eight for the briefing."

"I'll be there with guns on," he said.

Twenty-Six

Tex had finished up the affidavit by the time I got back.

"Sign," he said.

"Shouldn't I read it first?"

"Why start now?"

"Good point." We both signed the affidavit and then walked back to Winthrop's office.

"You're good," he said, after reading through the two pages quickly. "Rourke is at the courthouse now, said he'd wait there till five-fifteen, not a minute later. Go."

We went. It was just after five when we pulled up the courthouse on Obery Street, just behind Jordan Hospital. I left the Jeep in a spot reserved for law enforcement and we ran inside and took the elevator to Rourke's office.

His clerk, a young Asian girl with a hoop earring in her eyebrow, looked at our credentials and waved us into his office.

"Dave said you guys had a hot one," he said, coming around from behind his desk as we walked in. "Let's have a look."

He sat on the front edge of his desk, reading. He flipped back and forth between the pages a couple of times.

"Tell me about this vacuum thingy," he said.

"It's a big thing, with a central power unit with hoses connected to all the tools and it just pulls all of the sawdust and shavings and stuff into the bag," Tex said. "Pretty slick."

"And you think there might be, what, some bone or tissue fragments in there from the band saw?"

"Yes, sir. If he isn't too careful about emptying it out."

"Huh. Might have to get me one of those things," he said, then pulled out a pen and signed.

"Vaya con dios," he said, handing the papers back.

"Thank you, your honor," I said.

"Tell Dave I'll see him at the club this weekend," Rourke said.

"Yes sir," I said.

Back in the Jeep, I gunned it onto Obery and pushed through a yellowish-red light at South Street. I made the quick left onto the Route 3 on-ramp and nailed it.

"'Tell Dave I'll see him at the club,'" Tex said. "Bunch of Mayflower Compact-signing motherfuckers. Please."

"We got the warrant, right?" I said as I hopped into the left lane, squeezing between a Mini Cooper and a red Ninja. "Call Moore and make sure Alves is still there."

He dialed Moore and got the OK as I passed through Kingston, pushing eighty-five. I checked the time: twenty past five. Time to get there, do a quick search and get whatever we find back to the lab before the briefing. Killed my plans for a pre-raid nap, though. I kept the accelerator pinned and as we approached the Duxbury exit, I had to make a choice between dropping

356

back into the right lane behind a slow-moving septic truck or trying to get past him and still make the exit ramp. I jammed the gas pedal one more time, passed the truck, cranked the wheel to the right and whipped in front of him, making the exit by about ten feet. I braked hard on the way up the ramp and saw the truck coming behind me, the driver giving me the finger out the window. Sorry, homes.

Moore was still sitting where we'd left him earlier. I pulled alongside his car and he wound down his window.

"Need any help?" he asked. "I'm so fucking bored, I've been listening to NPR for the last hour. If you want to know what's going on with the Greek economy or the leitmotifs in Yo-Yo Ma's new record, I'm your man."

"Any talk of chocolate shweaty balls on there?" I said.

"I wish. A deer wandered past about forty-five minutes ago and I had a nice conversation with him. Hell, I've only got three years left till my twenty-five, maybe I'll move to Maine, become a park ranger after that. Animals are nice."

"Ayup. Listen, we should be in and out of here in like thirty or forty minutes. You want to hang around and then head back with us for the briefing?"

"Sounds good. If I'm not here when you're done, I might be wandering around in the woods, looking for poison mushrooms to eat."

"Enjoy," I said, and rolled down the road and on into Alves's drive. When we got out of the Jeep, we could hear him in the back, still going at the wood pile. The guy was persistent, if nothing else.

We walked around the house and over to where Alves was working. We waited while he finished what was in front of him. He had a steady, rhythmic stroke that obviously had been developed over a long period. His routine was metronomic in its precision and repetition. Bend, lift, place, stand, swing, throw. Lather, rinse, repeat. He was so intent on the work and the rhythm of it that he didn't even notice us for a good minute as we stood and watched. When he did, he straightened and looked at us with genuine confusion. Then he saw the warrant in my hand.

"Ah, you are here to search," he said. "There is nothing to find here, but it is your right, of course. Come."

He started walking toward the house, still carrying the ax in his hand, swinging it idly as he went.

"Not the house," I said. "We're here to search your shed."

That stopped him. He seemed to consider what that meant for a few moments, running through the ramifications, thinking about his options. At some point he realized he didn't really have any.

"I'd like to call my lawyer," he said.

"Sure, go ahead," Tex said, "but we don't have to wait for him to get here. The warrant lets us search whenever we want. But do what you want. All we need is you to sign the warrant and then we'll get on with it and get out of your way."

Alves leaned the ax against the side of the house and took the pen Tex offered and signed the warrant. He pulled an iPhone from the pocket of his khakis and made the call. He walked a few steps away, talking in a low voice. The shed was still open, so we got to work on it.

The shed was small and neatly kept. Tex took an eight-foot step ladder from against the wall, stood it in the center of the floor and went up to the gun rack. He handed down the guns one at a time. The first two were hunting rifles, a .22 and what looked like a .30-06. The third was a shotgun, which I laid on the workbench. Tex hopped down from the ladder and picked up the shotgun, racked the pump and came up empty. He looked it over and let out a soft whistle.

"Wonder where he got this," he said. "You recognize it?"

"Sure, Benelli M3. Not exactly your typical hunter's shotgun."

"No, it is not. Unless you're hunting men."

Tex tagged the shotgun and set it aside while I started poking around with the vacuum system. It took me a minute, but I finally found the release that opened up the big central sawdust collection bin. It looked like it held twenty-five gallons or so, and it was nearly full. There was mostly sawdust, but I could see plenty of other little bits of stuff in there, too.

"Here we go," I said. "That's a shitload of work he's done. Must be a few weeks' worth of stuff in there."

359

"Take it."

"Yeah...how?"

"Aw, hell. I guess I didn't think about that part. Can't we just lift that bag out of there and sort of tie it off somehow?"

"Thing's made of canvas and I don't think we have any industrial sized twist-ties with us. Hang on a sec..."

I rooted around on Alves's workbench for a minute and found a box of puncture-proof yard cleanup trash bags on a bottom shelf, next to a hard-sided case of saw blades.

"Here." I handed Tex one of the bags and I lifted the vacuum bag out of the holder. Tex flipped the trash bag upside down and shimmied it down over the top of the vacuum bag. He found a roll of duct tape on the workbench and wrapped it around the contraption a couple of times, tearing the tape off with his teeth at the end.

"Not great, but it should be OK till we get back," I said.

"Let's get that saw blade," he said.

I pulled on a pair of latex gloves and went over and popped the catch on the band saw blade mechanism and pulled out the blade. It looked fairly clean, but that didn't mean anything. We didn't need much in the way of residue in order to get a result. A tiny bit would do the trick. I picked up the shotgun on my way out of the shed. Tex was dragging the vacuum bag out into the yard as I walked out and saw Santos coming around from the front of the house.

"Lemme see it," he said. I handed him the warrant and he gave it a quick once-over and handed it back. He looked at the shotgun and other stuff we hauled out of the shed.

"What's the reasoning here?" he asked.

"Just a hunch," I said. "We'll see what we get. Two of our victims were killed with a shotgun, not counting Andres DeSilva. Alves is right in the middle of this whole thing, he has a shotgun and plenty of motive. So here we are."

"Lot of people have shotguns," Santos said.

"Sure."

"What's with the trash bag?"

"Treasure hunt. Look, we're almost done here. We'll show you the inventory before we leave."

"OK."

We took the shotgun and other stuff out to the Jeep. Quick time check: six-thirty. Getting tight. Time to go.

"Let's do a quick run-through of the house, just see if there's any other obvious weapons or stuff that grabs our attention," Tex said.

We did a cursory search of the house, with Alves and Santos standing in the doorway watching silently. Nothing much caught our eyes, so we showed Santos the inventory and headed out the door. As we got to the Jeep, I remembered something and snapped my fingers.

"Be right back." I said and jogged back to the shed. I grabbed the small case of saw blades I'd seen on the workbench shelf earlier and ran back around to the front of the house. I held it up for Tex.

"Never know," I said.

I went over to here Santos and Alves were.

"We talked to him about this earlier, we need Alves to come down to the morgue tomorrow sometime and have a look at a couple of bodies. There's a good chance that they're his wife and daughter."

Santos looked at Alves, who was expressionless, as though we were discussing where to go for dinner. "You think that's possible?" he asked Alves, who nodded.

"Everything fits in terms of timing and all of that," I said. "We can do it whenever you want tomorrow."

"It makes no difference," Alves said quietly. "This is irrelevant."

"It is?" I said. I was getting tired of his quiet, detached act, as if all of the madness going on around him was happening to someone else and was just an abstraction for him. "I don't think that's the way that the parents and families of those dead women would characterize the situation. I think they'd probably consider all of this pretty fucking relevant. And you, of all people, with your little sob story about waiting years to see your family again, I'd think you'd be interested in seeing this through and finding out the truth. Then again, maybe you already know what happened. Right? That would make this all pretty academic, I guess."

"Hey, Tobin, take it easy, will ya?" Santos said, his voice sounding weary and oddly small. "Everyone is tired and on edge right now. We'll be there tomorrow, OK? Let's say ten."

"Fine." I glanced at Alves, who was looking at the case of saw blades in my hand. "We're going to win, you know," I said to him. "Us, not you. Us."

Alves shrugged and walked back around the side of the house. A few seconds later we heard the sounds of him splitting logs again.

"I hear there's some heat coming down on you guys for this one," Santos said. "Sounds like Cooper is getting a little squirmy up there."

"Nothing new about that," Tex said. "She's a politician, not a cop."

"That's one thing she is," Santos said.

"We gotta run," I said. "We'll see you in the morning."

It was just before seven when we got back to the barracks. We took the evidence down to the evidence section and asked the attendant to ship it off to the lab over in Lakeville with a priority request on it. Even with that, it would likely be several days before we got even some preliminary results back. The shotgun wasn't going to be of much forensic value, since we didn't have any shells from the scenes or anything else that might help tie it to the killings. But showing in court that Alves had an assault shotgun would help establish him as a likely suspect. The real prize was the blade we'd taken from the saw, along with the others in the case. The lab would know quickly whether any of them had any blood on them. Once we knew that, then we'd start the process of trying to tie that blood to one or more of the suspects.

363

"We got an hour before the briefing," I said to Tex," so I'm gonna run home and change, grab something to eat."

"I'm gonna hang here and try to catch a few minutes sleep on the couch."

"Back in an hour."

Twenty-Seven

JD was taking a nap of his own when I got home. I kicked the couch on my into the kitchen.

"Just about play time," I said. "You want something to eat before we head out?"

"This work crap is getting in the way of my laziness," he said as he stood and stretched. "You got any microwave burritos in here, or a can of spaghetti-o's?"

"No, man. I have actual food. You know, like the kind that comes from the produce aisle and the meat department."

"Yeah, they don't have those aisles in the mini-mart. Lemme get a grilled cheese, then. Any tater tots in here?"

He was digging around the in the freezer, trying to find some sort of bullet-shaped potato product he could cover in ketchup and salt.

"This is a disgrace, dude," he said, when he came up empty. "Vita-Muffins? Smoothie mixes? This makes me want to cry."

"I'm trying to live past forty, man. You might wanna give the packaged crap a rest and try some *food* food."

"Plenty of time for that when I'm old like you."

"You're eighteen months younger than I am, man. You *are* old like me."

"Shut it. Where's that grilled cheese, Batali?"

We sat on the back deck and ate the sandwiches and talked over the plans for the night. JD's role was a small one, but it might make the difference between us succeeding and failing catastrophically. As we talked, the pair of herons flew in over the house, circling gracefully above the inlet for a minute before splashing down about fifty yards away from us on the edge of the water. We watched them wander around for a bit, flapping from spot to spot as they looked for their dinner. It was getting dark now and the white birds were about the only visible things moving out there. But I was pretty sure that there was at least one other hidden thing close by, watching, waiting.

"So when I call, you pull the trigger. Right then, and you make sure that it stays that way," I said.

"Yup. Then what?"

"Then you wait. I may need you to do one or two more things, but once I give you the OK, you drive to the airport, put the car in central parking and check into the hotel. Tomorrow, it's up to you. Go wherever it is you go."

"Simple enough."

"Should be, but who knows. Lots of things going on, which means there are a lot of things that can go wrong. None of that will matter to you, but for me and Tex..."

"I get it. I'd like to see Tex again before I go."

"Mmm, probably not the best idea," I said. I polished off the last of my sandwich and took a slug of diet Coke.

"He knows?"

"He does. I screwed up a little bit with some of the info you got on the meeting tonight and he figured it out. Not the end of the world, but he wasn't happy. I told him it was all me and you were just doing what I asked, but you know how he gets."

"So touchy about laws and rules and all that," he said.

"Right? You'd think he was a cop or something."

"Which brings up something I've been meaning to ask you..."

"Yeah?"

"Why are you still doing this? I mean, I know you like the action and the challenge and all that, but I sort of feel like you're wasting your time."

"How so?"

"Well, don't take this the wrong way, but the whole idea of truth, justice and the American way doesn't seem like it's your main motivator," he said. "You don't have a problem stepping from one side of the line to the other and doing things that other guys--like Tex-- wouldn't even consider. Don't get me wrong, I dig that and you know I don't mind doing a little of that myself. But you obviously spend a lot of energy battling the guys above you to let you do what you need to do. I'm guessing you get the results or else you wouldn't still be there, but what's the point? You're not going to keep your head down, make rank and put in thirty years. That ain't you."

"Did my dad call you or something? Jeez, man."

"No no, I'm just saying, there's a lot of other stuff out there you could be doing that is way less stressful and way more rewarding."

"Such as."

"Well, working with me. Hang on now, don't laugh. I have way more work than I can handle, and I turn down a ton of stuff that pays good money, just because I don't have time or it's not my thing or whatever. The point is, you could do ninety percent of these gigs in your sleep and you'd be making three or four times what you do now."

"You don't know what I make. Or do you?"

"I can make a pretty good guess, and I do know what I make, so a little simple math tells me that it could be a profitable move for you," he said. "And I think you'd enjoy the work. The challenge is there, and it beats the hell out of chasing assholes around the countryside and worrying about your pension."

"I don't know, man. I mean, I might sort smudge the line a little bit here and there, but I'm not sure I want to make a career out of it."

"Dude, the only non-legal stuff I do is for you," he said. "Well, maybe not the only..."

It sounded pretty attractive, honestly. I was worn out. Worn out and worn down. Tired of the job, tired of the people, but most of all, tired of the endless stream of depravity and malice and hate and greed and indifference that poured into my life every day. JD was right about one thing: I couldn't see myself doing this for the long haul. Not anymore. Maybe once, when I felt like closing a case and putting someone away made a difference somehow, but not now. Not when I knew how little difference any of it made and how little the people who should care actually did. It was worth thinking about.

"Kick it around, talk to your girl, think about it," JD said. "The offer is out there."

"Let me get through this mess and then I can think about it. But it doesn't sound awful."

"Have you seen my tan?" he asked, smiling. "Looks the same in December as it does in July. Hard to do that here."

"OK, OK. Ease up. I'm not saying no."

"Smart man."

While JD cleaned up, I took a quick shower and dressed. Jeans, a worn t-shirt that said "Everybody everybody" on the front and old running shoes. I opened the safe in the floor of my bedroom and grabbed three extra clips. By the time I got downstairs, JD was ready, backpack in hand. He was dressed the same way I was: jeans, light colored t-shirt and Nikes and a filthy Orioles cap with the smiling cartoon bird on the front.

"Time to go," I said. "Getting late."

He gave me a quick hug and slap on the back.

"See ya when I see ya, man. Keep your head down out there," he said.

"Will do. Thanks for the help. I'll be in touch. Oh, and I expect to be getting that hat back in the mail by next week. That's the real thing."

JD gave me a thumbs up and headed out the door. A few seconds later I heard the Jeep start and I watched as he backed out of the drive and rumbled up the dirt road toward the parking lot. I went out on the back deck and looked across the inlet, waiting. Twenty seconds later, a

369

car pulled out of the small parking lot behind the condos and out onto 3A, heading north into town. I gave it about ten minutes and then I locked up the house, leaving a couple of lights on downstairs.

I got into the Pathfinder, left the lights off and crept down the road as carefully as I could. It was a little hairy, but I took it slowly and got into the gravel parking lot safely. There were still a few cars in there, so I turned the lights on and turned onto 3A. I went south, just for the hell of it, and picked up Route 3 down at exit 4, pushing it hard up the highway and catching 44 west over to Middleborough.

If things had worked out, JD should be sitting in a coffee shop in Kingston by now, probably surfing porn, waiting for my call. Just as I accelerated onto 44, my phone buzzed. I grabbed it from the cup holder in the center console and checked the screen: Brendan.

"Hey, Brendan."

"You busy?"

"Sort of. We have something going tonight. What's up?"

"Ah, nothing really. Look, I'm not sure I really got my point across the other day. I wasn't trying to preach to you or make you feel guilty. I just...I don't know. You didn't sound like yourself," he said. "I know how you get when you're deep into something and it sounds like that's what's going on now. But I just need to make sure that you're thinking everything through and not jumping off a cliff here."

"I appreciate the concern, Brendan, but we're covered. We know what we're doing. I don't think there's much of a risk for you anymore. Especially not after tonight if things go well."

"What's happening tonight?"

"I can't really say right now, but I'll just tell you that we should have our arms around a lot of these guys in the next few hours," I said. "Things are moving quickly right now and I'm really looking forward to getting these guys off the map."

"Listen Danny, I know you know what you're doing, but I am still concerned that you're treating this as a kind of crusade to make up for what happened to Erin. And you know that's not right. They're two separate things, and one has nothing to do with the other."

"B, I know that. Give me some credit," I said. "We're doing what we need to do, OK? This isn't a hunting trip. You know I love you, but this isn't what I need right now."

"Fine, but the way you made it sound, these guys don't seem like they're going to just throw up their hands and surrender quietly."

"Maybe not, but that's what my job is. I need to get them one way or another. I'm not out here trying to get into a fight with them, trust me," I said. "It looks like these guys killed at least eleven people that we know about, and probably a lot more than that. So if I have the chance to take these guys out of circulation, that's happening."

"Is that what you want? You want to walk around with that on your head for the rest of your life? Come on, Danny. Don't be a child."

"I've already got one on my conscience."

He was quiet then, and when he spoke again his voice was low and even, unnaturally so. "I'm starting a novena tonight and I'll have you in my prayers, as always."

He may as well toss a bunch of chicken bones on the ground and do a dance around them, for all the good it would do.

"Thanks," I said.

"Danny, let me ask you something. What are you looking for?"

I sighed. I didn't need a spiritual debate right now. I needed to be clearing my head, not cluttering it up. But Brendan knew me as well as anyone did, and it wouldn't do me any good to try and BS him.

"Honestly? I don't know, B. I thought it was this, what I'm doing. But I can't say that's true anymore. I just want this to be over so I can sit back and gather my thoughts for a while and figure things out."

"Being a cop is what you always wanted. Is that not true anymore?"

"I really don't know," I said. And I didn't. "I just know I want this to be over. However that happens."

"I believe you'll do the right thing, Danny. And I believe God has a plan for you. Do you believe that?"

I sighed. "I believe in me," I said.

"You sound tired," he said.

"I am. I'm tired of all of the darkness, man. I'm just worn out. Look, I gotta run," I said. "Take care of yourself."

"I'll call you tomorrow. God bless."

I pulled into the barracks a few minutes later and left the Pathfinder in the back, out of sight. As I walked into the building, I tried to push Brendan's words out of my mind and focus on what was ahead of me tonight. I wanted to wring his neck for calling me now, of all nights, to give me a lecture about right and wrong. He was without a doubt the kindest and most thoughtful person I knew, and he was truly sincere in his faith and beliefs. But he dealt in the theoretical and the spiritual concepts of right and wrong, good and evil. He was working on a timeline that was thousands of years long.

I had to deal with the daily presence of actual, physical evil. It's one thing to sit in a room and contemplate these ideas and it's easy to come to nice, neat conclusions when it's just a thought exercise. But when you're right there, in the moment, and it comes down to it, the answer isn't always so clear.

In fact, most of the time it's a complete toss-up. Even after the fact, it's not always certain whether you'd made the right decision. Brendan knew none of this. He only knew what he read in the Bible and what Rome told him. The real world was a mystery to him. I loved him for his sincerity and honesty and I admired his faith and moral certitude, but we were different people.

And the way I figured it, the world needed both of us.

The briefing was in a large conference room near the cafeteria and it was mostly filled by the time I walked in. Murray was on one side of the table with his team, Winthrop was at the head of the table--even though he was barely involved--and Tex and Moore were on the other side. I took the chair next to Tex. There were briefing packets in front of each of us, and as I flipped through mine, I saw a detailed topo map of the area in Duxbury, a Google Earth aerial view with streets and houses marked and a detailed rundown on who we were after and what we expected to occur. I'd written that last bit with Tex, and we'd been as explicit as we could be about what DeSilva, Alves, Maglia and the rest of them had done and what we should expect from them.

"Let's get going," Winthrop said. "Teixeira, Tobin? Go ahead."

"Thank you, sir," Tex said, standing up. "Y'all have seen the briefing docs and you know what we're up to here. There are a few things I want to highlight, and then I'll let Murray talk about the tactical plan. First, there are two separate crews involved here and both of them have serious violent histories. On just this case, we have eleven bodies that we know about, and we think that DeSilva's group is probably good for another six or eight beyond that in the last few years. They don't look like much, but don't underestimate them. Expect them all to be armed and expect them all to start shooting at the first sign of a problem. Second, we don't know exactly how many people we're dealing with. Our best guess is something like ten. But we could be off by fifty percent either way. So be aware of that. And third, there's a decent chance that this thing is a set-up. The beginning of this case was basically a big fuck-up by DeSilva's people, who were supposed to deliver the women to Maglia's crew, but somehow ended up killing them instead. So you can imagine how that went over. This is supposed to be a kind of peace offering to make up for that mess, but there's no guarantee that it won't turn out to be a shitshow."

Murray: "If they start shooting each other before you guys make your move, what do we do?"

"I think we sit tight. If we wade in there, we either end up in the crossfire or we shoot all of our suspects. I don't want either one of those. If it comes to that, we're only really interested in DeSilva and his people. The others are just props."

"Won't be easy telling them apart out there," one of the tac guys said.

"No, but our CI says DeSilva's crew will be coming in all at once with the truck carrying the girls. So, at least at the start, we should have some sort of idea who's who."

"What else?" Tex said, looking at me.

"Just remember that there are a bunch of houses out there and we may have some citizens wandering around. Try not to shoot them, even though they are from Duxbury," I said.

Tex nodded to Murray, who walked to the rear wall, where a whiteboard was mounted. He sketched out a rough picture of the area, which was essentially a fat little peninsula hanging off the southern end of Duxbury's small land mass.

"Wait. This meeting is happening inside your prostate?" a tac officer said. The room broke apart with nervous laughter and even Winthrop gave a little smile.

Murray waited for the noise to die down. "That's actually a drawing of your wife's saggy ass," he said. "I know it's a little small, but I only have the one wall to work with here. Now, can I continue?"

"Yes sir."

"Uh huh. Not much to add to what Tex said, but I did want to point out that we've had a trooper in plainclothes in there for about two hours now, getting a read on the situation and trying to keep an eye on how many civilians are around," he said. "He won't be a hundred percent sure who's in there when we arrive, but it's better than nothing."

He pointed to the top of the whiteboard. "We come in from up here, split and set up on each side. My team: We wait for Tex and Tobin to move and then we go in fast and loud. We want to be on them as quickly as possible, overwhelm them and end it. The goal, as always, is zero shots fired. We've let the Duxbury cops know we're going to be in there tonight, but we're not bringing them in, just because we want to keep this tight and as quiet as possible. Questions?"

There were none.

"Let's go then."

Moore caught my arm as we filed out. "I'm gonna tag along," he said. "If Alves is going, he's going to go get DeSilva first, so Davis can handle that."

"He OK with that plan?"

"Yeah. I talked to him this evening. He's good."

"OK then. You remember how to fire your gun?"

"I point the part with the hole at the bad guys, right?"

"Last I checked," I said.

Twenty-Eight

I left the Pathfinder and rode with Tex and Moore in the Outback. The tac team rode in a black Expedition behind us. It was just after nine o'clock when we rolled out of the parking lot. It was a quick, thirty-minute ride over to Duxbury and we kept quiet most of the way. As we got off the highway and began to make our way through the residential area on the way to the meeting spot. Tex left the radio off and I could see the tension on his face as we passed underneath the street lights on the deserted streets of the small town.

The air was still thick and doughy, even though the sun had set more than an hour and a half ago, and I could see the yellow moon peeking out periodically as clouds swept past overhead. There were some thunderstorms banging around up in Brockton and Weymouth, and the weather service was making noises about them popping up down here later. I spent the ride going over the plan in my head and trying to avoid thinking about Caroline, and wasn't having any luck. I'd meant to call her this afternoon before we got going, but I got caught up in the planning and the discussions with JD and Brendan. By the time I'd remembered, it was in the middle of the briefing and I was screwed. Plenty of time for that later.

As Tex made the turn off Bay onto Standish, I could see the silhouette of the Myles Standish monument looming ahead. The huge pillar--and the oddly small statue of the bloodthirsty captain himself that stood atop it--were obscured by the darkness, but I could picture the little figure of Standish, one hand pointing out to the Atlantic. Why someone would build such an elaborate monument to such a miserable, brutal guy was beyond me, but I'd long ago given up trying to figure out what made people do what they do.

It made my head hurt.

We followed the road all the way down to where it turned into Crescent and bent back north and west toward the park and the monument. Tex made a full circle of the park and then stopped back at the northern edge where we'd come in. The park itself wasn't much to look at--a few acres of scrub pines with some hiking trails winding in and out. But I could see why DeSilva and Maglia had picked it: It was secluded, but not completely isolated, and even though there was really only one road in and out, there were plenty of other escape options.

The park was encircled by a small group of houses that lined the coast of the small peninsula. If things went badly, it wouldn't be hard for one or both of the crews to split up and find hiding spots in the area until they could get out. The water still worried me. Most of the nearby houses had their own private docks, and it would be simple enough for them to have a boat waiting a couple of hundred yards off shore ready to come in and pick up a load of people at one of the docks. By the time the owner of the house figured out what was going on--if he even noticed--they'd be on the boat and gone. I didn't think it was going to get that far, but operations like this tended to take weird turns and twists and I'd seen much simpler ones go south for no apparent reason.

Tex left the Outback on a dead-end side street that led down to the water and we hiked it back up the park. We waited at the southern end of the park while Murray and his team set up. He'd be placing three men near the entrance to the northern edge of the area, where Crescent met two other roads. Anyone coming into the park by car would have to come through that crossroads. Those guys had descriptions of the vehicles we knew each crew to drive and they would watch all of the traffic coming in and alert us when they started showing up. The biggest problem we had now, though, was that we didn't know what sort of vehicle the women would be coming in. There were only so many things that could carry fifteen or so people, though, so we'd just have to wing it and hope there wasn't a string of RVs and box trucks coming in.

A few minutes after Tex, Moore and I got into the park, Murray materialized out of the pines. Like the rest of his guys, he was dressed in the all-black tac team uniform, including a Kevlar helmet and body armor. The three of us were wearing vests, too, and I was sweating like a whore in church under mine.

"We're set," Murray said.

"What's the report from your advance guy?" I asked.

"Flynn. Mostly clear. There's a couple of teenagers sitting on one of the picnic tables, but we're going to go scare them off in a minute. He's going to go by acting like a crazy drunk and get 'em out of there."

"OK, we're going to make our way up toward the monument and wait to hear from you. We'll be ready."

Murray walked back into the trees and was gone. We went in after him, taking our time getting up to the center of the park. I knew that the other three tac guys were around here somewhere, but we'd never be able to see them. Tex was still quiet on the walk up to the monument. I couldn't see his face in the dark, but I had a good idea that it was wrinkled with concentration and tension. He often got like this before a confrontation or operation like this, and I'd learned to just let him be and not try to talk him out of it. We came to the edge of the clearing where the monument stood, and the moon was fully out, bathing the pillar in yellowish light, lending it an eerie glow. No one was around and we hung in the shadows of the pines, just inside the treeline, waiting.

After a few minutes, a quiet voice came over the radio. "Dark Cadillac coming in. Heading south on Crescent." Alves and DeSilva.

"Copy," Tex said. We stayed put and waited some more. I squatted down on my heels and bounced back up a few times, trying to keep my legs loose. Tex was walking in small circles in the trees, his running shoes making soft, muffled sounds on the carpet of pine needles underfoot. Moore sat calmly, his back against a tree. Intel guys knew how to handle the waiting.

Thirty seconds later, another voice on the radio: "Cadillac stopped halfway down Crescent in a turnaround. Still pointing south. No movement from the driver."

That was fifty yards to our west, through the trees. "On the way, heading in from the east," Tex said.

We started walking that way, moving slowly, picking our way through the pines, the moonlight filtering through the canopy and lighting our way. Halfway there, Murray popped up on the radio.

"Heads up. Tanker truck coming in. Looks like a septic truck or water wagon. Not sure. Headed south on Crescent."

We quickened our pace, moving into a half jog. We got to the edge of the park and could see the Caddy about thirty or forty yards south of us on the road. The driver was apparently still in the car. We stayed well inside the trees and crept from tree to tree, making our way slowly down the road. I could hear the truck coming up behind us, easing through in a low gear. We got to within about fifteen yards of the turnaround and took up positions behind thick pines. I could see the Cadillac clearly through the trees from my spot and hear the engine idling evenly.

Tex was six or eight feet farther down and was facing the opposite way, back up Crescent, watching for the tanker. He pulled his gun, holding it low pointed at the ground. I did the same, flicking off the safety and reflexively patting the rear pocket of my jeans where my extra clips were. We crouched like that for a minute or so as the truck rumbled down toward us. As it came even with us, I could see the writing on the side reading "Eastern Septic." Little bit late at night for a visit from the honey wagon. It stopped right in front of us, maybe fifty or so yards from the Cadillac and the driver cut the engine but stayed in the cab.

I pulled the disposable cell from my pocket and sent JD a text: STAND BY. He responded twenty seconds later: READY. We stayed in our spots for another four or five minutes and no one in either the truck or DeSilva's car moved. I snapped my fingers softly at Tex and spread my hands out wide: What's going on? He held up one hand: Wait. A minute later, Murray was in our ears.

"Here we go. Dark 5-series coming in. South on Crescent, coming at ya." Maglia.

Tex responded with a double tap on the radio key. Murray's team at the northern edge would be blocking off the road in now and Murray would be coming down Standish on the other side of the park in the Expedition. He'd stay out of sight on the lower end of the peninsula, waiting for us to move. His other three guys should be making their way toward us through the trees.

The moon had disappeared now, and there was almost no ambient light at all, just the glow of some streetlights farther up Crescent. I heard a low, long rumble of thunder that sounded like it was maybe a mile or so away. Headlights appeared around the curve, coming down from the park entrance. Just as the big sedan stopped about fifty yards behind the truck, the first fat drops of rain began to hit the pavement. It was sporadic at first, but within a half a minute it was a steady downpour. The rain wasn't reaching us through the trees yet, but I could see it splattering on the road

384

and the vehicles, and it was coming down hard. As we waited, I could see the glow of a cell phone screen come on in the BMW and a couple of seconds later the same in the Cadillac.

I pulled the disposable, texted JD: NOW.

A few seconds later, the driver of the BMW got out and started walking down the road toward the truck. I saw a bright flash of lightning off to the west and the trees trembled with the thunderclap that followed a second later. Water shook off the pine boughs above us, showering the forest floor with rain and needles. I was completely soaked now and getting antsy. My legs were stiffening and I could feel the adrenaline starting to pump. I needed to move.

As the driver of the BMW--who at this range looked a lot like Maglia--passed the front of the truck, the Cadillac's front doors opened and two men climbed out. The rain was pounding down now, hitting the street so hard it seemed to be coming up from the ground. The BMW driver was pointing at the phone in his hand and shouting something above the rain and thunder. The two men from the Cadillac stayed behind their doors and the driver put one hand up in a STOP sign, telling the other man to stay where he was. I crept over to where Tex and Moore were and put my hand on Tex's shoulder.

"Ready?" I asked.

He held up one finger, signaling me to wait. "I want to see the truck change hands," he said.

The phone in my pocket vibrated and I pulled out the disposable, expecting a message from JD. But the phone was dark. I felt the vibration again and yanked my iPhone from my other pocket. Davis was calling. What the hell? He knew what we were doing out here. Why was he bothering me? I hit ignore and shoved it back in my jeans.

"When we go," Tex said, "Tobin takes the truck driver, I take the BMW guy, Moore, you cover us."

Another peal of thunder detonated right on top of us and the rain was coming down sideways now. Out of the corner of my eye, I caught some movement to my right and glanced over to see the truck driver climbing down from the cab. In front of the tanker, Maglia, or whoever it was, stood shouting at the two other men, still holding his phone up. We slid a few steps forward and were no more than thirty feet away from him now, just inside the cover of the trees. I saw Maglia's free hand start moving slowly toward the small of his back. The two men outside the Cadillac stayed where they were, maybe too far away to see what was happening.

"Shit," Tex said. He keyed his radio. "Move, move, move. NOW!"

Twenty-Nine

As we came out of our crouches and broke from the treeline, the truck driver, seeing Maglia's move now, suddenly sprinted for him, pulling a handgun from underneath his t-shirt as he ran. We were only ten yards from the street, but it looked like we didn't have a chance to get there. I angled for the driver, my gun coming up. Tex went for the Cadillac, staying on the grass and out of the potential line of fire. The driver had a head start on me, but I had the angle and I was going hard. Only a few steps now, five, four.

I hit the pavement, two steps and launched myself at the driver. He saw it at the last moment and turned, his gun free now and coming up at me. My right shoulder slammed into his midsection, and I felt his gun hit my head as I threw my full weight against him. We were both airborne for a half second and I saw a brilliant flash of light and then heard a dull thud as we crashed into the front quarter panel of the truck. The driver was between me and the truck and his head bounced off the truck's fender and snapped forward, hitting the top of my head.

We skidded on the wet pavement, him on top of me, the gravel and blacktop tearing my shirt to ribbons. I could feel bits of rock and whatever else shredding my back as we came to a stop a few feet from the truck. I heard tires screeching somewhere and voices shouting and then a pair of gunshots, followed by several more. The driver was dead weight on top of me. He was out cold, so I rolled him twice, onto his stomach, pulled a

387

zip tie from my pocket and cuffed him and left him next to the truck.

I came up into a crouch, and peeked my head around the side of the truck. A body lay on the street near the driver's side door of the Cadillac. I could see the Expedition a few yards behind the car, its headlights on, doors open, shadows moving in front of the lights. My ears were ringing from the collision with the truck fender and I shook my head, trying to clear it. Duckwalked forward a few feet and saw Tex on the ground with the BMW driver, rolling around, a gun on the ground next to them. I took three long strides toward them and caught the driver in the ribs with a solid right foot. He went limp and Tex flipped him and banged his head off the pavement once, twice, flipped him again and cuffed him. It was Maglia.

Tex picked his gun up off the ground, looked at me. "You OK?"

"Yup."

Moore came over from the trees, eyes wide.

"What happened there?" he said.

We all ducked as someone unloaded an automatic weapon somewhere behind us. We ran to the side of the road near the treeline and got low. Another long burst. Sounded like an AR-15, one of our guys. I risked a look up and saw two of the tac officers advancing on the BMW, rifles up. I tapped Tex on the shoulder and pointed that way and took off in a low run, staying inside the trees. He came behind me, Moore behind him. The tanker was still sitting in the middle of the road, door open.

"This is Tobin. We are coming up through the trees from the south toward the BMW," I said into the radio.

"Copy," Murray's voice came back. "We have the Cadillac locked down. One bad guy down."

We got close and I could see that the two tac officers were trying to coax someone out of the passenger side of the car. The BMW was parked at an angle, so that it was pointed toward the trees and the driver's side was obscured from our view. I could see one person inside, but the rain pouring down the windshield made it impossible to tell what he was doing.

"Hands! Now, motherfucker! Hands out the window and open the door from the outside!"

The passenger didn't move. No one moved. The tac officers were still yelling at the passenger, screaming at him to open the door and get out. I was flat on the ground on my stomach, trying to stay out of the way. Tex was just to my left and as I crawled forward a few feet for a better vantage point, I saw movement underneath the car. I laid still and waited and saw it again. It was only visible as a disturbance of the pitch black behind the vehicle. Someone was back there.

I lifted up slowly and turned to Tex. "Behind the car. Someone is back there," I said. "Lay down and have a look."

He dropped to his stomach and popped up on his elbows a few seconds later. "I see it."

While we were talking, the tac officer closest to the BMW began moving around to the passenger side, gun pointed at the window. As he moved, still shouting at the passenger, the figure behind the car began moving in the opposite direction, circling away from him and toward us. His dark form blended with the Beemer, but as he cleared the rear corner nearest to us, I could see he was holding a long gun of some kind, maybe a shotgun. Couldn't tell for sure.

"Shit," I said softly.

"Aw hell," Tex said.

The car was maybe ten yards away from us and there was nothing between us and the gunman but sheets of rain and a couple of pine trees. The gunman was crouched on his heels, creeping forward bit by bit, the sounds of his movements obscured by the fury of the rain and thunder. I felt Tex shift next to me, and I moved with him, both of us crawling forward in the pine straw on our stomachs. The gunman was next to the rear driver's side door now, and because the front door was still open, he had good cover from the tac guy standing in front of the car. His back was to us, but he was still a few yards in front of us on the street, so we had a three-quarters profile look at him. As he shifted a bit on his haunches, I could see now he was holding not a shotgun, but an assault rifle, something with a long magazine. Jesus.

Tex on the radio, quiet as he could: "Armed suspect on driver's side of the BMW. Looks like an assault rifle. Tobin and I are in the woods on that side and have a clear view of suspect. Murray, please advise."

"Hold your position. I'm coming up from the south through the trees behind you. Units four and five, be advised there is an armed suspect on the driver's side of that car. You have two officers in the trees to your east. Get that passenger out of the car now."

The officer in front of the Beemer stood stock still, but I noticed him angle his head slightly to his right, toward us, and nod. The other officer was still on the other side of the car and the passenger finally reached his hands out the open window. I could see through the open driver's door as the trooper popped the door and yanked the passenger out and shoved him to the ground, all in one motion. He put his knee in the man's back, cuffed him and dragged him to the grass on the side of the road and then gave him a shove with his foot so the man fell sideways onto the grass.

The gunman snuck a look through the driver's door, saw what was happening, and made his move. He sprang to his feet, bringing the rifle up to his shoulder as he rose, and took aim across the roof of the car as the trooper stood up on the opposite side. I saw all of this happening and took note of the tac officer in front of the car swinging his AR-15 toward the gunman. At the same time, I was raising up on my elbows, leveling my gun at him. I was aware of Tex doing the same on my left, both of us firing at once. The tac guy cut loose in the same instant, and the gunman was thrown backward and hit the ground, the rifle clattering back toward us.

I popped up and kicked the gun back into the trees and the tac officer walked around the driver's door, his gun still pointed down at the suspect. I bent down and checked him for other weapons and then for a pulse. He was gone.

Thirty

Moore came out and checked the backseat of the car and found it empty. Murray came running up the road and looked at us and then down at the guy on the ground.

"He took a shot?" he asked.

"Yeah. Raised up on your guy. He lost." My voice sounded jittery and oddly high-pitched in my ears.

"Who dropped him?" Murray said.

I looked at the tac guy and at Tex, who shrugged. "We all fired," I said.

Murray bent down and looked at the man's chest, which was shredded, the red blood mixing with the rain to form a pink mess on his shirt. "OK. He's dead either way," he said. He turned to the officer who'd fired and said, "Tom, you OK?"

"Sure."

"Allright. Head back down to the Expedition, get some water, decompress and I'll be there in a few minutes."

"What happened down there with the other car?" Tex asked.

"When you guys took out the truck driver and the other suspect, the Cadillac guys panicked. They turned and saw us coming and the driver popped off a couple of shots as we came out of the truck. We took him down and then the passenger ran off into the trees. I had to chase his ass down. So we got two from the Caddy, one, two here and the guy from the truck. That it?"

"Doesn't seem right," I said. "We thought there'd be at least three or four others." I looked down at the guy on the ground, seeing his face for the first time. Didn't recognize him. "Lemme see the guys you got from the other car."

We walked down the road, the rain letting up some now as the storm moved off to sea. Maglia still lay on his back on the street, his eyes closed against the rain. I kicked his arm as we went by.

"The fuck happened?" he said, looking up at me.

"Don't know, but you're gonna tell me in a minute. Stay put."

"Ha ha."

"You guys clear the truck?" Tex asked.

"The cab, yeah. Haven't opened the tank. Thought we'd wait for you guys," Murray said.

The Cadillac driver was lying face down on the pavement, both arms pinned underneath him. He was too big to be Alves, and when Murray picked his head up and turned his face, I recognized him as one of DeSilva's bodyguards. I looked at Tex, who was running his hands over his head. What the hell?

"Where's the other one?" I asked.

"Back here," Murray said, leading us around to the rear of the Expedition. The tailgate was up and there was a man sitting on the ground in the shelter of the gate, his hands cuffed behind him and a pair of nasty red welts on his forehead.

"Ah, come on!" Tex said. "Who the hell are you?"

The man said something in Portuguese. Tex responded, the frustration clear in his voice.

"Christ. Guess what his name is. Go ahead."

"Whitey Bulger?" I said.

"Close. Armando DeSilva. He's a nephew or second cousin or some garbage," Tex said. He looked down at the man on the pavement, who was obviously confused by all of this, especially Tex's anger.

Tex kicked him in the leg. "Where is everyone?" he asked. "Why is no one here?"

The man smiled and nodded. "Yes," he said. "Hello."

"Let's go see what's in the shitwagon," I said. We walked up the street to the tanker and I climbed up the ladder on the back and twisted the wheel on the hatch. I braced for the smell and got it, but it wasn't what I was expecting. Instead of the stench of years-old excrement and decomposing varmints, I got human sweat, urine and rotting food.

"Hand me up a flashlight," I called. Tex tossed me his Maglite and I shined it down into the tanker and counted ten women that I could see squatting in the bottom of the tank. I couldn't see all the way to the front of the space because of the angle, but there was probably room for six or eight more anyway. The women were surrounded by crumpled soda cans, plastic wrappers and plastic water bottles. They shielded their eyes from the flashlight's beam and the rain coming in through the hatch.

A makeshift metal ladder was welded to the inside of the tank and reached down to within a couple of feet of the floor. One of the women began climbing up, and I put my hand out to stop her.

"No no, stay there. Stay," I said. To Tex: "Switch places with me. Need your language skills up here."

I went down, Tex went up and began talking to the women in Portuguese. My phone buzzed again and I looked at the screen and saw three missed calls and two text messages, all from Davis. I'd completely forgotten about his call from earlier. Damn.

I checked the texts first: DESILVA NOT LEAVING. NO MOVEMENT HERE. Oh man...

The other one: ALVES HERE IN THE S CLASS. MOVING NOW.

The last message was from about fifteen minutes earlier, when we'd been in the middle of the firefight. Alves wasn't coming here with DeSilva. So where were they going?

I looked at Moore: "Did you guys ever take the GPS tag off the Mercedes?"

"No. Why?"

"I think Alves and DeSilva are headed somewhere else. Davis texted me and said Alves showed up at his house in the S-Class and they're moving," I said. I handed my phone to Tex. "Check it out."

"How long ago?" Moore said.

"About fifteen minutes."

"I have the GPS receiver in my car."

"Lemme call Davis first, see where they are," I said. Tex handed back my phone and I hit Davis's number and got no answer. I hung up and tried again, still nothing.

396

"OK, let's go. Tex, lemme get your keys. I don't like where this is headed."

Tex tossed me his keys. "I'll stay here and process this mess. Call me when you figure out what's happening," he said.

"I'm gone."

Thirty-One

Moore and I ran back down Crescent to where the cars were parked, going pretty much all-out. I grabbed the GPS handset from him.

"Keep trying Davis," I said. "If you get him, call me."

"Got it."

I ducked into the Outback and checked the display. The triangle icon for the S-Class was damn near on top of my location. I fumbled with the handset for a second, found the right button and zoomed in. The triangle moved a little farther west and eventually came to a stop. On the cranberry pond. Alves's house.

I sped through the backstreets as quickly as I could. The rain had picked up again, and there was standing water everywhere in the low spots. I crossed over Route 3 on East Street and pulled up to the dirt road next to the pond. From what my headlights landed on, I could see there was no way I was going any farther in the car. I'd have to hoof it. The road was a complete quagmire, submerged under inches of water. Not a chance that the Outback was getting through there. The GPS showed the Mercedes as being right here somewhere. Probably either at Alves's house or bogged down on the way in. I grabbed an old Bourne Braves hat out of the back seat to give me a little protection from the rain and started walking in.

I called Moore; still no answer from Davis. I didn't want to think about the possibilities here, because none of them was good. If Alves had reached some kind of

399

inflection point and no longer cared what happened to him--and that's the vibe I'd gotten from him this afternoon--then this could be awful. Davis not answering gave me chills. Alves likely wouldn't think twice about taking out a cop at this point, not with everything else he'd done and what had been done to him.

I picked my way through the muck in the trees that ran parallel to the pond, staying close to the road.

The ground in the woods wasn't quite as muddy as the road, but it was slow going and I was getting frustrated quickly. Five minutes after I went in, my left foot went into a deep hole and when I pulled it out, my shoe was gone. Just gone. I pulled off the other shoe, stripped off my socks and started walking. I moved to the side of the road, near the edge of the trees where there was a small berm that was relatively dry. With the rain and darkness, I wasn't sure how far I'd gone but I had a sense that I was running out of time. It had been more than a half hour since Davis's last message. Gotta go.

I started running easily along the berm, trying to land as softly as I could. The ground was still sort of mushy, but I was moving much faster and within a couple of minutes I could see the small house taking shape through the trees. It was just a black spot in the middle of the dark woods, a series of right angles and straight lines where there should only be randomness and roundness. I saw just one weak light on in the window facing the pond, but couldn't discern any movement inside the house yet.

I slowed as I approached the clearing where the house sat and crouched down, trying to listen and watch, see if anything was happening. The rain had stopped again, and there was little sound aside from the water dripping off the trees. Nothing seemed to be moving in the house, or at least not near the window. Creeping along the treeline toward the front of the house, I saw the Mercedes in the driveway. I moved into the shadow of the car and looked inside. Empty. I had no desire to kick down the door on the house and surprise them, but I wasn't sure what the other options were. If Davis was in there...

I pulled my gun and rounded behind the car and slid along the driver's side, keeping the car between me and the house. I watched the front windows for a bit, but there was no signs of life, so I ran low and fast to the side of the house, staying close to the bushes. I could see the storage shed from there--both of the doors were open and the shop light was on. Stuck my head around the corner of the house--nothing. I didn't hear any sounds coming from the shed, so I took one more look around the back, counted to three and ran over to the shed, my bare feet hardly making a sound on the wet pine needles and scrub grass.

I crouched in the lee of the open door and peeked in through the opening between the door and the frame. It took a few seconds for my eyes to adjust to the light in there, but when they did I wished they hadn't. There was a large puddle of blood near the back wall, dark red splatters and drips dotted the rest of the floor. No one was inside. I took a glance at the rear windows of the house, decided it was too late now anyway and moved around the door and into the shed.

I stepped around the blood droplets and smears and went to the spot where the puddle was, beneath the band saw. A hand lay in the puddle, the fingers curled upward as if reaching for something. I bent down to get a better look and saw that the blood on the floor was still quite wet. The wound on the hand was jagged and raw, one of the bones sticking out sideways and the tissue was still warm to the touch.

The victim had still been alive when this was done. No doubt.

I looked up at the band saw; I thought we'd taken all of the blades during the search earlier. But there was a blade in there--a rusted one, the teeth dull and rounded off and now slick with blood.

My heart was pounding now, my thoughts spinning as I thought of Davis out here somewhere with Alves. No idea where they were or whether that was even his hand, but if it was, Davis would have probably ten or fifteen minutes before he bled out. Less than that before he lost consciousness. And I hadn't heard any screaming on my way here, so I'd already lost at least half of that time.

ShitshitshitshitSHIT.

This was not what I was here for. I did not sign up to be finding disembodied hands in the tool sheds of genteel, well-mannered engineers. I paced in circles in the shed for a few seconds, trying to gather my thoughts. OK. OK. The hand was just taken off, the doors to the shed are open, he's probably carrying or maybe dragging Davis, so Alves had to be close by. I hadn't seen any signs of them on the way in from the road or in the front of the property.

That left the house. And the pond.

I looked around the shed, grabbed a flashlight from a shelf over the workbench. All pretense was gone at this point, so I sprinted to the back of the house and looked in the window. It was mostly dark inside, with just a small table lamp glowing, but there was clearly no one in there. I listened for a second, just to be sure, then took off running toward the pond. The clear ground surrounding the house was ankle deep mud, but I was loose now and moved lightly, landing on the balls of my feet to avoid sinking into the muck. I felt my phone buzz in my pocket but left it there. No time.

No time.

The moon broke through the clouds as I ran, giving me a little light. I felt the ground under my feet change, growing harder and rougher, more rocks. Getting closer. I kept my eyes on the ground ahead of me, looking for pine cones and stones and other debris, and I had to stop short to avoid splashing into the pond. I stood and got my bearings for a second--I was at the northwestern corner of the pond, the opposite side of the water from where we'd pulled the bodies out last week.

Even with the intermittent moonlight, I couldn't see much of anything out here, but the sense of deja vu was overwhelming. The noise of the cars flying past on the highway. The smell of the pines in the background, overridden by the stench of the foul water in the pond. The sense that there was something hideous and awful and pitiless was waiting here. It was making my skin crawl. I wanted to be done with this place and these people. I wanted to rid myself of all of it and all of them.

Thunder rumbled off to the west again and I could see another line of clouds overtaking the clear skies. I needed to find Alves and Davis somewhere out here, but I didn't want to risk turning on the flashlight. He'd see me immediately, and I needed to hold onto the only advantage I had, which was the element of surprise. I moved to my right slowly making my way around the edge of the pond. Walking along the western edge of the pond, I heard what sounded like an animal whimpering. The whining was soft, but high-pitched, pained. It was ahead of me, but I couldn't tell how far. I went into a quick jog but didn't get more than a few strides before a gunshot cracked. The bullet hit the water to my left and I dove right, away from the pond and into the mud.

The muzzle flash had blinded me in the dark and I closed my eyes tight, trying to picture in my mind's eye where the shot had come from. It had to be in front of me. I stayed down, but raised my head. No movement, no sound. And then a flash of lightning across the sky. There. Two people. Maybe forty or fifty yards ahead of me, on the edge of the pond. One standing, the other sitting or kneeling. I crawled forward a few yards in the mud, trying to keep a mental picture of where they were. The second shot skipped off a rock to my right, pinging off into the woods.

"Far enough, detective. No more."

I was close now, no more than fifty feet I figured. Crawled another few feet, working it out in my head. I guessed there was a better than even chance that Davis was going to die out here, even if I got to him right now. I needed to get this done.

"That's a cop you have there, Alves," I shouted. "A cop. You need to make the right decision here."

"You are misinformed, detective. You are the only police here. This is just a small family dispute here."

"That's DeSilva with you?"

"See? I knew you were a good investigator."

If he was only out here with his uncle, where did that leave Davis? Nowhere good, I thought. More whimpering and groaning, I guessed from DeSilva. He sounded like he was in bad shape. I wasn't close enough yet to make a move, but I had the sense that it might be too late for him already. Either he was going to bleed out or Alves was going to kill him outright. This didn't feel like a scare tactic to me. I needed to keep him occupied long enough to get within range so I could make a move. What that move would be was the question.

"Look, Alves, we know what DeSilva did. We know he killed all the women we found here the other day, including your wife and your daughter. I don't blame you for being pissed here. It was me, I'd kill him. Without a thought."

405

I slid forward in the mud, staying low but keeping my head up, looking for movement. And shots. One yard, two yards, three. Closing in.

"But you don't want to do that. Don't make that mistake," I said. Still the whimpering from DeSilva.

"And why is that, detective? You want to do the job yourself?" Alves said.

He wasn't wrong. And he wasn't far away. Inside of fifteen yards now, probably.

"Because then you'll be just like him," I said. Another slither, another yard. "You'll be a piece of shit, a killer. And you can't take that back."

He laughed at that, a joyless dry chuckle. "Maybe I was wrong about you after all, detective. Maybe you're not such a good investigator, because as far as I can tell, you haven't figured out a single thing. You think killing my uncle would make me like *him*? I will *never* be like him!" Shouting now, pissed. "He's a disgrace, a child raper, a pathetic, disgusting man who has ruined more lives than you can imagine."

"I am not--" DeSilva said, the words cut off by what must have been a kick to the stomach. He made a hissing sound as the air went out of him.

"I could live a hundred years and spend the rest of my days doing nothing but killing and never come near the damage that he has done," Alves continued. "And you think you know the worst of what he's done? Tell me this: Who killed Andres?"

"Maglia. Or one of his people."

Another flash of lightning exploded just to our east then, and I nearly jumped when I saw how close I was to them. They were perhaps twenty or twenty-five feet ahead and to my left. Alves had flinched at the lightning and I could see that he was holding a handgun of some kind and DeSilva was sitting on the ground, his back to Alves. It was still too far, though. Even if I could recall exactly where they were, flicked on the flashlight and shot right away, I'd have as good a chance of hitting a car on the street behind them as hitting Alves.

"That's right. But that doesn't really matter. What matters is that Paolo allowed it to happen. Actually, that's not quite right. He *caused* it to happen. Yes, that's the correct word. He caused it."

"You're not making much sense here," I said. "Maglia killed him as payback for Paolo screwing up the delivery and all of the women being killed."

"You still don't see it. Andres wasn't payback, he was *payment*. Our business has been drying up for a year now, mostly because Andres was mentally unstable and had angered so many people we used to deal with, demanding more money or delivering sick and diseased women. We had almost no customers left."

"Except Maglia's people." Crawled forward another couple of feet, almost there...

"Yes. And when things...went bad the last time with them, that was it. They were done with us. There had been other problems recently, and they couldn't stand Andres," Alves said. "I believe he was somewhat retarded, to be honest."

407

"Shut up, Joao! My son was--" Another kick, and DeSilva groaned badly. I anticipated it this time, and moved quickly, closing another six or eight feet on them. I was close enough now that I could see Alves silhouetted against the moonlit sky. He was between me and DeSilva, so I couldn't get a sense of what shape he was in.

"I got that feeling myself," I said.

"Yes. But this one"--he gave DeSilva another shot to the ribs--"he couldn't understand how much damage Andres was doing until the women died. Then he saw it and he saw that his last remaining customer was going to leave, and that would be the end for him, too."

I saw it now. Ah, Christ. "So he set Andres up for Maglia. He handed him over," I said.

"Now you see? Now you understand what kind of man this is? A man who can kill his own son for money. For *money*."

Thirty-Two

Alves was feeling pretty talkative and I didn't want to discourage him from continuing. But I could think of only one reason for him to be telling me all of this: He knew that neither he nor DeSilva was leaving here alive.

He was here to end it. And I was in the middle of it.

"He killed your family, too, didn't he?" I said. "Your wife and daughter, they were in that shipment and he killed them all."

DeSilva spoke up. "I didn't kill them. He did."

Alves was quiet for once. No response, no kick to DeSilva's ribs. The more I heard from these two, the more I just wanted to push them both into the pond and walk away. Who lives like this? Was there some cave down in Brazil where they manufactured these shitheels and stored them in a cool, dark place until they needed a new one? Just plucked them from the ceiling and sent them up to the world to create chaos?

"My men might have ended up shooting them, but it was his fault," DeSilva said. "Without him, none of this would have happened and we'd all still be making money."

"The drugs were yours, right?" I asked. I was still laying behind them and to their left. I didn't know when Alves was going to snap and make his move, but it seemed to be coming soon. I couldn't see him standing here for long, eating this shit from the two of us. I would've shot me ten minutes ago.

409

"My retirement plan," he said flatly. All of the emotion was gone from his voice now. "It had been working for more than two years and there was a lot of money coming in. Everything was fine."

"What about Paolo's wife and daughter?" I asked.

"He stole from me, so I stole from him," Alves said flatly. *The hands*, I thought.

"You were working with Delia. He moved the drugs through the club."

"Yes."

"But that last shipment was delayed on the way here and the girls started dying off, right? The balloons were breaking open in their stomachs and they were being poisoned. So then the driver figures out what's going on, maybe he checks on them at a rest stop, sees that they're dying and sick, and calls your uncle. And he thinks about and says, fuck it, they're dying anyway. Kill 'em. That about right?"

Silence.

"And he knew full well that your wife and daughter were in there. I bet he didn't even think twice about it. Product is unusable? Dump it. Always more women willing to whore themselves out for a trip to America. No need to worry about one or two here and there."

More silence. Cars going by on the highway, bats zipping around overhead, collecting a midnight snack, pines creaking, branches rustling behind us. My phone vibrated again, but I couldn't risk Alves seeing the lighted screen, so I ignored it.

"I was there," Alves said after a while.

410

It was so soft I almost couldn't make out the words.

"When he got that call, I was sitting next to him. We were sitting on a bench at Nelson Park, eating ice cream cones. He took the call, listened for a few seconds, and said, 'Do it.' He put the phone away and continued eating his cone. I remember this, because I was watching the children on the playground while he talked, and I thought, Soon, I will bring my grandchildren here."

"No, you won't," I said. I wasn't sure why I was antagonizing him, but I just had no sympathy for either one of them. I didn't want to hear his sob story or start to feel bad for him. I just wanted this to end. I'd had enough of all of this, the excuses, the rationalizations, the fucking diseased mentality that all of these people had.

Enough.

I pushed up onto my hands and knees and then leapt to my feet, bringing my gun up and leveling it and the flashlight all at once at the spot where I figured Alves was. I was right about where he was, but he saw it coming and was faster. He had his own flashlight and gun pointed at me. He moved the beam up and down my torso, where my armored vest was plainly visible. I kept my flash focused on his upper chest. We were no more than ten feet apart. One shot from either one of us and this would be over. I tried to relax, letting out a deep breath.

"What now?" I said after an uncomfortable minute of silence.

"You've overstayed your welcome," Alves said. His voice was full of venom now, harsh and jagged. "Time to go."

"Go where? I'm here," I said. "Let me take him with me. Believe me when I tell you that thirty years at Walpole is a lot worse than a bullet in the head. We send him in there branded as a pedophile, he'll be begging someone to kill him. Lemme have him."

He laughed. "Your prisons are better than most people's homes in Brazil. Nice try. No, this is my affair and I will finish it myself. Now: go."

I looked down at DeSilva. He was sitting flat on the ground, his legs stretched out in front of him, head hanging down to his chest. He seemed completely resigned to his fate. I couldn't tell whether his arms were restrained, but I got the feeling that even if they weren't he'd still be sitting still. I thought about how difficult it would be to get a conviction on either one of these two in court with the evidence that we had right now. We might get them on the drug-smuggling and the human trafficking, but the murders...I didn't think so. A good lawyer would tear us up.

"What about you?" I said to Alves. "Do you think I won't be able to find you after this?"

"You won't need to look very hard," he said. There was something awful and pitiable in his voice. "As I said, this is a family dispute. And it's about to end. I'd rather not kill you too, but I will if you stay here. Please. Go."

Even with my body armor on, I didn't like my chances at this range. He could put two in my head before I heard the sound of the first shot. I sighed and put my left hand in the air and holstered my gun, letting him see it. I looked at the two of them for a long moment--Alves, no emotion on his face, and DeSilva, simply awaiting his fate, making no effort to escape or change Alves's mind. I tried to imagine how each of them felt in that moment, knowing that the end was here. And it struck me that they had stood by and watched--whether literally or metaphorically--while the same thing had happened to dozens of people in their lives. And they'd done it without a second thought. Why should I care any more than they did? Fuck 'em.

I turned and started walking toward the car. I counted my steps as I went: ten, fifteen, twenty...

The air cracked and I heard a soft thud. I flinched, but kept walking, picking up the pace as I went, trying to get as far away from them as I could. I was about halfway to the car when the second shot came. It reverberated through the trees, echoing against the pines and lingered in the thick night air.

I kept walking.

Thirty-Three

Walking in a daze.

I weaved through the parking lot toward the barracks, felt the eyes of the other troopers on me, didn't care. Couldn't care. Couldn't gather the energy or the emotion. Pushed through the doors and into the hallway, ears ringing, eyes blurry. Saw faces coming toward me, some looking at me, others at their feet. Kept walking. Down the hall, moving by muscle memory, feeling nothing. End of the hall, left turn, right turn, left turn. Knock, wait, open door, sit. Breathe, breathe.

"You have five minutes," Winthrop said. "Talk."

I rubbed my face, ran my hands through my hair. "I'm not sure I have much else to say, really. I mean, what's changed in the last four hours?"

He looked me up and down. "Not your clothes."

"Yeah. Am I here for this? Really? Because I just...I'm not..."

"You're here because I thought you might appreciate a chance to save your job. I thought that maybe you'd come up with some rational explanation for what happened last night. Hell, I'd even settle for a bunch of half-truths and fairy tales and stuff you've picked up in shitty cop shows. Because right now, all I have is what Tex and Murray and the others have told me and that doesn't fit together very well. There are a lot of blank spots here, most notably the giant fucking black hole where the arrests of Alves and DeSilva

415

should be. So why don't you go ahead and see if you can fill those in for me?"

"Captain, my story is not going to change from what I told you last night. Or this morning, or whenever it was. I got to the house, I was looking for Alves and Davis. I didn't see anyone around, checked the shed, found the hand and the blood and then went out to the pond. That's it."

"So why did it take you so long to get in touch with someone after you found the bodies?"

"I had to make sure there was no one else there. I wasn't sure what happened, I still didn't know whether Davis was there somewhere. Nothing was clear."

"Then why not call for backup? You had a half-dozen men five minutes away," he said.

"Look, that's not how I was thinking. I was concerned about the possibility of there being a shooter out there. That was my thought process. And I also knew that the other guys had their hands full over there."

Winthrop nodded. "OK. So you're maintaining that DeSilva and Alves were both dead when you found them? Is that correct?"

"Yeah." I didn't say it with much conviction and it sounded hollow even to me, but Winthrop just nodded again and wrote something on the legal pad in front of him.

"How's Davis?" I asked after a minute.

He shrugged. "Not sure yet. The skull fracture is the big concern. Surgeon said someone probably hit him with a pipe or a piece of metal, something like that.

They got in there and stopped the bleeding, but he was sitting there for a while before Moore found him. Could've been an hour or more. No one's really sure. They're moving him up to Mass General this afternoon to see a brain guy. Might be a while before they know about brain damage or whatever."

I felt nauseated and tasted the hot bitterness of bile in my throat and mouth. I rubbed the back of my neck and looked out the window over Winthrop's shoulder. I couldn't look at him and I didn't want to think about what my delay in calling Tex and Moore might cost Davis. I knew what it was going to cost me, but that I could handle. I never meant for any of this to corrode anyone else. I felt Winthrop's eyes on me and looked over. He gave me a thin smile.

"Not good. Not good." He stood up. "Come see me when you're done."

I left Winthrop's office and walked three doors down the hall to the big conference room. No one looked my way as I went in and depending on the outcome in here, many of the guys in here probably wouldn't bother to spit on me the next time they saw me.

Susan Cooper sat at the head of the long faux oak table, her hands folded in front of her. A laptop was open on the table and a large case file sat next to it. A man I'd never seen before sat to her right, dressed in a black suit, white shirt and thin black tie. He had a yellow legal pad in front of him with an expensive-looking gold pen resting on it. Even from across the room he smelled like a lawyer or a politician. He didn't look at me and the expression on Cooper's face was blank, unreadable. I stood in the doorway, waiting.

"Please close the door and take a seat, detective," Cooper said. Her voice was cool and confident.

I pulled out the chair at the opposite end of the table and slumped into it.

"Before we begin, you should know that there will be a formal disciplinary hearing later this week. This is just a meeting so that I can gather some facts and understand what happened. I've already talked with Captain Winthrop, as well as your partner and some of the other troopers who were involved, so this is your opportunity to explain what happened."

"Who's he?" I said.

"My name is Eric Masters and I'm an attorney with the union. I'm here for your sake, to ensure that everything is done fairly and in your best interest," he said.

"Go screw," I said. "I don't need you here."

"It's not a good idea for you to do this on your own, detective," Masters said. "You could incriminate yourself and put yourself in jeopardy of prosecution. I need to stay."

"Screw."

"Fine. Enjoy yourself." He gathered his things and walked out.

Cooper smiled and shook her head. "He's right, you know. You could get yourself into a lot of trouble here."

"Let's get on with this," I said. "I'm exhausted and I've pretty much told Winthrop and IAD everything I have to say. It's all right there in that file, I'm sure."

"It is, you're right," she said, glancing down at the file. "But I'm not really interested in what happened last night. I've heard all I need to hear on that. What I want to know is, why?"

"Why what?"

"Why were these guys so important? What was it about them that made you decide to chuck everything you've done up till now--whatever that was?"

"That's for me, not you. I did what I did and that's all there is. You don't honestly care why anyway, do you? You just want to feel like you've done your job-- whatever *that* is--so you can use me as a chit in the election to help your boy. 'Oh, look how tough I am on rogue cops. I won't tolerate this kind of behavior on my watch.' Well, tough shit. Find another issue."

"Oh, your name will definitely be coming up during the campaign, don't worry. I'll be kicking your ass all across the state," she said. "But the one thing I thought I knew about you was that you wouldn't do something like this without a good reason, however warped and misguided your thinking may have been. I didn't see you as the type to set another trooper up to nearly get killed, leave a couple of bodies in a pond and hack into a suspect's computer and monitor his activities--all without any actual direct evidence--just to settle a score."

I winced at the last bit and Cooper caught it.

"That was a pretty clever idea, I have to say. Honestly. Nice little end run around the wiretap laws. We'll have to remember that for the future. But, once Harris started poking around in there, it was pretty easy to put it together. You're not as good as you think you are, it turns out."

She was bluffing. JD pulled up stakes and removed his rootkit as soon as he was finished last night and none of what he did would've shown up in any of the logs on DeSilva's network. Even Harris wouldn't have found anything that pointed to me, if he found anything at all. The only other possibility was Tex.

"Look, I'm about done here. Whatever you want to tell the board is fine. Do what you want. But I have a question for you, if you don't mind."

"Go ahead."

"What was it about DeSilva and Alves that had *you* so interested? Why all the pressure on us to put this case down?"

She shrugged and looked away. "It's a high-profile case and it was right where I live. I didn't want people stopping me at Dunkin' every morning and asking why we hadn't found the killer. And, as you said, the election is only a few weeks away and we need a bump. This is it."

She hadn't looked at me at all while she spoke and was fidgeting with the mouse on her laptop. Nice try, though. I dug in the pocket of my jeans and came out with a USB drive.

"Nope," I said.

I slid the drive down the table to Cooper and it stopped on the edge of the table, teetering. She looked at it, watching it wobble back and forth for a few seconds until it tipped and fell over the edge. She caught it with her left hand and looked up at me.

"If that's the department's laptop, you may not want to open the file on there. Might leave some ugly breadcrumbs for Harris to pick up later. I can just tell you what it is, if you'd like. It turns out that DeSilva kept pretty detailed records on his customers. He may have been a nutbag, but he was pretty anal about that."

Cooper tapped the drive on the table a few times and looked out the window, considering. I couldn't read the expression on her face, so I waited. I figured it was fifty-fifty whether she'd call bullshit on me. Didn't matter to me either way. After a minute, she nodded slowly to herself and then tucked the tiny piece of plastic and silicon into her laptop bag.

"Huh. Allright. So I imagine you think this is going to automagically save your job," she said. Her voice was calm and without any particular emotion to it. Pretty impressive, given the circumstances. I sat forward in my chair and leaned my forearms on the table.

"You think this is about my job? Really? Please."

"What then?" she asked.

I rubbed my palms together and looked at her. "Two things: First, Tex. Leave him alone. He's the only one who acted like a cop in this whole thing. Not you, not Winthrop and not me. Tex. He did what was expected of him. He's a good cop and you need as

421

many of those as you can get, believe me. And B, when I leave today, I'm gone. I'll sign whatever paperwork I need to sign, but that's it. I'm resigning. No disciplinary board, nothing. You can spin it however you want. I couldn't care less. That's it."

"And I'm supposed to, what, trust that you'll just be quiet about this? Seems unlikely."

I shrugged. "Don't care."

Cooper stared at me. She clicked her fingernails against the table, rhythmically running them back and forth. She stopped after a bit, closed her laptop, placed it in her bag along with the case file and then stood up.

"You're a piece of work, Tobin, you know? Priceless. Who does this? Instead of just doing your job and keeping your head down like everyone else, you do this. Don't sit there and smirk at me like you have some moral high ground here. Because you don't. I do what I do, but no one gets hurt. You better hope that Davis makes it, because if he doesn't, I'll have a warrant out for you in ten minutes."

I smiled. "No one gets hurt? You mean except for the girls DeSilva had killed and the other ones he kidnaps in Brazil or wherever and brings up here in a fucking septic truck for you? Because they don't count, I guess. Not to you, not to him and not to anyone else, apparently."

"So you're their savior, is that it? Give it a rest, Tobin. You, the fucking white knight? The same guy who left Davis out there for dead while he played out his own personal revenge fantasies? The same guy who probably falsified evidence and probably broke into a

422

suspect's computer and maybe shot two suspects? That guy? Fuck you, Tobin. You're gonna lecture me on ethics and morality? Shut your mouth. You might have found an out here, but I'm not going to stand here and listen to you get preachy on me. You can save that shit for someone else."

I stood up and walked around the table and stopped a foot in front of her. I was a good eight inches taller than she was and I stared down at her, smiling. She tried to give it back but it wasn't in her and she simply looked down. I laughed, and it sounded awful and nasty.

"I'll say what I want, when I want. And you get to sit on your round ass and worry about whether that's going to hurt you at some point. And I *love* that. Because the difference between you and me is that I know what I am. I may not like it, but I have it figured out now. You? You still think you're some other person, some better form of yourself. The great thing is, some day you're going to realize that it isn't true, that you're exactly the person that you've feared you were all along. And it's going to just *crush* you. It's gonna hurt so fuckin' bad you're going to wish that you'd just been that person forever and owned it the whole time. And when that happens, when you're sitting in a chair by a window, wondering how this happened, I'll know. I'll know and I'll think of those girls and I'll smile."

I saw in her face that she knew. Her eyes moistened and her cheeks and throat reddened and she knew that I was right. She tried to brush by me and go out the door, but I didn't move. I kept looking at her, watched as the first tears broke free and made muddy mascara-black tracks down her cheeks.

And I enjoyed it.

Thirty-Four

"I don't even want to know what happened in there or what you said," Winthrop said as he walked back into his office.

I sat in his guest chair, gulping a bottle of diet Coke. He dropped a small packet of papers on the desk in front of me and put a pen on top of them.

"But apparently you're now resigning. And that's the end of it. Sign those and you're clear."

I signed a statement about the incidents the night before, admitting nothing, and then a bunch of HR forms and that was it. I stood and pulled my credentials and badge case out of my back pocket, dropped them on the desk. I removed my gun from the holster, pulled the clip, removed the round from the chamber and set it all on top of the papers. In less than a minute of writing and formalities, my career in the Massachusetts State Police was finished.

Winthrop had remained standing and when I turned to go, I was surprised to see him holding out his hand. I shook it.

"What now?" he asked.

"No clue. I need some rest, though, I know that. A long, quiet rest."

"Do me a favor?"

"What's that?"

"Move out of my jurisdiction. I hear Virginia is nice this time of year."

"You're not wrong about that," I said.

I wandered around the halls for five minutes, looking for Tex with no luck. I asked in the homicide unit and got dead stares. I took another lap around the barracks and didn't see him and then walked out to the parking lot and saw him leaning on the back of my Jeep.

"Heard you quit," he said as I walked up.

"Quit, resigned, escaped. Whatever you want to call it, I'm done."

He nodded and looked away, squinting into the afternoon sun. Eventually he looked back at me and pushed himself up off the bumper, dusting off his pants.

"Couldn't just leave it alone, right? Doing it the way we're supposed to and getting the results isn't enough for you. There's always some other motive, something else you have to do to make yourself feel better or make someone else feel worse or whatever the hell it is you do. I don't even know, man. All I know is that a week ago I thought I had things figured out pretty well, and now I'm standing in a parking lot lecturing my best friend after he just burned down his career and almost did the same to mine."

"Look man, you're not going to be harder on me than I'm going to be on myself, so you might as well stop. I have the next sixty years to think about what I did. Don't worry about it."

"Really Danny? You think I'm going to buy that self-flagellation act from you? You might feel bad about some of this, but I know that you'd do it all again tomorrow if it served your purpose. When that purpose was in line with your job, that made you a great cop. A fucking great cop. But when it wasn't? God help whoever gets in your way. I never thought that included me, but at least I know that now. So thanks for that, I guess."

I ran my hands through my hair, feeling the dirt and sand and filth in there and suddenly feeling the fatigue and pain pressing down on me. "Did you really stand out here waiting just so you could lecture me? Because if that's it, I need to go."

"No, actually I waited out here to tell you that I went to Rourke this morning and got an arrest warrant for JD. I'm sure he's in Bermuda or Marbella or wherever by now, but the next time he tries to come into the U.S., he gets a free ticket to Boston. So maybe there will be some justice in this after all."

"Classy. Nice move, man. You feel better about all of this now? Do you think Amy gives a shit about this now? Of course not. She moved on years ago. You did it for yourself, so you could get a little bit for you, to feel like you didn't get run over by a bus in all of this. Good for you. Believe that if you'd like, man. But it's not my problem anymore."

"Right. But you know what *is* your problem? Erin. She's been your problem for years and she's going to continue to be your problem until you stop acting like you can do something about it. You think I'm crazy for trying to get back at JD? Think about what you're doing for a minute. Erin's been gone for a long time now. Maybe you should've gone down there and done something earlier, when things started going bad. I think about that all the time, man. All the time. And she

427

wasn't even my sister. But you didn't. And so she's dead. Things got handled, but yeah, she should still be alive. That's a fact and I bet it hurts like a bastard. But I gotta tell you, what you're doing--what you did--isn't going to make it hurt any less."

He was right, of course, and I didn't have anything to counter him with.

He'd stuck with me through all the mess with Erin, all of the aftermath and all of the shit I'd stepped in since then. He and Kim had treated me like family. I couldn't even remember the number of nights I'd spent on their couch or how many Easters, Thanksgivings, Christmases and random Sundays I'd spent at their dinner table. Tex was really the only person I could call a true friend; even JD, as much as I loved him, was a fond memory most of the time. I could go a year or more without seeing him. But Tex had been right here, watching my back and bringing me along.

And now I'd repaid him for his loyalty and trust with...this.

I felt ill. I could feel the sweat beading on my scalp and my mouth felt like it was full of sand. My stomach was in knots. I couldn't even look him in the eye and I felt like a child who'd been called on the carpet by his father. I knew he was right, not just about what I'd done last night but about all of it. But the real killer was I'd known all of that before any of this even started. And I'd still let it happen. Wanted it to happen.

"Look, it's not going to mean anything right now, I know that, but I'm sorry," I said. The sentiment sounded ridiculous to me, even as I said it.

"Sorry for what you did or just sorry you got caught?"

"For all of it, man. For everything," I said. "I'm just...I'm sorry."

He looked at me, not with pity or contempt, but just plain sadness. "Were you ever really my friend?" he asked.

Sweat trickled down my back and my hands felt damp and tight. I rubbed them together and wiped them on my jeans. I looked back at Tex and knew that I had no answer for him.

I shook my head slightly and walked past him and climbed into the driver's seat, not meeting his eyes as I went by. My phone buzzed as I sat down and I looked at the display and saw Brendan's picture smiling up at me, St. Peter's Square in Rome in the background. I stared at it for a few seconds, then dropped the phone on the passenger seat and let it ring. I turned the engine over and Tex stood aside as I backed out.

"You'd do it again, wouldn't you?" he asked when I had pulled alongside him.

I took a deep breath, put the Jeep in gear and pulled away.

Epilogue

I made a call on my way out of the parking lot, spoke to the man on the other end for a few seconds and then dropped the phone the on the passenger seat as I accelerated onto 44, heading east. Twenty minutes later, I pulled into the small visitor lot at Plymouth Municipal Airport, sticking the Jeep in a slot next to a cherry '69 Camaro ragtop, the chrome mirrors and bumpers shining in the early afternoon sun. A heavy leather flight jacket hung on the passenger headrest and a cheap blue plastic rosary, the kind every kid gets on his First Communion, dangled from the rearview. I'd gotten one just like it on my day, my brother Brendan and sister Erin standing there with my parents, everyone smiling.

I stood for a second, watching the crucifix at the end of the chain twist and twirl in the breeze, reached into my pocket for my phone to call my brother. But I didn't know what I'd say, how I'd answer his questions. I locked the Jeep and walked into the terminal.

I found Trey Evans sitting in the pilots' lounge, a red can of Coke set on the table in front of him, beads of sweat running down its sides and pooling on the scarred Formica table. He nodded as I approached and stuck out his hand. I shook it, noticing how small and fragile it felt in mine, the bones almost birdlike. He pulled his hand back quickly and folded it, prayer-like, with his other hand in his lap. I pulled out the orange plastic chair across from his and sat.

"Thanks for doing this," I said. "You sure it's not a problem?"

"It's fine. My buddy only uses his chopper during the week, does some scouting for some of the land developers around here. Said it's mine for as long as I need it."

"Won't take long. Ready?"

He nodded and picked up his Coke, taking a long drink. I watched as his hand quivered, Evans fighting it hard to keep the soda from spilling down the front of his shirt. He tossed the can in a blue plastic recycling bin set on the floor by the door of the lounge and we walked out onto the tarmac.

The trees and groundcover passed silently beneath us, the heavy thrumming of the copter's rotors beating out a steady rhythm as we pushed north. Evans held the stick tightly in his gloved hands, and I'd noticed the mild shake in them as he'd gone through his pre-flight checks a few minutes earlier. It didn't seem to be affecting his skills, though. Smooth was the word. I kept my eyes out the side window as we made our way out of Plymouth and up into Kingston, Evans holding the powerful Bell chopper steady, a few hundred feet above the quiet cul-de-sacs and streets. He banked right as we got closer, following the grey concrete vein of Route 3.

"Coming up on the left here," he said over the intercom.

I looked out through the front windshield. Even before the clearing was visible, I could sense where it was, where it would appear, the trees becoming more sparse and sickly as we got closer until they finally gave up altogether near the edge of the pond. Dense forests of old pines with thick, heavy boughs dominated this part of the state, and there were still areas where you could find acre upon acre of undisturbed woods. This was one of those places, and this forest had sat quietly for decades, notable only for its calm grace.

And now it would also be known as a boneyard.

Evans held the Bell on a straight line, riding it up above the southbound shoulder of Route 3. As the last of the pines disappeared below the copter's skids, Evans made a wide sweeping left turn, bringing us around again to the right at the western edge of the clearing so that the pond was visible out my window. He eased the big chopper into a graceful hover and I pressed my face against the glass, looking down at the pond that had claimed more than a dozen lives and changed so many others.

Three state police cruisers were parked on the dirt access road and a small group of people were gathered near the edge of the water, at the spot where I'd left DeSilva and Alves the night before. The men looked up at us, shielding their eyes with their hands. I stared out at the pond, the twisted, charred trunks jutting out of the water at odd angles, the green algae and scum moving gently on the surface as the wind came out of the forest and skimmed across the pond.

I thought about the girls who'd been dumped into the water, bellies full of dope, heads blown apart. I thought of them driving up in that truck, praying that

433

the cheap plastic bags inside them wouldn't break, begging God to just let them make it to the end, to get the dope out, and whatever they had to do after that would be fine.

And then the first of the girls got sick, suddenly throwing up, the other girls instinctively moving away from her, to the corners of the truck. Trying to get away from the sickness, praying it wouldn't touch them, too. But it did. It got them all, one way or another. In some way, that first girl was probably the luckiest one. She probably went fast, the massive dose of pure heroin poisoning her body, putting her out within a few minutes and then killing her not long after.

The others, they would have had it worse. Much worse. Knowing what was coming for them, fighting to stay calm as the panic began to set in and another girl went down. And then another. The truck would've been filled with vomit and excrement by then, the remaining girls quickly losing it as they felt the truck come to a stop at last. Bursting out of the hatch as the men opened it, quickly pulling their heads back at the stench as the women clamored up the ladder, hysterical, shouting.

Then a quiet conversation, a quick phone call and an easy decision. Do it.

That's what DeSilva had said: Do it.

And so they had. One after another, the women had been pulled out of the truck, thinking they were clear, that they'd made it. And then the screams would have come.

My hand was wound tightly around the chopper's door handle, the knuckles white, as I thought about the women. And I thought about DeSilva and Alves last night, about the resignation in the voice of Alves, the educated man, as he'd called himself. I thought of him standing there in the wind and rain, the gun in his hand, his uncle sitting in the mud before him, just waiting.

And I waited for the anger and the hate to come, waited for it to wind me up, to get my head humming and my ears buzzing. I waited for the tingling in my skin to start, the sweat to break out on my palms. But it didn't come. It was gone.

"You good?" Trey Evans asked over the headset. His words sounded clear and crisp, as if they'd come not from him but as if they were my own.

I looked down at the troopers, one of them now waving his arm wildly, telling us to move off. I turned and saw Alves's cabin through the windshield, the little house standing on its own in the trees. I glanced over at Evans his face calm, but his hands trembling as he held the chopper in the hover. I nodded, and he put us into a quick climb, up and away from the pond and the cabin.

"I'm good," I said.

Caroline's father drove her down from Boston in the late afternoon and I met them at her apartment and we unloaded the rest of her stuff that he'd brought down and got her settled. They followed me back over to my place and while Caroline was upstairs in the bathroom, her father walked me outside to the deck and pulled the door closed behind him.

435

"I asked around about you with some of the guys I know on the staties," he said. "I heard a lot of things, and not all of them were so good. Actually, some of them were wicked ugly. I did hear you were a gifted investigator, but you sure didn't make a lot of friends with that shit last night."

Scott Nelson was a compact man, no more than five-nine or so, but he exuded the calm toughness that many veteran cops have. He'd already gone gray, but he was still in good shape. He was standing very close to me and I was not comfortable being alone with him out there.

"No sir, I didn't," I said.

"You quit the force?"

"Yes sir."

He nodded. "It's fifty-one point three miles from my driveway to yours. Caroline is my only daughter. You got it?"

I nodded. "Yes sir, I do."

He nodded, looking off toward the inlet and the marsh. "What do you plan on doing now?"

"I honestly haven't thought much about that yet," I said. "I just know I'm done with this for a while. Maybe for good. I don't know. I need to get my head right first."

"See that you do that."

"Yes sir."

Caroline opened the door then and looked at the two of us.

"Is it safe to come out?" She walked over and put her arm around my waist. Her father looked at me for a long moment and then at her.

"It's safe, honey."

A half hour later Caroline and I were sitting at a tall table on the top deck at the Cabby Shack, looking out at Plymouth Harbor, with Long Beach and Clark's Island in the distance. The sun was just dipping below the horizon and the air was already turning cool. Wouldn't be long now before the tourists were gone and the ice cream parlors and t-shirt shops were boarded up. The waitress came and set our beers on the table and moved off, tending to the sparse late-afternoon crowd. Caroline was leaning back in her chair, her bare feet up on the wooden railing.

"You were all over the TV this morning," she said, still looking out at the water. A lone lobster boat was making its way back into the harbor, idling quietly through the channel to the commercial wharf just below us. The smell of baitfish and diesel fuel and salt mixed together in the air, not unpleasantly. I waited.

"How much of that was true?" she asked after a minute.

"Don't know. I didn't see any of it. But I'll answer whatever you want to ask me."

She was quiet for a long while as she sipped her beer and watched the gulls and terns circle overhead. I had prepared myself for this, but I still wasn't sure I could handle it if she didn't like the answers I gave her.

"Did you kill those two men, DeSilva and Alves?" Her voice was low, but it was clear and firm.

"No, I didn't. But I was there when it happened."

"Could you have stopped it?"

"Yeah."

She kept her gaze on the harbor for a moment, then pulled her feet off the rail and turned toward me.

"I'm glad you didn't," she said. "I'm glad they're dead. They were disgusting, awful people. I never thought I'd hear myself say something like that, but it's true. Does that make me a bad person?"

"You're asking the wrong guy. I know how it makes me feel, but that's got nothing to do with you."

"And does it bother you?" she asked, her eyes fixed on mine.

I looked over her shoulder at the harbor, the boats and, just visible in the distance, the Myles Standish statue, the last rays of sunlight glinting off the old man's head. I thought about the last few days and what lay ahead of me, and I wanted to tell her the truth, to keep this one good thing I had clean and unspoiled.

I was dying to be honest with her, aching for it.

But instead I took a sip of my beer, looked her in the eye and lied to her for the first time.

"Yeah," I said, "it does."

440

Acknowledgements

This book would not have been possible without the patience and forbearance of my wife and family. I spent a lot of nights, weekends and holidays writing, and that's a pretty selfish way to spend your time. But my wife never complained about any of it. She's the best. I'd also like to thank my volunteer editors, Chris Gonsalves, Tara Kusamoto and Adam Torman, without whose edits, suggestions, not-so-kind words and encouragement the book would have been barely readable. If you don't like it, blame them. Thanks also to Peter Chernin, Mike Mimoso, Adam Shostack and others for reading early drafts. Several of my friends in the security community, who asked to remain anonymous, were kind enough to review the technical content of the book. If there are mistakes in that, they are mine. Special thanks to my friend Gene Kim for months of advice, coaching and encouragement on the book, the path to self-publishing and many other things. The cover photos are the work of my talented brother-in-law, Ryan Delaney, and the cover design was done by my equally talented sister-in-law, Lisa Chernin. Huge thanks to both of them for their awesome work. Finally, I need to thank my parents, who, once they discovered my lack of other discernible talents, encouraged my writing constantly and never let me think that there was something I couldn't do. Thanks.

A Few Words on Geography

Most of the locations--restaurants, bars and landmarks--
in the story are real places and are depicted as they
actually exist. The swamp where the bodies are found is
a real place and sits exactly where I've described it.
However, careful readers will notice that I've taken
some liberties with the geography of Plymouth, mostly
to make things easier for myself and to avoid putting
dead bodies in front of my friends' businesses and
homes. Otherwise, without too much effort, you could
find Danny's house, the pond in Duxbury, the Standish
monument, the BBC and just about everything else.
Except Plymouth Rock. I made that up.

CPSIA information can be obtained
at www.ICGtesting.com
Printed in the USA
LVHW021329150722
723529LV00003B/42